Reginald K. Write
www.ReginaldWrite.com

OTHER WORKS AVAILABLE BY THIS AUTHOR

Beyond the Breaking Point
Teacher's Pet
My Boyfriend's Brother
Playing with Fire
Playing with Fire Pt 2: Friendly Fire
Wicked Ambitions
My Son's Teacher

Copyright © 2013 Reginald K. Write

This book is a work of fiction. Names, characters, places and incidents are products of the author's imagination or used fictitiously. Any resemblance to actual events or locales or persons, living or dead, is entirely coincidental.

All rights reserved. No part of this book may be reproduced in any form or by any means without the prior consent of the publisher, excepting brief quotes used in reviews.

ISBN-13:978-1514650226
ISBN-10:1514650223

CHAPTER 1
RAYMOND

I nodded my head robotically as I listened to Keon's epic lunchroom rant. Even though I struggled valiantly to pay attention, I couldn't help but zone out. He had been rambling on ever since we sat down to eat ten minutes ago. Thankfully...mercifully...he abruptly stopped when he noticed the subject of his rant approaching.

"Speak of the Devil," he whispered.

Brianna, flanked by her two-girl entourage, strutted towards us. Stunningly gorgeous and arguably the most popular girl in our high school--Brianna was the captain of the cheerleading squad. Keon daintily dabbed the corner of his mouth with his napkin, smiled and waved graciously at "Queen" Brianna. She returned his saccharine smile with one of her own as she and her handlers glided past the peasants table carrying their trays, deigning to sit at the royal table behind us.

Keon or "Ke-Ke" (as some called him) returned his attention to me and rolled his eyes. "God, I can't take that fake ho." He was also on the cheerleading squad and Brianna was his arch-nemesis. He took a bite of his peach cobbler and continued his tirade. "She may believe she's Rihanna--thinking her reign just won't let up--but what that bitch don't know is that I'm the motherfucking Adele of that squad. This year, I'm going to set FIRE to her reign!"

"Uh, huh...I see." I gave him the blank stare that I reserved for his craziest comments. And boy, were there a lot of them. Ke was one of my best friends. Well, my only friend actually...but dude definitely had some issues. Considering he was approximately 200lbs (of mostly fat) and stood about 5'8, I concluded a long time ago that the bitter rivalry between he and Brianna was undoubtedly just a figment of his imagination. Although I would never actually tell that to him of course, since I didn't want to break up our friendship (or have to fight him to the death). We had known each other since our sophomore year. He was an outspoken, big fem dude and he couldn't give one fuck if anyone liked it or not. I was the exact opposite--a slim, masculine dude who was on the low-key reserved side. However, one thing we had in common was that we were both out with our sexuality.

"Oh, another hater, huh?" Keon raised an eyebrow.

"Um...did you forget to take your medication today?" I replied with a grin.

"Whatever," he smacked his lips and laughed. "So how's your first day going so far?"

I shrugged my shoulders and nonchalantly gulped my milk. "Meh, it's going alright. Same ole shit so far. I'm glad this is our last year."

"Wow, how exciting," Keon deadpanned. "Anyway, those are some cute First Day Fashions you got on."

"Oh, thanks." I smiled bashfully as I glanced down at my new Green Lantern t-shirt and skinny black Levis. I also had on a matching Green Lantern snapback and a pair of new glasses to top it off.

"Yes, very geek chic."

"Uh, thanks again...I guess." I laughed.

Suddenly, the "MVP's" also known as "The All-Stars," entered the lunchroom. A reverent hush instantly fell over the raucous crowd. All eyes immediately fixated on them. This was the most popular clique in the school. It consisted of Tim, the quarterback of the football team; Michael, star of the track team; and Aaron, captain of the basketball team and leader of the wolf pack. All of them were tall, cocky, always impeccably dressed, and fine as fuck.

Too bad they were also supreme assholes.

Where you would see one, the others would usually be nearby. If you got into a fight with one, you had to fight them all (not that anyone in his right mind would dare challenge them though).

I watched as they sat down at the table with Bri's squad of cheerleaders. Each member of the All-Stars dated one of the three "mean girls." Keon jokingly referred to the two power cliques collectively as "The Illuminati," since they seemed to run the whole school. Aaron slid into an empty reserved chair beside Brianna. He set his tray down and kissed her on the cheek. She giggled. Before I even realized I was still staring, Aaron called me out.

"Yo, what you lookin' at, Blackout?" He yelled loudly from across the table. Of course, both of his simple-minded cohorts burst out laughing like that was the funniest thing they had ever heard. "Blackout" was the nickname they had for me because I was dark-skinned. Unfortunately, Aaron was also in my homeroom this year, so there was no escaping his stupidity.

I just shook my head and turned back around to face Keon. "Dumbasses."

Keon bristled. "Um, so you sure I can't tell him 'bout himself?" Ke was very protective of me. He had been itching to go off on Aaron for years, especially since he didn't like Brianna. But I wasn't one for confrontation; I considered it pointless and immature.

"Meh, it's not necessary." I was used to being teased for my skin tone by stupid color struck people like Aaron, who was light-skinned.

"OK, if you say so." Keon smacked his lips. "When you change your mind, just say the motherfucking word and a bitch will go OWWF on Lite Brite's ass."

I laughed and put on a smile, even though inside I was a little hurt and pissed.

After lunch I had three more classes to go. During fifth period, I asked to be excused to use the restroom. When I finished peeing, I zipped up my pants and washed my hands. As I was drying them, the door suddenly swung open. Just my luck, in walked Aaron. When he saw me, a big grin spread across his face. *Great*. I diverted my eyes and tried to exit the bathroom, but he blocked my path, standing in front of the door.

"Where you flying off to so fast, Gay Lantern?" He burst out laughing.

"Wow. Funny," I retorted dryly.

"I know it was."

"You think you can get out of the way, please?" I said, getting angry.

"You think you can get out the way, please?" Aaron mocked me in a nerdy voice. "You sound like such a white boy." He chortled again.

I was furious now. I tried to push past him, but he blocked me with his tall, muscular frame as if he were guarding me in an imaginary basketball game. At six feet tall, I wasn't short, mind you. But Aaron still had a good three inches of height on me. And he outweighed me by probably 50lbs (of muscle, which I severely lacked).

"Where you going, Blackest Night?" He scoffed, forcefully pushing me against the chest. I stumbled back slightly. I gritted my teeth as I readjusted my glasses. My heart was pounding.

The door swung open at that moment, and another dude walked in. Luckily, it was someone that Aaron knew. They greeted each other boisterously. I used this distraction as an opportunity to promptly slip away from the bathroom.

I walked the hallway back to class feeling tight.

Adrenaline pumping.

Eyes watering.

Fighting back tears of anger and angst.

Well, it looks like this year is going to suck elephant ass, just like the last three. I couldn't wait for it all to be over. I couldn't wait to graduate and get the hell out of high school. I just wanted to put it all behind me, and get on with the rest of my miserable life.

CHAPTER 2
MATTHEW

I glanced at the clock on the wall and sighed. It seemed like time had stopped. The first day of school always seemed to drag, and my fifth period English teacher definitely wasn't helping the situation. He was short and dumpy, with strands of gray hair that were combed over his bald spot. Aside from resembling a hobbit, he also had the most irritating monotone voice I had ever heard.

Just then, the classroom door opened. The dude with the Green Lantern t-shirt came back in. He had asked to go to the restroom a few minutes earlier. I wish I had come up with that idea so I could've gotten out of this boring class for a little while. He briskly walked back to his seat. When he sat down, he accidentally knocked over his notebook. He let out an annoyed huff as it hit the floor. Guess he was having a bad day. He leaned forward to pick it up, but I reached over and grabbed it first. He looked at me warily, like he thought I was going to try to steal it or play keep away with it.

"Here you go," I said in a hushed voice, handing it back to him.

"Thanks," he replied with a look of relief. He smiled briefly as we made eye contact. His eyes looked watery behind his glasses, like he was upset.

"No prob, man," I said with a smile of my own.

"Is there something you would like to share with the class..." Mr. Hobbit interrupted, slowly scanning down the attendance list he'd taken earlier. "Matthew?" His beady eyes narrowed as he focused on me.

"Nope." I shook my head and slumped in my desk. *Asshole.* Muffled snickers filled the room.

"Good." He glowered and panned the room with a death gaze. "Everyone needs to pay attention. I will not tolerate talking in my class while I am teaching." He pulled a pen from his shirt pocket and wrote something on the attendance before resuming his lesson. Terrific. First day, and I've already been blacklisted. I looked over at Green Lantern and he gave me a sympathetic glance. I shrugged nonchalantly and grinned. Why could I suddenly feel myself blushing?

Thankfully, my sixth period class flew by and wasn't too painful. Aside from being punked in English class, my first day wasn't too bad. I pulled the straps of my book bag over my shoulders and promptly exited the classroom. As I entered the hall, I reached into my pocket and grabbed my cell phone. My face lit up when I saw I had a new message from one of my friends back in Cali. I was so wrapped up in my text that I wasn't fully paying attention to where I was going. The next thing I know, I bumped into something hard. I looked up from my phone to see this tall dude with a scowl on his face.

"Aye," he snapped, staring me up and down, "you better get your nose outta that phone and look where the fuck you goin', white boy." He had two other guys with him, who burst out laughing.

"My bad, man," I replied, raising my palms defensively. He didn't scare me, but I didn't want any trouble with the dude. This was my first day at this school. The last thing I needed was to get suspended and kicked out like I did at my old school. "Sorry," I reiterated.

He just glared at me silently. I backed up and prepared myself. I didn't want to fight over petty shit, but if it came to that, I was ready to throw hands. Being a white dude attending a predominately black and Latino high school in Cali, I had faced my fair share of bullies who liked to pick fights with me for no reason other than my race. After I got beat up a few times, my big brother made me enroll in boxing classes at the Y. I wasn't a fucking Ultimate Fighter or anything, but I could certainly hold my own.

"Yo, Aaron," one of his muscular friends chimed in. "Leave that dude alone. It's the first day and your ass is already starting trouble." He placed a hand on his shoulder and chuckled.

"I'm not causing shit." Aaron gave him a sideways glance. "John Cena here is the one slammin' into people and shit like it's Wrestlemania. You can't see me, dawg." He waved his hand in front of his face, comically imitating the WWE wrestler, John Cena. "So watch where the fuck you're going next time."

We engaged in an intense stare down. My heart raced as I anticipated his next move. His boys snickered. Aaron smirked and then continued on his way with his boys closely following. I watched them saunter down the hall. Everyone parted like the Red Sea as they passed. I guess they were supposed to be big shit in this school? I exhaled, allowing the tension to slowly seep from my body while I left the building.

On my way home, I noticed the dude from class with the Green Lantern shirt on, walking ahead of me. I debated if I should say something, or just pass him without speaking. I didn't want to seem like a creepy stalker or anything. But I also didn't want to come off rude, since we had met each other earlier.

"Hey, what's up?" I said, announcing my presence as I sidled up to him. He jumped.

"Oh, what's up, man?" He flashed a meek smile. He had a perfect set of teeth.

"Nothin' much. Just happy to be getting out of there and heading home," I lied. (Well, partially lied.) I was happy to be getting out of school, but I wasn't too thrilled about going home. "I can already tell that hobbit-looking Mr. Bailey is gonna be a bitch."

"Yeah, I know, right?" He laughed. Dude's voice was pretty deep.

"How was your first day?" I asked.

"It was all right." Either he was shy, or he just didn't want to talk to me.

"Yeah, mine wasn't too bad, considering this was my first day going to this school," I volunteered, trying to keep the conversation rolling.

"Really? This is your first year here?" He seemed genuinely interested.

"Yep. I'm originally from Cali. My family just moved here this summer."

His face beamed. "Wow, that's cool, man. I always wanted to visit there. I bet it's better than lame Augusta, GA."

"Yeah, it's real nice there. But not so great with no money," I joked. "My mom and dad moved here for work."

"Oh, I see." He titled his head sideways. "Uh, what was your name again?"

"Matthew, or Matt," I said. "Yours?"

"Raymond, or Ray," he replied with a coy smile, extending his hand. I grasped it firmly. Was I blushing again?

"So, how can you wear a Green Lantern shirt and hat in public after seeing that crappy movie?" I asked with a crooked grin on my face. He shot me a dirty look, and then chuckled.

"So you're a comedian, huh?"

"I can be," I said. He gave me a lingering look. I felt a tingle shoot up my spine. Something told me that this was the start of what promised to be an interesting friendship.

When I got home, I heard the TV on in the living room. That meant my dad was home. *Great*, I thought with a sigh. I heard him talking to someone. I moved through the kitchen into the living room.

"Hey dad," I said as I walked by him. He was sitting in his recliner with a beer in one hand, and a cell phone pressed to his ear. Of course, he couldn't trouble himself to acknowledge me. I didn't care. I'd rather him ignore me than talk to me anyway. He had an authoritarian and regimented personality, which most likely stemmed in part from the time he'd spent in the military. My dad had served in the army for fifteen years before being dishonorably discharged due to his drinking problem.

I went to my room and locked the door. I put in a Drake CD, making sure the stereo volume was low as possible. After stripping down to a pair of basketball shirts and a wife beater, I proceeded to work out. I did some reps with the dumb bells, fifty pushups, and fifty crunches. By the time I was done, my muscles were burning. I removed my beater and posed in front of the mirror. My eyes studied my biceps, before traveling down to my six pack. *Not bad*, I thought. After being slim for most of my life, I was finally starting to fill in. I was contemplating trying out for the basketball team; that way, I would have something to do after school instead of come home.

Suddenly, there was a loud banging at the door. I startled. I don't know why. I should've been use to this by now. I pulled on my beater. I took a deep breath and opened the door. My dad was standing there with a furious expression. His eyes radiated anger.

"Didn't I tell you to make sure you lock the fucking door when you come in?" He slurred, reeking of beer. "In case you haven't noticed, this isn't Beverly Hills around here!"

I knew I locked the door. I always made sure to lock it. I didn't want to give him anything to bitch about. Too bad he always found or made up an excuse to do so anyway. I just nodded.

"And turn that ghetto music off, too!" He yelled. "Dumbass." He placed the palm of his hand against my forehead and shoved me. I stumbled back into the room as he slammed the door. I stood there shaking with anger. I walked over to my bed and sat down.

I hated my life.

I held my head in my hands. Tears welled in my eyes, but I refused to let them fall. My father may have controlled me physically, but I wouldn't allow him to control me mentally or emotionally.

He wasn't going to break me.

Fortunately, this was my last year of high school. I swore to myself after I graduated, I would do just like my older brother did. I would join the Army, leave my dysfunctional family behind, and never look back.

CHAPTER 3
RAYMOND

I was sitting in homeroom, texting back and forth with Keon's greedy behind. He was always talking or texting about boys or food. Or his favorite fantasy--boys AND food.

Keon: Is it lunchtime yet?
Me: Um, we just got here
Keon: And? A bitch starving. I need to put something in my mouth ASAP
Me: What else is new? Don't your jaws ever get tired?
Keon: Fuck you ho. And FYI, no they don't. Ever. Now run tell that :-P
Me: stupid. Lml

I couldn't keep a straight face reading Keon's foolishness. My smile quickly evaporated when I heard Aaron's loud mouth come into the class with his boys. It was like he needed to announce his presence whenever he entered a room. Of course they had to sit right behind me. I lowered my head as they passed, and pretended like I didn't notice him. Hopefully, he wouldn't say anything to me.

"Sup, Gayday?"

I sighed. It seemed like he just lived to ridicule me. I pictured him staying up all night, eagerly brainstorming and jotting down new gay-themed nicknames in a journal, then giddily rushing to school the next day to taunt me with them. Ugh. Why couldn't my life be like one of those gay teen high school novels where all of the good looking jocks were secretly gay, and crushing on the nerdy unpopular dude?

Hmm...maybe Aaron was actually a repressed homosexual who had a crush on me, and that's why he was always fucking with me? He'd been aggravating me my entire high school career, so according to the tried-and-true plotline, it should only be a matter of days before he corners me in the bathroom and passionately kisses me, staring into my eyes longingly as he reveals that he has always wanted me. After that, we'd carry on a torrid secret affair. Of course, a whole bunch of crazy off-the-wall drama and wacky hijinks would ensue, eventually forcing him to out himself and profess his undying love for me while a shocked student body looks on. Everyone would hate us at first, but then they'd come around to accept us and even vote us Homecoming King and Queen...er, King.

Yeah, right. The preposterousness of that fantasy scenario made me chuckle aloud.

"Aye, look at this corny ass dude over here laughing by himself," Aaron blurted out. His fan club guffawed it up.

I just put my head down and sighed. Graduation couldn't come soon enough.

The next three periods were uneventful. Fast forward to lunch. As usual, I was sitting there listening to Keon run his mouth like a marathon. This time it was about the horrors of his French class.

"I was like, 'Damn, bitch! It's only the second day, and you're already assigning homework and shit?'" He said, scrunching up his face in an animated fashion.

"Thank God, no homework for moi so far." I grinned and bit into my burger.

"Oh, you trying to be cute, huh?" Keon pursed his lips. "Anyway, have you seen Duke today?"

"Um, his name's Matt."

"Whatever. Duke, Brett, Matt, Zack—it's all the same thing. Typical Caucasian guy name."

I rolled my eyes. "No, I haven't seen--"

Suddenly, I noticed Matt coming down the aisle carrying his tray. My eyes widened and I almost choked on my burger. I took a gulp of my chocolate milk. I didn't know we had the same lunch period. I lowered my head and prayed that he didn't see me. I didn't know why I felt so nervous. Ke looked at me like I was crazy.

"That's him," I whispered, motioning my head in Matt's direction. I had already told him about Matt walking me home from school yesterday. Before Keon could even turn his head in the direction I was indicting, Matt was standing right in front of us.

"Hey, what's up, man?" He asked. His green eyes twinkled as his smile beamed. "Is this seat taken?" Before I could even reply, he set his tray on the table and slid into the chair next to Keon, across from me. He grinned. "So what's good, Ray-Rey?"

I was speechless. I was never one to go all crazy over white dudes, but Matt was so damn cute. He wore his dark hair in a low buzz cut. Aside from a faint five O'clock shadow, which lined his strong jawline, his skin was smooth and clear. As we talked on our way home, I couldn't help but notice that he had a confidant sexiness about him. He had a "chocolate flavor," but he wasn't trying to "act black" or anything.

"Ahem." The sound of Ke loudly clearing his throat snapped me out of my trance.

"Oh," I startled, breaking the stare with Matt and turning to Ke. "Uh, this is my friend, Keon. Matt's in my fifth period," I said, introducing the two.

"What's up?" Matt smiled and nodded at Ke.

Keon pursed his lips to the side and looked at Matt as if he were invading his space. *Rude ass*, I thought. I shot him a look. He put on a fake smile, and then fixed his face. I rolled my eyes.

"Nice to meet you," he said, offering his hand for Matt to shake.

If this were one of those corny romance novels, this would be the point in the story where the protagonist and his best friend would try to subtly figure out if the hot newcomer was gay or not.

"So, just to give you a heads up, if you're seen sitting here talking to us, you're probably gonna be labeled a homo," Keon said, punctuating his statement with a smack of his lips.

O...M...GGGGGGGGGGGGGGG!!!!! I gave him the most incredulous look I could muster.

"What? I'm just saying." He shrugged.

Matt laughed. "That's cool. I'm TeamGay myself."

"You're...?" I replied, trying not to sound too happy.

"Yessir." He gave me a crooked grin. "And I don't give a fuck who knows either." Wow! Matt was out and proud. From looking at him, I would've never guessed.

"Oooweee! I like you already!" Keon exclaimed, clasping his hands together. The whole table turned in our direction.

"Um, do you really have to be all loud and shit?" I raised an embarrassed eyebrow.

"Yes...I do. And you already know this." He stuck his tongue out at me. "Now, as I was saying before I was so RUUUUUdely interrupted--welcome to the Bitch Clique, Matt. Your membership card and welcome packet is in the mail."

I shook my head. Keon was in rare form today. I felt like crawling under the table and dying a quick death.

"Oh, thanks! I'll keep an eye out for it." Matt burst out laughing.

Well, at least he has a sense of humor, I thought. That was a good thing. If he was going to hang around Keon's crazy ass for long, he'd need it.

"Hey, who's that?" Matt asked. I followed his eyes. It was Aaron and the other All-Stars walking back to their exclusive table.

"Oh, that's just his majesty--King Aaron--and his royal jesters," Keon replied.

Matt smirked. "We had a run-in yesterday. Dude seems like a real jackass."

"You don't know the half of it," I said. I was liking him more and more every time he opened his mouth.

Of course, Aaron had something smart to say as he passed. "Stop raping me with your eyes, Gaymond!"

"Hey, man, leave him alone," Matt said.

The whole table turned in our direction again. A hush fell over the lunchroom.

My heart froze.

Aaron stopped in his tracks and squinted at Matt. "You again, John Cena? Who are you--*Captain Save-a-Fag*?" Laughter came from the peanut gallery. "That's your boyfriend?" Aaron asked with a sly grin. He was enjoying the hell out of this.

"Nah. Not yet anyway," Matt fired back. He stood up. "Anything else you wanna know?"

My mouth fell open. I looked at Keon with bug eyes. *Did he just say, not yet?*

Aaron sneered. "I see you gotta death wish, huh, white boy?" He set his tray on the table. What happened next seemed to be in slow motion. Aaron shoved Matt in the chest. The next thing I know, Matt hauled off and punched Aaron dead in the face!

CHAPTER 4
MATTHEW

Aaron and I sat in the administrative area outside the principal's office. I couldn't believe it was only the second day, and I'd already gotten into a fight. Well actually, it wasn't much of a fight. More like a minor skirmish. After I punched Aaron in the face, he staggered and then came back at me swinging like a girl. Most of his punches were so wild they didn't even come close to connecting. Seconds later, security swarmed us and broke it up. Of course, Aaron was yelling, cursing, and acting like he was trying to get to me while the security guards were conveniently holding him back. Even while we were waiting for the principal to show up, he was still talking shit.

"You're just lucky security came before I had a chance to whoop your ass," he said in a low voice.

"You mean before your boys had a chance to jump in?" I replied sarcastically.

"What the fuck are you saying?" Aaron twisted his lips. "I don't need any help to beat your punk ass."

I laughed. "Whatever, man. It sure looked like it." I was getting a kick out of pushing his buttons.

"Oh, trust me, we can finish this right now." He looked like he was about to explode.

Before I could needle him any further, a tall black dude in a nice suit blew into the room like a tornado. With his solid muscular frame and imposing disposition, he resembled a drill sergeant more than a principal. His eyes shot bullets at me. He halted in front of us long enough to spit out a command.

"Come with me," he said.

We followed him into his office. Aaron and I sat down in front of a mammoth, mahogany desk. There was a glass nameplate sitting on it which read "Dr. Perry". The principal closed the door and took a seat on his desk, facing us with one leg hanging off the edge.

"What's good, Mr. P?" Aaron said in a chirpy tone.

"You tell me, Mr. Thomas." The principal folded his arms across his chest and furrowed his brow. "I hear you two had an altercation in the cafeteria?"

"Yeah, this crazy white boy sucker punched me, Mr. P."

The principal gave me a stern look. "Is this true, son?"

"No sir, I didn't sucker punch him." I cut my eyes at Aaron and gave him a screw face.

"But you did hit him first, correct?" Mr. Perry shifted on his desk. His eyes were now burning holes in me.

I squirmed in my seat. "But Mr. Perry, he started--"

"I don't want to hear it!" The principal bellowed, cutting me off in mid-explanation. "And the name's DR. PERRY." Aaron snickered. "Everybody around here knows I have ZERO tolerance for fighting. I don't like troublemakers in my school. Since you're new here, and it's only the second day, I'm letting you off with a warning. THIS TIME." After a lingering glare, he returned his attention to Aaron and gave him a warm smile. "And you know you should be busy focusing on your game, son. The season's kicking off soon. Hopefully, you intend to lead us to a championship this year?"

"Of course, Mr. P!" Aaron sprouted a cocky grin. "Don't I always?"

I groaned and slouched in my chair. Dr. Perry looked at me and grimaced. I quickly sat up in my chair and flashed a coy smile.

"Anyway, as I was saying: Matthew, don't let me see you in my office again, son. GOT IT?" I wanted to tell him to kiss both of my hairy ass cheeks, but I bit my tongue. I simply nodded my head instead. The big smile returned to his face when he addressed Aaron. "And Mr. Thomas, this is your last year. I'm expecting big things from you!" He winked at Aaron. "Don't disappoint me, son."

"Aight, I got you, Mr. P." Aaron was all teeth as he leaned in and dapped Dr. Perry up.

"Good, now both of you get out of here and go to class."

We stood up and headed toward the door. Dr. Perry reached over and swatted Aaron on the ass as we were walking out the door. Aaron chuckled. *What the hell?* This dude was definitely the principal's pet.

As we exited the office and walked into the hallway, Aaron stared at me with evil eyes. "This shit isn't over, bitch."

I squared up with him. "Whenever you want it."

We stared each other down for a few seconds. Then, Aaron smirked and sauntered down the hall in the opposite direction. I shook my head and went to my locker to get what I needed for the rest of my classes.

When I walked into my fourth period Algebra class, everyone stopped talking and stared at me as I walked by. Shit felt real awkward to say the least. The teacher came in seconds later and began scribbling on the board.

This pretty chick sitting next to me tapped me on the arm and whispered. "So I heard you beat Aaron's ass?"

"Well, uh, not really..."

She smiled flirtatiously. "Cute and modest, too."

After class, she handed me a folded piece of paper. I opened the note and looked at it. It was her name and number.

"Um, thanks." I looked at her and smiled halfheartedly.

She bit her bottom lip seductively. "Text me." She whipped her long hair and strutted off like a super model. (Even though I'm not into girls, I had to admit this was one bad chick).

As I walked down the hall, it seemed like everyone was gawking at me and chattering when I passed. *Damn, word traveled fast around this place,* I thought. When I made it to fifth period, Raymond was already at his desk. He beamed when he saw me walk in. I slid into the desk next to him.

"So, how was the rest of lunch?" I joked. I leaned over and clasped hands with him.

"Man, rumors are flying around that you're crazy. I can't believe you went off like that. Everybody's calling you 'Machine Gun Matt' now."

"Really???" My eyes got wide. I was already becoming a legend here?

"Nah, I just made that last part up." He grinned.

"Ah damn, you had me all gassed up for a minute," I said with a laugh.

Mr. Bailey, aka The Hobbit, stood up from his desk and cleared his throat loudly. "Matthew, class has begun! NO TALKING OR LAUGHING!" He scowled as he picked up the attendance and scribbled something on it.

I sighed and rubbed my temple. *Great.* Strike two. Or was that three?

At the end of the today, me and Raymond walked home from school together again.

"Thanks for standing up for me, man," he said sincerely.

"It's cool, bro. That dude Aaron's a serious asshole. He had it coming."

"Knowing him, being embarrassed like that is just going to make him even more of a pain."

"Eh, he's all bark and no bite. I'm not worried. And you shouldn't be either." I gave him a reassuring look. He smiled. "So, uh, since I stood up to Aaron for you, I was wondering if you could give me something in return." I grinned at him mischievously. Raymond raised an eyebrow. "Nah, it's not that, perv." I playfully scrunched my face.

"Oh." He snickered. "What then?"

I reached in my pocket and pulled out my phone. "Your number." I looked at him with puppy dog eyes. "Your mom does let you talk to strange boys, right?"

"Um, sometimes." He laughed. "Not that I have any boys calling me anyway; unless you count Keon."

"No. I don't."

He playfully shoved my arm. I looked away and tried to hide my goofy smile as he took my phone and input his number. I wanted to do a backflip into a handstand. *YES!!!* "So, uh," I began, trying not to sound overly enthusiastic, "does your mom know about you?"

"Yeah, she knows," Raymond said nonchalantly. "She's cool with it."

"That's what up. So that means she won't be too alarmed when she sees a shifty-looking white dude hanging around all the time." He looked at me like I was crazy. "What?" I shrugged and gave him an ear-to-ear grin.

By the time I got home, I was still feeling amped. I even did a little happy dance up the driveway. I unlocked the door and went in the house. I was so excited about the prospect of talking to Ray and eventually spending time with him outside of school that I was practically giddy.

"Hey, dad," I announced cheerfully.

My dad was in his recliner like always. He was talking to someone on the house phone. He glanced up with a peculiar look on his face as if he'd just noticed me standing there.

"I'll call you back later." He said in a hushed tone. I wondered who he could be talking to so secretively. He set the cordless phone on the cradle and shot up from his chair. "Don't be eavesdropping on me like that." *What the fuck is he talking about?* I wondered. He stomped up to me and backhanded me across the face so hard I saw dancing stars. The sting of his slap made me tear up, but I took a deep breath and held them in. I wouldn't let him see me cry. Before I could even react, he wrapped his hand around my throat and slammed me up against the wall. We were roughly the same height and build, but I was pretty sure that he was stronger than me. His face was inches from mine.

I could smell the liquor on his breath.

I could see the hatred in his eyes.

"And if I get another call from your damn school about you causing trouble, I'm throwing your sorry ass outta here. Now get the fuck in your room, and don't let me see you for the rest of the night! If I catch you sneaking in that kitchen, I'm going to kick your ass all over this house!" He huffed and shoved me away from him.

I rubbed the side of my face. I cautiously knelt down to pick up my book bag while my dad stood there glaring at me. I was careful to avoid eye contact with him, for fear of pissing him off further. I hastily made my way to my room and locked the door. I leaned up against it and took a deep breath. I slowly let my bag slide from my hand to the floor, as tears slid down my face.

CHAPTER 5
RAYMOND

After I got home from school, I ate and took a quick nap before going to work. Six hours later, my shift was just about over. I was beyond ready to go. I checked my phone for the umpteenth time. No missed calls or texts from Matt. I shook my head at myself. I couldn't believe I was geeking over this dude like this.

"Bitch, put that phone away." Keon's voice rang out from behind me. We worked together. "Stop worrying about Maverick; he'll get at you before the night's over."

"Matt."

"Same difference." He smacked his lips. "You're going to be getting some of that 'other white meat' soon enough. Or, should I say--some 'COCK'?!" Keon blurted out shamelessly.

I recoiled and put my finger to my lips. "Shhhh." I cringed and looked to make sure nobody had heard him. Thankfully, no one else was around. I almost exhaled until my eyes landed on our supervisor, Melanie. She stood there with her flabby arms folded across her broad chest. As usual, she was sporting her signature scowl. She was a hefty, butchy woman in her 50's who wore her badly-dyed-blonde hair in an 80's-style-rocker mullet. She seemed to stay in a perpetually bad mood. (I guess I would too if I'd spent my entire life working my way up the ladder at Dairy Queen.)

"I'm sure you two can find something better to do than stand back here gossiping," she growled.

"Well, um..." I didn't know what to say. (Mind you, the place was all but empty since it was only fifteen minutes till closing.) We had already cleaned up out front, and were basically just waiting out the clock. Of course, Melanie wouldn't be Melanie unless she worked us right up to the last second. God, I hated that woman. I had been working here for the past two years to save up money for college. Much like my high school career, my job at Dairy Queen was another facet of my life that I couldn't wait to be finished with.

As always, Keon was quick on his feet. "Of course, Ms. Melanie," he replied with a smile. Melanie glowered and ambled off to probably graze, and then harass another unfortunate employee's life. I felt sorry for whatever poor man, woman, relative, and/or animal who called her "lover". After she was out of earshot, Keon made a face. "Chile, fuck that ole Honey Boo Boo Bear-looking bitch." He waved his hand dismissively. "My shift is ova. This girl is DONE for da nyyyght."

I snickered as I grabbed the broom and began sweeping up...again.

After escaping purgatory, Keon and I walked out to the parking lot. My sister Kim was waiting in her car with a sour face. "Bout damn time," she snapped as soon as I opened the door. Whenever my mom had to work overtime, she made Kim pick me up from work. This only happened sporadically, but Kim always groaned and groused whenever she had to do it.

"What's going on, girl?" Keon said, squeezing his girth into the backseat.

"Hey," Kim replied flatly. She always gave Keon attitude because of his femininity. Of course, Keon was aware of this. Kim's attitude was only an incentive for him to be extra over the top gay. In fact, he reveled in it just to push her buttons and annoy her. Once she dropped Keon off, she turned to me with a scrunched up face. "I don't know why you hang with that fat faggot."

"Don't call him that," I replied, my heart rate ratcheting up. An attack on Keon was like an attack on me — and vice versa. I was probably closer to him than I was to my own sister.

"That's part of the reason why Aaron and them be picking on you all the time." Kim had graduated high school two years ago, but still kept an active grapevine of nosy friends to keep her in the loop and informed about my trials and tribulations.

"Aaron doesn't bother me anymore," I lied.

"That ain't what I heard." She held out her hand. "Anyway, you got my gas money?" I looked at her incredulously. *Is she serious?* She just sat there with her lips pursed and her hand in my face like some money-grubbing hood rat. She obviously wasn't going to budge from this spot until I paid the fee.

I grudgingly reached in my back pocket and retrieved my wallet. I thumbed through the meager contents. "I only have four bucks." She did the "gimme" gesture with her hand. I plunked the crumpled bills into her grimy paw.

She rolled her eyes and cranked up the radio, putting Gucci Mane on full blast. She bobbed her head and ignored me for the rest of the ride home. I just looked out the window watching houses whiz by. As much as I hated it, my sister was yet another facet of my life I couldn't wait to escape. Thankfully, Kim was always over her boyfriend's house, so I only had to deal with her occasionally. She pulled up to the curb and stopped abruptly.

"Thanks for the ride," I said, getting out of the car. I smiled at her and closed the door. She sucked her teeth and shook her weave as she hit the power locks. I barely had time to back away from the car before she sped off down the street. "Bitch," I muttered as I walked up my driveway. Being nice to Kim was like trying to pet a rabid wolverine; she'd hiss and growl, and then your hand would be gone. I couldn't wait until I got my license so I wouldn't have to rely on her or my mom for rides. (Of course, then there would be the small obstacle of obtaining wheels.) I sighed hopelessly. Why did I always have to be at someone's mercy?

When I got inside, I heated up some leftovers. I sat at the kitchen table and ate in silence. I put my phone on the table, hoping it would make a peep (it didn't). Once I was done, I dragged myself to my room and tossed my lousy phone on the nightstand. I kicked off my shoes and lay back on my bed. I clicked on the TV with the remote. Suddenly, my phone chimed. I sprung up in bed and grabbed it. It was Matt! *Finally.* I struggled to suppress my enthusiasm.

Matt: Ray-Rey
Me: Machine Gun
Matt: Lol. Wyd?
Me: Relaxing. Just got home from work.
Matt: Home alone?
Me: Yep.
Matt: Can I see you?
Me: Um, I guess you'll see me on the way to school?
Matt: lol. I meant before then
Me: ???
Matt: U scared?
Me: Should I be?
Matt: Yes ;)
Me: lol

A chill of excitement shot up my spine. I bit my bottom lip in consternation. I was eager to see Matt again, but I wasn't expecting it to be so soon. *What should I say?* I wondered. My mom was working tonight, so I would have the house to myself. But then again--

Matt: It'll only be for a minute. I just need to get out the house

I contemplated for a few more seconds before relenting and texting him my address.

Matt: Thanks *does happy dance* see you in a few
Me: K

I set my phone on the bed and stared off into space dreamily. A huge smile sprouted on my face...until I remembered what I was wearing. I grabbed at my uniform and took a whiff. My nose instantly turned up. I smelled like I'd bathed in a vat of grease. I jumped off the bed and bolted to the bathroom. I quickly showered and dried off. Just as I finished throwing on some sweats and an old, faded *Flash* t-shirt, the doorbell rang. I briskly walked to the door feeling ridiculously nervous. I composed myself and peeped out the little window.

Matt contorted his lips and made a silly face. I cracked up. I took a deep breath and let him in.

"You didn't have to get all dressed up for me, man. I'm just here to kill ya." He made a semi-serious face and playfully extended his hands toward my throat like he was going to strangle me. He laughed as I swatted his hands away. He stepped inside and greeted me with a warm bro-hug. The smell of Irish Spring and Head & Shoulders invaded my nostrils.

Thank God I took that shower, I thought, locking the door behind him. I walked over to the fridge and grabbed two sodas. "Hope you like Sprite, cause that's all we've got."

"*Sprite?*" He squinched his face. "Ain't nobody got time for that!" He exclaimed. He burst out laughing. "I'm just joking; that'll work."

I chuckled and handed him the can. We walked through the living room and down the hall to my room. "Whelp, this is my humble abode," I announced, extending my arm and sweeping it about in grand fashion.

"Hmm...not bad." Matt removed his jacket to reveal a snug white t-shirt. From the way it hugged his chest and arms, it was obvious he put a lot of work into his body. He haphazardly tossed the jacket on the desk chair, kicked off his sneakers, and plopped down on my bed.

"Well, I was going to say 'make yourself at home,' but I guess it'd be a moot statement at this point?"

"Pretty much," he replied with a shrug. He leaned back and looked around at the posters on my wall: *Green Lantern*, *Batman*, *Superman*, and of course, the entire *Justice League*. "Damn, you really are a comic fanatic, huh?"

"And?" I folded my arms across my chest and gave him a semi-serious look. "You have a problem with that?"

Matt grinned. "Nah, I just don't know how I feel about dating a dude with a DC fetish. Where's *Spidey*, the *X-men*, or hell--even the *Fantastic Four*? And by the way, you do know that the *Avengers* kick the *Justice League's* ass all day, every day, and in every way, right?"

I laughed and adjusted my glasses. "Are we talking old Avengers or new Avengers?

"Both."

Okay, NO ONE puts down the League in my presence and gets away with it. I was about to go into full-blown Sheldon Cooper-geek mode. "Okay, that's where you're wrong. The Trinity (aka, Superman, Batman, and Wonder Woman for the uninitiated) could easily beat the Avengers all by themselves! And furthermore--" I stopped in mid-sentence when Matt's words came ricocheting back into my mind...*I just don't know how I feel about dating....*"Um, who said anything about us dating, Machine Gun?"

"Come on, it's inevitable. I know your Spidey-sense tingled when you saw me the first day of school. I know I felt something tingle when I saw you." He flashed one of his signature crooked grins.

He was so corny and cute trying to spit game at me using comic book lingo. "Maybe." My anxiety was starting to dissipate, but I was still a little nervous. I placed my hands in my pocket and rocked on my heels. "So, what do you wanna do?"

"Not 'what'...more like *who*." He flashed his gleaming teeth.

"Ummm..."

He exploded with laughter. "I'm kidding, man. I just wanted to chill with you and get outta my damn house for a little bit. My dad was on my case all day."

"Really? Why?" I asked as I removed his jacket from the chair. I hung it on the coatrack attached to the back of my door.

"The school called him and told him about the fight I got into. He was so fucking pissed when I got home...." He trailed off as if he were reliving whatever altercation he and his father had had. My mood suddenly dampened. I felt bad that he'd gotten into trouble on account of me. Matt exhaled and perked up. "It's cool though. It was worth pissing my pops off to knock that smug grin off of Aaron's stupid face." A smile played at his lips.

I laughed, but I was still a little concerned. "So your dad's mad at you, but he let you come out this time of night?"

"Well, I actually snuck out through my window," he said nonchalantly. I looked at him in disbelief. I didn't want him getting into any further trouble because of me. "It's OK. He's passed out now anyway," he said in a sullen tone. His eyes lowered and his shoulders slumped. It was like the energy had been sucked from his body again. It was obvious he had some issues with his dad. I didn't know him well enough to pry, so I changed the subject. I walked over to my desk and grabbed a bag of potato chips.

"You want some?" I asked, waving the bag in the air.

His face lit up. "Toss that shit over here, bro." I snickered and threw him the bag. He tore into it like a buzz saw. I stood there and quietly observed him like it was feeding time at the zoo. He paused and glanced up at me. He removed the potato chip wedged in his mouth.

"What? I'm a growing boy." He waggled his bushy eyebrows and flexed his bicep. The t-shirt tightly gripped at the muscle.

"I guess so," I replied. *Geez, his body is everything*, I thought, trying not to drool. I took a seat next to him on the bed.

We talked, laughed and played *Call of Duty* for an hour before I began to yawn. I was thoroughly enjoying Matt's company, but it was time for a brother to hit the sack. Matt slipped on his shoes and jacket. I walked him to the door.

"Alright, man, thanks for letting me invite myself over tonight." He turned to me and smiled.

I snickered. "You're welcome. Invite yourself over anytime."

We stood there in awkward silence with big goofy smiles.

"Alright, I'm going to take you up on that." Matt bit his bottom lip and stared into my eyes. I held my breath as his face got closer and closer. We were a few scant inches apart. I reflexively closed my eyes. Our lips connected. The moist, suppleness of his lips was like tasting cotton candy. I opened my eyes to see Matt with a toothy grin on his face. "Night, Ray-Rey." He hugged me tight again, and then opened the door.

"Later, Machine Gun," I replied breathlessly as I watched him leave. I closed and locked the door. I was beaming inside and outside. *Maybe this school year won't be so bad after all?*

The next day, Matt and I walked to school together. He cracked jokes the entire way. Dude was so funny he had my stomach hurting from laughing so hard. I was wearing a Batman t-shirt, so of course he gave me all kinds of grief over that. By the time we got to school and parted ways, I was still smiling at his silliness. Even though I tried not to, I couldn't help but sit through homeroom daydreaming about him. I was so preoccupied with my fantasies that I was blissfully unaware of Aaron and his crew. He tried to get my attention a few times, but I just ignored him. Before I knew it, homeroom was over.

As soon as I walked out the door and rounded the corner, I felt a hand shove me in the back. I spun around to see Aaron and his boys sporting wicked grins.

"What's up, Dark Knight? Boy Wonder ain't here to protect your ass now." He snatched the glasses off my face.

"Stop playing, Aaron!" These were the new frames my mom had just bought me over the summer. I wasn't about to let him play around with them. I tried to grab them back, but he kept the glasses out of my reach--agilely maneuvering them around his body like we were playing a game of hoops. Barely able to see, I reached for them. My hand accidently brushed against his chest.

Aaron pushed me back against the wall. "Aye, don't be tryin' to feel on me, homo."

His boys howled.

I let out a deep breath. I could feel myself tearing up out of anger. "Just give me back my glasses so I can go to my next class, man."

Tim snorted with laughter. "He's about to cry and shit."

Aaron sniggered. "I know, right?" He extended his arm to hold the frames out to me. "Here, man." Just as I was about to take them from him, he turned his body slightly and let them drop. They hit the floor with a loud crack. I glared at him through squinted eyes. "Oops! You need to work on that hand-eye coordination, bruh." He mushed my head and walked off with his toadies in tow. The pack of hyenas cackled their way through the hall.

My heart thumped in my chest. I knelt down and blindly felt around the floor for my frames. I picked them up and examined them with my fingers. I sighed.

The lenses were completely shattered.

CHAPTER 6
MATTHEW

I was still smiling to myself as I changed into my gym clothes for third period. I couldn't get Raymond off my mind. Aside from my empty stomach, he was practically all I could think about since I'd gotten to school. I was nervous as shit when I first got to his house last night. But the more we conversed, the more relaxed and comfortable I became around him. Aside from our sarcastic sense of humor, I found out we had a lot more in common: we both loved cartoons and comic books (well, he was more of a DC comics guy than a Marvel fan, but I guess I could live with that small flaw), and we also shared the same eclectic tastes in music. And the best part of all was that he seemed to be feeling me as much as I was feeling him. I still didn't know what the spontaneous kiss between us meant or where it would lead. All I knew was that I couldn't wait to do it again. Just thinking about Ray's soft, full lips was getting me worked up. I slipped into my shorts and tossed my stuff into the locker before I got a hard-on.

(*Fuck!* It was too late.)

With my back still turned to everyone, I subtly adjusted myself and pulled my t-shirt out to cover my bulge. I quickly exited the locker room and took a seat on the bleachers. It didn't take long for everyone else to do the same.

Seconds later, the coach entered the gym from the side door holding his trusty clipboard. He was a dumpy, middle-aged man with a big bushy handlebar moustache. Everyone got deathly quiet as he approached. He stood at the bottom of the bleachers and began calling roll.

My stomach growled (or more like roared).

Coach stopped taking attendance and looked at me with a raised eyebrow. The entire class burst into laughter.

I wanted to melt and ooze underneath the bleachers like a formless blob. I could feel my face turn 50 shades of red. I was still starving from not having eaten the night before because of my dad barring me from the kitchen. The only little snack I had before going to bed were the chips at Ray's house and a candy bar. Luckily, my mom had left me some lunch money under my door this morning when she came home. She worked crazy hours as a registered nurse at her new job at the hospital, so I barely got a chance to see her anymore. I wish I could say the same for my dad. He was up bright and early this morning after finally having awakened from his drunken coma. Too bad sobering up didn't do anything to change his rotten attitude towards me.

After Coach finished taking attendance, he left to go get the equipment we would need for activities. Everyone started chattering away as soon as he was gone. I was just glad my noisy stomach didn't seem to be the topic of anyone's conversation.

"Damn, your stomach was loud as fuck," the dude seated next to me said.

Great. I turned and looked at him as his lips curled up into a slight grin. "It's gotta mind of its own." I returned his smile and pat my belly.

"Sounds like it's got a stomach of its own, too." He snickered.

I turned 50 more shades of red.

"Name's Savion."

"Matt," I replied.

His eyes widened. "You're the crazy dude that they say punched Aaron in the face yesterday???"

"Uh, yeah...that's me...I guess. 'Crayaazay' Matt." I chuckled. Geez, it was like this psycho rumor was picking up steam.

His face beamed with excitement. "Ohhhhh, shit!" He practically yelled, covering his mouth in disbelief. The way he was acting, you'd think I had just confessed to slaying a dragon. He enthusiastically shook my hand like I was a movie star or something. "Bout time somebody put that motherfucker in his place!" He was obviously another member of the Anti-Aaron Association.

"So I take it you don't like him either?"

"Fuck no," he replied, his voice full of disgust. "I can't stand that dude. We play ball together."

My ears perked up. "You're on the basketball team?"

"Yeah," he said. He smiled meekly. "I haven't gotten much playtime in since I've been on it though."

"Why not?" I leaned forward.

"Depends on who you ask." He flashed a sidelong grin. "Some people say because I suck." He sat back and ran his hand over a neat row of braided hair. "But I say it's because I haven't gotten a chance to prove myself yet, thanks to Aaron." He took note of my forehead crinkling in confusion. "Aaron's the captain of the squad. Coach listens to practically everything he says. Aaron doesn't like me, so the coach makes me ride the bench."

"Wow, he has that kind of pull?" Not only did Aaron have the principal eating out of his hand, but the coach too?

"Pretty much." He shrugged nonchalantly. "That motherfucker got the whole school up his ass--right along with his own big head."

I couldn't help but laugh at the word picture. "Damn. And I was thinking about trying out for the team. If Big Head is calling shots like that though, I guess I shouldn't even bother, huh?"

"Oh, you play ball, too?" His face lit up again.

"Yeah."

"You any good?"

"I played for my old school." I puffed out my chest. "I can do a lil' schumin', schumin' on the court."

He laughed. "What position did you play?"

"Shooting guard," I proudly proclaimed.

"Ohhhh shit!" He covered his mouth again. "Me, too!"

Before our little meet and greet could continue, Coach came back and crashed the conversation. The rest of the period was spent on the floor playing volleyball. By the time we were done, I was D-U-N-N. I was so hungry I was nearly delirious. Savion and I changed and left the gym together.

"Aight, man, I'll see you tomorrow. Take it easy," he said as we entered the bustling hallway. He dapped me up. Before I could respond, my stomach rumbled...again. Savion grinned and playfully swatted my belly. "You too, big homie." He laughed as he walked away.

I blushed and slinked away in the opposite direction. Savion seemed like a pretty cool dude to befriend. I just hoped my stomach tremors didn't scare him away. Lunchtime couldn't come fast enough.

****

Once I paid for my food, I nearly ran down the damn aisle with my tray. I slid into the seat next to Keon and across from Ray. I dove into that food like it was The Last Supper. I kind of noticed something different about Ray, but I was too delirious to figure out what it was. At that moment, all I could think about was eating. I hunched over my tray as I shoveled food into my mouth.

"What's up?" I mumbled with a mouthful of spaghetti. Once I gulped it down, I looked up. Raymond and Keon were staring at me like I really was crazy. I wiped my chin and grinned. "What?"

Keon pursed his lips and shook his head. "Chile."

Ray gave me one of his cute shy smiles.

That's when it hit me. "What happened to your glasses?"

"Nothing." He lowered his head and began playing with his spaghetti, twirling it around on his fork listlessly. "I broke them in gym this morning."

"Damn, how did you do that?" I asked, chugging down my milk.

"They just fell and broke, alright?" He snapped. I could tell by his somber demeanor and testy tone, there had to be more to the story.

"Oh," I replied softly. My eyes connected with Keon's. The look on his face confirmed my suspicions; something had happened to Ray earlier.

"Doesn't he look like rugged trade without his glasses?" Keon said with a cackle. I could tell he was trying to cheer his friend up.

"Yeah, he should go without the glasses more often," I chimed in. "He has some sexy eyes."

Raymond glanced at me and let out a little giggle. "Shut up, man."

"I'm serious," I replied, maintaining eye contact as I bit my bottom lip. He smiled bashfully. I could feel myself getting hard again.

Keon cleared his throat. "Um...ya'll two are about to make me gag."

Ray and I cracked up.

At that moment, Aaron the Asshole and his two stooges walked by. He waved his hand in front of his face like John Cena and smirked. One of his boys patted him on the shoulder and looked back at us with a smug grin.

I glanced at Ray. He was seething with anger. It didn't take a genius to realize that Aaron had something to do with Ray's missing glasses. The thought of a big dude like Aaron picking on Ray pissed me off to no end. I wasn't going to push the issue with Ray right now, since he didn't seem to want to talk about it. But I was going to find out the truth...even if I had to confront Aaron himself to get it.

CHAPTER 7
RAYMOND

After lunch I went to my fourth period class. I pulled out my iPhone and texted Matt while I waited for class to start. I felt bad for the way I'd spoken to him when he questioned me about my glasses. I didn't tell him what had really happened because I didn't want him to say anything to Aaron. I couldn't have Matt getting into trouble again for fighting my battles.

Me: *Sorry about barking on you at lunch. Just mad about breaking my glasses.*

Matt: *It's cool...I like Ragin' Ray :)*

Me: *lol. Stupid*

I nearly dropped my phone when the teacher entered the room. I fumbled to put it away. Ms. Rios was a hardnosed, no-nonsense Latina who had a reputation for taking phones and giving detention. She closed the door. Her heels clacked loudly against the floor as she walked over to the board and began scribbling in Spanish.

Suddenly, the door creaked open. Ms. Rios stopped mid-scribble and whipped her head in the direction of the noise. The look on her face seemed to say: *Only a fool would dare to disturb my classroom once it was already in session.* When I saw who the "fool" was, I felt a pit in my stomach. I shuddered as he walked up to Ms. Rios and handed her a folded piece of paper.

"I got transferred to this class." He flashed a cocky smile.

Ms. Rios frowned. "You're late. Don't let it happen again. Take a seat."

He nodded and strutted away from her. Everyone watched as he made his way down the row to one of the few empty seats. I watched in horror and prayed that he didn't pick the one next to me. Of course, he did. He plopped into the desk.

He turned to me with a grin and whispered, "What's up, Ray?"

"Sup, Savion?" I mumbled and cut my eyes. As if this day wasn't already going bad enough. Now I had the "joy" of looking forward to sitting next to my ex-boyfriend the entire year.

He bit his bottom lip and winked at me. As much as I couldn't stand him, I had to admit that Savion was an attractive guy. He was a pretty boy, thug wannabe who stood about 6'1, with a lean toned frame. He kept his hair in braids and maintained a meticulously trimmed goatee that connected to a thin moustache. He had an ingratiating smile that was accentuated by his dark chocolate skin tone. He was one step down from Illuminati/All-Star status, but a few rungs up from the unpopular chattel caste that I was regulated to.

I ignored him and pretended to focus on Ms. Rios. The sound of Savion sucking his teeth brought a thin smile to my lips that I struggled to suppress. This was the first time I'd spoken to him since we broke up--or more aptly--since he dumped me. He was my first...and only. Just thinking about the whole sordid affair with him brought back bad memories that I didn't want to relive.

When the bell rang I quickly gathered my books and left the class. As I walked down the hallway I heard Savion call out from behind me.

"Aye, Ray!"

I kept walking like I didn't hear him, hoping he'd get the hint. Of course, he didn't.

"Why're you in such a hurry, Slim?" He fell in step with me.

"Oh, was I supposed to be waiting for you?" I asked sarcastically. The question had more meanings than one.

He ignored my tone. "Where you headed now?"

"English."

"Aight." A few silent seconds passed as we continued to walk. "So, can I text you sometime?"

I stopped abruptly. I almost adjusted my glasses (until I remembered I didn't have any.) "For what?"

He licked his lips and lowered his voice. "Maybe we can chill sometime." I glared at him like he was stupid. I couldn't believe he was actually trying to push up on me.

"No, thanks. I'm good." I walked away from him--just like he had done to me.

I was still fuming when I got to my fifth period class. Fortunately, I shared this period with Matt, who managed to get my mind off Savion. We spent the entire hour hiding our phones under our desks so we could text jokes about the teacher.

After this period and then Chemistry, it was time to head home. When the final bell rang, Ke and I practically ran out of the room like it was on fire. Once he got his stuff from his locker, he walked with me to mine. I stuffed the books that I would need for homework in my bag and closed it.

"Come on, bitch. I gotta bus to catch," he said, turning to walk away. Ke lived on the other side of town and caught the bus to and from school.

"Hold up. Let's wait here for a second. I told Matt I'd meet him by my locker so we could walk home together," I replied bashfully.

A smile crawled across Keon's face. "Awwww!"

I just stared at him with a raised eyebrow. "Please stop."

"It's only been a few days and ya'll already too cute." He clutched his book bag to his chest. "First it was 'TomKat,' then 'Brangelina.' Now, make way for 'Raythew'!" He grinned. "Nah. Maybe 'Mattmond'?" He pursed his lips in contemplation. "That has a nice ring to it. Which one do you like best?"

I shook my head and squinted in the direction behind him. I groaned at the sight of King Aaron and his royal handlers, Tim and Michael, striding down the hall towards us. I swear, it was like these dudes were joined together at the hip. Although I couldn't prove it, I highly suspected they shared a collective hive-brain like The Borg from *Star Trek*. I quickly turned to my locker, hoping they hadn't seen me.

"Aye ya'll, look—it's two broke bitches!" Aaron yelled out as he approached. Tim and Michael yucked it up.

Keon smacked his lips and pointed at The MVP's. "Hey, look—it's a Destiny's Child reunion!"

"What the fuck did you say?" Aaron sneered, stopping in front of us.

"I enjoyed your performance at the Superbowl Halftime show, King Bey. You slayed for the GAWDS, hunty!" Keon punctuated his over-the-top delivery with a smirk.

Aaron glared at him. "That shit ain't funny."

I unsuccessfully tried to stifle a snicker. Aaron turned his gaze on me.

"Oh, so you're laughing now, huh? You weren't laughing this morning."

"Yeah, he was about to cry and shit over them ugly ass glasses," Michael scoffed.

I clenched my jaw and balled my fists.

"What you gonna do, Blackout?" He backed me into the locker. "Hit me?"

Keon sighed loudly. "Why don't you go on somewhere, Aaron? Ain't nobody got time for your shit today."

"Shut the fuck up. This doesn't have anything to do with you," he replied. Without taking his eyes off me, he removed his backpack and handed it to Tim. He jutted out his chin, daring me to hit him. "Go ahead, bruh; swing and see what happens."

I trembled slightly as I looked up into Aaron's taunting face. I swallowed hard. The temptation to punch him was almost unbearable. But there was no way I could hit him. I would be slaughtered. I glanced around. A small crowd was beginning to form. All eyes were on me, waiting for me to make a move. My panicked mind raced. *How am I going to get myself out of this???*

"Leave him alone, asshole!"

Aaron turned to see Matt standing behind him. His face was red with anger.

"Make me, white boy," Aaron spat. Matt calmly raised his fists in front of his face and squared up with him. The gawking crowd looked on in eager anticipation. I knew I had to stop Matt from getting himself in trouble again because of Aaron.

"Matt, he's not even worth it, man," I said, hoping to dissuade him from fighting. From the look on his face I could tell my words had fallen on deaf ears. Aaron threw his hands up and cautiously approached Matt.

Suddenly, a teacher came out of the adjacent classroom.

"Alright boys, break it up!" He pushed his way through the crowd and got in between them. "Unless you want me to get security involved?" He folded his arms and looked from Matt to Aaron.

Aaron continued to leer at Matt. If his eyes could shoot vaporizing Omega Beams, Matt would've been a pile of smoldering ashes at that moment. He snatched his bag from Tim's grasp. "This ain't over, dawg," he proclaimed and stomped off. His entourage quickly followed his lead.

Matt brushed Aaron's threat off with a cool smirk and a casual shrug.

The teacher cleared his throat. "Alright, everybody--show's over!"

The blood thirsty mob grumbled with disappointment as it began to disperse.

After accompanying Keon to his bus, Matt and I trekked home. I invited him to come to my house to hang out and play video games for a little bit. He was still pissed about the whole Aaron affair.

"Damn, I wanted to fuck him up so bad." He pounded his fist into his palm.

"Get in line," I replied.

His emerald eyes locked onto mine. "So did that asshole have something to do with your broken glasses?" I looked away, not wanting to answer. I didn't want to lie to him, but I knew if I told him the truth it'd only stir up more trouble. "Did he?" Matt reiterated his question, his probing gaze still on me.

"No," I said softly. All I heard was the sound of passing cars and some rowdy kids walking in front of us. Matt remained silent, as though he was pondering his next words. I just hoped he would drop it.

He let out a long breath. "So how was the rest of your day?" He asked. From the sound of his voice I could tell he was reluctant to change the topic.

"Meh, it was OK," I quickly answered. I was happy to talk about anything besides Aaron's aggravating ass. "Well, aside from my ex transferring to my Spanish class," I added.

Matt stopped abruptly on the sidewalk. "Ex…as in boyfriend?"

"Yep. Remind me to tell you the story sometime," I said nonchalantly.

"Damn. That's suuucky." He laughed. "Well, if he tries anything, tell him to kick rocks cause you're about to be taken."

"I am?" I smiled at him flirtatiously.

"Uh, huh." He flashed his signature grin and proceeded to walk. "You'll see."

I felt something stir in my pants.

When we got to my house, my mom was cooking. The smell of sizzling ground beef and onions greeted me before she did.

"Hi, ma," I said, walking into the kitchen.

"Hey, Mookie," she replied with her back turned to me. She had her long hair tied up in a blue scarf, and she was wearing her favorite housecoat. Matt looked at me with a silly expression. I groaned inside at the childhood nickname she wouldn't seem to let die a humane death. "I'm making hood burgers tonight!" She continued, adding insult to injury.

O...M...GGGGGGGGG!!!! "Uh, ma," I said to get her attention, "this is my friend, Matt."

She finally turned around. "Oh, hey." She let out an embarrassed chuckle.

"Hi." Matt nodded and smiled. "Nice to meet you."

"Likewise." She looked from Matt to me and flashed a silly smile. I wanted to shrivel up and die. "So as I was saying--I'm making *hamburgers*. You're welcome to eat, too, if you want."

Matt's face lit up. "Sounds like a plan to me, ma'am."

My mom smiled. "You go to school with--"

"Well, we're going to hang out in my room for a minute," I said, trying to make a quick getaway.

"Okay. I'll call you when it's time to eat." She gave me a furtive glance and grinned. I could tell she was dying to know if Matt was gay or not. I already knew she was going to be all in my business as soon as he left.

We made a hasty retreat to my room and fired up the Play Station while Mom finished cooking. In the midst of a pitched video game battle, we talked and got to know each other some more. We sat on the carpeted floor side-by-side.

"So, besides reading comic books and playing video games, what else do you like to do for fun?" He asked.

"Watch porn." I chuckled. "What about you?"

"I knew you were a pervert. Well, let's see; I like to watch porn, too," he said with a snicker, "lift weights, play basketball, and write." I stole a glance at him. The last part of his statement tickled my ears. I loved creative people. "What kind of stuff do you write?"

"Mostly short stories," he replied, not taking his eyes off the screen. He furiously pounded the buttons on his controller.

"What genre? Romance?"

"No, that's corny." He laughed. "Sci-fi and Fantasy." His video game character shot a fireball at mine.

"Oh, cool!" I exclaimed, prompting my character to block his character's assault. "You've gotta let me read some sometime." My man delivered a flying roundhouse kick.

"Yeah, man. That'd be cool. No one's ever asked to read my stuff before." Matt looked over at me with a toothy grin. Our characters stood motionless on the TV as we got lost in each other's eyes.

"Uh, yeah, cool." I snapped out of the trance and focused back on the game. While Matt was still distracted, I went in for the kill. My character delivered a lethal, spine-ripping finishing move.

"Hey, man! You cheated!" He whined.

"Never take your eyes off the target, Machine Gun." I smiled victoriously. He nudged me with his shoulder.

"Okay, time for round two! I'm gonna show you NO mercy this time."

We continued to talk as we tried to out game one another. During the course of our conversation I learned that we both had an older sibling, and we both had just recently turned eighteen.

Once the burgers and fries were ready, we joined Mom at the kitchen table. Matt woofed his food down. From the way he seemed to eat, I was surprised he didn't look like Keon.

My mom looked over at me. "That's all you're going to eat?"

"I'm full, ma," I replied, leaning back in my chair and patting my belly.

She shook her head. "Boy, you eat like a lil' anorexic bird."

I shrugged. "I have a small stomach." My mom was always complaining about me being too thin. Hell, I couldn't help that I had a high metabolism.

"Mmhmm. I'm going to fatten your ass up yet." She took a bite of her burger. "So, how's school going so far?"

"Eh, it's going good," I replied, lying through my teeth.

"Where're your glasses?" She asked as if she'd just noticed something was missing.

"Um, I broke them in gym today," I mumbled, grabbing a fry from my plate.

"Boy, you know how much I paid for those frames?" She barked.

"Yeah, I know." I lowered my head. "Sorry."

"Nobody stole 'em, did they?" She asked.

"Noooo, ma." I averted my eyes.

"Alright. You know I don't have no problem coming up there and slapping the shit outta somebody."

Matt let out a burger-muffled snicker. I gave him a slight smile and rolled my eyes. My mom was crazy over protective of me.

After we finished eating, we put our plates in the dishwasher. Mom went in her room to take a nap before her shift started. Matt and I went to my room and closed the door.

"Your mom's no joke." He laughed.

"You don't know the half of it," I replied. "She works as a correctional officer at the county jail, if that tells you anything." I was about to grab the controller from the floor and resume the game, but Matt grabbed my arm.

"Come here," he said in a low voice. "Let's play something else now." He smiled seductively as he pulled me into him. I closed my eyes and shuddered as his muscular arms embraced me. He brushed his jawline against the side of my face; the light stubble on his face grazed my skin as he brought his lips to mine. A jolt of pleasure shot up my spine. He slowly backed me up as we continued to passionately kiss. I fell back onto the bed. Matt crawled on top of me, carefully lowering his body onto mine. I reached under his shirt and felt his strong pecks. He positioned his body so I could feel the bulge in his jeans pressed against my own. I ran my palms over his smooth abs. I worked a hand into in his pants and underwear, gripping his hardness. It was thick. I began massaging him gently. Matt moaned softly into my mouth as we continued to kiss. He reached under my t-shirt and sensually rubbed his palm along my stomach, down to my crotch. He gently squeezed it and grinned. I smiled back bashfully. I was harder than steel. He tugged at my belt. I took the hint, hastily unfastening the buckle and unzipping my Levi's. He pulled his shirt over his head, exposing his toned chest and defined abs. He tossed it to the side and helped remove my shirt. His hand glided into my boxers and firmly gripped my erection. Matt started jacking me off as his lips found their way back to mine. I took hold of his shaft once more and returned the favor.

His tongue invaded my mouth.

We stroked each other in unison.

His breathing quickened.

My body began to tense.

We both shot off almost simultaneously.

My body spasmed as cum shot from my dick onto my chest. Matt grunted, ejaculating a stream of cum onto my stomach. He collapsed beside me. Seconds later, I heard snoring.

I turned and looked at him incredulously. Sure enough, he was lying there on his back with his eyes closed and his mouth wide open. *You've got to be kidding me*, I thought.

Suddenly, one of his eyelids slid up. He looked at me out the corner of his eye as his mouth morphed into a silly grin. "Told ya' that you were taken, Mookie."

I laughed. This dude was definitely a nutcase. "I guess I can live with that. Just don't call me 'Mookie again."

"Okay, I'll think about it." He rolled over and kissed me on the cheek. "Mookie."

CHAPTER 8
MATTHEW

A big smile was plastered on my face as I walked home from Raymond's house. I didn't plan for the steamy jackoff session to pop off, but I was more than glad that it had. I'd been feeling Ray like crazy from the first day we met. When we went back to his room after dinner, I couldn't help myself. I spontaneously grabbed him and kissed him. *Man, that was hot!* Just thinking about it was getting me hard again. However, my euphoric mood began to sour the closer I got to home. I dreaded having to deal with my dad. As I rounded the corner and approached our little house, I noticed his car wasn't in the driveway. Only my mom's car was there. I breathed a sigh of relief. Once I entered the house, I walked into the kitchen. My mother was sitting at the table with her head lowered.

"Hey, mom."

She turned to face me with a weary smile. "Oh, hi, Matty." I cringed inside. (Ray wasn't the only one with a silly mom-made nickname that wouldn't go away.)

I took a seat across from her at the table. I removed my backpack and dropped it on the floor. "No work tonight?"

She shook her head. "No, I'm off today." She sighed. "Although I wish I wasn't. We could really use the money." A Bible sat on the table in front of her. She had become more active in church since we moved here. She would always try to get me to come along on Sundays, but religion wasn't really my thing. I prayed to God plenty of times over the years. He was nowhere to be found when I needed him most. Her long dark hair was swept up in a disheveled bun. Her eyes were red and puffy, like she'd been crying. Her hand trembled as she raised a lit cigarette to her lips. She only smoked when she was stressed about something.

"Where's dad?" I asked, not that I really cared.

"He said he was going to the shooting range to blow off some steam." She sounded skeptical. Aside from being an alcoholic, my dad was also a gun nut. Besides drinking, his favorite past time was practicing with one of his many firearms down at the local shooting range.

"Oh. Are you okay?" From the way she was acting, I knew she and my dad had yet another argument.

"Yes." She looked away. "Just a little fight with your father."

What else is new? I thought. They were always having screaming matches. Since we'd moved to this new city, the fights only seemed to be escalating, becoming more frequent and violent.

"It was nothing serious, just a little spat." She let out a long breath. "Your dad is just frustrated because he hasn't been able to find a job," my mom said, wiping her face with the back of her hand. Ever since I could remember she was always making excuses for my dad's abusive behavior. In spite of the weariness that was etched on her face from years of mistreatment, she was still a beautiful, intelligent woman. She was petite, attractive, and only in her late thirties. She'd had me and my brother, and married when she was a teenager. For the life of me I couldn't understand why she continued to put up with dad's bullshit all these years. I know it probably sounds bad, but when I was young I would actually pray that she'd pack me and my brother up, and leave my father.

"Yeah, like he'll ever find one sitting on his ass in the recliner drinking beer and chain smoking all day," I said, sounding more sarcastic than I'd intended.

"Watch your mouth, Matthew!" She pointed a stern finger in my direction. "And don't talk about your father like that. In spite of all his flaws, he's still a good, decent man."

I let out a low sardonic laugh. "Yeah, right. Are we talking about the same guy?" I knew my tone was disrespectful, but I couldn't contain my anger. With each passing day, it was getting harder and harder to hide my contempt for my dad. I loved my mom, but her unwavering devotion to a monster was beyond frustrating.

"He took care of this family and stuck by me even when..." she paused as if biting back her words. She shook her head and sighed softly. "If you only knew all your father did for us...for you..." she trailed off. I could tell she was tired and under tremendous strain. I felt like a Grade A Jerk for adding to her worries.

"I'm sorry, mom." I meekly apologized, not wanting to stress her out any more than she already was. "Maybe I can get a job or something to help out?"

"No." She smiled thinly and shook her head. "I just want you to focus on school, Mr." She took a drag of her cigarette and exhaled a ring of smoke. "Have you started researching colleges yet?"

I closed my eyes and scratched the back of my head. "Not this again," I whined. "Ma, I already told you my plans after I graduate." We'd had this conversation a thousand times already.

"I know. That still doesn't mean you can't change your mind. I can hope and pray, right?" She smiled at me. My mom was dead set against me enlisting in the Army. She didn't want to give up both of her sons to Uncle Sam. It wasn't something that I genuinely wanted to do either. But deep down, a part of me hoped that me joining the military would earn my father's love, or at the very least, his respect. "Are you going to get something to eat? I made macaroni and pork chops." Her head motioned to the stove.

"I already ate at my friend's house. I'll get something later." Ms. Reynolds' bronto burgers would be enough to tide me over for a few hours. Grabbing my bag from the floor, I stood up and walked over to her side of the table. "I'm about to knock this homework out." I leaned down and kissed the top of her head. She gently grabbed my wrist as I was about to walk away.

"I'm sorry about blowing up at you like that. I've just got a lot on my mind." She looked at me with a contrite expression.

"It's all right, mom. I understand." I said with a thin smile on my face. I was used to far worse. I went in my room and lay down on the bed face first. I felt like the weight of the world was on my shoulders. I groaned into my pillow. Things had to get better, I told myself.

My phone chimed. With my head still buried in the pillow, I reached in my pocket and pulled it out. I brought it up to my face and turned my head slightly to look at the screen. It was a new text from Mookie.

Ray: U got home OK?
Me: Aside from the alien abduction and probe, yeah
Ray: lml. Alrighty then. Hope it was as good for u as it was for them
Me: lol. Freak
Ray: Don't forget to email me ;)

An uncontrollable smile sprouted on my face. I was so happy I'd met Ray. I'd just left his house and I already couldn't wait to see him again in the morning. With him in my life, maybe this year won't be so bad after all, I mused. I set my phone on the dresser and changed into a pair of basketball shorts and a beater. After doing some pushups and a set of sit ups, I sat down at the small desk in the corner. I turned on my computer and emailed Ray one of my stories. I couldn't wait for him to read it.

About thirty minutes into my math homework, I heard the sound of loud voices coming from the kitchen. I exhaled. The asshole was home. I reached over and turned the volume up on my radio, hoping to drown out the arguing. It didn't do any good. In fact, it seemed like their voices ratcheted up a few decibels. I took a breath and tried to block out the noise.

I heard something crash to the floor.

It sounded like a chair.

Without thinking, I sprung from my desk and bounded out the room. When I got to the kitchen, my mom and dad were shouting at the top of their lungs. He held her by the wrist as he yelled, his finger in her face.

"Dad, let her go!" I commanded as I raced to Mom's side. He released his grip on her and turned his attention to me. He walked up to me with burning hatred in his eyes.

"Don't you dare tell me what to fucking do in my own house, boy." I could smell the liquor on his breath. I guess he must've stopped off at the bar before he came home. He sneered at me and shoved me in the chest, pushing me out the way. I was relieved when he staggered out the room without incident. Seconds later, I heard the door to my parents' bedroom slam.

I glanced over at Mom. "Are you all right?" I touched her shoulder. She wiped her mouth and nodded her head. Her eyes were glassy. "It's going to be OK, ma," I said softly, attempting to console her.

"I know." She nervously ran her hand through her hair. I watched her silently as she walked over to the stove and prepared a plate of food for my dad. She put it in the microwave to warm it up. "He'll sleep it off after he eats." She grabbed a bottle of water from the fridge and nestled it under one arm. Like a dutiful wife, she took the plate and the water into their bedroom and softly closed the door behind her.

I just stood there with my arms at my side. I looked up at the ceiling and fought back the tears that had welled in my own eyes. I refused to let them fall. I had to stay strong, I reminded myself. I had to remain strong for myself. But more importantly, I needed to remain strong for my mom.

Things will get better.

They had to. I didn't know how much longer I could live like this.

CHAPTER 9
RAYMOND

Matt's eyes narrowed into slits. He boldly walked up to me and shoved my chest. I stumbled backwards as I raised my fists in front of my face. I gritted my teeth and stared him down with the angriest grimace I could muster.

"Oh, so you're gonna hit me now, punk?" He snorted, tilting his head to the side. "Go ahead — hit me — so I can knock you the fuck out." He cracked his knuckles. I shook my head in dismay. I couldn't believe things had actually come to this. He stood before me with a smirk, daring me to hit him. I knew what had to be done, but I just couldn't bring myself to do it. "I thought so...Gaymond." He released a condescending chuckle. That was the final straw--I charged at him and swung--connecting with his face. Matt blinked in astonishment. The mocking grin was gone. Before he had a chance to react, I pressed my attack, unleashing a flurry of lefts and rights. He raised his hands to shield his face. "That's all you got? Stop being a pussy!" He taunted as he rushed towards me. He wrapped his arms around my waist and tackled me to the ground, landing on top of me.

"Get off me, jackass!" I growled in defiance. Matt straddled my chest. His green eyes glared down at me.

"Or what?" His scowl slowly shifted into a smile. "Nice. But you still have much to learn, my young turtle."

I snickered. "Gee, thanks, Splinter."

He folded his arms across his chest. "That's 'Sensei Splinter' to you."

I rolled my eyes. "Um, do you think you can get up now, 'sensei'?"

Matt slid off me. He removed his boxing gloves and his headgear as I struggled to do the same. He looked at me in quiet amusement. "Here, let me help you." He took hold of my hand and effortlessly unlaced the oversized boxing glove. He yanked it off and quickly went to work on the other hand.

"Thanks," I said. With my hands finally free, I unfastened the Velcro straps under my chin and pulled the snug leather gear from my head. I wiped the sweat from my brow with my forearm.

"Not bad." He sat on the ground next to me. "You should've knocked my block off while I was trash talking instead of waiting though. When you're at a disadvantage with an opponent, always seize the element of surprise. Don't be afraid to fight dirty." We lay on our backs in the lush green grass of my backyard looking up at the clear blue sky. A month had passed since we met. The leaves on the trees were beginning to turn red and yellow; it was the last weekend of summer.

"I see," I replied unenthusiastically. I still couldn't believe I'd let Matt talk me into letting him give me some boxing lessons. It wasn't like I would ever actually use them. I just wasn't a fighter. Violence never solved anything.

Matt rolled over and rested a hand on my stomach. "I just want you to be able to protect yourself in case I'm not around."

"I know, man." Even though Aaron still picked on me, it wasn't to the extent that I felt a need to stoop to his level and get into a physical altercation with him. Matt's hand moved from my stomach and gripped my waist. He pulled me closer to him. He nestled his stubbly face into my neck. "Ouch!" I flinched as his five O'clock shadow grazed my skin. "When are you going to shave those whiskers, Splinter?"

He positioned himself on top of me and raised an eyebrow. "Oh, so now you're calling me scruffy?"

I bit back a smile. "Yep."

"Take that shit back, Gaymond." He looked at me with a serious expression.

"Nope," I replied.

"You've got five seconds, punk."

I struggled to keep a straight face.

He began counting down. When he got to one, he started tickling me.

I squealed with laughter. "Stop playing, man!" I pleaded.

"So I'm not scruffy, right?" He asked, still tickling me.

"Yeah you are--but I like it," I said, barely able to breathe.

"OK...I can live with that." He got off me and then gripped my hand.

"Asshole," I mumbled as Matt pulled me to my feet.

"That's my middle name." He flashed a satisfied grin.

We dusted ourselves off, and then gathered up the boxing gear. Once we were done, we went inside to escape the sweltering midday heat. After grabbing two cold sodas from the fridge we migrated to my room. Matt popped open his can and chugged it down while I turned on the window-mounted air conditioner. The old A/C unit hummed to life, filling the air with a cool breeze. Matt pulled off his t-shirt and stood in front of the A/C with his arms out-stretched. He tilted his head back and moaned like he was having an orgasm.

"Really, man?" I sat on the bed and stared at him incredulously. "Is it that serious?"

He turned and walked across the room. He stopped at the foot of the bed and kicked off his sneakers. A fine film of perspiration coated his bare chest and abs, making them glisten in the light. "Hey, I'm a Cali boy; I'm not used to this southern heat, like ya'll," he replied, pronouncing "ya'll" with a fake southern drawl. He flopped down on the bed next to me. "So...HOT..." he groaned in a muffled voice, his face buried in the pillow.

"Stop being a pussy," I said, imitating the taunt he'd used against me earlier during our sparring session. I leaned over and swatted him on the behind.

"Yeah, smack that!" He wiggled his butt a little. "May I have another?" He looked up at me with a silly grin. "You know you want to. I got a nice lil' phatty for a white boy, right? Come on, make it rain on me, Ray-Rey." He playfully gyrated his pelvis against the bed.

"No, freak." I laughed and smacked him on the ass again. "And stop dry humping my bed, please."

"Fine!" Matt pretended to pout and buried his face back in the pillow. He made whimpering puppy sound effects. I smiled and rubbed my hand across his buzz cut. He and I flirted every chance we got. However, aside from jacking off a few more times, we hadn't done anything else sexual. I was attracted to him like crazy, but I just didn't want to rush into anything. I'd told Matt about my previous relationship (that ended with me being dumped on my birthday). I was still leery of getting in too deep with anyone, too fast. He told me he fully understood and respected that. He was willing to take things slow, which was another thing I liked about him.

My laptop suddenly came to life. I got up from the bed and walked over to my computer desk. It was an incoming Skype call from Keon. My face lit up as I plopped into the seat.

"Happy Saturday, bitch!" Keon exclaimed. "What're you doing today, ho?"

"Just hanging with Machine Gun." I pointed behind me and moved to the side so Matt would be visible in the webcam.

"Hey, Ke!" Matt momentarily lifted his head from the pillow and waved to the webcam, cheesing like it was paparazzi.

A big grin engulfed Keon's face. "Chiiillle...I'm not interrupting anything, am I?"

I chuckled. "Nah."

"Oh." He twisted his lips in disappointment. "That sounds boring."

I shook my head. "So what're you up to?"

"I got my mom's car today; I was thinking about hitting the mall. I was calling to see if you wanted to go, but it looks like you already have plans." He jokingly pursed his lips and gave me the side-eye. I sniggered bashfully. "Anyway, have fun RayMatt. Make sure you leave the camera on," he said with a wink.

I rolled my eyes and laughed. "Bye, Ke." I ended the call and closed the laptop. I got up and climbed back in bed. I lay down next to Matt, draping my arm around his waist. He rolled over unto his back, propping his head up with his arm. I rested my head on his chest, feeling the warmth emanating from his body. It felt soothing as his fingers gently stroked my low cut hair. We laid there quietly for a minute, cooling off. "So what do you want to do now?" I asked, looking up at him.

His face lit up. He sprung from the bed. I watched him curiously as he knelt down and grabbed his book bag. He rummaged around in it before finding whatever he was digging for.

"Ah, ha!" Matt announced. He proudly held up a blunt and a lighter.

"Where did you get that?" I asked with a raised eyebrow.

"This dude that I'm cool with in my gym class," he replied, sitting back down on the bed. "I've been saving it for the right moment."

"So in addition to being mentally unstable, you're a weed head, too?" I asked jokingly.

"You didn't know me and Snoop Dogg are like this, mon?" He said in a fake Jamaican accent. He twisted his fingers together and grinned. "Nah. I only light up occasionally. I haven't blown any since I moved from Cali. So let me guess: You've never smoked before, Nerd Boy?"

"Yeah, I have," I said, recalling the times I'd smoked with my ex, Savion.

"So do you want to fire this bad boy up?" He waved the blunt under my nose.

My annoying sister wasn't home, and my mom was at work till midnight, so the coast was clear. "Go ahead."

Matt beamed. He hurriedly put the blunt to his lips and sparked it. He took a deep pull and closed his eyes, letting the smoke fill his lungs. He passed it to me. I put it to my lips and inhaled. The next thing I know, I was coughing uncontrollably. Matt took the blunt from me and laughed.

"Easy, my little turtle," he said, rubbing my back.

"That's some strong stuff." I pounded my chest. After I regained my composure, I took another hit. Fortunately, the second time went much smoother than the first. By the third pull, I felt like I was floating. I was normally a shy, quiet guy, but once the weed kicked in, I couldn't shut up. We talked and talked, and laughed and laughed about everything; comics, politics, music, and a bunch of other stuff I can't remember. Matt also bounced some story ideas off me. I'd read plenty of his stuff over the past several weeks, and I was enamored with his creative mind. I loved the way his eyes twinkled when he told me about a new character he'd come up with. It felt like we were talking for hours. Time seemed distorted. It was like we were in another dimension. I turned on the radio and the music enraptured me like it was in surround sound. It felt awesome! We sat there bobbing our heads to the beat. When the latest Lil Wayne song went off, Matt spoke up.

"So why do you think Aaron is always on your case?"

I shrugged. "The hell if I know."

He shifted on the bed. "Do you think it's because you hang with Keon?"

I shook my head. "Nah, he was messing with me before I even met Ke." I frowned. "He actually seems to pick on me more because of my skin tone than my sexuality."

Matt gave me a confused look. "Isn't he black, too?"

I chuckled a little at his naïve question. "Some people in the black community have this mindset that a lighter skin tone grants them some sort of superiority to those of us with darker skin." I held up my forearm and rubbed my hand across my skin to illustrate my point. I paused for a moment. This was an extremely sensitive subject for me to talk about, especially with someone who wasn't black. It was like I was divulging a dirty family secret to a stranger. "It's a pretty complicated phenomenon to fully explain. But in a nutshell, it's a deep seated, ingrained hatred for one's own race."

Matt's eyes gleamed with understanding. "Damn, that's messed up."

"Yeah, it really is. It's a screwed up mindset born out of centuries of slavery and racial segregation—a legacy that's been passed down from generation to generation." He nodded, staring at me intently. His full attention was focused on me. I suddenly felt shy again and clammed up.

"Why'd you stop?" He asked.

I smiled awkwardly. "Because I was about to start preaching up in here."

He grinned. "So you were about to go in on us white folks, huh?"

I laughed and playfully shoved his head to the side. "Stupid."

"Maybe Aaron secretly likes you." His eyes glinted as he snickered.

I stroked my chin in contemplation. "The bully crushing on the person he bullies? Meh, that's too cliché." I lay back on the bed and stared at the ceiling. "Some people are just assholes who get off on bullying others for no good reason."

Matt smirked. "You don't have to tell me...I live with one." He pulled his knees up to his chest and wrapped his arms around them. "My dad's the same way," he said somberly. He always seemed to get down whenever he mentioned his father. Since we were high and being candid with each other, I figured this would be the perfect time to find out why.

"Why do you say that?" I inquired, propping myself up on one elbow.

"I don't know." He let out a long breath. "It's like I can never please him. Nothing I do is ever good enough for him." His eyes were glassy, but not from the weed. "He always pushes me around and treats me like a fuckup," he said, burying his face in his knees. I could hear the anguish in his voice. *His home life must be a lot worse than he lets on*, I surmised.

I leaned upright and touched his ankle. "Does he hit you?"

Matt slowly raised his head.

Our eyes met.

He turned away. "Sometimes."

At that moment I saw a side of him I'd never seen before. Underneath the tough exterior and cavalier attitude was a scared little child desperately yearning for his father's approval. I reached out and took hold of his hand, gently caressing it. He looked at me dejectedly. I wanted to say something, but no words came. I'd only known him for a short time, but I already cared about him immensely. I knew how he felt in spades. I wanted to comfort him, but I didn't know how. What do you say to someone who's being abused by the person who's supposed to love and protect him? Everything will be OK? *Sure it will.* It'll get better? *When?* All I could do was give him a sympathetic stare as my mind raced to come up with an appropriate response. The only thing that came out was, "Damn." *Wow, Raymond. That was helpful.* I immediately wanted to slap myself.

"It's cool. I can handle it." He swallowed hard. He kept his eyes down as he attempted to regain his composure.

I scooted in between his legs, forcing him to make eye contact with me. "Whenever you need someone to talk to or a safe place to go--I'm here for you," I said softly. It wasn't profound, but it was from the heart.

"Thanks," Matt said with a faint smile. He took my hand in his and squeezed it. We sat there in utter silence, gazing at each other. I could feel the love and gratitude radiating from his eyes. It was like we were communicating telepathically. Gradually, the distance between us disappeared. Our lips met in a rousing, passionate kiss. Waves of warmth rippled through my body. He slowly pulled back. He flashed that crooked grin that I was used to. Happy Matt was back. "So uh, I don't know about you, but I'm hungrier than a kid in a fat camp."

"What else is new, Greedy?" I patted his flat stomach. This dude was a bottomless pit.

"I'm a growing boy, remember?" He flexed his bicep. "Plus, I've got the munchies like a motherfucker."

I chuckled. "Yeah, I feel you there, Snoop."

"Come on, let's raid the fridge before your mom gets home!" Before I could even reply, he bounced off the bed and sprinted for the door. If he was a cartoon character he would've left a trail of dust behind.

I shook my head and laughed at the mental picture. Just as I was about to get up and walk to the kitchen, my phone chimed. I grabbed it from the nightstand. My face scrunched up. It was a text from my ex.

Savion: We need to talk. Can I come through?

CHAPTER 10
MATTHEW

"Alright, dawg—let's see what you got!" Savion chucked the ball at me. He pulled up the edges of his basketball shorts and crouched down in a guard stance. He watched me intently, anticipating my next move. I caught the ball before it could slam into my chest. I began dribbling it against the concrete. I maintained eye contact with him as I bounced the ball. Suddenly, I exploded toward him. He flailed his arms trying to steal the ball. I charged by him like a bull on fire with my tongue lolling out of my mouth. He tried to stop me by positioning himself between me and the goal. I drove the ball to the hoop. Savion furiously tried to block me. He got a face full of sweaty crotch for his efforts as I leaped through the air, slamming the ball into the hole like I was at an NBA Slam Dunk Contest.

"Now what?!" I barked at him, all amped. "Mad Matt strikes again!" I started doing a victory dance. Savion watched me from the ground with a pissed off expression on his face. Besides Ray and Keon, Sav was the only person from school whom I hung out with. Although a little cocky, he was cool for the most part. He also had a wicked competitive streak. We were practicing for the school basketball team tryout which was coming up.

Savion glared at me. "Man, go on somewhere with all that noise." He dusted himself off and stood up.

"Why you mad though, bro?" I continued to jig. Savion ignored me and retrieved the ball. I grinned. I loved getting under his skin and throwing him off his game.

We played ball for about an hour before succumbing to the heat. We walked over to the patio to cool off a bit. I sat down at the table under a big canary yellow canopy umbrella. Savion went inside. I wiped my brow and took the opportunity to take in my surroundings. Sav had a nice crib—a basketball court and rim, a patio, and an in-ground swimming pool. Whatever his folks did for a living, they were obviously making some serious dough.

A few minutes later, he returned carrying a towel and two bottles of Gatorade. He handed me one as he pulled out a chair and took a seat. He had a joint tucked behind his ear.

"You wanna smoke?" He asked, wiping his face with the towel.

"Nah, I'm good," I said. I unscrewed the cap off my grape Gatorade. I turned it up and took it to the head. Once I finished chugging it down, I wiped my mouth with the back of my hand. "I had enough yesterday."

"Ole lightweight ass." Savion snickered. "I told you--my brother got that fiyah!"

"You can say that again," I concurred. "I can't fuck with that too often."

"Yeah, man. My brother can get anything you want."

"Uh, okay. I'll remember that." I put my hands behind my head and leaned back in the chair.

While Sav sparked up, I found myself reminiscing about the time I'd spent with Ray on Saturday. I couldn't help but smile as I relived the magical experience. It was like he and I had bonded on a whole different level. It felt strange to tell someone about my fucked up relationship with my dad.

At the same time, it also felt good to finally get it off my chest. I had no intention of burdening Ray with my issues, but it was still a great relief to know that I had someone to confide in if I needed to. I loved me some Raymond Reynolds. I was determined to make things official between us when the time was right. However, I knew he still had some mental hang-ups over the way his last relationship ended. He wanted to take things slow. I understood. If some douche had dumped me on my birthday, I would be skittish too about jumping into another relationship.

A blaring ringtone suddenly snapped me out of my daydream. Savion picked his phone up from the table and frowned. "This annoying ass bitch here." He sent the call to voicemail and tossed the phone on top of his towel.

I shifted in my chair and chuckled. "Who was that?"

"That chick from our gym class that I've been fucking with." He glowered.

"Nikki?"

"Yeah, that bitch."

"What's wrong with her?"

He shrugged. "She's aight...just not feeling her like that though. I'm trying to get back with my last girl."

"Your last girl broke up with you?"

His face twisted up as if I'd just called his mom a bad-breathed, buck-toothed bitch or something. "Ain't nobody dumped me. I broke up with her ass."

A mosquito buzzed by my ear. I swatted at it. Those little bloodsuckers seemed to be everywhere down here. "Why?"

"It's complicated." He took a pull from the joint and let the smoke simmer in his lungs. "But enough about me; what's going on with you in the pussy department, playa?"

"Not a damn thing," I replied with a laugh.

"That girl Tracy with the big booty likes you. You need to hit that, man."

"Eh, I'm good," I said, scratching the spot on my arm where the micro vampire had bitten me.

"You gay or something?" He snorted.

"Well...actually...yes." I grinned. I wasn't ashamed of my sexuality; I just didn't broadcast it. However, if someone asked me I had no problem telling them.

"Stop playing, dawg!" Savion looked at me with a wide smile. "Are you serious???"

"So serious."

His face dropped. "Fuck outta here. You joking, right?" The look on his face was hysterical. I burst out laughing. "I ain't with that homo shit, man." He scowled, his body suddenly tensing up.

"Don't worry." I folded my arms and leaned back in my chair nonchalantly. "You're not my type."

He stared at me silently.

Was he about to swing on me?

The tension was almost unsettling.

"For real though; I ain't with all that gay shit." He seemed to slowly decompress. "But you're cool peoples, so I guess I can overlook it. Just don't try no funny shit, or I'll have to bust your ass."

"You might want to rephrase that last sentence. It sounded a little gay to me." I laughed.

"No homo." He grinned bashfully and took another hit of the joint.

He acted a little weirded out for a minute. But the more we talked, the more he seemed to be OK with it. I just hoped me coming out to him hadn't ruined our fledgling friendship. We sat around and chilled for fifteen minutes, and then practiced some more.

Once Sav sobered up, he gave me a ride home. I could see the hood raised on my dad's car as we pulled up to the curb in front of my house. We dapped off. My dad poked his head out from under the hood and leered at me as I got out of the car. Savion pulled off. I took a deep breath and began walking up the driveway. Hopefully he wouldn't start with me today. I smiled at him as I approached.

"Hey, dad. Need some help?"

He wiped his hands on a dingy rag. He just glared at me and shook his head. I sighed. *Well, I tried*, I thought. I turned to walk to the house when my dad spoke.

"Don't bring any of *those* people around my house again, got that?"

I stopped and looked back at him in disbelief. *Those people? Racist asshole*. I turned and continued walking in the house. Before I could shut the door he burst in behind me. He grabbed my white t-shirt with his greasy hands and yanked me back. He slammed me against the wall and got in my face.

"Did you fucking hear me, boy?!"

I clenched my jaw. I could smell cigarettes and beer on his breath. Sunday afternoon and he was already drunk. Pathetic. We peered into each other's eyes. The disdain we shared for one another was mutual. I nodded my head. He slowly released his grip on me.

"Good." He took the rag he had used to wipe his hands and smushed it against my face, leaving an oily smudge on my cheek. He stomped back outside and slammed the door behind him. I balled my fist and trembled with anger. I knew he was my father, but he had no right to treat me the way he did.

I clenched my teeth and punched the wall.

I didn't know how much longer I could take his abuse without fighting back.

CHAPTER 11
RAYMOND

After having an awesome time with Matt on Saturday, it was back to the monotonous drudgery of work the following day. It was an unusually busy day at the restaurant for a Sunday. I was happy to clock out and go on my lunch break. Unfortunately, I had to spend my break there. I ordered my food from Keon, who was working the register. I handed him a ten dollar bill. He twisted his lips as he held it up to the light and scrutinized it.

"This ain't real. I'm 'bout to call Moose Melanie on your ass," he said, jokingly referring to our boss.

I folded my arms. "Boy, if you don't give me my change."

"Eww." He clutched imaginary pearls. "No need to get all hostile." He opened the register and grudgingly handed me four crisp bills.

"Bitch," I said in a low voice, snatching the money from his hand.

He wagged his tongue at me and laughed. Minutes later, he slid me a tray with a large soda and a chicken strip basket on it. I grabbed the tray and walked to an empty table in the back near a window. I pulled out my phone to check my messages as I stabbed a straw into my drink. There were two new texts; one from Matt...and one from Savion. I rolled my eyes. I didn't even bother to reply to the text he'd sent me Saturday asking if he could come by and talk. He followed up with another text later that night which simply read: question mark. I ignored that one, too.

As far as I was concerned, he'd told me all I needed to hear when he dropped me on my birthday several months ago.

Savion: So you can't even respond to me now?

I shook my head in disbelief. I couldn't believe he was carrying on like this. We'd broken up a few weeks right before school let out for summer break. Those weeks were the worst. I pretty much spent the entire summer sulking over the breakup and working to get over him. Now he was back and trying to act like it had never happened. I'd been ignoring him since the day he showed up in my Spanish class. Apparently he still hadn't gotten the hint that I wanted nothing to do with him. I guess I was going to have to make it crystal clear when I saw him Monday, I concluded. I dipped a chicken strip in honey mustard sauce as I opened Matt's message.

Matt: Sup Double R?
Me: On break. Wyd?
Matt: Scratching my nuts and doing homework
Me: Eww
Matt: What's wrong with doing homework? :P

I laughed to myself. I loved Matt's playful banter. I had an ear-to-ear smile on my face.

Until I glanced up and saw Savion walk through the door.

He turned his head from side-to-side like he was looking for something. His sights landed on me and his face lit up. I groaned as he sauntered towards me. I lowered my head and continued eating like I hadn't noticed him. He casually slid into the chair across from me.

"What's up?" He announced, smacking his hand on the table.

"Nothing," I replied dryly. I shot him a death glare. Unfortunately, he didn't die.

"When you stop wearing glasses?" He was all smiles.

"When I started wearing contacts," I said in a sardonic tone. Instead of getting a new pair of frames to replace the pair Aaron broke, I persuaded my mom to buy me a pair of contacts. I'd gotten used to the feeling of not wearing glasses and kind of liked it. (Not to mention, Keon was right for a change; I did look less geeky without glasses.)

"Oh...cool." He licked his lips and stared at me with a silly grin.

"So, umm, are you stalking me now or something?"

He laughed a little. "Mane, ain't nobody stalking you. I just came from playing ball and stopped by this joint to get some ice cream."

"Okay. You have to place your order up there." I motioned to the counter with my head.

He reached across the table and helped himself to one of my french fries. "Damn, that's cold, bruh."

I looked at him incredulously. "No colder than breaking up with someone on his birthday."

"Look, that's what I've been wanting to talk to you about," he replied, smacking on the fry. "I've been trying to holla at you for--"

He stopped abruptly, his eyes fixating on something. I turned to see Keon wiping down the table behind us. I couldn't believe his nosy ass had conveniently slipped from behind the register just to wipe down a table that was already clean (well actually, I could). Up until that point, I hadn't even noticed him. *How in the hell did he get back there without me seeing him?* I thought. It was like he had some sort of invisibility or teleportation powers. I shook my head at him. He grinned, shrugged innocently, and then strutted away.

"So like I was saying," Savion said, picking up where he left off, "I just wanted to apologize. All that gay shit was new to me when I first met you. I'd never been with a dude before you, man."

"Just like I'd never been with one either before you; so what's your point?"

He exhaled. "I know. But you always knew you liked dudes. Up until we met I was only curious. When I started having all these feelings for you, it scared the shit out of me."

"Which still doesn't explain why you dumped me." I looked at him with a blank face. "On my birthday."

He ran his hands over his braids and grinned. "Alright, I know that part was fucked up, but I just panicked. Me celebrating some dude's birthday like he my girl and shit. Things were getting too deep, and I didn't know how to deal with it, feel me?"

As he spoke, I couldn't help but think back to how it all had started. Savion and I met on a gay social network during winter break. He sent me a message saying that he'd seen me around school and wanted to get to know me. I clicked on his profile and saw he didn't have a picture. He used the classic line about being "too DL" to have pics online. Usually, I wouldn't even waste time with someone like that. But he was persistent and kept hitting me up relentlessly.

After chatting online for a few days, we exchanged numbers. We quickly went from texting to talking on the phone. The first time I heard his voice I nearly melted like a pot of protoplasm, it sounded so smooth and masculine. He finally agreed to meet me in person on the first day of the second semester. I was happy to see that the face matched the voice. Savion was just as handsome and confidant as he sounded.

Over the next five months we would discreetly chill at my place after school. Out of respect for his privacy, I agreed to keep our relationship a secret from everyone. I didn't like it, but I liked him, so I reluctantly went along with it. Aside from a brief glance and a smile in the halls, he didn't even acknowledge me in public for fear of being associated with an openly gay dude. It hurt, but I tried not to take it personally. I knew he was on the basketball team with Aaron, who'd jump at the opportunity to have another "homo" to taunt. I didn't even tell Keon about us until it was over. In his typical dramatic fashion, he scolded me, telling me how "shocked, appalled, offended, and betrayed" he felt. (Of course, a few seconds later he proceeded to ask for all of the juicy details.)

"I was trying to convince myself that I was only going through a phase. But now I realize," he looked from side-to-side and then leaned in to whisper, "I'm bi." He stared at me anxiously, as if expecting me to applaud his revelation and start fawning over him.

I shrugged my shoulders. "I'm glad you've had an epiphany and all, but what's that got to do with me?" Maybe he was sincere, but that didn't change anything. I wasn't angry at Savion for being confused or scared because of his sexuality. I was just mad at the way he handled things. It was bad enough that he broke up with me, but then I had to witness him walking with his arm around some girl and kissing all on her just a few days later.

"Damn, Ray." His eyebrows furrowed. "You ain't going to make this easy, are you?"

"Make what easy?" I asked, playing dumb. I already knew what he was getting at, but I just wanted the satisfaction of hearing him say it.

"I miss what we had. I'm ready to get back with you." He looked me in the eye and bit his bottom lip. Several months ago, that gesture probably would've had me eating out of his hand, but not anymore.

I nonchalantly finished the last of my drink before responding. "I'm glad you're ready, but I'm not." I smirked. "I've got somebody in my life who isn't confused about who he is or what he wants."

Savion had a smug, unfazed look on his face. "Stop lying, bruh. You ain't with nobody."

"Believe what you want." Even if Matt and I weren't officially together-together, there was no way in hell I'd ever go back to Savion.

He blew air through his teeth. "Whoever it is, tell him to kick rocks. Ya boy is back now." He flashed a cocky grin.

I saw my supervisor standing near the front looking at her watch. "Look man, it's over between us. I'm glad you've found yourself and all—and maybe we can be friends—but as far as us getting back together, that isn't going to happen." I stood and picked up my tray. "I've got to get back to work now."

"You need me to scoop you up later when you get off?"

I looked at him like he was insane. *Was I speaking in Vulcan or something?* "No, thanks. I already have a ride home." As I was about to walk away, he grabbed my arm.

"Alright, I'll hit you up later." He licked his lips again.

"Don't bother." I snatched my arm from him and proceeded to empty my tray in the trash. After I finished washing my hands and returning to my station, Savion was at the counter holding a chocolate ice cream cone. When he saw me, he seductively licked the cone. I rolled my eyes. He winked at me and grinned, and then left the store. Keon turned to me with his mouth wide open.

Great, just what I needed: A stalker ex-boyfriend.

CHAPTER 12
MATTHEW

"**What's up, fellas?**" I shouted as I slid my tray on the table.

Keon jerked his head in my direction and clutched his chest. "Damn, you almost gave a bitch a heart attack!" He laughed. "Turn it down a notch, please."

"MY BAD!" I sat down next to him and winked at Ray. "I'm in hype mode today!" I started tearing into my lasagna.

"Yeah, I can tell," Keon said, sticking his index finger in his ear. "My eardrum is bleeding."

Ray stroked the few strands of hair on his chin. "Why're you so wired?"

I stopped mid-chew. "Tryouts, remember?" The first day of basketball tryouts were being held after school. I couldn't wait to get out there on the court and show my stuff.

"Oh yeah, that's right," he replied with an embarrassed expression. "You did tell me that."

"Wow, one of the biggest days of my life, and my dude forgets about it." I pretended to sulk.

"Don't worry." Keon placed an arm around my shoulder. "Cheerleader tryouts are being held today too, so I'll be there to give you all the moral support you need."

"Aww, thanks." I playfully rested my head on his arm. "At least someone cares."

"Oh, Lord." Raymond rolled his eyes. "I know you're going to do well." He gave me a reassuring smile. Hearing my baby-to-be voice such confidence in me made me feel all warm and wavy inside. "So how's your day going so far?"

"It's been alright." I frowned. "Although, my boy was acting kind of funny today."

"The one you came out to yesterday?" Ray asked.

"Yeah, him," I said somberly. Ray and I had talked on the phone last night after he got home from work. I told him about coming out to my friend. "He hardly said anything to me the entire period." Before yesterday, Savion and I always used to bug out together during gym class. Today it was like he was giving me the cold shoulder.

"He's probably still a little freaked out. Just give him some time, he'll come around," Ray replied.

"I hope so." I enjoyed our burgeoning friendship. It was cool having a friend who shared my love of basketball. This was exactly what I feared would happen by telling Savion I was gay. I guess I was hoping that he'd handle it a little better.

"Chile, fuck that bitch," Keon interjected. "If he can't accept you for who you really are, then he's not a real friend anyway."

"Yeah, I know." Ke was right. I'd lost friends before because of my sexuality. If Savion couldn't deal with it--too fucking bad. I turned my attention to Ray. "So how's your day been going, Double R?"

"Eh. It's going." He took a sip of his chocolate milk.

"Have you seen your stalker today?" During last night's conversation, Ray had told me about his ex popping up at his job. Just thinking about it sent a ripple of rage through my body.

He chuckled and shook his head. "Not yet. Unfortunately I'll see him next period."

"You sure you don't want me to say something to him?" I was just dying to have a word with this punk. However, I didn't know who he was. Whenever Ray talked about the asshole, he always referred to him as "my ex". I never asked him the dude's name (I was new here, so I doubted it was anyone I'd recognize anyway).

"Nah, I got it, Killer." He grinned a little. "I already told him to get lost. I think he got the message."

Keon smacked his lips. "What makes you think that? From the way he was licking that--" Ray shot him a look and he instantly clammed up. It was too late. My curiosity had already been piqued.

"The way he was licking what?" I asked, starting to feel some kind of way.

Ray sighed. "He was just flirting with me...by licking an ice cream cone." He mumbled the last part, but I still heard it.

I could feel the blood rushing to my face. "And you forgot to mention that last night?"

"I didn't think it was that big of a deal." He shrugged. "And I didn't want you getting all bent out of shape about it like you're doing now."

"I'm not getting 'bent out of shape'!" I replied, much louder than I had intended. Everyone at the table turned in our direction. I lowered my voice. "I just don't like some dude trying to push up on you when I'm not around." I knew we weren't officially together yet, but I couldn't help feeling a little possessive when it came to Ray. I trusted him, but I didn't want even the slightest possibility of his ex fucking things up for us.

"I can handle it, Matt," Ray said in an exasperated tone. "Don't worry about it, OK?"

"Alright. I'll keep my mouth shut then." An awkward silence lingered in the air over our little section of the table. Keon tried to lighten the mood by changing the topic and the tone of the conversation. I pretended to smile and laugh along with him, but inside, I wasn't feeling it. For some reason, I no longer felt as amped as I had before.

*****

I was still pissed when I walked into fifth period. Ray was already sitting at his desk when I came in. We were the only ones there. Without saying a word, I took my seat. I opened my notebook and proceeded to write. (Yeah, I know I was probably being a little childish, but oh well.)

"Sorry about not telling you everything last night," Ray said in a meek voice. "I just didn't want things to be blown out of proportion. Trust me, my ex is a total non-factor."

"I believe you," I said nonchalantly. I continued to write in my notebook.

I felt him gently grab my wrist, stopping my pencil. I finally turned to face him. "You forgive me, Machine Gun?"

"Yeah, I guess...Mookie." A begrudging smile appeared on my face. I couldn't stay mad at my Ray-Rey. "You can make it up to me by giving me a good luck kiss."

He raised an eyebrow. "Now?"

"Yep." I grinned and bit my bottom lip. "You owe me."

He huffed and looked from side-to-side. He slowly leaned towards me. Our lips were inches and a second away from touching. Suddenly, the Hobbit came hobbling into the room. Mr. Bailey loudly cleared his throat. Ray and I quickly repositioned ourselves and pretended like we weren't just moments away from tonguing each other down.

"Uh, hey, Mr. B." I saluted him with a chirpy tone.

"Hello, Matthew," Mr. Bailey replied dryly. He set his bag down and pulled out his trusty clipboard. He took a pen from his shirt pocket and began writing a novel. I groaned. I could only imagine what he was scribbling about me on that fucking thing. I looked at Ray. He was stifling a laugh.

As always, Mr. Bailey's mediocre teaching bored me to tears and nearly put me to sleep. Thankfully, after bolting from his class, my remaining period was art class, which I enjoyed and excelled at. By the time the bell rang signaling the end of school, I was so hype I was practically bouncing off the walls. Ray and I had "made up," now it was time to tear some shit up on the court!

After stashing my books in my locker and grabbing my book bag that contained a change of clothes, I walked to Raymond's locker. We chatted a little as I walked him to the exit.

"I'll let you know how everything went when I get home," I said.

"Okay." Ray gave me a bro-hug. "Good luck."

"Thanks. So...can I get that good luck kiss now?" I looked at him expectantly. He looked at me like I had a giant octopus on my head. "I was just joking, wuss." I squinted my eyes like I was focusing on something. Ray looked at me with a confused expression. "You've got something right here." I pointed at a spot on his forehead.

His eyes widened with concern as he scrubbed his palm against the area I'd indicated. "Did I get it?"

"Nope." I motioned with my hand for him to come towards me. He wearily leaned closer. I caressed the side of his face and planted a sloppy wet kiss on his forehead. He pulled back and wiped the spot I'd kissed with the back of his hand. I couldn't help but crack up at the look on his face. "Had to kiss my good luck charm." Just then, I noticed Savion coming down the hall. "Sup, Sav? Ready to do this?" I asked, trying to re-break the ice. He simply nodded his head and glared at me as he kept walking. I took a deep breath and exhaled. "Whelp, looks like that bromance is DOA."

Ray looked at me funny. "*That's* the friend you've been telling me about?"

"Yeah, that's my boy, Savion." I smirked. "Well, 'was my boy,' I guess I should've said." Ray looked as if he'd seen a glowing, giggling, green ghost. "What's wrong?"

He gulped like Scooby Doo. "Umm...*that's* my ex."

I looked at him dumbfounded. "What?"

"Savion is my ex," he repeated barely above a whisper. Okay, so I wasn't hearing things.

"Oh, man, it's about to be on," I said with anger already building in me. I was just about to walk off when Ray grabbed my hand.

"No, Matt. Just let it go."

"What do you mean, 'just let it go?'" I asked, throwing my hands up in frustration. This was the evil ex who was pushing up on him and he expected me to just let it ride. "No way."

"Just leave it alone. I don't need you to fight my battles. I can deal with him," he implored.

"But--" I protested. He looked into my eyes. He knew his eyes could make me melt inside.

"It's not worth it. You don't need to ruin your tryout over him." Cool, calm, collected, logical Ray.

"Fine." I rubbed my hand over my head and huffed. "I won't say anything to him."

Raymond smiled and gently squeezed my hand. "Thanks. Now go get'em Machine Gun."

I was fuming as I walked to the gym. It was going to take everything in me to keep my word to Ray and not bark on Savion. I walked into the locker room to change my gear. I made my way over to the benches. Savion looked up and gave me the screw face. Apparently, he'd seen me kiss Ray and wasn't too thrilled about it. *Stay cool, Matt*, I told myself. I kept walking. I went to the other side of the locker room.

Once I finished changing into my basketball shorts and a t-shirt, I walked out into the gym. The sound of chattering and laughing filled the air. It looked like approximately 20 dudes standing around. Most were in groups of three or four, talking and bullshitting. There were a few loners standing off to the side by themselves. I noticed Savion talking with two other dudes. One of the dudes was speaking to him, but Savion's eyes were fixated on me. We were locked in an intense stare down when I heard a voice from behind.

"Aye, what the fuck are you doing here, white boy?"

I exhaled. I already knew who it was without even looking back. I turned around to see Aaron with a devious grin on his face.

"Oh, I'm just here to take your spot," I replied confidently. His grin disappeared. He was about to respond when the sudden shrill shriek of a whistle pierced our eardrums. We both turned to see Hard Ass, aka, Coach Smith approaching.

"Alright, gents! Everybody line up!" He commanded like a drill sergeant. Everyone hustled to line up on the court. Aaron glared at me for a few seconds before walking away. I followed behind him to get in line. Coach Smith paced up and down the line with his arms and clipboard folded behind his back. "For those of you who don't know me, my name is Coach Smith!" He eyed each of us as he spoke. "I see a lot of returning faces, and some new ones." He stopped in front of me and looked dead in my eyes. "I don't care if you were on the team last year, the year before, the year before that, or three years before that, for you super seniors." He stopped in front of a dude with a full grown beard. "No one's spot is guaranteed. If you want to be on this team, you're going to have to earn your spot! This will be a level playing field—everyone will have an equal opportunity to show what he can do."

After he finished his rousing speech, he instructed us to stretch for a few minutes. Then, he made us run laps around the gym to test our endurance.

As we ran, I saw Keon in the far corner of the gym practicing with the cheerleaders. He was the only dude there. I'd heard about his epic, fabled rivalry with Aaron's girlfriend Brianna, the squad captain. From the way Ke was mean mugging her on the sly, you could tell that he had it in for her. He was matching her move for move, beat for beat. Even from a distance, I could tell they were in fierce competition. Ke was a big boy, but to his credit, he was giving the girl a run for her money. It was hilarious. I gave him a small wave as I passed. He smiled and dropped into a split. *Ouch.* I chuckled to myself. Most of the dudes running were busy staring at the cheerleaders. Except for Savion. He was too busy competing with me. Whenever I poured on the speed to try to break away from him, he would speed up too. Even though there was no finish line, he and I were racing each other as if there was.

After a few minutes, Coach blew the whistle. We all went back and collapsed on the bleachers. I'd barely wiped the sweat from my brow before the whistle sounded again. Coach Smith didn't let up for a second, he was a fucking taskmaster. He made us do some shooting and ball handling drills for thirty minutes before making his next announcement.

"Now we're going to play a little game of four-on-four. Two newbies will be paired with two veterans." Coach called eight dudes up. Savion and I traded angry glances as we sat in the bleachers. Coach took notes as he watched the first pair of teams play, obviously checking for their ball handling skills and teamwork. Once he saw enough, he blew his whistle, signaling the end of the competition. He scanned his clipboard for the next victims. "OK...Thomas," Aaron sauntered to the court like he was walking to the stage to receive a plaque at a hip hop awards show. I shook my head. "Simon," a lanky dude with a high top fade shuffled to the floor. "Daniels," a stocky kid got up. "And Richards—front and center."

Richards--that was me.

Great, I was on a team with the Asshole Supreme. Could this day get any more randomly coincidental or sucky? I took a deep breath. *Alright, here goes everything*, I thought. My anger was offset by a twinge of nervousness. I popped up and scurried onto the court with the other three dudes on my team.

"And your opponents will be..." Coach paused, looking down at his clipboard again. He rattled off more names. Four more guys got up from the bleachers. One of them was Savion. I couldn't help but smile to myself. If I couldn't literally kick his ass, at least I'd now have the opportunity to do it figuratively. Our eyes locked as he approached.

"I'll guard him," I said, pointing to Savion before Aaron could even say anything. It was tip off time. Being the tallest member on our team, Aaron was elected to represent our side. The other team got the ball. I wasted no time aggressively going after Savion. I was all over him. He guarded me just as intensely whenever we had the ball. At times, things were getting real physical between us.

During the entire game, I hustled up and down the court with Savion doggedly on my tail. I went out of my way to show off my defensive and offensive skills (without looking like I was trying to show off, of course). Coach casually observed from the sidelines and jotted notes on his clipboard. I glanced over at him, he had that same poker face. I couldn't tell if he was impressed, distressed or just flat out ready to go. While I was busy focusing on him, a player on the opposing team managed to steal the ball from us and score. *Fuck! If this was a real game, we'd be losing.*

Play time was over. It was our ball again.

Surprisingly, I was wide open. I flailed my arms in the air, desperately attempting to get Aaron's attention. He looked my way. From the sour expression on his face, I could tell he would rather have his nuts smashed with a hammer than pass me the ball. He hesitated for a moment, and then reluctantly tossed it to the stocky dude. Just as it touched the tips of his pudgy fingers, Savion came out of nowhere and stole the ball from his grasp. Before we even knew what had happened, he was already speeding down the court like a bullet. He slammed the ball in the hole and hung onto the rim for a second to show off. He had a smug expression on his face as he walked back up the court. He looked at me and flashed a smarmy grin.

Easy Matt, I told myself. I wanted to knock his head off right there. We got the ball once more.

The other members of our team were wrestling with their defenders, jockeying for position. Stocky dude and I managed to break free of ours. Savion was on my back hard and heavy, but I was able to keep him at bay. Our bodies forcefully bumped and pushed against each other as I frantically extended my hands to Aaron. His pink lips twisted. His eyes ricocheted from me to Butter Fingers. His expression was one of pure ambivalence. From the agonizing look on his face, you would've thought he was mulling a decision to hand over his first born child to the devil in order to save the world. I stared at him with wide eyes. I wanted to scream at him, *Give me the ball already, jackass!* He exhaled. He turned and faked like he was going to pass it to Butter Fingers, but hurled it at me instead. Fortunately, I was paying attention and caught it. Judging from how hard he threw it, he was clearly hoping to hit me with it. It was all good though--I could take it and dish it out too. I bolted down the court, dribbling the ball in front of me. I leaped into the air and smashed the ball in the hoop. Savion grilled me as I strode past him. I nodded and smirked.

Minutes later, the opposing team had the ball. Savion got it and went for a layup. I jumped in front of him and smacked the ball out of his hands hard as fuck. Our bodies collided. He crashed to the floor in slow motion.

A chorus of "oohs and ahhs" erupted from the onlookers in the bleachers.

I looked down at Savion and gave him a smug look that said, *"What, bitch?!?!"* One of his teammates extended a hand and pulled him to his feet. He dusted himself off and scowled at me.

At one point, there was a loose ball. I bust my ass to rebound it. Aaron was open. Without hesitation, I passed it to him. Even though I didn't like the guy, I wasn't going to be unsportsman-like like him and let it interfere with teamwork (Although, I did launch it at him extra hard as payback). He caught the ball with a grimace, and made an easy shot from the three-point line—it was all net.

He flashed a cocky grin. "Take notes, punk."

I just looked at him and shook my head. I now realized what he was trying to do. He wanted to provoke me and piss me off to the point where I lost it. If we came to blows, there was no doubt that the coach would side with him and kick me out of the tryouts. This was clearly what Aaron wanted to happen. I wasn't dumb enough to give it to him. I was a hothead, but I wasn't going to lose my cool. I had to redirect my anger. Neither he nor Savion were going to knock me off my game. My thoughts were shattered by the sound of Coach's whistle.

"After you've been up, you're free to leave," he yelled. "A list will be posted on my office door in the morning. Those of you who make the first cut are to come back for round two tomorrow."

As Savion and some of the other guys headed to the back, Aaron went over to talk to the coach. They both looked in my direction. Coach nodded his head as he listened to whatever Aaron was saying. Coach still had his poker face on. I could only imagine what lies Aaron was pumping his head with. I made my way to the water fountain. After drinking like a dehydrated camel in the desert, I walked to the locker room. I sat on the bench and took off my sneakers. Savion was on the bench across from me changing his clothes. Neither of us said a word, but tension filled the air like locker room funk. I was just about to pull off my t-shirt when High-top Fade came up to me.

"You were good out there, dawg!" He exclaimed.

I dapped him up. "Thanks, man."

Savion blew air from his mouth. "He ain't all that."

I knew Ray told me not to say anything to Savion, but I just couldn't hold my tongue any longer. "You gotta problem with me?"

Savion quickly finished dressing and stood up. "Yeah, I gotta problem with your faggot ass. You need to stay away from my bitch." *Did he really just say that?* I thought. I sprung to my feet. He walked over to me and got in my face. We stood chest to chest. He shoved me. I bumped into the locker behind me. I cracked my knuckles. *Game on!* I pushed his ass back. He stumbled a little and then threw himself at me. He took a swing. I ducked and punched him in the stomach. We started throwing blows at each other in rapid fire. The other guys scrambled to pull us apart. It took a lot of effort, but they were finally able to separate us. Savion and I glared at each other, breathing hard.

The dude with the high top looked at Savion. "Sav, if the coach catches ya'll beefing he's going to ban both of you on the spot."

"Yeah, Sav, you know the coach don't play that shit," the dude holding Savion said. "There's too much pussy out here to be fighting over some bitch." Everybody laughed except me and Savion.

"You heard the man," I chimed in. "Kick rocks. And stay the fuck away from Ray, too." The guys gave each other confused looks. "He doesn't want anything to do with you."

Savion stared at me with a scowl. He snatched his arm from the dude restraining him and grabbed his bag from the bench. He mean mugged me as he pulled the straps of his book bag over his shoulders. "We'll see about that." He said under his breath. He smirked and promptly exited the locker room.

"Oh yeah, trust me, we will," I said to myself. I was always up for a good challenge. Game fucking on.

CHAPTER 13
RAYMOND

"But he started it," Matt whined like a child. He and I were Skyping about the basketball tryout. I was annoyed that he'd gotten into it with Savion even after I'd asked him not to.

I leaned back in my chair and just shook my head at the laptop. "Man, you can't go around getting into fights over every little stupid comment."

Matt's forehead crinkled. "And what was I supposed to do? Just let him disrespect me in front of the entire locker room and not say anything?"

"You could've just ignored him."

"I don't think so," he said with a snort. "I don't like people trying to play me." He moved his hand along his bare chest and rested it on his shoulder.

One thing that I'd noticed about Matt was that he had a bit of a stubborn, pigheaded streak. "I'm just saying, you can't go around letting simple-minded people goad you into fighting. You have to control yourself."

"I do control myself." His face became serious. "I have to control myself all the damn time! Just because you let people walk over you--" he abruptly stopped in mid-sentence, but the damage was already done.

"Just because I don't go around punching everyone out at the drop of a hat doesn't mean I 'let people walk over me'," I shot back, my voice tinged with anger.

"I didn't mean it like that, man," he said contritely.

"So how did you mean it?"

"Well..." He ran his hand over his head. "You just let things slide. Your ex pushes up on you--I tell him to get lost—and you get pissed at me?" He shrugged like he'd just made a profound point.

"Like I said before—I don't want or need you fighting for me." I knew his heart was in the right place, but I was just sick of always being treated like a hapless weakling. "I'm not some damsel in distress who needs saving. I can fight my own battles, my own way."

"Like the way you're fighting the battle with Aaron?" His tone sounded a little too sarcastic.

"What's he got to do with this?" I asked. I didn't know if this was a "lover's spat" or what, but I wasn't liking the tone of this conversation. I hated arguments, and that's what this was beginning to feel like.

"Raymond, the dude's been busting your chops for years, and you just let him get away with it. Has controlling yourself and being all nonviolent stopped him from picking on you?" He leaned into the screen and peered into my eyes as if he was right in the room with me. "The only reason why he's not bullying you as much as he used to is because I stood up to him for you and decked his ass."

He had a point. But still, I just didn't believe in violence. I loathed physical aggression. I'd witnessed enough of it when I was a child. Those traumatic memories still haunted me to this day. Violence was just something that I was opposed to with every fiber of my being.

"You're wrong," I retorted.

Matt folded his arms across his chest in a defiant posture. "How am I wrong?"

"Aaron still hasn't changed. He's still the same asshole he was before you hit him. He still broke my--" I caught myself before I spilled the beans about my glasses that Aaron had shattered a month ago.

"He broke what?" Matt's eyes narrowed.

"Nothing," I muttered. "Look--" I attempted to change the subject, but Matt interrupted me.

"What did he break, Ray?"

"Don't worry about it." My voice cracked. "It wasn't anything serious." I just wanted him to let it go.

"Bullshit." I should've known it wasn't going to be that easy. "You can't keep leaving me in the dark about stuff, man!"

I took a deep breath. "Can we just drop this, okay?"

"No, we're not going to just drop this until you tell me what it was that Aaron broke." Matt was like a pitbull who'd sunk his teeth into a steak. There was no way he was going to let it go without a fight.

"He broke my glasses, alright!" I blurted out indignantly. I didn't know if I was still angry at Aaron for breaking them, angry at Matt for forcing me to relive the humiliation...or angry at myself for allowing it to happen in the first place. Was I really too passive? The thud of Matt slamming his fist down on his desk snapped me out of my introspection.

"I fucking knew it! Oh, man, just wait until I see him tomorrow!" His face seethed with anger.

"No, Matt! This is exactly what I was just talking about." I waved my hands demonstratively. "You can't allow idiots like Aaron to make you stoop to his level."

He stared at the screen incredulously. "You're way too passive and peaceful for your own good, ya know that? All that 'turn the other cheek' stuff is good in theory, but it doesn't work to well in real life."

"And what should I have done, Matt?" I asked in annoyance.

"Knock his fucking head off!" He replied as if it was the most logical and obvious answer in the world.

"And what would that have resolved?" I was seriously frustrated now. We were stuck in a perpetual loop of philosophical disagreement. I was yin and he was yang. "We both probably would've gotten suspended, and we'd still be enemies. He'd eventually do something else to me, I'd retaliate, and it'd just keep going on and on in a vicious, pointless circle," I said emphatically. "That's just not something I want to do. I don't want to waste time and energy on petty conflicts."

"So you're saying if we get together, I just have to stand by and let assholes like Aaron push you around, and not get involved?" He scratched his forehead. "I can't do that, man. I care about you way too much."

I let out an exasperated sigh. It was like he and I were Romulans and Klingons—alien races from totally different worlds who spoke completely different languages. Why couldn't he see that violence only led to more violence?

Suddenly, I heard a voice yell Matt's name in the background.

"My dad's calling me." His face dropped. "I'll hit you back later, okay?"

"Alright," I said somberly. I was relieved that the arguing was over, but disheartened at the same time. I didn't like ending our conversation on such a sour note. Our differing views on how to deal with conflict seemed to be at the root of all the disagreements we'd had. Was this something we could ever work out?

I slid back from my desk and went in the kitchen to get something to eat. My mom had made some meatloaf and mashed potatoes before I got home. Once I finished eating, I went back to my room and got to work on my English homework. I had a three-page essay due the following week. After getting midway through the first page, I began to get distracted. My mind drifted to Matt. *What am I going to do with this hothead?* A smile crept across my face. I really liked him, but he was going to have to respect my wishes. I mean, was I wrong for not believing that you can punch your problems away? I caught myself yawning. I needed a break. I got up and clicked on the TV. I lay down in my bed. I closed my eyes and slowly drifted off to sleep.

The sound of my phone ringtone startled me awake. I looked at the big red digital numbers on the clock sitting on the nightstand. It was 10:35PM. I rubbed my eyes with one hand as I jumped up and grabbed my phone off the desk. *Savion*. I sucked my teeth and sent it to voicemail. I tossed the phone back on the desk and made my way to the bathroom.

Just as I finished taking a leak, I heard the bell ring. I wondered who could be ringing the doorbell at this hour. I quickly made my way down the hall. The door to my mom's room was wide open and the light was off, which meant she'd already left for work. I hadn't seen my sister around in a few days, so I was home alone. We lived in a pretty decent neighborhood, but still, you never know. I cautiously approached the door and peeped through the little window in it.

I gasped at the face looking back at me.
It was Matt.
I whipped open the door. He was wearing a hoodie, some basketball shorts and flip flops. He was standing there with his hands tucked in his hoodie. Even though he had the hood over his head, I could see his face was a little bruised. His eyes were red and watery.

"Sup, Double R?" He looked down bashfully as he shuffled his foot. "You said if I ever needed a safe place, I could always come here." He lifted his head and gave me a faint smile. "Well...here I am."

"Dude, stop playing and get in here. What the hell happened to you?" I asked. I stood to the side to let him enter.

"My dad," he replied in a subdued manner. He exhaled softly as he came inside. I closed and locked the door behind him. He pulled back the hood, revealing the full extent of his injuries. He had a small cut under his right eye, and some bruising on his left cheek.

"He did this to you?" I was damn near hysterical. Violence and bloodshed always made me panicky. "Why???"

"Cause he was drunk and needed something to hit?" He said with a shrug. "I guess he was in an even more rotten mood than usual tonight." I couldn't believe how calm he seemed. He was so nonchalant--like this was an ordinary occurrence.

"This isn't a joke, man." I shook my head and folded my arms. "You need to tell somebody." I gave him a pleading look.

"Like who?" He asked in a flat tone.

"I don't know...." I nervously shifted my weight from one foot to the other. "Maybe a relative?" He smirked and shook his head. "Maybe a school counselor, or something?"

He snickered a little. "This isn't some after school TV special, man. If I told someone and it got back to my dad, I'd really be dead. Not only would he kick my ass, but he'd probably throw me out, too."

"Your dad using you as a punching bag isn't cool, Matt. We have to do something." I felt anger surging through my veins. My father used to beat my mom all the time. Even though he never directed his aggression at my sister or me, just witnessing it being unleashed on my mom was traumatic enough. The psychological and emotional pain of being a little kid and helplessly standing by as your father brutally beat your mother was probably just as damaging as physical abuse. At least physical scars would eventually heal and disappear. (Thankfully, she eventually packed me and my sister up one day and fled. She promptly got a restraining order against him and filed for divorce.)

"Look, don't sweat it. I can handle this." He stared at me imploringly. I opened my mouth to reply, but the expression on his face told me it'd be pointless. I sighed. I hated feeling powerless like this. "I have less than a year until I graduate...then I'm out." He paused and averted his eyes. "I hope I didn't overstep my boundaries by coming here without being invited? I texted you, but you didn't respond." His voice wavered as he looked up. "I didn't know where else to go. I just had to get out of there."

"Man, you know it's OK." I gave him a sympathetic smile. I just wanted to reach out and hug him. "Come on, let's get you cleaned up." I motioned for him to follow me to the bathroom. When we got there, I flipped on the light switch. Matt sat down on the toilet lid. I opened the medicine cabinet and grabbed the bottle of rubbing alcohol. I reached around him and took a handful of toilet paper. I poured some of the alcohol on it. Gently clasping his cleft chin, I knelt down so that we were eye-level. I carefully dabbed the cut under his eye with the tissue. He winced.

"Ow, shit...that stings," he said through clenched teeth.

"Stop crying, you big ole baby," I joked, attempting to lighten the mood. I squeezed the sides of his face until his lips puckered, the same way my grandma used to do to me when I was little. I made the annoying cooing sound that old ladies always make over babies and puppies.

"You got jokes, huh?" He said with his lips still puckered like a fish. "I got your 'baby'." He straightened his back and swatted my hand away. "Go ahead, I can take the pain. GRRRRR..." He playfully flexed.

I chuckled. It was amazing that he was in such good spirits. I knew it was an act though. He was just trying to make me not worry. I could tell by his body language--the way his shoulders slumped--that he was hurting inside. I finished cleaning the cut and then applied a small band aid to it.

"Thanks, Nurse Ray."

"No problem. The $1000 bill will be in the mail tomorrow," I replied. I tossed the tissue in the trashcan next to the toilet. As I glanced down, I noticed a thick print had developed in Matt's basketball shorts. I looked up at him. "Freak." He grinned bashfully and licked his lips. They looked so succulent. That was all it took. Just like the first time we kissed, our lips gravitated to each other. Once again, he had the Magneto Effect on me. I wrapped my arms around his neck as we greedily devoured one another.

After a few heated minutes, Matt broke the lip lock and pulled away. "Ray, you have no idea how bad I want you," he said between breaths. He wrapped his hands around my wrists. "But, I want us to wait until you're ready." We silently peered into each other's soul. His mouth was saying stop (or at least proceed with caution), but his traffic light-green eyes were signaling for me to keep on going.

"I am ready." I caressed his face and smashed my lips back against his. The softness and the sensuousness of his kiss almost made my knees wobble. As our tongues intermingled, his hand found its way to the bulge now protruding in my sweat pants. After gently gripping it and massaging it through the thin barrier, he pulled the sweats down along with my Batman boxers. I was fully erect.

Matt looked up at me with that signature sly grin on his face as he took hold of my stiffness. "Damn, dude, this thing is almost bigger than you." I let out a shy laugh. He stroked it for a few seconds, and then inserted it in his mouth. I closed my eyes and tilted my head back. A low moan escaped my lips as Matt worked his mouth and tongue, gliding them along my shaft. I took his hand and led him back to my bedroom.

We continued to kiss ravenously while pulling off clothes. Once Matt slipped out of his shorts and underwear, we climbed in bed. We felt each other up and down like...well, the two horny teenagers that we were. We wound up in the 69 position, sucking each other off. After a few minutes of this, I was hungry for more. I knew it was a big step, but I was ready.

It was time to take it to the next level.

I reached over and pulled open the drawer to the nightstand. I rummaged around under some comic books until I found a condom and some lube. I handed the condom to Matt. He blew on it and pretended like he was wiping it off.

"Dusty." He winked and flashed a stupid grin.

"Um, you better hurry up before I change my mind," I replied as I lubed myself up. I hadn't been penetrated since I broke up with Savion, so I already knew it was going to hurt like hell at first.

"Gotcha." He wasted no time tearing into the wrapper with his teeth and rolling the condom on. He slid in between my legs, positioning his solid body on top of my slight frame. The warmth of his skin was exhilarating. I could feel his heart beating as his muscular chest pressed against mine. He proceeded to softly nibble on my neck. I reached down and took hold of his thick manhood, carefully guiding it to its destination. I flinched and grit my teeth as he worked himself inside.

"Ah, shit...take it easy, Machine Gun," I murmured.

"Stop crying, you big ole baby," he teased. Our fingers interlaced. He gyrated his hips, slowly opening me up. Things went much smoother once I finally relaxed. It didn't take long for Matt to get into a nice steady rhythm. I shut my eyes and savored the sensation. Once again, his lips found their way back to mine. His tongue pushed into my mouth as he pushed into me. He pumped harder and faster. Dude's stroke game was phenomenal. I palmed his firm, fuzzy ass cheeks; they were nice and plump.

"Told you I had a phatty," he said with a grin, as if reading my mind. I snickered. Matt leaned upright on his knees while still inside me. He grabbed my dick and began jerking me off without missing a beat. I was instantly teleported to a parallel dimension of pleasure.

My nut was building.

It didn't take long for this two-pronged assault on my body to overload my senses. Before I knew it, my toes curled and my body convulsed. I shot off, ejaculating all over my stomach and chest.

Matt bent forward. "Almost there, baby," he said. His pace quickened.

After a few more thrusts, his body tensed. I could feel his dick pulsating as he spilled his warm juices into the condom. He grunted and collapsed on top of me.

We were both sweaty and spent.

We lay there motionless, silently basking in the experience. I gently rubbed his back. His skin felt so soft and still warm to the touch.

"Thanks for being here for me, Ray," he whispered. "No matter how dark the rest of my world is, you're like my little ray of light." A big cheesy smile materialized on his face as we made eye contact. "Imagine that...Ray is my ray of light...HA!"

I groaned and pushed him off me. "Ugh...can you get anymore corny?"

He snickered and grabbed me by the waist. "Shut up, Ray-Rey. You know you like that sappy stuff." He started tickling me. I squirmed uncontrollably. He was right; deep down, I was a bit of a hopeless romantic. He stopped and suddenly got serious again. "So...does this mean we're finally official?"

"Yeah..." I placed my hand on his chest and smiled. "I guess it does."

"Alright! Take that, Savion!" He exclaimed, jumping up on the bed like Tom Cruise on Oprah's couch. He looked so adorably silly. He pumped his fist and elbow back as if he were celebrating a victory at some golf tournament. I rolled my eyes. "What?" He asked, looking down at me with a goofy grin.

"Umm...I'm having second thoughts now. Can I get my money back?"

"Sorry, buddy. It's too late for buyer's remorse. No refunds." He laid back down next to me.

"Oh, no! Dear God, what have I done?!" I playfully covered my face with my hands.

He snuggled up closer and kissed me on the cheek. "I love you, too, Mookie."

*****

I slept well last night.

"Raymond, I know your ass still ain't in that bed?!"

Apparently a little too well.

The sound of my mom's voice blasting through the door jarred me from my slumber. Shafts of sunlight filtered into my room through the closed blinds. *What time is it?* I thought. My eyes glanced at the clock on the nightstand.

"Fuck!" I mumbled, slapping my palm against my forehead. After Matt and I had sex last night, we showered (and fooled around some more) and got back in bed. He was only supposed to chill with me for a few minutes before heading home. I guess we were both pretty tired, because the next thing you know, we were both sound asleep. *Dammit!*

I looked over to see him lying on his stomach with his arm draped around me. Even though he was snoring up a storm, he looked so cute and peaceful that I almost hated to disturb him. I gently poked him in the side. He groaned, smacked his lips and kept snoring. I rolled my eyes. *So much for subtly.* This time I shoved his shoulder. He cracked open one eye and looked at me groggily. He wiped the slobber from his mouth and grinned.

"I-I'm up, ma!" I replied in a shaky, raspy voice.

"You better hurry up and get ready! Your ass is gonna be late." I heard her go in her room and close the door.

"Mornin', Mookie!" Matt beamed. Someone was definitely a morning person. "What time is it?"

"Ssshhh." I put my finger to my lips to indicate he needed to keep his voice down. He gave me the "my bad" face. Mom was cool with me being gay, but I doubted she would be thrilled with me having my boyfriend sleeping over, especially on a school night. *Boyfriend*...the sound of that brought a smile to my lips. I still couldn't believe I was in a relationship again. "A little after seven," I said in a hushed tone.

"Oh shit!" Matt blurted out, and then clasped his hand to his mouth. "Sorry," he whispered with an apologetic smile. "We're gonna be late, man."

"I know," I replied frantically. I whipped the cover off of us and planted my feet on the carpet. I reached down and retrieved his and my underwear from the floor. When I turned to Matt to hand him his boxer briefs, he was lying there nonchalantly with his hands behind his head. He looked at me mischievously. My eyes traveled down to his dick. It was standing straight up in the air like a flag pole.

"Morning wood." He flashed a crooked grin. "It's yours now...go on and tell it hello."

I just shook my head at him. He made it jump and wiggled his eyebrows. *Oh, what the hell?* I thought. I was already going to be late anyway. What's a few more minutes? I gripped and gently stroked his dick. It was brick hard. My mouth began to water. *Breakfast is served.* I leaned over and opened wide, preparing to engulf the meal I was about to receive.

"I DON'T HEAR YOU GETTING READY IN THERE!"

I hastily let Matt go and jolted upright on the bed. God, I hated living with a correction officer! Matt stifled a laugh as he slipped on his underwear. I pulled on my sweat pants with an annoyed sigh.

"We better get out of here before she kicks the door in and catches us." I got up and searched my dresser for a clean t-shirt.

Matt smiled. "I have to go home and change." Crap, I'd forgotten that he came over wearing only a hoodie and some basketball shorts.

"You can wear some of my stuff," I proffered, looking back at him.

He twisted his face. "Your clothes can't fit me."

"Okay, Mr. Hulk," I quipped. "You're not THAT much bigger than me." Matt was more muscular than I was (well, I had no muscles), but our waists were practically the same size. And he only had an inch of height on me. I was sure I could find something in my closet to fit him.

"Aww...we just made it official and we're already wearing each other's clothes." He ran over and playfully hugged me.

"Oh, Lord." *Sooo stupid.* I pushed him off me before I got turned on again.

"Shit. I forgot, I came over here with flip flops." His face grew concerned. "I can't go with those on."

"Hmm..." I put my hand to my chin. "What size do you wear?"

"Eleven." He glanced down at his bare feet and then looked up at me with a proud grin. "I got man's feet, baby boy."

I shook my head. "Looks like you're out of luck, Sasquatch. I wear 9 ½."

"Fuck. It's all right. I'll run home real quick. I gotta get some books from my place anyway. Um...so how're we going to get out?"

My heart fluttered. I hadn't even thought about that. Mom had the hearing of a cybernetically-enhanced canine. I glanced at the window. The AC was blocking that escape route. It looked like I was going to have to sneak him out. I quickly formulated a plan.

"Wait here," I murmured to Matt.

"Okay," he whispered. His stomach suddenly growled. "Aye, can you bring me back a bowl of cereal or something?" He rubbed his belly and grinned a little. I rolled my eyes. This boy was always thinking about food. I slowly creaked open the door and poked my head out. I looked from side-to-side to ensure the coast was clear. I briskly walked to the bathroom and turned on the shower. Hopefully, the sound of the running water would provide us sufficient cover to distract Mom while I smuggled Matt out undetected. I snuck back to my room.

"Come on, let's go," I whispered, motioning for him to follow me. He grabbed my hand.

"Hold up," he said. He pulled me back and kissed me on the lips.

I balled up my face. "Ugh, morning breath."

"Like I said last night—no refunds, buddy." He sniggered.

I turned to Matt and placed my finger to my lips once more. We tiptoed into the hall.

This was a highly dangerous gambit that would require the utmost care.

We would need ninja-like stealth and cunning to elude capture and complete our mission.

My mom's door sprung open.

BUSTED.

She cleared her throat and took a sip from the coffee mug she was holding. *Oh man, I'm so dead.*

"Good mornin', Ms. Reynolds," Matt chirped with a broad smile.

Mom pursed her lips. "Good morning, Matthew. You're here mighty early." She turned her eyes to me. I swallowed hard. Yep, I was definitely a goner.

"Hey, ma." I gave her a shy grin as my mind raced to come up with a lie. "Uh, he came over last night after you left for work. We, um, watched a movie and ended up falling asleep." I punctuated my fabricated evening with a nervous laugh. I searched my mom's face for a reaction. There was none. She just stared at me and calmly took another sip from her mug. I could feel my hands starting to sweat. Mom's gaze could make even the hardest criminal crack under the pressure.

"Mhmm." She smacked her lips. "Ya'll better get your butts to school." She turned to go back in her room and closed the door.

Well, that wasn't as bad as I expected. I looked at Matt and breathed a sigh of relief.

My celebration was premature.

"We'll talk when you get home from school, Ray."

I groaned at her ominous decree. I should've known she wasn't going to let me off the hook that easily. Matt shrugged, giving me a sympathetic smile.

Fifteen minutes later, after getting dressed (and heating up two Pop Tarts for Matt's greedy behind), we were out the door. Once I locked up, we made our way to the street.

"I'll see you at lunch," Matt said, extending his hand to me.

"Alright," I replied. We dapped off and went our separate ways. Matt's house was on the block behind mine. It was like a twenty minute hike to school from where we lived. I hastened my stride and began speed walking. Not long after Matt had left, I came to a stop sign. I anxiously waited for the cars to go by before I crossed the street.

Suddenly, a horn beeped. I looked to the side just as a pimped out blue Maxima pulled up. The bass from the sound system rattled the whole car. The tinted passenger window rolled down. I rolled my eyes.

"Sup, bruh?" Savion yelled out the window. "Want a ride?"

I smirked. "No thanks."

"Man, get in here." He flashed a disarming smile. "You're gonna be late."

I glanced at my watch again. I blew out a long breath. Grudgingly, I got in the car and closed the door. I knew I was going to have to face him sooner or later. I guess now was as good a time as any to have that talk.

After I strapped in, Savion pulled off. He drove for a few seconds before coming to a stop at a red light. He reached to turn the volume down on the stereo system. An awkward silence filled the air.

"So, why can't you give me another chance?" He licked his lips and stared hard into my eyes. This was my opportunity to nip this in the bud once and for all.

"Cause…I already have a boyfriend," I replied, breaking his gaze.

"Who, Matt?" He smirked.

"Yep. We're together now. So that means you can stop calling and texting me trying to get back together, because it's not going to happen."

He gave me an incredulous sidelong glance. "That whack ass dude? Pssh! You tellin' me you're choosing him over me?"

"All day, every day," I proudly retorted. "And he's far from whack. In fact, the reason why I'm running late this morning is because he kept me up all night." I gave him a sly grin to rub it in his face.

Savion sucked his teeth as he continued driving. "Man, he's mad corny."

"Whatever, Savion. If anyone should know what corny is, it's you. At least Matt doesn't treat me like a pariah in public." He looked at me with a puzzled expression. "That means he's not scared to acknowledge me in public," I clarified.

We pulled into the school parking lot. He put the car in park and killed the engine.

"What the hell are you talking about? You're with me in public right now, aren't you?"

"Yeah, so I guess that means I better get going. Thanks for the ride. We don't want anyone to see me in your car now, do we?" I asked sarcastically. The few times when Savion had given me a ride to school back when we were dating, he'd always drop me off a few blocks away from school so people wouldn't see us together. I'd have to walk the rest of the way. Just recalling the way I allowed him to mistreat me made me want to backhand myself. What the hell was I thinking?

"Ain't nobody worried about that." He looked away and stared out the window at some students passing by before continuing. He pulled the brim of the hat he was wearing down over his eyes, and crouched in his seat a little. In spite of what he said, I could tell he was still paranoid about being seen with me. "Quit playing, bruh." He leaned closer to my face so his lips were inches from mine. I could feel his warm breath against my skin. He smiled seductively, then reached over, grabbed my hand and placed it on his dick. Even through his jeans, I could feel it was rock hard. "Now tell me you don't want this shit?"

OK, this dude was seriously tripping and doing way too much right now. "Me and you are finished, Savion." I snatched my hand from his grasp. I shot him an angry glare. From the look on his face, he obviously realized I meant business. I grabbed my book bag from the floor board and reached for the door handle. All the locks in the car instantly clicked shut.

He reached over and cupped his hand under my chin. "I didn't say you could leave yet."

I swatted his hand away. "Stop playing and open the damn door, Savion," I demanded as calmly and confidently as possible. My eyes locked on to his. I was tired of people not taking me seriously. I was nervous, but I tried my best not to let it show. I had to stand my ground. "I'm in a relationship with Matt now. Period."

He didn't say a word. He stared at me with his nostrils flaring. From the way his jaw was clenched, I could tell that he was grinding his teeth in anger. He suddenly slammed his fist down on the leather steering wheel cover. "Fuck you, dawg! I didn't want you back anyway." He hit the switch to open the locks.

I quickly got out of the car. "No, fuck you!" I shouted back at him, slamming the door with all my might. I smiled to myself as I walked through the parking lot towards the building. It looks like I finally got my point across to Savion's thick head, I mused. It felt good to assert myself and speak my mind for a change. Maybe being aggressive and outspoken weren't such bad things after all?

CHAPTER 14
MATTHEW

    After parting ways with Ray-Rey, I sprinted home--my flip flops slapping against the pavement as I ran. I was praying my dad wouldn't be outside watering the grass or working on his car when I got there. Usually, he'd still be passed out when I left for school in the morning. He'd blow his fucking lid if he saw me just coming home, especially since he didn't know I snuck out last night. Thankfully, there was no sign of him as I approached the house. My mom's car was still gone from last night, too. She was probably working another double. That meant she wouldn't be home for another two hours or so. I felt bad for Mom; she was always at work trying to keep a roof over our heads while my dad sat on his ass, drinking and berating her.
    I went around to the side of the house. I climbed over the fence into the backyard and walked to my room. The window was still ajar, the way I'd left it. I gently slid it up, careful not to make too much noise. I pulled myself up and shimmied through the window.
    Once inside, I rushed to my closet and grabbed the least wrinkled pair of jeans and shirt I could find. There wasn't time to iron anything. I heard the shower going.

Good, I thought. At least that meant my dad wouldn't hear me in here. I hastily put on my jeans and shirt. I ran the brush over the light fuzz on my head and grabbed my book bag from the floor. I shoved my books and notebook in it and pulled the straps over my shoulders. I was just about to climb back out the window like a thief, when I heard the doorbell ring. I paused out of curiosity, wondering who it could be.

Seconds later, the water stopped running. Heavy footsteps raced from the bathroom. I tiptoed to my door and pressed my ear against it. I heard the kitchen door open. My dad greeted whoever it was.

"Hey, beautiful!" He had an excitement in his voice I'd rarely heard.

"Hi, baby." The person returned the greeting just as cheerfully. It was a woman's voice. But it wasn't my mother's. "Why do you have this towel on?"

I heard giggles and kissing sounds.

My stomach turned and my blood ran cold. I stood there motionless with my hand on the doorknob. What should I do? For the longest moment, I pondered bum rushing my dad and the bitch he was cheating on Mom with. I decided against it. Instead, I proceeded to make my way back out the window.

I walked to school in a fog.

I arrived thirty minutes late, missing homeroom. I went through all of my morning classes in a total daze. It was like I was in a trance. I was trying to wrap my mind around this fucked up situation, but I just couldn't.

How could Dad do this to Mom?

I spent the first two class periods mulling over that question. I couldn't come up with an answer.

When gym class rolled around, I got dressed, but didn't participate. I wasn't in the mood to play volleyball. I just sat on the bleachers staring into space.

After gym, it was lunchtime. I got my tray and sat in my usual spot with Keon and Ray.

"What's up, boy?" Ke greeted me with a big smile.

"Hey," I replied solemnly.

"Eww." He twisted his face. "What's the matter with you?"

"Nothing," I lied.

"You all right?" Ray asked.

"Yeah, I'm good." I exhaled softly. "Just got some stuff on my mind."

"Is something wrong?" Ray looked at me with worry in his eyes. I wanted to tell him, but I just couldn't bring myself to verbalize it yet.

I shook my head. "No." I lifted my fork and listlessly picked at the food on my tray. I didn't have much of an appetite. Keon and Ray looked at me for a second, and then reluctantly resumed the conversation they were having before I had sat down. I wasn't paying them much attention, but Ray seemed to be halfheartedly engaged in the conversation. I could tell he was troubled by my bizarre behavior. Their conversation and the rest of the noisy lunchroom chatter took a back seat to the whirlwind of thoughts and emotions swirling in my head.

How could my dad cheat on my mom after all these years? How was she going to react when I told her? Should I confront him first?

"Matt." Ray's voice snapped me back to reality. I looked up to give him my attention. "You sure you're OK?"

"Yeah." I laid my fork down. "Just not hungry today."

Keon gasped and clutched his chest. "Okay--what have you done with the real Matt?" I cracked a faint smile. He placed the back of his hand to my forehead. "You sick or something?" Ray looked on with a concerned expression.

I let out an annoyed sigh. "I'm fine." Thankfully, everyone began getting up, sparing me from any further interrogation. Lunch was over. I picked up my tray and emptied it in the trash.

By the time the bell rang to signal fourth period had begun, I was still in a fog. I just stared into space as the teacher rambled on and scribbled on the board. My phone vibrated. It was a text from Ray.

Ray: Did I do something wrong?
Me: No

I put my phone away. I tried to put everything out of my mind and focus on the teacher for the rest of the period.

When I walked into fifth period, Ray was already seated at his desk.

"So, are you going to tell me what's going on with you?" He asked as I sat down next to him.

"I'll tell you later," I said. He stared at me apprehensively. I could tell not knowing what was bothering me was eating him up inside. I knew I had to open up, but I just couldn't. Not yet.

After school was done, I got my books and met Ray at his locker. I didn't feel like going to the second day of basketball tryouts, but I figured it'd do me good to get my mind off of things for a little while at least. As Ray and I were talking, Savion walked by with a broad smile on his face.

"Aye, bae, hit me up if you need another ride to school in the morning." He winked at Ray and kept going.

"'Bae,'?" I turned to Ray for an explanation. "'Another ride'?"

"He's just trying to cause trouble," he replied dismissively. "He saw me walking to school this morning and offered me a ride."

"And you got in the car with him???"

"Nothing happened, Matt. Don't go blowing things out of proportion. He tried to push up on me again, but I told him that I was with you."

"And you couldn't mention this to me before now, huh?"

He sighed. "I was going to tell you at lunch, but you were acting all mopey and EMO."

"You'd be acting 'EMO' too if you caught--" I stopped myself in mid-sentence. The anger had been simmering in me all day. I was this close to exploding. I didn't want to take it out on Ray. I shook my head. "I gotta get going. I'll hit you up later." Without another word, I made my way to the gymnasium. I heard Ray call my name, but I just kept walking. I couldn't deal with this right now. I already had enough on my plate.

Once I changed, I walked out to the basketball court. Everyone stood around talking and bullshitting except me. I was in my own world, and the weight of that world was squarely on my shoulders. When the coach arrived, he wasted no time running us ragged. He made us run some drills and play a few scrimmages. I just went through the motions. I knew my performance was lackluster, but I didn't care. My heart and mind weren't into it.

During the tryout I noticed Savion smirking and giving me dirty looks whenever I glanced in his direction. I paid him no mind. I wasn't going to let him get under my skin. In the emotional state I was in, I was liable to snap and do God knows what. Thankfully, I was able to make it through the tryout without incident. I didn't even bothering changing back into my jeans. I just grabbed my bag from the locker and left the premises as fast as I could. The entire walk home I debated what I should do. I thought about calling my brother, but I knew it'd probably be a few days before he got back to me.

When I got to my house, I saw only my mom's car was there. I opened the door and found her in the kitchen making dinner.

"Hey, Matty," she said with her back to me.

"Hey, mom," I replied somberly. She set the big wooden spoon that she was stirring the contents of the pot with down on the counter. She turned to face me.

"What's wrong, honey?" She looked at me with a worried expression.

I took a deep breath. As I stared into her loving eyes, I realized I had no choice. That bastard didn't deserve such a compassionate and devoted woman. Even if it hurt her and ended up destroying their marriage, I had to tell her the truth. And I had to do it now. "Mom...I have to tell you something."

"What is it?" She pushed a strand of hair from her eyes. Her tone was more urgent.

I exhaled. "Dad is...having an affair." I looked at her expectantly, bracing myself for an emotional meltdown.

Mom's shoulders slumped. Her arms hung lifelessly against her petite frame. She gave me a sympathetic look before averting her eyes to the floor. Her voice was barely above a whisper when she replied, "I know."

I stood there in utter silence. "How..." I was so stupefied I could barely speak. "How long have you known?"

"I found out a few weeks ago." She slowly lifted her head. "I overheard him making plans with her on the phone one morning."

"And what did he say when you confronted him about it?" I asked.

"I haven't told him I know yet."

"Why not?" The blood was really flowing through my veins now. "You're just going to let him get away with this?"

"I blame myself for him cheating. I've been working so many hours lately that I've been neglecting our marriage. If I start being a better wife, he'll--"

"Mom, do you hear yourself?!" I'd never raised my voice to my mother before, but after all of today's craziness my anger had reached the boiling point. "The reason why you've had to work so much is because Dad isn't helping you! While you're at the hospital killing yourself, he's out here messing around behind your back!" I gestured emphatically with my hands as I tried to talk some sense into her. "Please tell me that you're not OK with this!"

"Matt," she sighed and shook her head, "you just don't understand all your father has done for us."

Just then, I heard my dad's car pull into the driveway. *Speak of the fucking devil.*

"Please don't say anything about this to your father." My mom was panic-stricken. I looked at her like she was crazy. "Matt, please, just go to your room, OK?" She looked at me with pleading eyes.

I didn't respond. I calmly set my book bag on the table. There was no way I was going to just stand by and keep my mouth shut. Just like with Ray--I couldn't stand to see someone I loved being mistreated. I folded my arms and anxiously awaited my dad's entrance.

A minute later, I heard the sound of keys jangling. The door unlocked and opened. My father stepped in and saw us standing there; One with a fearful face and the other with a furious face.

"What the hell's going on here?" He looked from Mom to me with a perplexed expression.

"Go on and tell him," I said to my mom. She swallowed hard, but didn't say anything. *Fine, if she won't tell him, I will.* "She knows you're cheating on her. And don't try to deny it, because I heard you this morning!" He looked at me with an evil glare. "That's right, asshole--I was in my room when your mistress came over. I heard everything!"

"Sharon, you better tell this little punk to watch his damn mouth." He scowled as he walked towards me. I balled my fists. Mom stepped in between us and faced my dad. I glared at him over her shoulder.

"Joshua, how could you?" Her voice cracked.

"You should ask yourself that question." He smirked.

"That was over nineteen years ago, Josh!"

"Yeah, it's bad enough that it happened in the first place. But what's even worse is that I've gotta be reminded of it every day of my fucking life!"

"That's enough!" Mom implored him to stop his abusive tirade. He turned his eyes from her and stared at me with a look of disgust. "Please, leave him out of this."

"Why? It's out in the open now. You might as well tell him everything."

"Joshua...please," she begged. He just stood there with a smug expression.

"Mom, what's he talking about?" I asked anxiously, looking from him to her. "What happened nineteen years ago?"

She slowly turned to face me. Her eyes were filled with tears. "Matt...before you were born...I had an affair."

"What?" I stared at her in wide-eyed disbelief. My whole world seemed to be crumbling.

The tears began to fall. "I admitted it to your father a few months after it was over. By the grace of God, he took me back after my unfaithfulness. Things were rough at first, but with the Lord's help, we were able to get through it."

So many things made sense now.

"So this is why you put up with all of his abusive bullshit over the years--because he was holding an affair over your head?!" I lost it. "Mom, I understand you probably felt guilty about what you did, but that was almost two decades ago! That's no reason to let him walk over you the way he has all these years!"

"Matt, you don't understand...." She wiped her eyes.

"I don't understand what?" I yelled. She kept taking up from him. I was sick of her making excuses for the way he treated us. "I understand how this asshole pretended to forgive you for making a mistake when you were young, just to turn around and use it as a convenient excuse to treat you like shit!" I pointed an accusing finger at my father.

"I already told you to watch your fucking mouth, boy!" His face twisted. "All things considered, I think I did pretty good by your mom. That affair wasn't the only mistake she made that caused friction in our marriage."

"Josh, don't!" She clasped his arm and looked into his eyes.

"It's just as well all of this is finally out in the open now." He snatched himself away from her. "I was just biding my time living here anyway."

"Wh—what are you saying?" My mom's voice was soft, yet filled with desperation.

"I'm moving out at the end of the month," he replied calmly.

"No, you can't leave us."

"Watch me." He looked at her with icy indifference.

I touched Mom's shoulder. "Fuck this bastard! If he wants to leave, then let him!"

"I'm not the one who's the bastard, boy." He stared me down for a second before storming off to the bedroom and slamming the door.

Mom exhaled as she turned to me. Her expression was one of soul-crushing sorrow and ravaging regret. Whatever dark secret she was hiding was tearing her up inside, and had obviously been eating away at her for all these years.

"Mom, it's okay." I wrapped my arms around her. "We don't need Dad. We can make it without him." She lowered her head into my chest and wept softly.

"Matt..." she looked up at me with tears streaming down her face. She cupped a trembling hand to her mouth. "Joshua isn't your real father."

CHAPTER 15
RAYMOND

Later that night, Keon and I were at work on our lunch break. We sat at a table in the back as we ate and rehashed the day's events. I was still concerned about Matt. He was acting out of it all day. And the way he stormed off after finding out Savion had given me a ride really bothered me. I texted him, but I hadn't heard anything back. And that was over five hours ago.

"I don't know what's gotten into him. He was fine this morning when we left my house."

"You must've put it on him too good. You know bomb sex be having the boys goin' cray cray!" Keon laughed. I didn't. Realizing that I wasn't in a joking mood, he got serious. "Well, just give the boy some space."

"I know. I'm just worried about him though." I hadn't told Keon about Matt's issues with his dad. I just hoped his father didn't do anything to him when he went back home to change clothes before school.

"I'm sure he'll tell you what's up with him when he's ready."

I sighed. "Yeah, I guess you're right."

"Duh." He smacked his lips. "That goes without saying."

"Anyway." I sipped my soda.

He grinned, taking a bite of his burger. "So, what about your stan, Savion?"

I grimaced. "Well, I reiterated to his ass that I don't want him. And after that stunt he pulled in the hall this afternoon in front of Matt, I blocked his number from my phone to show him I mean business."

"Mmhmm. We'll see if that takes." He gave me the side-eye. "So in other blog news: I practically dragged that bitch Brianna at cheerleader tryouts today."

"I take it you let her have it?" I cracked a smile for the first time tonight.

"Did I?!" He exclaimed triumphantly. "That ho just lucky I ain't a real fish cause I'd be captain of that squad, honey!"

"You mean you're not a real fish?" I flashed a sly grin.

He pursed his lips. "Bitch, don't make me take off my lace front and beat your ass!" I burst out laughing. Joking around with Ke was a welcome respite from thinking about Matt.

Once our lunch break was over, we went back to work. We stayed till closing and clocked out. My mom was already at work, so Keon's mom picked us up. When I got home, I jumped in the shower to get that restaurant smell off me. I changed into some Superman pajama bottoms and a t-shirt. I was sitting at my desk doing homework when I got a text from Matt.

Matt: Can I come over?
Me: Sure
Matt: Be there in a few
Me: K

I don't know why, but my stomach fluttered with nervousness. *What if he's coming to breakup with me over that Savion crap?* I wondered. I tried to calm my nerves as I waited for him to arrive.

Fifteen minutes later, the doorbell rang. I quickly walked to the door. I took a deep breath and opened it. My mouth dropped. Savion was standing there with a big grin on his face.

"What's good, dawg?"

"What are you doing here?" I asked in a dry tone.

"I was driving through your hood. I ain't see your mom's car here, so I figured since she wasn't home I'd drop by and see what you were up to." He licked his lips. "So why you blocked my number?" I just stood there looking at him like, *Are you serious right now?*

"To keep you from bugging me. Clearly you didn't get the hint though, huh?"

He was unfazed. "Let me come in for a minute. I just wanna talk."

"We don't have anything to talk about." I stepped back inside and started to close the door. Savion put his hands up to block it. I struggled to shut the door, but he was too strong.

"Don't be trying to close no door in my face, dawg." He laughed like this was a game.

"Let go of the door, dammit! I'm not playing with you!"

He barged his way into the house. "Damn, why you actin' like a lil' bitch?"

"If you don't get out of here right now--"

He gripped my arm and got in my face. "You lucky I like you. If I didn't I would've fucked your shit up when you slammed my car door this morning."

I pushed him off me. "Get the fuck out of here, Savion!" My mind raced to come up with an adequate threat. "Before I call the cops!"

He snickered. "Bruh, stop playing." He licked his lips again. "Come here and give me a kiss."

Matt suddenly appeared in the doorway like a flash of lightning!

His face radiated rage.

He grabbed Savion by the arm and yanked him away from me.

"What the--" Savion started to exclaim in surprise before Matt's fist collided with his jaw. Before he could react, Matt punched him again. He then gripped Savion by the collar of his shirt and slammed him back against the wall.

"I swear...if you ever come near him again...I will break your fucking jaw," Matt growled in a raw, husky voice. He had a crazed look in his eyes that I'd never seen before. I worried about what he might do next. I could see the fear all over Savion's face.

"Matt." I placed a hand on his shoulder to get his attention, but he still didn't let go. He was breathing hard as he kept Savion hemmed up. "Baby, that's enough."

After a few tension-filled seconds passed, Matt reluctantly loosened his grip. They both scowled with their eyes locked on each other. Savion straightened his shirt as he cautiously eased out the door.

"This shit is fucked up, Ray. Don't bother calling my phone again." I looked at him incredulously. *What the fuck was this dude smoking and/or popping???* He spit a glob of blood on the grass. He turned on his heels and stomped back to his car which was parked along the curb.

His tires let out an angry squeal as he sped off.

I closed the door while shaking my head in disbelief. "I'm sorry about that." I scratched the back of my neck as I nervously glanced to the floor. "I had no idea he was coming here." I abruptly stopped talking when I looked up and into Matt's eyes. All I saw was pain. Whatever was troubling him was much larger and more important than this Savion drama. "Are you...okay?" He shook his head. "What's wrong?"

"Everything," he whispered. "My life is so fucked up, man." His lips began quivering. He took deep breaths as if he were hyperventilating. I'd seem him angry and upset before, but never like this. It was like he was falling apart. He was always good at maintaining his composure and keeping his feelings bottled up. I rushed to embrace him. His body quaked. He gripped me tightly and lowered his head on my shoulder.

Seconds later, I could feel the dampness on my shirt from all the tears he'd fought so hard to hold back.

CHAPTER 16
MATTHEW

It was the first game of the season.

Coach put me in during the last twenty minutes. I came off the bench like a wild man. I was a beast out there on the court, rebounding and sinking shots left and right. There were five seconds left on the clock. We were down by two points. Aaron lobbed me the ball. I caught it and trotted down the court. With two seconds left on the clock, I positioned my body — lining it up with the basket. I took aim and let it fly. A hush fell over the auditorium. I watched with baited breath as the ball sailed through the air. I shut my eyes at the last second. I couldn't bear to look.

The crowd erupted.

I opened my eyes to see the students from my school pouring onto the court in celebration. All my teammates (except Aaron and Savion) bum rushed me and congratulated me on the buzzer beater.

"Yeah! That's what I'm talking about, boy!" My teammate Jarell screamed in my face as he patted me on the butt.

We all stood in the middle of the jubilant crowd and did a little victory dance. I was so happy at that moment. I glanced up in the bleachers and saw my mom cheering wildly. A wide smile sprouted on my face. I looked down a few rows and spotted Ray. My smile grew bigger at the sight of my baby. He waved at me. I loved that dude so much.

A month had passed since I'd found out the truth about my "dad." I was just now getting back to normal (or at least as normal as possible, all things considered). When my world was crumbling around me, Ray was there when I needed him most. His love and support helped guide me through my depression.

After getting changed up and bullshitting around with the guys in the locker room for a minute, I made my way back out to the gymnasium. I looked around until I found Ray chatting with Keon. When Ke saw me approach, he burst into a cheer.

"M-A-T-T!!!" He clapped his hands in the air and stomped his feet as he spelled out my name.

I chuckled and blushed. "Uh, thanks, man."

"Aww, he's so adorable when he turns red." Keon laughed and pinched my cheek.

Ray playfully swatted his hand away and gave me a bro-hug. "Awesome game, Machine Gun." He smiled broadly.

"Thanks, Ray-man." We stared lustfully at one another. Damn, I wanted to tongue him down right here. "Come on, my mom's over here." I was anxious for the love of my life to meet my mother.

"So, can I be in the wedding?" Keon grinned. "I already got my bridesmaid dress."

Ray rolled his eyes. I said bye to Ke and led Raymond to where my mom was standing. Her face lit up when she saw me approaching.

"Mom, this is my best-est bud, Ray," I said, introducing them to each other.

"Hi, Ray. It's nice to finally meet you!" She said enthusiastically. "Matty--" she caught herself and gave me an embarrassed glance. "Matt, talks about you all the time." I could feel myself blushing again.

He smiled coyly. "You should only believe the good stuff."

Mom laughed and started walking back to the car.

Ray nudged me in the side with his elbow as we followed behind her. "Good game, *Matty*." He grinned slyly. *Cute little smart ass.*

I raised an eyebrow and let out a little laugh. "Thanks, *Mookie*."

We stopped by Dominos on the way home and picked up a pizza.

A few days after I'd found out that Joshua wasn't my biological father, he packed up and moved out to live with his mistress. I was relieved that he was finally out of our lives. I was excited to be able to bring Ray to my house for a change. That was something I wouldn't dare do when my stepdad was there.

After we ate, Mom went to get ready for work. Ray and I retreated to my room.

"Whelp, here we are." I flipped on the light switch. "Welcome to the Matt Cave!"

Ray walked around with his hands behind his back, perusing the room like he was a housing inspector. He picked up a framed picture on my dresser. It was an old photo of me, my brother, my mom, and the man I thought was my dad. Even though our family was fucked up back then too, I was too young to know it. He silently studied the picture and sat it down. "You look a lot like your mom, Matty." *Ugh, why did Mom have to call me that in front of him?*

"Yeah, from what I can tell, I got most of my facial features from her." I sat down on the bed and unlaced my sneakers. My mom had one old photo of my real father which she eventually showed me. You could imagine my surprise to find out that he was Latino. She hadn't had any contact with him in over eighteen years.

Ray came and sat next to me. "Your mom seems to be doing well."

"Yeah, she's getting better. She's still getting over all those years of living with that abusive asshole." I said, kicking off my shoes. As big of a jerk as my stepdad was, Mom still loved him. Even though he treated me like shit and disrespected her constantly, she still held him in high regard for taking on the responsibility of raising another man's child. Looking at it from his perspective, I guess I could see why he would harbor some bitterness. But that still didn't give him the right to take it out on me the way he had.

"You can't stay angry at him forever, Matt. The bitterness in your heart will just fester and eat away at you just like it did to him," Ray said, placing a hand on my thigh.

"I know." I let out a long breath. "It's just hard to get over something like that, man." We stared into each other's eyes. He licked his sexy lips.

"Matty!" My mom's voice rang out through the door startling us. "Er, Matt--I'm leaving for work now. You boys don't get into any trouble, OK?"

My mom didn't know I was gay.

No one in my immediate family knew.

As open as I was about my sexuality with strangers, I'd never come out to those closest to me. It wasn't that I was scared or anything, it's just that it never really came up. I wanted to tell my mom, but with all of the recent craziness going on in our lives, I didn't feel it was a good time. I didn't want to add to her mental and emotional distress. I figured I would tell her when the time was right.

Ray snickered. I gave him a sidelong glance.

"Alright, ma. Don't work too hard. I'll see you in the morning." I waited until I heard her leave, and then turned to Ray. "Something funny about my nickname, punk?" I started tickling his ribcage. He rolled around on the bed laughing and snorting like a kid. I pinned him down with his hands above his head. I slowly traced my tongue along his neck, making circles. He moaned softly. I brought my mouth to his. I gently nipped at his bottom lip. I sucked on it and then traced my tongue along the inside of his lip. He motioned for me to roll over onto my back. I obliged and pulled my t-shirt over my head. Ray planted feather kisses on my chest. I shuddered and moaned when he lightly bit my nipple. He licked all the way down the light trail of hair on my abs and back up to my pecks. When his nose brushed against my arm pit, he suddenly froze and looked up at me.

"Pits of Doom." He scrunched his face.

"My bad." I flashed a coy grin and lifted my arm to take a whiff. *Whew! Guess I didn't put on enough deodorant in the locker room.* "Excuse my manly musk, baby boy. That's just the sweet smell of success."

"Um, if you say so." He pinched his nose. I laughed.

"Come on, let's hit the shower." We got up and stripped down to our underwear. I stood back to admire Ray's slender physique for a second. A flirtatious smile played at my lips.

"Stop screwing me with your eyes, sicko," he quipped. Dude was so freaking modest. That was one of the things I found so sexy about him.

We walked down the hall to the bathroom. I turned on the shower. We started kissing again as we waited for the water to heat up. We slipped out of our underwear and got in. I shampooed my hair. (Winter was coming, so I was letting it grow out.) Meanwhile, Ray lathered me up with the soap, making sure to give special attention to mini-Matt between my legs. My package grew to its full length in a matter of seconds. The slightest touch from him always had that effect on me. He stroked me using the soap as lubricant. I stiffened even more as his hand glided along my shaft. Once the soap was rinsed off, Ray knelt in front of me. He gripped my dick and licked around the swollen head. I gasped as he took all of me into his warm mouth. I held his head between my hands and pushed in and out of his mouth. He created a tight suction around my dick with his lips and bobbed his head up and down on it. I could've came from just that alone, but I had other plans.

After a few minutes of him sucking me off, I pulled him up and turned him around. I knelt down and spread his firm cheeks with my hands. I licked my lips and dove in, pushing my tongue into his wet hole. His fingers squeaked against the wet tiles as he grasped the wall. I kept working my tongue, flicking it against his hole. He let out a guttural, masculine moan.

Now clean and totally turned on, we migrated back to the bedroom, both of our dicks bobbing in the air. We fell back onto the bed ravenously fondling each other. I reached in the nightstand and pulled out a condom. I ripped open the package and rolled it onto my thick rod. I lubed Ray up and went to work making love to that tight hole. He lay on his back with his hairy legs resting on my shoulders. He moaned and gripped the bedspread as I slowly burrowed my way into his tunnel, opening him up. Before long, I had that slim little body of his twisted up like a pretzel while my mushroom head massaged his insides. When I saw his eyes roll back in his head, I knew I was hitting the sweet spot. *Just call me "Magic Matt."* I grinned in my head and doubled my efforts, ratcheting up the intensity.

Once we both came, we just laid there, basking in the sex afterglow. I rolled over onto my elbow and looked him in the eye. "I told you that I love you, Ray-Rey, right?" I meant it with all my heart.

He rolled his eyes. "Oh Lord, don't start with the mushy stuff."

I laughed. "Let's go get those last three slices of pizza." I grinned mischievously. "And then maybe we can go for round two."

"Is your appetite ever satiated?" He asked, getting up. I got out of bed too and playfully smacked him on the butt. I came up behind him and pressed my front against his backside. I wrapped my arms around his slim waist.

"Nope." I planted a kiss on the back of his neck. "How many times do I gotta tell you that I'm a growing boy?"

CHAPTER 17
RAYMOND

When I got home the following morning, Mom was sitting at the kitchen table sipping her coffee and eating breakfast. She looked up at me with a wide smile. "Well, look what the cat hacked up."

"Morning to you, too, ma." I tried to slip away before she got nosy, but no such luck. I had called to let her know I was spending the night at Matt's house after the game, so I knew she was going to grill me for details.

"How was your night?"

"It was great. Matt scored a basket at the last second, and we won the game," I replied excitedly.

"Mmm...just look at you glowing. My little Mookie's in love." *Hoo, boy.*

"Mom. Stop." She'd drawn blood, now she was going in for the kill.

"What? I'm just telling it like it is." She grinned. "Admit it; you know you love that boy." I let out a modest snicker and averted my eyes. "That's alright. You don't have to say anything. I know you like the front and back of my hand. I can see it all over your face." She bit into a piece of bacon. "Walking around here with that big Chester Cheetah grin."

"Oh, Lord." I rolled my eyes, but she was right. I was head over heels for Matt. We'd grown even closer over the past month. After he'd found out the truth about his dad, he was really down. I couldn't even imagine what it must've felt like for him to have his reality shattered to pieces in one day. With everything he was dealing with, I honestly feared he might do something to harm himself. I made sure I was there to listen to him and console him as much as I could. I thanked God when he began to pull through. I knew it was going to take a long time for him to fully recover from the mental and emotional trauma, but at least he was turning the corner. The Matt that I knew and loved was back. My Machine Gun was happy again. And seeing him happy made me happy.

"What ya'll do at your little sleepover?" My mom continued her interrogation.

"Just watched a few movies."

"What movies ya'll watch?"

"Umm..."

"Uh, huh. Caught you in a lie!" She laughed. "Ya'll using condoms, right? Like I tell your sister: I'm too young and sexy to be a grandma."

I groaned inside. I was NOT about to have this conversation with my mom on a Saturday morning. "And on that note, I'm going to my room."

She laughed. "Boy, sit your little narrow butt down and get you some of this food first."

"I'm good. I already ate before I came home. Matt made us breakfast before I left." I sprouted another spontaneous smile.

"He's cute, AND he cooks, too?" She recoiled in her chair with wide eyes. "Damn. I might need to find me a piece of white chocolate. You said he got an older brother in the Army, right?"

I laughed and proceeded to my room. "Bye, ma." My mom was a mess. I loved her, but she definitely needed to get herself a man and some business of her own ASAP.

Once I took my coat off and hung it up, I sat down on my bed and texted Keon. We both didn't have to work, so hopefully we could hang out. Since Matt and I had become an item, I'd been kind of neglecting Ke. I didn't want to be one of those dudes who banished his friends to the Negative Zone whenever he got in a relationship.

Me: Wyd
Keon: Pussy popping on a headstand :p
Me: Eww *chokes on vomit*
Keon: lol. Just relaxing. Got my mom's car today. Want to hit the mall?
Me: Sounds like a plan my man

After I finished texting with Ke, I crawled under the covers and got a few more hours of shuteye. (I didn't get too much sleep at Matt's house, if you know what I mean). When I woke up, I took a shower and got dressed. I shot Keon a text to let him know I was ready.

Twenty minutes later, he was outside blowing the horn like a lunatic.

"I'm glad you could actually join me today!" He exclaimed as I got in the car. "I thought you had kicked a bitch to the curb to fend for herself. Not returning my calls or texts. Got in the witness protection program; got a new name and identity. Moved and changed your number." He sighed loudly for dramatic effect.

"Exaggerate much?" I deadpanned, buckling my seatbelt.

He smacked his lips. "I'm just saying, I'm surprised you found time for lil' ole me. I know you'd usually be somewhere taking COCK right now."

"Umm...can you not say that word?"

"What? He doesn't call his pecker a COCK?" He looked at me with a crooked grin.

"No. The words 'pecker' and 'COCK' have never come out of Matt's mouth. Thank you very much."

"Oh yeah, I forgot you said he's not a purebred white dude."

I rolled my eyes. Keon looked at me out the corner of his eye and burst out laughing. He cranked up the stereo volume. The sounds of Rihanna's lastest CD filled the car. Of course, he had to sing along to each…and…EVERY…song. Sure, he sounded like an un-spayed cat on fire, but I wasn't about to tell him that. He was having fun, and so was I. It felt good to be spending time with my crazy ass friend again.

Once we arrived at the mall, Ke dragged me to Macy's, Foot Locker, and a million other stores. He dropped his whole paycheck on a pair of shoes and two outfits. (Call me cheap, but I just browsed and window shopped.) As we strolled through the mall, we happened upon a neat novelty store that I had never noticed before. I picked up a cool pair of Spider-Man boxer briefs for Matt. I couldn't wait for him to model them for me.

Before leaving the mall, we decided to stop by the food court to grab a bite to eat. Since Keon had to double his order as usual, I finished eating before he did. I sat there patiently staring at him, my elbow on the table and my fist propped under my chin.

"So, um…will you be finished anytime soon?"

He froze with the soft taco a few inches from his mouth. "You're gonna back up off me today, bitch."

I snickered. "While you finish stuffing your voracious hole, I'm going to use the restroom. Watch my bag for me, OK?" I stood up and placed my shopping bag in my seat. I gathered up the empty burrito wrapper and stuffed it back in the bag it came in. After tossing it in the trash, I made my way to the bathroom to let out the super-sized soda I'd just gulped down. Even though the restroom was empty when I walked in, I still went straight into a stall. Maybe it was because I was so shy, but I just had this weird aversion to urinals. As I was peeing, I heard the bathroom door open. Someone came in and went to the urinal. Once I was done, I shook twice, flushed the toilet and exited the stall. When I saw who had entered the bathroom, I wished my molecules would miraculously disperse so I could vanish. Even though his back was turned to me, I instantly recognized Aaron.

Just fucking great, I thought to myself. The Raymond Reynolds Anti-Luck strikes again!

Luckily, he was facing the wall, so that meant I could sneak by without being noticed. The sound of a steady stream of urine hitting porcelain masked my movements. I lowered my head and quietly shuffled to the sink, praying he didn't turn around and see me. I was tempted to just slip out the bathroom without even washing my hands, but I was too much of a germaphobe to do that. I trembled a little as I hit the button on the soap dispenser, and shuddered at the sudden noise it made. I glanced up. King Aaron was still facing forward, draining his royal penis. *Good.* I hastily lathered my hands and rinsed them off in the water.

My heart was racing now. Did I dare activate the hand dryer?

Nah, better not chance it.

I'd just wipe my hands on my pants, I concluded. The steady stream of urine was now a few trickles. *Shit.* I had to get the hell out of here--like now!

Just as I was about to rush out the door, Aaron called out.

"What's up, Reynolds?" I froze in my tracks as if I had been ensnared in a tractor beam. I would never have a career as a ninja, that was for sure. I slowly turned around. Aaron was still facing the urinal with one hand holding his junk.

I stared at him with a deer caught in the head lights expression. *Wait a minute; did he just call me by my name?* I was so nervous that it took a second for it to register. "*Fag*," "*Homo*," "*Fagmo*," "*Gaymond*," "*Blackout*" – Aaron had called me everything except my actual name over the years. Hell, I was surprised he even knew my real name. I sheepishly looked away as he shook his dick and stuffed it back in his jeans. He hit the handle to flush the urinal and walked over to me as he zipped up his pants. I wanted to get the hell out of there, but I couldn't move.

He walked over to the sink. "So, what's good?"

"N-nothing," I squeaked. OK, so this was way awkward.

Aaron studied himself in the mirror as he casually washed his hands. "Why're you actin' all scared, Ray?" So he just used my name **twice**. What the hell was going on here? Why was he being cordial to me? Was this restroom a portal to the Twilight Zone???

"Scared of what?" I replied nervously.

He turned towards me with a serious look on his face. "Why were you staring at my dick just now, bruh?"

And here comes the bullshit. I sucked my teeth. "I didn't even know you were in here until you spoke to me." I turned up the bass in my voice.

Aaron stepped forward. His 6'3 frame stood right in front of me. He looked down with a blank expression. "Man, stop lying. I saw you stealing looks at my shit out the corner of my eye."

I shot him an exasperated glance. "I was washing my hands." My anger overtook my anxiety. "Nobody wants to see your small ass dick," I blurted out. As soon as those words escaped my lips, I immediately regretted them. I was shocked that I had recklessly mouthed off to Aaron like that. That was something I would've never dared do before. I guess Matt's boldness was rubbing off on me.

"You must be talking about that white boy you're with. There's nothing small over here." He grabbed me by the collar of my coat and pulled me closer. "I bet if I pulled this shit out right now, your gay ass would drop to your knees." His hazel eyes stared into mine with an intensity I couldn't identify. Was it hate...or something else?

Just then, the door to the bathroom whipped open. A man entered holding his little boy's hand. They both gave us puzzled looks. Aaron released me and put on a fake smile. He patted me on the arm like he was playing. I quickly exited the restroom; Aaron followed behind me. Once we got outside he passed me, bumping me with his shoulder.

"Faggot," he murmured. His girlfriend Brianna was standing against the railing on her phone. When he approached, she put her phone away and gave him a kiss. Aaron put one arm around her waist and led her away. He glanced back at me with a peculiar grin.

I just stood there in a daze. One second, he's using my name and speaking to me like a civilized member of the human race. And the next, he's back to acting like the same asshole he's always been. *What the hell was that about?*

CHAPTER 18
MATTHEW

After Ray went home Saturday morning, I spent the rest of the day just chilling around the house--lifting weights, doing homework, writing, playing video games, and of course engaging in every teen boy's favorite past time, jacking off. The weekend seemed to breeze by. Before I knew it, it was the beginning of another school week.

I typically hated Mondays, but this one was different. From the moment I walked in the door, everyone was all on my jock praising me for my buzzer beating shot that won the game. I'm not even going to lie, I was enjoying the hell out of all the adulation and attention.

"Qué pasa, mi amigos?" I slid my tray on the table and claimed my usual spot across from Ray. He and Keon looked in my direction. They both raised an eyebrow simultaneously. "What? A dude can't embrace his Hispanic half?" I flashed my teeth.

"Chile, I guess," Keon replied with a shake of his head.

"How's your day going, compadré?" Ray asked, taking a sip of his milk.

"Bro, my day's been awesome!" I couldn't contain my excitement. "In every class and in between every class, someone was giving me pounds and props. After my performance on the court Friday night, the whole school finally recognizes the magnificence of Matt." A proud smile graced my face. "Mattmania is runnin' wild, brotherrrr!"

"Well, at least he's still modest," Ray said to Keon.

"I know, right? He must have some strong neck muscles to be holding up that big head of his." Keon was quick to join in with his own sarcasm.

"Yep, it's practically big as a boulder." Ray looked at me with a comical smirk.

"Haters," I retorted. The All-Stars walked by as we laughed. Aaron shot me a dirty look. The smile instantly vanished from Mookie's face. "That asshole bother you today?" Ray had told me about the incident that took place in the mall over the weekend. I was still heated about Aaron accosting him in the restroom. This dude was always fucking with somebody. I wanted to say something to his him so bad, but I knew Ray would get pissed at me for fighting his battles for him. I was trying my hardest to respect his wishes. Lucky for Aaron, he didn't put his hands on Ray. If he had, it would've been a whole 'nother story.

"Nah. He made a stupid snide remark in homeroom, but I just ignored it," he replied casually. I had to force myself not to get angry. It was subtle, but I could see the boxing lessons I'd been giving Ray the past few months were definitely building his confidence. He was finally growing a backbone and becoming more assertive. But I was still aggravated by his docile acceptance of Aaron's bullshit. I guess he'd been picked on by Aaron for so long he'd just grown to accept it and take it in stride.

"I'm telling you, all you've gotta do is pop him in the mouth one good time." I demonstrated my point by smacking my fist into my palm. "And I bet you he'd leave you alone then."

Keon snickered. "Boy, hush. You know Ray is a lover and not a fighter." He took a bite of his apple cobbler. "Me, on the other hand...I'll come looking for that ho with a gaggle of gangsta girls and fuck his world up, hunty."

Ray and I both shot him a blank stare. I turned my attention back to Ray. "So yeah, like I said, talking shit is one thing, but if he puts his hands on you, just let me know."

"Yeah, I know. Um...can we drop this subject now?" He looked down and fiddled with his fork. I'd seen him react like that before. I wondered was there something more that he wasn't telling me.

Before I could verbalize that thought, a loud voice shouted my name. I looked up to see Jarell and Quinton, two of my teammates, approaching the table with their trays. They greeted me raucously as they sat down in the empty seats next to me and Keon.

"This my boy right here!" Jarell beamed, playfully throwing an arm around my shoulder. He was the lanky dude with the high top fade who'd complimented me on my ball handling skills the first day of practice. We were cool and all, but he'd never been this friendly towards me. He'd definitely never eaten lunch with me before.

"What's good, fellas?" I said with a smile, a little taken aback by their sudden arrival. It felt kind of awkward having my personal friends and my basketball buddies around me at the same time.

"Ain't shit, Mr. Magic." Quinton replied, shaking his juice. He cast a quick glance at Ray and Keon.

"Oh yeah, Quin and Rell--these are my boys, Ray and Keon." I said, introducing everyone to each other. "Ray and Ke, these are my teammates, Jarell and Quinton."

They both said "what's up?" to Ray and Ke. Ray smiled and gave them a nod of his head. Keon pursed his lips to the side. He gave them that same annoyed *"Why are you here? Please die."* look he'd given me when we first met. Hopefully, he would warm up to them like he did to me. Ray nudged him under the table with his elbow, prompting Keon to put on a faint smile.

Well, I suppose it was better than nothing.

The uneasiness I'd initially felt slowly subsided as my teammates and I started talking. Ray and Keon talked amongst themselves, having no interest in our conversation.

"Man, you know Aaron was popping mad shit when you left out the locker room," Jarell said, taking a big bite out of his hamburger. "Talkin' 'bout he set up all your shots." I laughed and shook my head. I wasn't surprised. "He's always gotta take credit for shit."

"He can't take nobody else getting any shine," Quinton chimed in.

"I know, right? I can't stand his ass," Jarell said. "He wants somebody to be all under his nut sack and shit, kissing his ass."

"Fuck that dude. He's two-faced anyway," Quin said. "He acts like he's cool with you in the locker room, but he doesn't know you when he's with his two butt buddies."

Jarell laughed. "The 'All Stars'--fuck outta here with that corny shit."

The topic of conversation drifted to what we had done over the weekend. As always, Quinton had to brag about his latest sexual conquest. He was a pretty good looking guy, who undoubtedly had his pick of girls.

"Man, I finally fucked that bitch Myra yesterday." He was all teeth.

"It's about time," Jarell said boisterously, slapping hands with him. The two of them were rowdy as hell. I noticed Keon turn to them and roll his eyes, and then he went back to talking to Ray. *So much for him warming up to them.* "What about you, dawg?" Jarell looked at me. "I know you had girls throwing the pussy at you after the game?"

I blushed. "Yeah, I got a little somethin', somethin'."

"HA, HA! That's what's up, dawg!" Jarell whacked me on the back. I glanced at Ray and gave him a coy smile. He smirked and resumed his conversation with Ke. *Whelp, that was dumb, Matt*, I thought. Hopefully I didn't just put my big foot in my big mouth.

We moved on to discussing college football games we'd watched on TV over the weekend. Jarell and Quin were busy arguing over who was going to win the upcoming GA Tech/UGA game. I just sat back and watched them in amusement as they passionately went at it, debating which school had the best team this season.

Suddenly, I felt my phone vibrate. I pulled it from my pocket. It was a new text message.

Ray: A little something, something? Smh. Jackass :)

I snickered a little and looked up at him. He gave me a slick grin. Well, at least he wasn't mad or anything. We continued to shoot the shit until lunch was over.

Fourth period went by pretty fast. When I got to fifth period, Ray was already sitting at his desk as usual.

I sat down next to him. "So, what you think of Rell and Quin?"

"They seem alright," he replied with a shrug. "A little obstreperous though."

Ray and his big words. I stared at him with a puzzled expression. "Can I get the earthling translation please?"

"They're crazy loud."

"Who're you telling?" I chuckled a little. "They're cool people though."

"If you say so." He flashed a sly smile. I couldn't tell if he actually liked them or was just being nice.

Once all of our classes were done and the final bell rang, I walked Ray to his locker. We said our goodbyes and went our separate ways. He had to work after school, and I had practice. The fact that we had won our first game didn't mean shit to Coach. He still ran us ragged as if we'd lost. I'm telling you, this guy could make a Marine drill sergeant cry and beg for mercy. I was so happy when practice was over. My legs and my arms felt like they were about to fall off. My whole body ached. I just wanted to go home and soak in a nice hot bath. The team wearily staggered into the locker room to get changed.

"Aye, I wanted to ask you something," Quinton said. He was sitting next to me on the bench, unlacing his sneakers. "Why I always see you sitting with them gay dudes at lunch?"

"Cause they're my friends," I said defensively. "Is something wrong that?" I was always ready to pounce whenever homophobia reared its head.

"Cause he's a fag, too," Aaron's voice rang out from across the locker room. Everybody burst out laughing. Savion was laughing harder and louder than anyone.

"And you got a problem with that?" I stood up from the bench and glared at Aaron.

He scowled as he started walking towards me. "Yeah. What you gonna do about it?" I smiled inside. It looked like I was going to have an excuse to kick his ass after all.

Coach Smith suddenly appeared out of nowhere.

"Alright, ladies—knock it off—before I make you both run 20 laps!" He barked.

Aaron and I mean mugged each other while Coach proceeded to lecture us. After he was finally done, Aaron angrily went back to his side of the locker room, got changed, and left.

"Man, don't worry about that dude," Jarell said to me in a low voice. He pulled his t-shirt over his head, exposing himself. He was slim like Ray, but with a worked out body. Dude's abs made my six pack look like a beer gut.

"Trust me, I'm not," I huffed. My blood was still boiling as I got dressed.

After we finished changing, the three of us exited the gym together.

"You need a ride, cuz?" Jarell asked Quin.

"Nah, I'm good." Quin shook his head. "I'm getting a ride with Myra." He flashed a cocky grin.

Jarell snickered and turned to me. "What about you, homie?"

"Yeah, man. I'll take a ride. The way my legs feel, I think they might give out before I even get out the building," I replied. We both dapped off with Quin and walked to the parking lot. As Jarell was unlocking the door, a green Jetta cruised by. The passenger window rolled down. Aaron stuck his hand out the window and flipped me the bird before speeding off.

"Dumbass." I shook my head as I got in the car.

"Like I said, don't pay that fool no mind." Jarell closed his door and cranked up the car. "He's just jealous that someone else is stealing his limelight for a change." He pulled out of the parking lot and off the premises. "He's always calling somebody gay and shit." He laughed. "Don't take it seriously."

I didn't reply at first. Then I thought, *if he's a homophobe, I might as well find out now.* "Actually, I'm not offended about being called gay...since I am." I looked at his face for a reaction.

"So, you really are gay?" He turned to me with a stunned look on his face and a glimmer in his eye. "I thought that Savion was playing when he told me that shit." He laughed loudly. "It's all good. I ain't got nothing against gay people though." I was glad to hear that. I wondered if Quin would have the same reaction. When we got to my house, Rell put the car in park and turned to me. "Well this you, man. Aye, give me your number. Maybe we can hang out sometime?"

"That's cool man," I replied. We exchanged numbers.

"Aight, I'll see you tomorrow." Jarell gripped my hand.

"Bet." I got out the car feeling good about the developing friendship. Hopefully this one would actually work out. I walked up my driveway and turned to look back.

Rell was still there.

When he saw me turn around, he smiled and saluted, and then pulled off.

Hmm. That was a little...strange. I did a Ray Shrug and went inside.

CHAPTER 19
RAYMOND

"I'm telling you: Hide yo' dog! Hide yo' kids! Hide yo' husband—cause it ain't nobody safe out here!" Keon exhorted. I just sat across from him at the table staring at him vacantly. He noticed my eyes glazing over and reiterated his point succinctly. "You better watch yo' man, ho. That's all I'm saying."

"Okay...I got it." I fought the urge to roll my eyes. Ever since we'd gotten out of school, Keon had been going on and on about Matt's teammates. In particular, he was convinced that Jarell was not only gay, but also had a thing for Matt. Here we were, hours later at work on lunch break, and he was still pulverizing the same dead horse. "Can we drop this topic already?"

He pushed the straw in and out of his milkshake, causing the plastic lid on the cup to make that irritating squeaking sound. "Oh, so you don't wanna hear the truth, huh?" He slurped his shake as he awaited my reply.

"Ke, you have no idea what you're talking about it." I leaned back in the seat and folded my arms. I knew Keon meant well and I loved him to death, but I wasn't about to take relationship advice from someone who'd never had one. Considering I'd only been in one quasi-romance before myself, I definitely wasn't a relationship expert either. However, from observing my sister's dating trials and tribulations over the years, I'd managed to glean a few things about what NOT to do to foster a healthy relationship.

My sister Kim was the jealous, argumentative type. Every boyfriend she had, she never trusted. I'd always overhear her yapping to her girlfriends about how she'd run this one's phone looking for evidence he was cheating, or cursed that one out because he chose to hang out with his friends instead of her. She was one of those clingy females who believed that just because you were in a relationship with somebody, you had to be under each other every day. And if you weren't, you had to be on the phone together every hour of the day. It doesn't take a Starship Enterprise engineer to know the quickest way to wreck a relationship is to smother your partner and not give them any space. I didn't want to be that way with Matt. I wasn't the jealous type, and I definitely wasn't going to be one of those dudes who didn't trust his lover out of his sight.

"Mmhmm." He leaned in and grinned. "You know that boy feeling Matt."

I finally gave in to the temptation to roll my eyes. Sure, Jarell seemed a little touchy feely, but that didn't mean anything. Just because he was gregarious didn't automatically mean he was after Matt. "Dude, you think everybody's gay."

He smacked his lips. "No, I don't. I don't think Quinton is family. Even though I wish he was. He's so alpha-manish. Chile, he know he can get all my cakes and the pans they were baked in." He paused and fanned himself. "But I can pretty much guarantee his boy is 'How You Doin'?'"

"Meh." I chuckled and shook my head at Ke's Wendy Williams impression. I still wasn't convinced anything was up with Jarell. He didn't trigger my "Spider-sense." But then again, my gaydar wasn't as honed and in tune with the "queer cosmo" as Ke's was. Eh, I guess it wouldn't hurt to keep an eye on him anyway.

After getting home from work, I Skyped with Matt for a little while. The thought of bringing up Jarell crossed my mind, but I decided against it. I wasn't even going to entertain Keon's madness. Once we finished, I took a shower, did some homework, and hit the sack.

It seemed as soon as I hit the pillow, the alarm clock went off. Before I knew it, I was back in homeroom. I was feeling seriously groggy, so I put my head down on the desk before the teacher arrived and the announcements started. For some dumb reason, I set my phone on the edge of my desk.

Seconds later, I heard Aaron enter the room. When he passed, he bumped against my desk, knocking over my phone. I lifted my head and leaned down to pick it up. Before I could reach it, he kicked it, sending it sliding across the floor to the back row. I turned and glared at him as he sat in the seat behind me. I knew he did that shit on purpose.

"What the fuck, man?!" I blurted out, my face twisted with anger. He just smirked. I got up and retrieved my phone. Thankfully it had a protective case on it, so it didn't break.

"What the fuck, man?!" Aaron imitated me with a California surfer voice. His cohorts erupted in laughter.

"Asshole," I muttered, reclaiming my seat. Even though I had said it under my breath, he still heard me.

"What's that? You got something to say?" I turned and gave him an annoyed look. His smirk soon gave way to a sneer. "What the fuck you staring at?"

Everyone around us snickered. I faced forward and sighed in frustration. God, I hated him. While I did tell Matt about Aaron accosting me in the bathroom at the mall over the weekend, I left out the detail about him roughing me up. If he knew Aaron had actually put his hands on me, he'd flip. I didn't want him going ballistic and confronting Aaron. (However, I was starting to regret that decision.)

After homeroom let out, I got up and made my way out the room. As soon as I got in the hall, I suddenly felt a pair of hands shove me in the back.

"Out the way, Mr. Softie," Aaron's voice yelled out.

I stumbled forward, barely catching myself from tumbling over. My books and notebook flew from my hands, scattering all over the floor. I quickly bent down and began gathering them up before they got trampled. I blew out hot air as I stared Aaron down. He turned and gave me a half smile before continuing on his way.

"I saw that. You aight, bruh?" Savion appeared out of nowhere. Before I could respond, he knelt down and began helping me pick up my books.

"Yeah, I'm good," I replied weakly, a little taken aback. "Thanks," I said as he handed me my notebook. I couldn't believe he was actually assisting me in a busy hallway. He didn't even look around once to see if anyone was watching. I was shocked. Maybe he was finally getting over his DL paranoia?

"No prob." He stood up, winked at me and walked off.

Well, that was a lot more...cordial...than I expected, I thought as I proceeded to first period. Wow, maybe Savion actually was growing up after all. (Either that, or he'd been replaced by a doppelganger from an alternate reality.)

At lunch, I sat with the usual suspects. Before Matt and I could even ask how each other's day was going, Jarell and Quin came over in all of their rowdiness. I let out a little sigh as they invited themselves into our space, taking seats on either side of us. Matt was immediately swept up in conversation with them. Keon looked at me with a silly smirk. I rolled my eyes. Apparently lunch with "Beavis and Butthead 2.0" was going to become a daily routine. I focused on my food and tried to ignore the dull pang of jealously that I suddenly felt in my chest.

*****

As Matt and I walked home, I figured it would be a good time to raise Keon's suspicions about Jarell. I felt a little silly bringing it up. I still didn't believe Keon's crazy theory, but I figured Matt would probably get a kick out of it when I told him.

"So, uhh...you want to hear something funny?" I chuckled a little.

"Do you even have to ask?" Matt gave me his undivided attention. "Lay it on me."

"Well, Keon thinks--"

The sound of a honking car horn interrupted me. We both turned our heads at the same time. A gray Toyota Camry pulled up alongside us on the shoulder of the road. The driver side window rolled down.

"Whatup, fellas?" Jarell exclaimed with an ear-to-ear smile on his face. "Ya'll want a ride?"

Matt looked at me. These dudes were really starting to get on my nerves. I wanted to say no, but that would've come off shady. Instead, I just shrugged. Matt took that as a yes. Jarell popped the locks on the doors. Quinton was sitting in the front. Matt and I slid into the backseat. Once we strapped in, Jarell got back on the road.

"Aye, we're about to go to my house and chill for a minute." Jarell looked at us in the rearview mirror. "Ya'll wanna come through and smoke one?"

"Hell yeah, man!" Matt responded enthusiastically.

I groaned inside. I'd already had my fill of these guys at lunch. I definitely wasn't about to spend my afternoon with them, too. "Uh...I've got a research paper I have to work on when I get home," I lied. "Thanks for the invite though." Matt gave me a peculiar look.

"Oh, aight. What about you, Matt Attack?" Jarell asked.

Matt glanced at me again, as if seeking my approval. I gave him a subtle smile to let him know I was cool with it. His green eyes gleamed like a kid who'd just been given permission to play with his buddies. It was so cute. Even though I didn't want to hang around with his friends, I didn't want to be a wet blanket. It would be unfair of me to keep him from spending time with his boys just because I didn't really care for them.

"Yeah, I'm down," Matt replied.

"That's what's up!" Quinton howled. He and Jarell started talking about some girl in one of their classes who they both wanted to fuck. I tuned them out and stared blankly out the window. While I was busy watching the houses pass by, Matt snuck his hand behind my back and playfully pinched me. I yelped a little and swatted him away. He wiggled his eyebrows and flashed a silly grin.

A few minutes later, Jarell was pulling into my driveway. I thanked him for the ride and dapped him and Quinton up.

"Alright, Machine Gun," I said to Matt, casually clasping his hand as if we were merely friends. I knew Matt wasn't ashamed of his sexuality, but I didn't want to put his business out there. I didn't know if he was out with his teammates or not. I opened the door and began to get out the car.

"I'll hit you up later, Ray-Rey," he replied. He pulled me back and gave me a peck on the cheek. I struggled to suppress a smile as I closed the door. I wasn't one for PDA, but that kiss made me feel all warm and s'mores-type gooey inside. It felt awesome to be with someone who was comfortable enough with his sexuality to express his love for me in front of his straight teammates. Savion and he were like night and day. I knew I didn't have anything to worry about with my Matty. I actually felt kind of silly for feeling jealous earlier.

As I walked in the house, my phone chimed. I pulled it from my coat pocket. I had a new message.

Matt: Thanks for putting up with my boys, baby. I'll make it up to you :)

The edges of my lips curled up into a smile. Before I could reply, an alert popped up. Someone had hit me up on Facebook. When I saw who sent the message, my heart nearly stopped.

It was from Aaron.

I stood in the doorway, staring at the message in disbelief. Why was my greatest foe sending me a message on Facebook? I guess picking on me in person wasn't enough. Was he now about to resort to cyber-bullying as well?

"Boy, close that damn door before you let all the heat out!" My mom's bark snapped me back to reality. I looked up from my phone and saw her coming into the kitchen fastening her Bat Belt. (That's what I jokingly called the utility belt that she kept all of her CO gadgets, like her stun gun and pepper spray, in.)

"Hey, ma," I said, quickly closing the door. "Going to work already?"

"Yeah. One of those lazy bastards called out sick, so I'm going in early." She grinned and rubbed her hands together. "More overtime for me." I could see where my sister got her money hungry ways from. "I don't have time to cook, so you're gonna have to fend for yourself."

"Okay. I think I can manage without starving to death."

She chuckled and grabbed me by the back of my neck. She pulled me down and kissed me on the cheek.

"Maaaaa!" I whined, wiping my face. It was one thing to get a kiss from your boyfriend; it was a whole other story to get one from your mother. "I'm eighteen for God's sake."

"Boy, hush. You not too old to give your momma some sugar." She pinched my cheek and rushed out the door.

I smiled and shook my head. I rummaged in the freezer and found a salisbury steak TV dinner.

"Ah, the food of the gods!" I quipped as I took it out and popped it in the oven. I went to my room while I awaited my feast. I pulled off my coat and hung it up. I plopped down in front of my computer and logged on to my Facebook account. I was going to just delete Aaron's message, but I guess my morbid curiosity got the best of me. It had to be one heckuva put down since he couldn't wait to unleash it on me at school tomorrow. I took a deep breath and clicked the message open.

Aaron: What's good Ray?

So he remembered my name again? I thought. I debated whether I should respond. Once again, my curiosity won out. I just had to know why my mortal enemy would go out of his way to track me down on Facebook.

Me: Nothing. Chilling.

Aaron: Cool. You have Ms. Rios 4th period, right?

Me: Yeah. Why?

Aaron: I got her for fifth period. I need some help getting ready for this test Friday. You think you can help me out?

My face crumpled up. I gave the screen a dirty look. Was this dude crazy? All the crap he puts me through, and now he wants me to help him? I laughed to myself. *Sure, I'll help you*, I thought. *When hell freezes over and thaws out, and refreezes again.*

I deleted the message and logged out.

Kiss my Mr. Softie ass, Aaron.

CHAPTER 20
MATTHEW

Aside from the radio, an awkward silence lingered in the car as we drove to Jarell's house. After I kissed Ray, everybody had gotten quiet. I guess they weren't used to the sight of same-sex affection.

"So, that dude's your...uh...?" Jarell began to ask, pausing as if the words in his mouth were glue.

"My boyfriend." I proudly finished his sentence for him.

"Oh. Um, what's that shit like—kissing another dude?" Jarell's question caught me by surprise. "No homo," he quickly added. "It just looks mad funny."

Quinton laughed. "Why you care, dawg? You thinkin' about switching sides?"

"Man, fuck outta here with that," Jarell snapped back. "You know I stay getting pussy."

"Why you getting all defensive? You actin' like you on your period!" Quinton kept ribbing him.

"Keep that shit up, and your ass is going to be walking in a minute."

"Yeah, right." Quinton snickered. "You must be forgetting that I bought the goodies today." He pulled a plastic bag containing weed from his coat pocket and waved it under Jarell's nose in a tantalizing manner. Jarell tried to snatch it from his hand, but Quinton swiftly withdrew it, placing it back in his coat. "Ah, ah. Keep your hands on the steering wheel, punk."

Jarell glowered. "I can't stand your big headed ass." He poked his lip out and pouted.

I just sat in the backseat watching them in amusement. These dudes needed their own Youtube show for real. It didn't take long for us to get to Jarell's crib. I was surprised to learn that he actually lived pretty close to me. We walked inside and dropped our book bags on the granite-top kitchen island.

"Ya'll make yourselves comfortable," Jarell said, leading us to the living room. He took our coats. "I'll be back in a minute."

"Aight," Quinton replied. He flopped down on the plush sectional sofa and I followed suit. He grabbed the remote from the coffee table and turned on ESPN. We sat there watching the TV in silence. I didn't want to read too much into it, but he seemed to be a little uncomfortable being around me alone.

"So, what you think about Duane Wade?" I asked, trying to break the ice.

He blew air through his teeth. "He's aight, I guess. He's got nothin' on LeBron though."

I chuckled. "You're joking right?" I pretended to look at him incredulously.

"Man, are you serious??? Everybody knows LeBron is the truth!" He exclaimed. I just gave him a smirk. "What—you don't think he is?"

I put my hands behind my head and casually leaned back on the sofa cushion. I deliberately took my time responding. "Well, now...I wouldn't say that."

"OH MY GOD! Are you playing right now?!" Quin replied, getting more animated. He proceeded to launch into an endorsement of Duane Wade, singing his praises and rattling off all of his career accomplishments. I just sat there looking unimpressed, which riled him up even more. I was inwardly laughing inside. I didn't necessarily disagree with Quin. I just wanted to get a rise out of him to get him talking. From observing the way he interacted with Jarell, I could tell that Quin loved to argue and disagree with people—especially over sports. If I had to engage him in a heated debate to be cool with him, I was game.

I enjoyed pushing buttons.

Once he finally shut up and let me get a word in, I eagerly countered his argument.

Seconds later, we were in each other's face, flapping our arms and yelling.

"Man, you're gay anyway—what you know about hoops?" He scoffed. Straight guys always assumed that just because someone was homosexual, that meant they had no knowledge of or interest in sports. It was time to put him in check.

"Well, since I actually scored the winning shot in our last game, I'd say plenty. And how many points did you score from the bench?" I gave him a wry smile. I wasn't sure if he was serious or not, but I was going to let him know I could take it and dish it out just as hard.

He waved me off dismissively. "Alright, so you got skills...for a gay dude."

I smiled inside. *Whelp, that shut his ass down*, I thought. I knew it pained him to give the gay guy his props.

"But we ain't talking about me," he quickly rebounded. "We talkin' about LeBron James!"

We picked up where we left off in our debate. Our voices got louder and louder as we tried to talk over each other to get our points across.

"Aye, ya'll need to shut the fuck up!" Jarell said, walking back in the room. He was now wearing a black wife beater, some black and red basketball shorts, and a pair of Nike slides with ankle socks. He sat down in between us and placed an herb grinder and a pack of blunt wraps on the table. Quinton leaned back into the sofa and folded his arms across his chest. "And for the record, both of ya'll are wrong; everybody knows Ray Allen's the man." Quinton and I grudgingly laughed, easing the tension between us.

"It took your ass long enough to come back," Quin said. "I thought you were in there jacking off." He burst out laughing.

Jarell gave him a sidelong glance as he began rolling. "I had to change. I don't want to get no smoke in my new clothes."

Quin snickered. "Oh yeah, I forgot, you a prima donna and shit."

"Man, fuck you," Jarell mumbled, as he finished the blunt. He produced a lighter and sparked it up. He took a hit and handed it off to Quin, who puffed and passed it to me. I took a pull and my eyes widened in amazement at its potency. I looked over at Jarell who had a big grin on his face. "That shit's good, right?"

All I could do was smile wistfully and nod my head in agreement. "Where you get this from, man?"

"Savion," Quin replied. "His brother got all the good stuff."

"Yeah, I know," I said with a grimace. Just the mention of that dude made me bristle.

Jarell picked up on my dry tone. "Didn't you and Sav used to be cool?"

"Yeah, we WERE," I said bitterly. "Not anymore."

"Why not? What ya'll beefing about?" He asked, taking another hit of the blunt.

"Well..." I paused to collect my thoughts. I wanted to be careful to word my response properly. "Dude's homophobic. When he found out about me, he didn't take it too well." I glossed over the part about us feuding over Ray. Even though Savion had no qualms putting me out there, I wasn't that type of person. I wasn't going to out him to his teammates like a bitter queen.

"Oh," Jarell said. From his nonchalant reply, I wasn't sure if he bought my explanation or not. He propped his legs up on the table and rested his hand on his junk.

Minutes later, I was in my own zone, looking off in space. Quinton got up to use the bathroom, leaving Rell and I alone. We continued to pass the blunt, getting higher and higher. It seemed like his long fingers would graze mine every time he passed it to me. I figured it was just the weed playing tricks on me though, so I didn't read anything in to it. At one point, I glanced over and noticed him staring at me peculiarly.

"What?" I asked, curious to find out what was on his mind.

"So, how long you and homeboy been kicking it?"

I sat up on the couch. "Who? Raymond?"

"Yeah?" He snuffed the clip out in the ashtray.

"We've been talking since school started. We just made it official about a month ago."

"Oh, that's what's up. I need to get me a serious shorty for the winter," he said with a laugh.

"Yeah, man, I love that dude." A cheesy smile sprouted on my face.

"So, uh...no homo," he paused and made eye contact with me. "Do you shoot the ball...or are you the basket?"

I looked at him awkwardly for a second and then exploded in hysterical laughter. I'd heard of "Who was the pitcher? And who was the catcher?" before, but never *"Who was the ball?"* and *"Who was the basket?"* What the hell??? Man, the shit straight dudes say when they're high!

"Well, if you must know--" Before I could finish, Quinton came back in the room.

"Aye ya'll, can we talk about something else? Ain't nobody tryin' to hear all that," he interjected. His face was contorted. I could see this topic was making him uncomfortable. But hell, it wasn't like I was the one constantly bringing it up and throwing it in his face.

"Don't get your panties all in a bunch, princess," I joked. If we were going to be boys, he was going to have to lighten up. Me and Jarell laughed while Quin sat with a screw face.

"Gimme that." Jarell reached over and snatched the remote from Quin's lap. He clicked on the Cartoon Network.

For the next hour, we watched TV, talked about school, sports, and just bugged out. I eventually started getting drowsy and of course, hungry. That was my cue to leave. I stood up and stretched.

"Alright, fellas. I'm about to head home."

"You need a ride?" Jarell asked, looking up at me with red eyes.

"Nah, I'm good. I wanna get home in one piece."

He laughed. "Fuck you, bruh." He rose from the sofa and adjusted his dick in his shorts. "I'll get your coat."

"Alright." I turned to Quin. "So are we cool, man?" I asked as I clasped his hand. "I know you're still mad cause Wade can't even carry Lebron's jockstrap."

"Yeah, we're good." He gave me a faint smile. "You're alright...for a gay dude."

"Not that there's anything wrong with that," Jarell chimed in as he came back with my coat.

I laughed and dapped Quin up. These dudes were a trip. Jarell escorted me to the door and gave me a bro-hug. I could still feel the effects of the weed as I walked home. The sun was just beginning to set. I inhaled the crisp autumn air, and enjoyed the scenic red and yellowing trees that lined the streets. I was in the best mood ever. Thanksgiving was a week away and I had a lot to be thankful for; I had an awesome boyfriend, some cool new homies, and my brother was supposed to be getting military leave time to visit. My life was finally going well for a change.

Or at least it was until I got to my house and saw my stepdad's car parked in the driveway.

The hairs stood up on the back of my neck. That dreadful sense of impending doom that I always felt whenever he was home returned. It was something I hadn't felt in months, and hoped to never experience again once he moved out.

Calm down, Matt, I told myself. *He's probably just here to pick up the rest of his crap.* I took a deep breath and exhaled as I put the key in the door. I slowly turned the lock and went inside. I found my mom and stepdad sitting in the living room. When they saw me, they stopped talking.

"Hey, Matt," my stepdad looked up at me with a smile. Totally ignoring him, I turned to my mom.

"What's he doing here?" My voice was low and razor sharp.

"Honey..." She let out a nervous breath. "Joshua may be moving back in with us."

I went ballistic. "Mom, are you crazy?! This is the same guy who cheated on you and treated you like crap for years!"

She rose from the sofa and walked over to me. "Matt, just hear us out." She gently gripped my forearm and looked into my eyes imploringly. "Josh has changed. He realizes he made a mistake and he wants to make amends."

My stepdad got up and stood behind her. "Son, I'm sorry for--" I wasn't even trying to hear whatever bullshit he was spewing.

"Oh, now I'm your son?" I snapped. "I thought I was a 'bastard' or 'mistake' that should've never been born?!" Even over a month later, the memory of those words still pierced my heart like bullets. He remained silent as my eyes cut through him. "What's the matter? The woman you were cheating on Mom with found out how lame you are--and now she's about to put your sorry ass out?"

"Honey, please." Mom squeezed my arm to get my attention. I looked down into her big, Bambi-like eyes.

"Why, Mom? Why would you even consider letting him move back in here after everything he's put us through?" I couldn't even begin to fathom what could possibly be going through her mind.

She sucked in air, and nervously chewed her bottom lip. "Your father deserves a second chance, Matt. He gave me one when I cheated." She let out a long sigh. "And I still love him."

I couldn't believe my ears. What kind of hold did this man have over her? "Apparently, you don't know what love is then!" I pulled away from her.

"Don't speak to your mother like that, boy," my stepdad interjected.

"Shut the fuck up!" I yelled at him. The mere sight of this manipulative creep filled me with a primal rage. He clenched his jaw. I focused on Mom. "I'm telling you now, if he moves back in--then I'm moving out!" I had nowhere to go, but at least the threat sounded good. Hell, I would live on the damn streets if I had to. Anything would be better than being forced to live under the same roof with this tyrant again.

"Matthew, you can't be serious?" She replied, her eyes wide with concern.

"I've never been more serious in my life," I sniffed. I stormed past her to the door. I had to get out of this house. I couldn't stay there for another second. I was about to snap.

"Where are you going?" My mom called after me.

"For a walk. I need some fresh air. The smell of stupidity in this house is suffocating me." I knew that my words were harsh, but I didn't care. As far as I was concerned, I was just calling it like I saw it.

CHAPTER 21
RAYMOND

I was engulfed in the latest issue of *Justice League* when the sound of my ringing phone yanked me back to reality. I reached over and grabbed it from the nightstand.

"What's up, Matt-man?" I answered cheerily.

"Sup, Ray-man?" He replied in a subdued tone. From the sound of his voice, I instantly knew something was wrong.

"What happened?" I wondered if he may have had an issue with Jarell or Quinton.

I heard him breathe a heavy sigh. "My stepdad's back."

"Oh, man. Are you for real?"

"Unfortunately, yes. He was there when I got home from hanging with my boys. My mom is actually considering moving the bastard back in." I gasped in disbelief. "You know me; I hit the fucking roof."

"Damn, I don't blame you." I couldn't help but put myself in his shoes. If I came home from school one day and found out my mom was getting back with my dad, I don't how I would deal with it either.

"You mind if I come by for a minute?"

I sat up on the bed. "Of course not. Just ring the bell when you get here."

"Okay." The doorbell suddenly chimed. "Uh...that's me."

I shook my head and ended the call. I got up and made my way to the door. I opened it to let Matt in. He was standing there with a somber expression on his face. "Come on in, stalker," I joked.

"Sorry about just dropping in unannounced." He cracked a little smile. "I just had to get away from that mad house."

"I feel you." I stood to the side. "So, are you going to come in before you let all the heat out?" God, I was sounding like my mom now.

"Actually, I was thinking you could come out here." He grinned. I looked at him with a raised eyebrow. "You're always cooped up in that house. It's nice out. Come take a walk with me."

"Um...alright," I replied hesitantly. I went back in my room to put on my shoes and throw on a coat. When I came back to the kitchen, Matt was raiding my fridge. "Looking for something, greedy?"

He closed the refrigerator. "No leftovers?" He asked.

"Nope. My mom didn't cook squat tonight." I grabbed an apple from the bowl on the counter and tossed it to him.

"Damn," he replied, catching the apple and taking a bite out of it. "That sucks." He scarfed it down in a matter of seconds. I just leaned against the counter and watched him in amusement. *Well, at least his stepdad's return hasn't affected his appetite*, I thought.

After I locked up, we walked to a nearby playground. It had a jungle gym, a rusty swing set, and some metal benches. The area was illuminated by a single, dim street lamp. At this time of night it was totally empty. A beautiful full moon hung overhead. Aside from the sound of chirping crickets and crunching leaves under our feet, it was perfectly quiet. Matt sat down, swinging his legs on either side of the bench. He patted the space in front of him.

I sat down in between his legs with my back facing him. He wrapped his arms around my waist and rested his head on my shoulder. Our fingers interlaced. He exhaled softly.

"Baby, I don't know what to do. If he moves back in, I'm going to lose it. Either I'm going to run away, or one of us is going to end up dead."

I turned my head to look him in his eyes. "Come on, man. Don't talk like that."

He let me go. "I'm serious, bro. I gave my mom an ultimatum: Him or me."

"What do you think she's going to do?"

He shrugged and lowered his head. "The scary part is, I honestly don't know. At this point, I wouldn't be surprised if she chose him over me. He's always come first. She obviously loves him a lot more than she does me." He looked up at me with moist eyes. "Nobody gives a fuck about me."

"Matt, don't say that. I love you," I said. He gave me a weak smile. He propped his knees up on the bench and lay down on his side, resting his head in my lap. He closed his eyes. I traced my fingers along his strong jawline, feeling the stubble on his face. I tenderly stroked his head, gently running my fingers through his inky black hair. We sat in silence for five minutes before I spoke. "Somebody needs a cut."

He rolled over onto his back and cracked open one eye. "You know you like my luxurious mop." He smiled again, this time more enthusiastically. We gazed into each other's eyes. He leaned up and cupped his hand under my chin to pull me in to a passionate kiss. I glanced down and saw his dick bulging in his jeans. I took hold of it and massaged it through his pants. A moan escaped his lips.

"Come, on. Let's get outta here and take care of this thing." I stood, pulling him up along with me by his dick.

"Aww...can't we do that here?" He looked at me with a mischievous grin.

I cocked an eyebrow. "Don't push it, Machine Gun."

*****

After fooling around at my place, I asked Matt if he wanted to spend the night. He declined. He said his mom would probably be worried sick about him after the way he'd stormed out of the house. Fortunately when he got home, his stepdad was gone. He told me he just avoided his mom and went straight to bed. I was happy to see that he appeared to be in a pretty decent mood when we linked up in the morning. I could tell he was still pissed, but at least he wasn't letting the anger consume him. When we got to school, we dapped off and went to our respective homerooms.

As I waited for the announcements to begin, I pulled out my phone and texted Keon. Seconds later, Aaron walked in. I looked up at him as he passed my desk. He smiled and nodded his head. I made a face and focused on my phone. I still couldn't believe he had the audacity to hit me up on Facebook asking me to help him study for a test! I was going to bring it up to Matt, but with all of his family drama, I didn't want to bother him with this.

"Psst." Aaron tried to get my attention. I just ignored him.

Once homeroom let out, I grabbed my books and got up. Aaron and his boys stood, also.

"Aye, I'll catch up with ya'll later," he told his friends. As they walked off, he grabbed my arm. "Yo, Ray, let me holla at you real quick."

I spun around to face him. "What?"

"You get my message?"

"Yeah," I replied in a curt tone.

"So, will you help me?" He bit his lip bashfully. "I gotta pass this test, man. I already flunked the last one."

"And I should care because...?" I retorted. "After all the grief you've put me through over the years, why should I help you?"

"I'm sorry about all that, alright? I was just fucking with you." He sighed and ran a hand over his ripples of wavy hair. "Ms. Rios told me you get good grades in her class. I just need a little help with that Pluscuamperfecto shit, or whatever it's called."

Umm...why don't you ask her to tutor you?" I looked at him skeptically.

"Man, that old bitch won't help me. She doesn't care if I pass or fail." He was right; Ms. Rios was a notorious hard ass. "And she doesn't like me anyway." Finally, a teacher he couldn't work his "magic" on. This was making my day. He looked at me with the biggest, most pitiful puppy dog eyes. It was weird seeing Aaron show humility instead of his usual cockiness. "Come on, Ray."

I knew he was just being nice only because he wanted something. But if I refused to help him, he would undoubtedly revert back to full-blown jerk mode with a vengeance. He'd torment the hell out of me and he'd probably try to get Matt kicked off the basketball team, too. Unless...

A light bulb suddenly lit up in my head like a green lantern.

Maybe I could use this to my advantage. Perhaps this was the way to finally resolve my war with Aaron through nonviolent means? I deliberated on these thoughts.

After a few seconds, I reached a decision. I couldn't believe what I was about to say.

"All right...I'll do it, but on one condition."

His eyes lit up. "What's that?"

"You have to promise to leave me and Matt alone. No more bullying. No more name calling. None of that." I squared up with him as I awaited his answer.

His facial expression became serious as he mulled my demands for a second. "Okay, you got a deal." He extended his hand. I looked at it warily. "Don't leave me hanging, homie." I hesitantly shook his proffered hand. I was expecting him to strike like a viper at any moment. To my surprise, he flashed a gleaming smile and pulled me into a half-hug. "Thanks, man."

As I looked up into his beaming face, I couldn't shake the uneasy feeling that I'd just made a deal with the devil.

I spent the next several hours second guessing myself. As I schlepped from one class to another, all I could do was wonder if I'd made a huge tactical error by agreeing to help Aaron. Initially, it seemed like a good idea, but now I was having doubts. I was anxious to get someone else's opinion. When lunchtime came, I found Keon and told him what I'd done as we stood in line to get our food.

"Bitch, are you crazy?" He blurted out with wide eyes. Everyone in line turned around and looked at us. He put his hands on his hips and gave them an unapologetic glare. They all went back to minding their own business. "What did Matt say?"

I glanced down at my blue Converses and tapped my foot. "Um...I haven't had a chance to tell him yet."

He shook his head and tsked me. "That boy is gonna have a baby when he finds out!"

I massaged my temples. "Please, don't say that." Sure, Matt was a bit of a hothead, but he was still reasonable. Once I explained why I'd agreed to help Aaron, he would acquiesces and see things my way. Or at least that's what I was hoping would happen. (Who the hell was I kidding? Ke was right; Matt was going to have twins when I told him.)

"I wouldn't do it, if I was you."

"I already told him I would. I can't back out now."

"Chile, please." He twisted his lips. "Fuck Aaron. The only thing you owe him is a kick in his yellow ass."

I snickered a little. A part of me thought it was a good idea to take Ke's advice. But I was the type of person who always tried to honor his promises. My word was my bound. I'd given Aaron my word that I would help him. I couldn't renege now, could I? And if I did, what would the repercussions be? There was no doubt in my mind that Aaron would go on a vindictive rampage if I told him to go fuck himself. I was caught between the proverbial boulder and a brick wall. No matter what I did, I was going to catch some flack--either from a mad Matt, or an angry Aaron. *Geez, what I wouldn't give for a time machine right now*, I mused.

"Just do me a favor," I said. "Don't mention this to Matt, alright? I want to tell him when the time is right."

"My lips are sealed." Keon made the zipper motion across his mouth with an imaginary key. "And I'll hide it in my bosom for safe keeping." He pretended to tuck something in his shirt. I rolled my eyes.

We got our trays and sat down at our usual table. It wasn't long before Matt joined us.

"What's up, peeps?" He sat down and began devouring his lunch. "So, how's your day going?" He asked through a mouthful of sloppy joe and french fries.

"It's going okay, I guess," I replied in a low voice.

He took a gulp of his fruit punch and looked up at me with a curious expression. "Everything cool?"

"Yeah..." I replied unconvincingly. Keon cleared his throat. He was obviously trying to prompt me to tell Matt about the Aaron dilemma. I scratched the back of my head. Well, I guess this was as good a time as any. I took a deep breath. Just as I was about to open my mouth, Jarell's ass swooped down on us. It was like he had materialized out of thin air.

"Fellas!" He exclaimed as he sat down next to Matt. I pretended to focus on my food like I didn't notice him.

"Relly-Rell!" Matt clasped Jarell's hand in an enthusiastic greeting. "Where's bighead Quin?"

"Oh, he cut school today to chill with some bitch," Jarell replied. "Sup, Ray?"

I looked up and gave him a weak smile.

Matt wagged his head ruefully. "Man, that must be some good pussy. Coach is going to go apeshit on him for missing practice."

"That dude doesn't care about that. He'd miss his own momma's funeral for some pussy." Jarell let out a hearty laugh. (Was it just me, or was his voice annoying as hell?)

They continued to banter back and forth, alternating between sports talk, and more sports talk. I exhaled softly. I felt like a third wheel sitting across from them. I'm not going to lie, I was also a little irritated that Matt's boys were encroaching on my "turf," but I just sucked it up. As I reminded myself that there wasn't a jealous bone in my body, I lifted my head just in time to see the All-Stars coming down the aisle in all their splendor. Aaron gave me a subtle head nod as he passed. I quickly averted my eyes. My stomach lurched.

He's actually acknowledging me now?

This was too weird. I ate a few fries and nibbled on my burger. For some reason, I didn't have much of an appetite anymore.

Following lunch, I went to my remaining classes. I was still in such mental disarray that I couldn't even focus on the teachers. Before I knew it, the bell rang and fifth period was over. Once class ended, Matt and I walked out together. I decided I was going to tell him now. I was tired of straining my brain over this.

"Hey, I've been meaning to talk to you about something."

"Uh, oh. I don't like the sound of that." He gave me a leery look. "You're pregnant?" A silly grin spread across his face. He stopped and grabbed me by the waist. "I'm about to be a daddy!"

I pushed him off me. "Who said it was yours?"

He laughed. "Oh, that's cold. Don't expect to get a dime of child support outta me then."

Even though I was tense over what I was about to tell him, I couldn't help but laugh at Matt's comment. "But back to what I was saying," I took a deep breath before continuing. "Aaron and I have the same Spanish teacher."

"Yeah?" Matt focused on me while we weaved our way through the packed halls.

"Well, he's been having trouble with some of the material." My mouth suddenly felt drier than Mars. "And," I paused and swallowed, "he asked me to tutor him." I wasn't sure he'd heard the last part, since the words barely escaped my throat.

"And you told him *no*, right?" His green eyes locked on to mine.

"Um...actually...I told him I would." I let out a nervous chuckle.

"Are you crazy???" He stopped abruptly, causing a girl to almost bump into him. She gave him a stank glare and kept walking. "Dude, you know him. He has to have something up his sleeve. He's probably trying to set you up!" He flailed his arms as he spoke.

"I'm not stupid," I fired back. I stepped closer to the lockers to get out of the way of oncoming traffic. Matt followed suit. "You don't think I've already considered that? I'm just going to study with him in the library or something. It's not like I'm going to his house or anything. There's nothing to worry about," I reasoned.

Matt grimaced. "I don't believe you right now, Ray. Why would you even think of doing something like this without talking to me first?"

I smirked. "Well, I was going to discuss it with you at lunch today, but you were too preoccupied to talk to me." The resentful edge to my tone surprised even me. Maybe some jealously was seeping through after all?

He threw his hand up. "You already told him you would help. So what would've been the point of discussing it with me after the fact?"

I let out an exasperated breath. Deep down, I still believed having Aaron indebted to me would work in our favor. However, if it was going to be this big of a deal and cause friction between us, then I wouldn't go through with it. "Look, I only told him yeah because I thought it would be a good opportunity to bury the hatchet and get him out of our hair. I even made him promise not to mess with us anymore if I helped him. But if you think it's a bad idea, then I won't do it."

"What difference does it make what I think?" He had a clenched jaw and a red face. "Hell, it's not like anyone gives a damn what Matt wants anyway, right?"

I realized he was referring to the situation with his mom and stepdad. I knew he was going through a lot at home, but it wasn't fair that he was taking it out on me. I didn't want to further incite him by vocalizing that sentiment though. "Come on, man." I turned on my soothing voice instead, hoping to calm him down some. "You know it's not even like that."

"Whatever, Ray," he huffed "Do whatever you want! Don't worry about me. No one else does, so why should you be any different?"

Before I could say another word, he stomped off.

I leaned with my back against the lockers.

My heart ached.

I watched him round the corner, and disappear from view.

CHAPTER 22
MATTHEW

Was everyone losing their damn mind? First my mom wants to take my stepdad back, and now this shit! I couldn't think clearly. My thoughts were so all over the place, it took me a few tries to get the combination to my locker right. Any other time, I could open it with my freaking eyes closed. I angrily transferred books in and out of my locker, and into my book bag. Once I was done, I slammed it so hard it nearly fell off the hinges. People turned around and looked at me like I was crazy. I pulled the straps of my bag over my shoulders and marched down the hall to the gym. Usually, I would've stopped by Ray's locker at the end of the day before going to practice, but not today. I wasn't ready to see him yet. I knew I needed to cool off some before we talked again.

After Ray told me he'd agreed to tutor Aaron, all I could see was red. This shit was fucked up to the ninth degree. To put it mildly, it felt like he had just kicked me in the nads. I went to my sixth period class and just stewed in my seat. By the time the final bell sounded, I'd simmered down a little, but not much.

What could possibly possess him to do something so stupid?

I remembered learning about something in one of my classes before called "Stockholm Syndrome," where someone develops emotional ties to another person who intermittently harasses, beats, threatens, abuses, or intimidates them.

Could that be what was happening with Ray and Mom?

"Great. You're psychoanalyzing people like fucking Freud, now," I said to myself as I pushed open the door to the gymnasium. I entered the noisy, smelly locker room. I walked past a few rows of lockers until I found Jarell. He was sitting on the bench with his shirt off and his belt unbuckled.

"Damn, what's wrong with you?" He asked.

"Nothing, man." I dropped my bag on the bench and sat down next to him. I started to unlace my sneakers.

"Stop lying. Your face looks like you wanna kill the guy who killed your cat." He snickered.

"Me and Ray had a fight," I said in a low voice. I kept my eyes to the floor as I pulled off my shoes.

"Why?"

I was about to explain what happened, when Savion suddenly came around the corner. I instantly clammed up. "I'll tell you later." The last thing I wanted was for him to overhear that Ray and I were fighting. Knowing him, he'd see that as a golden opportunity to try and worm his way back into Ray's life. He nodded his head at Rell and ignored me as he kept walking.

"Aight." Rell gave me a quick quizzical look. "Aye, Sav!" He called out, springing up from the bench. "You got it?"

Savion paused momentarily and looked back. "Yeah, I got you after practice."

"Cool." Jarell turned to me and started doing the Dougie dance. From the way he was carrying on, I could only surmise he was looking forward to a weed transaction.

"More HIGH-jinks after school today, huh?" I looked at him with a raised eyebrow.

"You ain't know?" He grinned from ear-to-ear. "420--24 hours a day, 7 days a week, 365 days a year."

I shook my head as I pulled off my striped rugby shirt. This dude was a bigger pothead than my friend back in Cali. We got dressed and hustled out onto the court with the rest of the team.

As usual, Coach worked us like Dalmatians at a dog show, making us jump through hoops and perform tricks. We had a game coming up Friday, so he really went HAM on our asses. Believe it or not, I was actually thankful for the distraction. We were so busy with drills and playing pickup games that I didn't even have time to think about my argument with Ray. However, I'd instantly be reminded of it whenever I saw Aaron.

I'm going to have a few words with that snake before we leave out of here, I promised myself.

Once practice was over, the team trudged back to the locker room like weary troops returning from war. Everyone immediately hit the showers. The steamy water felt good on my throbbing, aching muscles. I heard Aaron's big mouth, laughing and joking with some teammates on the other side of the shower wall. My face reflexively contorted.

"You all right, man?" Jarell's voice startled me. I glanced over to see him soaping up his chest and cut abs. His eyes were focused on me.

"Yeah." I sulked and faced forward. I lowered my head so the soothing water could wash over my body. Too bad it couldn't ease the tension that was building inside of me.

After leaving the shower area and drying off, we went to get dressed. I quickly put on my clothes and sneakers.

"I'll be back," I said to Rell as I got up from the bench. I stalked through the rows of lockers until I found my target.

Aaron had already gotten dressed and was just putting on his coat. My eyes zeroed in on him like heat seeking missiles. I marched up to him. He looked at me with a blank face.

"What are you up to, Aaron?" I asked tersely.

"What're you talking about?" He covered his mouth and let out a fake yawn.

"Don't play dumb. You know exactly what I mean. Why did you ask Ray to tutor you?"

"Obviously, because I need help," he said sarcastically. He calmly zipped up his coat. "He doesn't have a problem doing it, so why're you worried about it? Mind your business."

"Ray is my business, asshole." I stepped closer to him. "So what are you planning to do, huh? Get him alone so you can beat him up or something?" I balled my fists. I was ready to start throwing blows and elbows. Then it hit me; that was exactly what he wanted me to do. "Oh, I get it now. This is some sort of scheme to push my buttons, right? You're trying to use him to get back at me. You want me to break on you so you can get me kicked off the team." I smiled triumphantly, convinced that I'd seen through his plan.

"You? Break on me? Please." He snorted. "I already told your boy I wouldn't fuck with you anymore. Don't make a liar out of me."

I narrowed my eyes and pointed a finger in his face. "Whatever, man. Look, I don't know what you've got up your sleeve, but whatever it is, it's not gonna work."

He held his hands up in a placating manner. "Man, just drop it, alright? Trust me, I'm not going to do anything to the dude." He casually adjusted the knit hat on his head. "If I don't get my grades up in this class, I could be kicked off the team. I'm just glad homeboy agreed to help me after all the shit I've given him. You got yourself a good dude." He looked me up and down with a scowl. "You better keep your eye on him before some other homo snatches him up." He closed the locker and started to walk off. I grabbed him by the arm and pulled him back.

"I swear, if you do anything to hurt Ray, you're going to have to answer to me," I said through gritted teeth. "If I get kicked off the team for kicking your ass, then oh-fucking-well."

He looked at me with a sly smirk. "Whatever." He snatched his arm away and exited the locker room. I smacked my fist into my palm. I might not have decisively won that psychological tug-of-war with Aaron, but at least I got my point across.

I walked back over to where I'd left my bag. Jarell was busy combing his high top with a hair pick. "You straight?" He asked, putting the pick in his back pocket. He patted his hair to make sure it was perfectly square.

"Yeah, I'm good," I mumbled. I pulled on my coat and grabbed my bag. "Let's go."

Rell and I walked out of the school together to the parking lot. When we got to his car, Savion was sitting on the hood with his arms folded.

"Damn, 'bout time you got here." He looked at his watch with an irritated expression.

"Man, kill that noise," Jarell replied, stopping at the bumper. I stood back a few feet and silently observed. He dug in his pants pocket and pulled out a crumbled bill. He handed it to Savion.

"Where's the rest?" Savion eyed the money with his lips twisted.

"This is all I got right now. Q was supposed to have the rest, but his ass didn't come to school."

Savion shrugged. "What's that got to do with me?"

Jarell sucked his teeth. "Come on, Sav." I couldn't stand to see him pleading with this jackass like a crack addict.

"Hey man, how much do you need?" I interjected, walking up to them. Since I smoked with him and Quin last night, I had no problem chipping in.

"Good lookin' out, dawg." Jarell said gleefully. "Just $10."

I fished my wallet from my back pocket. I pulled out two five dollar bills and held them out to Savion. He stared at them as if they were counterfeit and then brushed my hand away. He pushed off the hood of the car and turned to Rell like I wasn't even there.

"Here," he turned his head from side-to-side to make sure no one else was around, and then subtly slid something into Rell's hand. "You'll pay me back later, right?"

"Yeah, man. No doubt." Jarell beamed. "Aye, you wanna come smoke with us?" Savion shot him a weird look. The smile vanished from Rell's face. "Uh, okay. Maybe next time then."

Savion left without saying another word. Once Rell popped the door locks, we climbed into his car. He cranked up the engine and allowed it to warm up.

"Damn, that dude makes me sick," I huffed, strapping on my seatbelt.

Rell snickered. "Ya'll need to squash that beef, man."

"Tell that to him," I retorted. I really didn't have a problem with Savion anymore. He probably felt differently, but as far as I was concerned, there was no competition between he and I. Ray had a choice between us, and he picked me. Not to sound like a cocky prick or anything, but the best man had won. Savion was just carrying a grudge because he was a bitter hater.

"He's generally a cool dude if you stay on his good side."

"If you say so. How long have you known him?"

"Uh...we go back a long time. But forget about him." He reached over and fidgeted with the radio. "You gonna chill with me for a minute?"

"Yeah, sure. Why not?" I wasn't originally planning to smoke again today, but I figured what the hell. Lighting up was just what I needed to clear my mind.

When we got to Rell's house, he went to his room to change clothes. While I was waiting, I pulled out my phone. I had a text from Ray from a few hours ago.

Ray: What happened to you after school?
Me: I just went straight to practice

I let out a heavy sigh. Just typing that made me feel like a grade A jerk. Even though I was mad, that still was no excuse for blowing him off the way I did.

Me: Sorry

After waiting a few minutes without a reply, I put my phone away. I knew Ray was probably at work by now and couldn't text me back. *I'll just hit him up later tonight to hash things out*, I thought.

"You gonna have to snap out of that funk, bruh," Jarell said, coming back into the room. He was now wearing a wife beater which showed off his broad shoulders, and some basketball shorts. He flopped down on the sofa next to me. "You gonna fuck up my high before it even starts with all that mopin' and shit." He chuckled. "You know how to roll?"

"Of course," I replied, sounding almost offended.

"Good. Make yourself useful then." He handed me the bag of weed and a blunt wrap. I went to work while he flipped through channels on the flat screen TV. As I finished licking and sealing the blunt, I could feel his eyes on me.

"What?" I asked, stopping in mid-lick.

"Nothing. Just tryin' to see if you know what you're doing." He laughed.

"Hell nah. You're not going to sit here and insult my rolling skills, bro." I handed him the blunt and playfully nudged him with my shoulder.

"Not bad." He sparked it up. He took a long pull and nearly choked to death.

"Punk," I quipped, taking the blunt from him while he tried to regain his composure.

It wasn't long before we were both floating on cloud ten. We talked and laughed about all kinds of stupid shit, half of which I couldn't remember. During lulls in the conversation, my mind would constantly drift back to Ray. As much as I tried not to think about him, I couldn't get Mookie out of my head. I hated it when we argued.

"So, what did you and your boy fight about today?" Jarell chimed in as if reading my mind.

I took a deep breath and told him the whole story. He just sat and listened attentively, his big round eyes fixated on me like I was the only thing in the room.

"Ray is just so nice and bighearted—almost to a fault. But then again, that's one of the things I love about him." I scratched the back of my neck and sighed. "I don't know, Rell. Maybe I was wrong by going off on him like that?"

Jarell took another hit and passed to me. "I don't blame you for flipping out, man." He lifted his beater and scratched his flat stomach. "No homo, but if he was my dude and he did some shit like that behind my back, I'd be tight, too." He shoved his hand down the front of his shorts. "He's basically sleeping with the enemy."

I nodded my head in agreement. *So it wasn't just me?*

For a little while, I wondered if I may have overreacted. However, Rell's words had reaffirmed my belief that my reaction was justified. Sure, I was wrong for taking my home life problems out on Ray—and I fully intended to apologize to him for that. But I was now more convinced than ever that I was right to react the way I had. I loved my baby, and I didn't want to even risk the chance of him getting hurt.

I was going to put my proverbial foot down.

For Ray's own good, there was no way I would let him tutor Aaron.

CHAPTER 23
RAYMOND

"He's just being a drama queen!"

I burst out laughing at Keon's unequivocal pronouncement. "Well, I don't know if I'd call him that, but he did go overboard with the theatrics." We were at work on our lunch break. As usual, my romantic life was hot gossip. "Well, at least he did finally text me back." I tapped the screen on my phone to lock it and then set it down on the table. I knew Matt was pissed about me agreeing to help Aaron, but he'd definitely overreacted in my opinion. "I still can't believe how he just blew up and stormed off like that, and then left me standing around after school looking like a dope."

Keon poked at his grilled chicken salad with his fork. "I can see where he's coming from though. Imagine if it was the other way around."

"Honestly, if he came to me and told me he'd agreed to give Aaron some basketball pointers and coach him after school to help him get ready for a game, I wouldn't get all bent out of shape over it," I said with a shrug. "Especially if he was doing it with the intention of ending all of Aaron's asinine antics."

"But that's you. Ya'll are different. You know that boy's got a short fuse. He likes to shoot first and ask questions never." He took a bite of his salad and made a face. He pushed the bowl away in disgust. "Chile, this nasty thing ain't going to do nothing for me. I wonder if I got time to order a burger."

I laughed and bit into my sandwich. "I doubt it."

"Damn." He shook his head, pulled the bowl back, and continued eating. "The things I have to go through to keep my figure looking tight so I can compete with that bitch, Brianna."

I gave him a crazy look. "Um, yeah...so like I was saying: Do you think I shouldn't have told Aaron yes?" Matt had a tendency to be rash and impulsive, but did that automatically always make him wrong?

He smacked his lips. "Well, I didn't say that either."

"Okay. So what exactly are you saying, oh Cryptic One?"

He chuckled. "Well, on the one hand, I can see why Matt would be pissed about you not discussing it with him first before agreeing to do it." He stabbed at his salad. "But on the other hand, Aaron is your problem. You were dealing with his bullshit long before you met Matt. If you feel helping him is a way to resolve whatever issue he has with you, then why not do it? If Matt loved you and trusted your judgment, he would still support you, regardless of if he completely agreed with you or not. Hell, he ain't your daddy. You don't need to get his permission."

I nodded my head vigorously. "That's what I said." I was still convinced that being diplomatic was the way to go. "But I don't want to let this come between us. If it's going to cause problems, I just won't do it."

"Sounds like somebody's dick whipped!" Keon grinned.

I balled up a napkin and hit him in the face with it.

When I got home from work, I immediately got out of my smelly uniform and took a shower. Once I freshened up, I changed into some sweats and a t-shirt. Sitting down at my computer desk, I opened my laptop and logged onto my Facebook account. I had a new message from Aaron. *Shit.*

Aaron Thomas: Can we study tomorrow after school?

I buried my face in my hands. *Guess I'm going to have to let him down gently,* I thought. Just as I was about to reply and tell him I'd changed my mind, I got an incoming Skype call from Matt.

"What's up, Mookie Man?" His smiling face filled the screen.

"What's going on, Mr. No show?" I said jokingly.

He blushed and scratched his forehead. "Hey, I'm sorry about earlier, man. My temper just got the best of me."

"What else is new?" I quipped. I wasn't mad, but I wanted to play around with him a little before I let him know I wasn't going to tutor Aaron anymore.

"I only flipped out like that because I love you and because I care so much about you." He stared into the camera and gave me a sincere smile. My heart leapt with joy. I felt like I was on a spaceship blasting off into the stratosphere. "I don't want to see you do something stupid."

Excuse me?

That space ship suddenly lost power and altitude.

My brow furrowed. "Just because you don't agree with my idea doesn't mean I'm being *stupid*," I replied, taking offense to Matt's last remark.

"Dude, I didn't say *you* were being stupid. I said your idea was," he clarified, shoving his foot deeper down his throat. "I mean come on, Ray; I bet even your boy Ke thinks it's dumb?"

I was coming to a slow boil, but I tried not to show it. *Calm down, Ray. Cooler heads should always prevail*, I reminded myself. I would just tell him I wasn't going to tutor Aaron anymore before I said something I'd regret. "Look, I'm not--" Before I could finish, Matt butted in.

"Even Rell agrees with me that you shouldn't do it." That was the last name I wanted to hear right now. It was also the last straw. I was beyond annoyed.

"Who cares what Jarell says?!" I snapped. My simmering irritation with Matt's newfound bromance had finally bubbled to the surface.

"You should care! He's making a lot more sense than you are right now," he fired back. Man, this conversation had gone south in a flash. That spaceship I was on was now plummeting back to earth. "At least he realizes that when you're in a relationship with someone, you gotta take your partner's feelings into consideration before just doing whatever the hell you want."

First Jarell encroached on my relationship, now he was turning my boyfriend against me. Maybe Keon was right about this dude after all?

"Just because we're in a relationship doesn't mean you can tell me what to do." I detested being treated like a child, especially by someone who was only a few weeks older than me. "If I want to tutor someone or be friends with somebody, then that's my prerogative. I don't need your approval, and I damn sure don't need Jarell's!" I was spitting fire like a dragon. "He probably just wants you anyway."

He looked at me incredulously. "Stop being silly. All that dude talks about is pussy and playoffs. He's not interested in me like that."

"You never know," I said with a smirk. "That's all Savion used to talk about too." I didn't really believe Jarell was gay, but since he apparently had so much to say about me behind my back, I figured I'd just throw his ass right under the bus too.

Matt let out an exasperated breath. "Look, I'm tired of fighting with you over this. I don't want you tutoring Aaron, and that's all there is to it. End of discussion." He folded his arms. His face was stern.

"Yeah, this discussion is definitely over. Good night, *Dad*," I said sarcastically. Matt rolled his eyes and threw up his hands. Before he could say something else to further piss me off, I logged out of Skype.

That emotional spaceship I was on had crashed and exploded, leaving nothing but a fiery wreckage.

I'm not usually one to react rash or impulsively, but his pigheadedness had managed to work my last nerve. I wasn't going to tutor Aaron, but after this latest argument with Matt, I'd changed my mind. I felt like I had something to prove now. My pride was on the line.

I opened Facebook and re-clicked on Aaron's message.

Aaron Thomas: Can we study tomorrow after school?

I hastily typed my answer and sent it.

Ray Reynolds: Yes

Seconds later, he hit me back.

Aaron Thomas: Cool. See you tomorrow, homie. I leaned back in my chair and huffed in bittersweet satisfaction. *This will show Matt (and Jarell) that Raymond Reynolds is his own man, and he doesn't take orders from anybody!*

*****

As per our usual routine, Matt and I met up on the way to school. Aside from a dry "good morning," neither of us said anything. We walked side-by-side in total silence for the first five minutes.

"So you couldn't even hit me back last night?" He asked in a flat tone. He'd called me after our argument, but I sent it to voicemail. I wasn't in the mood to deal with him after our disastrous Skype session.

"I didn't feel like talking," I replied nonchalantly.

He let out an annoyed sigh. "Well, did you change your mind about tutoring Aaron?"

"Nope," I said with defiance in my voice. "We're studying together today after school."

He reached in his coat pocket and pulled out a pair of ear buds. He plugged them into his phone and inserted them in his ears. He looked straight ahead and didn't say another word. I shook my head. Guess I was getting the silent treatment again. *No problem*, I thought. *Two can play this game.* I took off my book bag and grabbed my headphones. I put them on and blasted my music. We walked to school together, but we might as well have been worlds apart.

Once we got to the building, Matt mumbled something. I didn't even bother to remove my headphones to hear it. When we walked inside, we dapped off and went our separate ways.

I went through my morning like usual. Before I knew it, it was lunchtime.

"You and Mr. Matt still haven't made up yet?" Keon asked in astonishment.

"Nope." I casually took a sip of my milk.

"Chile, ya'll a mess." He shook his head and pursed his lips. "Here he comes now. Of course he's got that bumpy face, block-headed bitch with him."

I looked up and saw Matt, Jarell, and Quinton approaching. They sat down in their regular spot at the table.

"Hey," Matt said to no one in particular. He didn't even look in my direction. He immediately started talking to his boys. I rolled my eyes and went back to conversing with Ke.

Throughout the course of lunch, I would occasionally glance at Matt and catch him glancing at me—and vice versa. We'd both quickly look away. (Yeah, this was a juvenile game, but if he wanted to take it there, then so be it.) We were engaged in a silent war. I wasn't going to budge on this. I was sticking to my guns. I had to.

The war dragged on through fifth period, with both of us giving each other the icy shoulder.

At the end of the day, I walked back to my locker and loaded up my bag. It was time to meet up with Aaron.

"So, are you actually going to go through with this?" Matt was leaning against the locker next to mine with his arms folded. His sudden appearance startled me.

"Yep," I replied smoothly.

He pushed off the locker and walked down the hallway. More silent treatment. I watched him disappear into the crowd. Once again, he was behaving like a spoiled kid who didn't get his way. Sadly, I was getting used to it. I was also getting sick of it. I pulled one strap of my bag over my shoulder and proceeded to make my way to the classroom where I was to meet Aaron.

By the time I arrived, I was a bundle of nerves. I tried to relax by taking a deep breath. My heart was fluttering as I entered the empty classroom. It was like I was meeting someone on a blind date or something. I took a seat and pulled out my Spanish textbook and my notes. I sat there patiently.

Five minutes passed. I was still waiting.

Five more minutes passed. I looked at my watch.

He wasn't going to show. This was just a ruse.

He was going to "stand me up" and laugh about it later. I felt stupid.

Just as I was about to get up and leave, Aaron walked in the room with a big smile on his face.

"Sorry I'm late, Reynolds. I had to walk my girl to the bus and wait till she got on. She wouldn't stop talking my damn ear off." He slid into the desk next to me and placed his leather book bag on the floor.

"Oh, that's alright," I replied. I was relieved that I hadn't been played like a chump after all. I immediately launched into the lesson. I wanted to get this over with as quickly as possible. (Being in the close proximity of my archenemy was too unnerving.) I went over the different verb tenses he was having trouble with, slowly breaking each one down for him. "And you conjugate it like this. See?" I moved my notepad over a little. I made sure to keep a safe distance between us, so he had to crane his neck to take a look.

"Man, I can't see that. Come over here." He gripped the back of my desk and the front part that you write on. Before I even knew what was happening, he pulled me closer to him in one swift motion. The protective force bubble had been popped. My buffer zone was gone. "That's better. Now, what were you saying?" He placed his right arm behind me and rested his hand on the back of my seat. We were now uncomfortably close. We were so close that his long right leg was pressed against my left leg. I could smell his minty fresh breath and the tantalizing scent of his cologne. I could feel the warmth from his sinewy body. He casually reached under his desk and adjusted his dick. I was so nervous that I fumbled my pencil.

"You aight?" He asked, leaning over and picking it up from the floor.

"Uh...yeah," I squeaked as he handed me the # 2. "Thanks."

Why was I getting turned on? *This is your nemesis, Ray. Get ahold of yourself, dammit!* I exhorted myself. Unfortunately, chastising didn't work. I now had a raging hard-on. Ugh, I couldn't believe my body was betraying my brain and my hormones were hijacking my thoughts. With a great deal of effort, I managed to push the lust out of my head and focus on the school work.

Surprisingly, Aaron picked up on it pretty quickly. Seeing how easily he seemed to catch on, it was hard to believe he was having difficulty with the material. After thirty minutes of studying, I suggested we take a break. At first, we just sat there in awkward silence.

"Damn, it's hot in here," Aaron suddenly announced. He removed his hoodie and hung it on the back of the desk next to him. He was wearing a v-neck t-shirt underneath. The tee hugged his chest and arms snugly. He had an interesting tattoo covering a portion of his arm.

"That looks cool," I said, complementing the intricate body art.

He grinned. "Thanks, homie. I actually designed it myself."

"Really?" My eyebrow shot up in disbelief.

"For real, no lie. I drew a detailed schematic of what I wanted the tattoo guy to do."

"You can draw?" I asked, still doubtful.

"Yeah, I've been drawing since I was little." He leaned over to his left and rummaged through his book bag. He pulled out a notebook and placed it on his desk. "This is my sketch book." He opened it and my jaw practically crashed through the desktop. It was a breathtaking, manga-style drawing. I was flabbergasted.

"Woah...that's amazing, man." With each flip of the page, I was becoming and more impressed. The shading, the depth and the texture of the artwork were unbelievable. "Dude, you're crazy talented."

"Thanks," he replied modestly. I could've sworn he blushed a little. He put the notebook back in his bag.

"Geez, I had no idea you could draw like that."

"Nobody does. It's just something I do as a hobby."

"But you're really good, Aaron. You should consider pursuing that professionally or something."

"You think so?" There was a glimmer in his eyes.

"Definitely." I nodded my head.

"I've thought about studying graphic design in college," he said enthusiastically. "But my dad's pushing me to follow in his footsteps and go into the medical field. He's not going to be happy unless I become a pro ball player or a doctor." There was a twinge of sadness in his voice.

"You can't live for your parents, man. You should follow your heart and pursue your passion."

A goofy grin appeared on his face. "You sound like a teacher and shit."

"I'm serious. You have a gift. You shouldn't waste it."

"Yeah, right. Maybe I can get a job in Japan working on *Naruto* or something." He laughed.

"You like anime?" My jaw crashed through the floor this time.

"Hell, yeah! Dragon Ball Z--and especially Naruto-- that's my shit right there!" He beamed. Who'd ever guess that Aaron had a bit of nerd in him? First I find out he draws; now I learn he's an anime fan. Will wonders never cease???

My mind had just been vaporized.

If he wasn't at the top of the pecking order and I wasn't at the bottom, maybe we could actually be friends?

Nah, I wasn't going to delude myself.

Even though I was glimpsing a different side of Aaron, I couldn't lose sight of the fact that this was the same guy who'd made my life hell since freshman year. It was something that I laid awake wondering about many a night. I had to know why. *I may never get another chance to ask him this, so I might as well do it now.* I took a deep breath and psyched myself up. *Here goes nothing.*

"Why are you always bullying me?" I blurted out before I lost my nerve.

"Man, I just be playing around with you." He snickered. "You make it sound like I'm beating you up and taking your lunch money."

"You've been harassing me since the first time you laid eyes on me," I retorted. I bristled as I recalled all the times he'd made fun of me, knocked my books out of my hands and tripped me in the hallway. One year, the bullying was so bad I even went to the principal, hoping that would help. It only made things worse. The principal told Aaron, and Aaron came down on me even harder.

"That's just how high school is, bruh," he said coolly. "You were always an easy target. If you'd ever spoken up for yourself, I would've left you alone. Sure, I might've whopped your ass first, but I would've left you alone after that." He placed a hand on my shoulder and laughed. Although I didn't see the humor in his explanation, I realized he was being honest. Even in the animal kingdom, those who are perceived to be weak will be treated like outcasts. That was my problem—I'd always been a pushover and easy prey for others in the food chain.

"But why me, though?" There were hundreds of socially awkward kids at this school; why was I always the focus of his mocking and intimidation? His forehead crinkled like I'd just posed a complex riddle. I looked at him with anxious anticipation. I was on pins and nails as I awaited his answer.

He gave me a nonchalant shrug. "I don't know."

I don't know. That was it???

I wasn't sure what I was expecting to hear, but I was hoping for a response that was at least halfway logical. I was convinced that Aaron harbored a deep-seated hatred of me for some unknown reason.

All the gay gags; maybe because I reminded him of a gay uncle that molested him as a kid?

The endless skin tone taunts; maybe because my complexion matched that of a black Labrador who bit him or chewed up his toys when he was a baby?

It didn't have to be earth shattering or profound--but give me something to work with here!

For years, I'd spent countless hours agonizing over the way he treated me. It hurt to even think about it. But to him, it was all only in good fun. It was nothing more than "harmless" entertainment for his audience.

"Look," his voice snapped me back to reality, "like I said before—I'm sorry about all of that. I was just fucking with you. I ain't mean anything by it." He extended his hand. "We cool?" I just stared at him. "You gonna leave me hanging again, homie?" I reluctantly shook it.

I still didn't trust Aaron further than I could throw him (without the aid of telekinetic mutant powers), but I was at least willing to give him the benefit of the doubt. If he was truly trying to turn over a new leaf, I wouldn't hold a grudge. The way he treated me going forward would reveal if he was sincere or not. He held on to my hand as a smile spread across his face, showcasing a deep set of dimples. I'd never been this close to Aaron's face before without seeing a scowl on it. His skin looked so soft and clear. Aside from a uni-brow, (which he kept waxed into submission) his face was smooth and hairless.

"Thanks for helping me. I know I'm going to kill that test tomorrow!" He finally let go of my hand. "I'm going to look over this some more later though. Aye, can I get your number just in case I have any questions?"

"Um...yeah." *The Twilight Zone* theme played in my head. I gave him my digits as I closed my book.

After putting away his phone, Aaron stood and took a big stretch. As tall as he is, his mid-section was thrusting right in my face. His t-shirt rode up, exposing a ripple of hard abs. There was a fine glaze of hair on his tight stomach which disappeared into the band of his underwear. The head of his dick was visible in his sweats. I didn't know if he was hard or not, but it looked huge. I gulped and quickly looked away. The last thing I wanted was for him to catch me staring at his crotch. That would instantly destroy the fragile truce we'd just established. We got our book bags and left the room together. We talked about our favorite fights from Dragon Ball Z as we walked down the hallway. I still couldn't believe Aaron was a closet geek! I could now see why everyone was so enthralled by him. He was charming and captivating when he wasn't being a jerk. We exited the doors into the parking lot.

"You need a ride home?" He asked me.

"Uh..." his question caught me totally off guard. A week ago, I wouldn't have been surprised if Aaron tried to run me over with his car. Now he was offering me a ride in it? I was flattered...and leery. After my ordeal with Savion last month, I wasn't taking any chances getting into enemy cars.

"What, you scared?" He asked with a serious expression.

I chuckled nervously. "Nah, I'm good." I extended my hand. He took hold of it with a tight grip. He had that same indescribable intense look in his eyes that I'd witnessed in the mall restroom. His gaze was mesmerizing and intimidating at the same time. He released my hand and cracked a smile.

"You know you were scared." He lightly shoved me in the chest.

"Leave him alone, Aaron!"

What in the blue blazes? I thought. I swiveled my head in the direction of Matt's voice. He was standing next to a Camry with his face balled up in anger. *Really, Matt? You're spying on me now?* The passenger side door was open. I could see Jarell sitting in the driver's seat looking on.

I stared at him incredulously. "Relax, Matt. He was just playing."

"Stay out of this, Ray. This is between me and him." He kept his eyes locked on Aaron as he spoke.

"Aye, you need to calm down," Aaron replied. "Like I told you before: Mind your own business."

"And like I told you before: Ray is my business." Matt turned to me. "Get in the car." *There he goes again trying to boss me around.*

"Damn, you going to let him talk to you like that?" Aaron chimed in.

Actually, I wasn't. Matt was going to have to learn a lesson the hard way. I hated that he was forcing me to act this way, but I had no choice. Once again, my pride was on the line.

"No thanks," I said to Matt in a sharp tone. "I'd rather walk home." His face went blank. "Later, Aaron."

Matt's behavior was off putting to me. I knew he was just being overprotective. It was cute in a way, but it was almost bordering on possessive. It brought back bad memories of how controlling my dad used to be of my mom.

Just like I was seeing a different side to Aaron, I was also seeing a whole 'nother side to Matt. And it wasn't one that I was fond of. It was time to give him a dose of his own bitter medicine.

It was my turn to walk away.

I heard him call my name.

I ignored him and kept it moving.

CHAPTER 24
MATTHEW

"Damn, that was fucked up the way homeboy disrespected you in front of Aaron."

I didn't respond to Jarell's statement. I just glared out the car window as we drove from the school parking lot. I still couldn't believe Ray had just dissed me like that. A few feet from the school, I saw him walking on the side of the road with his headphones on. I had to say something to him to make this right. "Quick--pull over."

"Man, give that dude some room to breathe. He said he'd rather walk home, so let him," Rell said.

I opened my mouth to respond, but quickly closed it. It was probably a good idea to give Ray some space. I stared at him forlornly when we passed. I didn't know what I could say to him to fix things anyway. It seemed like every time I opened my mouth, it would backfire and he would take it the wrong way. Trying to talk to him didn't work, and just keeping quiet didn't work either. What else could I possibly do to make him see things my way? Why couldn't he see I was only trying to protect him?

"You're right." I sighed and sank into my seat. "He probably already thinks I'm a stalker or something now, anyway."

"Man, don't sweat that shit," Jarell said. "You were just trying to look out for the dude. It's not your fault he's all hyper-sensitive. He should be happy he has somebody like you who's got his back."

"Yeah, I guess," I replied dejectedly. In hindsight, waiting for Ray in the parking lot was probably a boneheaded stunt. However, it seemed like a good idea initially. After I had left Ray's locker at the end of the day, I met up with Rell in the weight room to blow off some steam. I told him that Ray was going to go through with tutoring Aaron. When I expressed how concerned I was that this was possibly some sort of setup to hurt Ray, Jarell suggested we wait for him in the parking lot next to Aaron's car, just in case he tried anything. I watched them with eagle eyes as they came out of the building. When I saw Aaron push Ray, I sprang into action like Superman. Unfortunately, I came off looking like a crazed idiot in the process. (How was I supposed to know Aaron was only playing?)

"Don't let this shit get you down. Just let him be. He'll get over it when he realizes he was in the wrong, and not you." Rell turned to me. "Aye, you wanna come by for a minute and smoke one?"

"Man, I don't know. We just smoked yesterday." I didn't know if Rell was trying to turn me into a straight up pothead or what. At this rate, I was going to be able to smoke Snoop under the table by the end of the week.

"And your point is...?" Jarell asked. He gave me a sidelong glance. "Come on, dawg. This will help you mellow out and get your mind off ole boy."

I exhaled. It definitely couldn't hurt. "Alright, I guess I can chill for a minute."

"Now that's more like it!" He looked at me with a big grin on his face.

We got to his place a few minutes later and went inside. Once we grabbed a few sodas, we walked into the living room. I was just about to sit down on the sofa when Jarell stopped me.

"We're not smoking in here today. My dad's supposed to be coming home early tonight. If he smells anything, he'll have a fucking heart attack." He led me down the hall to his bedroom and closed the door. "Make yourself at home." He hung our coats in the closet as I plopped down on a blue bean bag chair in the corner. "Now, to seal in the freshness." He rummaged through his clothes hamper and pulled out a towel. He folded it up and placed it against the bottom of the door. Once every crevice was covered, he walked over to the dresser and opened the top drawer. He took out a small bag of weed and some rolling paper. "Care to do the honors?"

"Sure, why not." I took the supplies from him and went to work.

I looked around at his room while I rolled. In addition to a bed and dresser, there were also a few pieces of IKEA furniture. He had an old school Michael Jordan poster on the wall above his bed. There was also a life size, cardboard standup poster of the wrestler Randy Orton against the adjacent wall.

"I thought you were only a basketball fanatic. I didn't know you liked wrestling, too," I said, licking the joint.

His face lit up. "Where the fuck have you been? I've been watching that shit since I was a kid!" He sat down on his bed and began unlacing his sneakers. "Me and my cousin used to think we were the Rock and Steve Austin." He laughed.

"Looks like someone's got a man crush on the 'Viper'," I quipped, referring to Randy Orton's nickname.

"Man, fuck you. My mom bought that for me last Christmas," he replied. He kicked off his shoes. He kept his black ankle socks on. He proceeded to unbuckle his pants and pull them off, stripping down to the basketball shorts he had underneath. He then took off his shirt and t-shirt, exposing his bare chest.

"Ugh, cover up, bro! Nobody's trying to see that lil' bird chest," I said, looking up from what I was doing. I was just fucking with him. In actuality, Jarell had a nice, slim athletic body.

"Whatever, dawg." He stood up and walked over to me. "Feel that shit!" He flexed his bicep in my face. "Go on--feel that."

"No, thanks. I don't want to get busted for child molestation for feeling up a little boy body," I said, looking up at him with my lips twisted. I handed him the joint.

"I bet my shit is tighter than the dude you fuck around with." He took a deep puff and exhaled before passing it back to me. "No homo."

I took a hit and laughed. "If you say so." After a few more hits, I began to feel the effect of the weed. I sank into the bean bag with my arms and legs hanging listlessly. My eyelids drooped. My thoughts immediately went back to Ray. I pulled my phone from my pocket, hoping to see a text from him. *Nothing.* I frowned. Was I wrong or was he wrong? *Or maybe we were both wrong?*

"Why're you sitting over there with that long ass face, man?" For a second, I'd almost forgotten Rell was still in the room.

"Oh," I said, snapping to attention. "I was just thinking about something."

"Don't tell me you still worrying about ole boy?" He was lying back on the mattress, propping himself up on his elbows. His slender, hairy legs were hanging off the edge of the bed.

"Yeah, a little. I just feel like such a dick, man. It seems like everything I say or do just pushes him further and further away, ya know?" I shook my head and sighed. I placed the joint to my lips again.

"Uh, you think you can pass that this way, bruh?" He sat upright on the bed.

"Oh shit, my bad. I didn't mean to hog all the fun." I rolled off the bean bag. I walked over to Jarell and handed him what was left of the joint.

"You can sit over here," he said, patting the space on the bed next to him. I sat down as he finished the clip and blew out a ring of smoke. "So let me ask you something." I looked at him, waiting for him to continue. "Why do you like that dude so much anyway?"

"Well, he's smart, he's funny, and not to mention, he's mad attractive to me." I sprouted a wistful smile as I pictured Ray's face. "On top of that, he loves me. I'm not the easiest dude to get along with, but he still puts up with me. He's been there for me whenever I needed him." My eyes began to get watery just thinking about the night that I'd broken down in Ray's arms after I found out the truth about my parentage.

"Aww...ain't that touching?" Jarell said wryly. "You sound like a pussy-whipped punk, dawg!" He suddenly put me in a headlock and pulled me down. We started wrestling. We laughed hysterically while thrashing about on the bed, each of us trying to get the upper hand and exert our dominance. We peppered each other with playful taunts as we horsed around. Rell was a slim dude, but he was pretty strong. Not stronger than Mighty Matt though!

After a few minutes, I managed to flip him over. I straddled his chest, putting all my weight on top of him to hold him down. I pinned his wrists above his head until he stopped squirming.

"Who's the punk now?" I said, breathing hard. I looked down into his red, glassy eyes and smiled triumphantly. He licked lips. My heart fluttered. I don't know if it was the weed, the physical contact, (or just the fact that I was a horny teenager), but I suddenly felt myself getting hard. I quickly let Jarell go and sprang from the bed. I positioned my hand in front of my crotch, hoping nothing was visible. *Man, this shit is sooooo embarrassing.*

Rell sat up and gave me a peculiar look.

"Uh...I just remembered, I told my mom that I'd fix something around the house today. I better get going," I stammered.

"Oh, aight. That's why you jumped up like that. For a second, I thought you wanted to fuck me or something," he said with a laugh. "No homo."

I blushed and snickered a little. "Don't flatter yourself. Even if you weren't straight, I still wouldn't hit that flat ass."

"If that's the case..." his eyes glanced down at my hands, which were still covering my erection. He flashed a wide grin. "Then why's your dick hard?"

Busted.

"Dude, whatever." I tried to play if off. "Why the hell are you looking at my junk anyway?"

"Ain't nobody looking at that shit. I couldn't help but notice it when I felt it poking me in the ribs." He burst out laughing. I felt myself blushing and changing shades like a chameleon.

SO, SOOOOOO EMBARASSING!!!

"You wish, bighead. Those were my keys," I lied. "Anyway, I gotta go." I turned to get my coat from his closet. Before I could take one step in that direction, I heard the bed's box spring creak. A second later, I felt Jarell jump on my back. His unexpected weight caused us both to crash to the floor.

"I got your ass now, punk!" He gripped me in a rear chin lock. "No homo."

This kid played around more than my big brother. "Damn, you still haven't learned your lesson yet?" I asked through clenched teeth; he still had the move applied to my chin, restricting my jaw's movement. *Time to nip this in the bud*, I thought. With lightning speed, I broke his hold. I then gripped his arms and gave him a hip toss, softly slamming him onto the plush carpet. He managed to hold on to my shirt, and pull me down with him. I landed on top of him with my hands planted on either side of his head. Rell was laughing hysterically. "Alright, so I've kicked your ass twice now, man. You give up yet?" I looked into his face with a cocky grin.

His laughter faded. He looked into my eyes and licked his lips.

"Yeah," he breathed. The next thing I know, he bent forward...and kissed me???

All I could do was blink in shock. *What the fuck just happened?*

Rell looked at me expectantly, as if awaiting my reaction.

I quickly stood to my feet. "What the hell was that?!"

He slowly got up from the floor with a worried expression on his face. "I'm sorry." He lowered his head in embarrassment. "I don't know what came over me."

I placed a hand on top of my head and stared at him in disbelief. "Dude, are you gay?"

His head shot up. "Of course not!" He looked offended.

"Well, why in the hell did you just kiss me?"

"I...I don't know why I did it," he said in a low voice. "I just..." He couldn't finish his sentence. The mental turmoil was written all over his in bold, bright letters.

"You can tell me the truth," I said, stepping closer to him.

An eternity of silence seemed to pass before he replied. "I've just been having all these crazy feelings lately. I can't believe I just did that. I've never kissed another dude before." He paused and took a deep breath like he was about to hyperventilate. "My head is all mixed up right now, man. With the weed and all, I just wasn't thinking clearly." He turned his back to me. I heard him sniffling. "I'm not gay though," he said, sounding as if he were choking on his own words.

He was confused about his sexuality, and waging a war within himself. It would take some time for him to sort it all out. "Rell...calm down. It's okay," I said softly. I placed a hand on his shoulder. "I understand what you're going through. I've been there. You can always talk to me, if you need to."

He exhaled and wiped his eyes with the back of his hand. He then turned back around. "Please don't tell anyone about this."

I looked at him sympathetically. Dude was probably scared out of his mind. "Don't worry, I won't."

Relief washed over his face. "Yo, I'm sorry for coming at you like that, man. I know you have a dude and shit. I didn't mean to disrespect you or him like that." His shoulders slumped. "You're not mad, are you?"

I shook my head. "Nah, I'm not mad at you. Just make sure you don't try that shit again though, or I'll bust your ass." I gave him a reassuring smile. "No homo."

He let out a little laugh. "Aight, I hear you."

"Cool. Well, let me get out of here before I get raped."

"Fuck you, bruh!" Jarell cracked a smile. After giving me my coat, he led me to the door and gave me a bro-hug.

As I walked home, I still couldn't believe what had just happened. *So, Raymond was actually right about Rell liking me*, I mused. *How could I have missed that?* I shook my head at my own blindness. The kiss was a spur of the moment thing. It was innocent and almost funny. I doubted Rell would try it again. But still, it probably was a good idea to watch myself around him and put some space between us. I didn't want to put either of us in a compromising position.

When I got home, I tried to put the whole thing out of my mind. I made myself a plate of left over tuna casserole and chowed down. After I finished, I worked on some homework for a minute, and then hit Ray up on Skype. When his face appeared on the screen, we just stared at each other in awkward silence.

"Hey," I bit the inside of my bottom lip. "You all right?"

"Yeah," he replied in a subdued tone.

"Ray, about earlier," I paused, "I didn't intend for that to happen."

He smirked. "And what exactly do you expect to happen when you spy on someone from a distance and jump to conclusions? And then, run up on him and try to drag him away like an ogre?"

I sighed in irritation and ran a hand through my hair. "I just wanted to make sure you got home safe."

"I don't need you to babysit me, Matt," he replied. "I don't need you trying to act like you're my daddy, either."

"I'm just trying to look out for you, man." I know it seems like I was being stubborn, but in my heart of hearts, I just didn't feel I was wrong for wanting to protect him. I mean, isn't that what you're supposed to do for someone you love?

"I understand that. But you've got to back off some. You're too overprotective, and it's kind of overbearing," he said meekly.

I leaned back in my chair and stared up at the ceiling. I was seriously frustrated. We still weren't on the same page. (Hell, we weren't even reading the same book.) Instead of belaboring the point I figured it'd be best to just change the subject for the time being.

"So, are you coming to my game tomorrow?" I asked, focusing my eyes back on the screen.

"I wish I could, but Big Boss Lady has me on the schedule to work."

"Damn," I said dejectedly. Ray was my good luck charm.

"Yeah, I know. But have no fear--Keon will be there to cheer you on and give you all the support you need."

I laughed. "Gee, thanks."

"Anytime, Machine Gun." It felt good to hear him call me that. "But don't worry, if we win, we can have a little post-game victory celebration." A mischievous smile appeared on his face. I was still in the dog house, but at least he'd thrown me a bone.

"Alright, Mookie Man. I'm gonna hold you to that," I replied, feeling amped. I talked to him a little while longer before signing off and getting ready for bed.

The following day was Friday. Like always, Ray and I walked to school together. Our conversation was a little strained in the morning, but by the time lunch rolled around things were slowly getting back to normal. I could tell that he was waiting on me to apologize for how I'd behaved regarding Aaron, but I just couldn't bring myself to do it. I honestly didn't believe I was wrong. I refused to say I was so sorry for standing up for my principles. I would just have to find another way to smooth things over with Ray.

Fortunately, I had the perfect plan.

*****

Once game time came, I went into beast mode and unleashed a full-scale Matt Attack! Of course, we won. The score wasn't even close. It was a fucking massacre on the court.

After showering and changing, I got a ride home with Rell and Quinton. They were going to celebrate with some of the other guys and asked if I wanted to join them. I politely declined. I had other plans.

Operation: Mookie Makeup was about to go down.

When I got to my crib, I threw on some clean shorts and a fresh tank top. I quickly went to the kitchen and whipped up something to eat. As the food simmered on the stove, I vacuumed and tidied up a little. I was preparing for a nice "romantic" evening with Ray (which would be capped off by a night of hot make-up sex!). Hopefully, all of this would make up for everything he thought I did wrong. I was just taking the biscuits out the oven when I heard the doorbell ring. I ripped off the oven mitt and ran to the door. Just before I opened it, I placed my hand in front of my mouth and nose to do the ole breath test. Yep, it was still minty fresh.

"Greetings, dearie," I said in my best evil old witch voice. "Enter." I stood to the side, rubbing my palms together and cackling wickedly.

Ray laughed and clasped my hand as he entered. He still had on his work uniform. I closed the door and gave him a bear hug from behind, pressing my lips to the nape of his neck. He groaned. "I don't know why you insisted that my mom drop me off here right after work. I wanted to go home and get freshened up first. I smell like a vat of day-old grease."

"Actually, you smell like three-day old grease," I teased. "But don't worry about it. I've smelled worse in the locker room after practice." He laughed. I continued to hold him by his waist from behind. "Anyway, I figured we can take a nice, hot bubble bath together after we eat." I led him to the kitchen and pulled out a seat for him. When he sat down, I placed my hands on his shoulders and began massaging them.

He tilted his head back and moaned softly. "Mmm...that feels good."

"You hungry? I cooked." I asked, continuing to knead his neck and shoulders.

"Well, I did eat earlier. But it's not like I have to watch my figure or anything," he said with a snicker.

"Cool." I walked over to the cabinet and grabbed two plates. I piled them high with Hamburger Helper beef mac & cheese. "Voila!" I set a plate in front of him and smiled proudly.

"I never knew you were a gourmet chef?" He gave me a sideways grin.

"Hey, it was all I had time to make! Get off my back, Gordon Ramsay!" I sat down next to him. While we ate, we talked about our plans for Thanksgiving, which was coming up next week. He was going to be spending it with his family at his aunt's house in Atlanta. I would be spending it with my mom and brother. I was totally psyched about getting to see my big bro again! This would be the first Thanksgiving without my asshole stepdad around to ruin things, so I was definitely looking forward to it. After I stormed out that night, Mom had cooled on the talk of letting him move back in. I was just hoping she'd finally come to her senses.

"So, I should be hearing back from some of those colleges I applied to soon," Ray said, wiping his mouth with a napkin. "I can't wait till I get accepted somewhere, so I can finally get the hell out of this place."

"I feel you." I gave him a faint smile and looked down at my empty plate. I tried not to put too much thought into the future after graduation. Whenever I did, I got a little down. Ray would be going off to college, while I would be enlisting in the military. What would become of our relationship? I pushed the thought out of my mind. I didn't want it to dampen my mood. I stood up and gathered the empty plates. "Ready for desert?"

"Oh, wow! Desert, too?" Ray beamed. "Did my mom put you up to this? That woman will do anything to try to fatten me up."

"Nah, I'm just trying to get that lil' phatty of yours nice and plump for my own selfish reasons," I replied with a wink. We both laughed. I opened the fridge and grabbed a small white box from the top shelf. I walked back over to Ray and placed it in front of him.

He looked up at me with a quizzical expression. "What's this?"

I grinned. "Just a little something I picked up from the bakery this afternoon."

He eagerly opened the box like a kid on Christmas morning. His eyes lit up when he saw the cupcake. "Aw, man! This is my favorite flavor! How did you know?"

"Telepathy." I wiggled my eyebrows. I'd actually pulled Keon to the side earlier and asked him if he had any suggestions for getting back on Ray's good side. His exact words were: *"Chile, red velvet cake is to Ray what cheese cake was to the Golden Girls."* Who could argue with advice like that? "You can call me Professor M."

"Eh, okay." He snickered. "I guess that's better than 'Jean Grey'."

"Smartass." I gave him a soft smack on the back of the head.

"Thanks, Matty. Man, this has been a pretty awesome night so far. Can't wait to see what else you've got up your sleeves...and under these." He placed his hand on my leg and slowly rubbed it up my thigh underneath my shorts. My dick immediately began to grow. "Let's take that bath so we can get the victory celebration started."

A broad smile spread across my face. "Your wish is my command." I did a happy dance in my head. "While my teammates are out celebrating with each other, I'm spending the night with my baby." I kissed him on the forehead. "And I wouldn't have it any other way."

"Aww...so you're choosing to spend the night with me over Jarell and Quin? I'm flattered," he quipped.

"Ha, ha, very funny. But seriously, you were right about Rell."

"How?" He gave me a curious look.

"The dude likes me."

Ray's eyebrow went up. "How do you know that?"

"Uh," I nervously scratched the back of my head, suddenly wondering if I'd made a mistake by bringing this up. I wasn't initially going to tell him, but I figured why not? I assumed he would get a chuckle out of it and have the pleasure of saying, *I told you so.* "He, uh... kissed me yesterday."

"So, that's why you're doing all of this tonight?" His nostrils flared. "You fooled around with that dude, and now you feel guilty?"

"No, I don't feel guilty--" I realized I was digging myself into a deeper hole. "I mean—we didn't do anything. He just kissed me, but I didn't kiss him back."

"And you couldn't have told me this last night when we Skyped?"

"I didn't want to make a big deal out of it."

"So, the two of you just sat at the table smiling in my face today at lunch like nothing happened?" He was getting angrier.

"It's not even like that, Ray," I said defensively. "The dude is a closet case trying to come to grips with his sexuality. He was high and kissed me in the spur of the moment. He probably likes me a little, but it's not that serious."

He stared at me like I was crazy. "How would you feel if I told you my friend liked me?"

I shrugged. "I'm not jealous. I'd trust you to not do anything with him."

He shook his head. "I can't believe you right now, Matt. So you're just going to remain friends with the dude and expect me to be OK with it?"

"What? So you're saying I can't be friends with him anymore? I already set him straight. He knows I'm committed to you. It's not like we're going to fuck around or anything."

He stood up, shaking the table as he rose. "You know what? I'm going home." He stomped to the door. I grabbed him by the arm before he could open it.

"Ray, don't be stup--" He glared at me, causing me to auto-correct myself. "Ridiculous."

"You're the one who's being ridiculously stupid," he snapped as he pulled away from me.

"Rell was right," I blurted out. "You are hyper-sensitive." Ray was always blowing shit out of proportion and taking things the wrong way. And I was sick of it.

"Whatever, Matt. Since Rell's obviously got your mind, then go be with him!"

I scowled. "Yeah, maybe I fucking will!" He looked at me with watery eyes. I instantly regretted what I said. "Ray, I didn't mean that."

Without saying another word, he turned and began walking. I chased after him. I grabbed his arm again, but he broke away.

"Leave me alone, Matt!" He yelled. I let him go. I knew there was nothing else I could say. I stood at the end of the driveway barefoot. I sighed.

With a heavy heart, I watched Ray disappear into the night.

Once again, one of us had walked away from the other in anger.

However, I had a sinking feeling in my stomach that this time, it was for good.

CHAPTER 25
RAYMOND

I stormed out of Matt's house faster than a bolt of lightning. When I got home, the first thing I did was strip off my clothes and jump in the shower. I just wanted to wash away the scent of my monotonous job, and the stench of Matt's mess. I stood with my head under the jet spray shower nozzle, letting the hot water wash over me. It felt physically soothing to my tired and aching body. Unfortunately, it didn't do anything to assuage the emotional pain I was feeling. Tears escaped the corners of my eyes and ran down my cheeks.

They were hot tears, born of betrayal and mixed with anger.

Once the water works were finished, I stepped out the shower.

After drying off, I wrapped the towel around my waist and walked back to my room. I threw on some pajama bottoms and a t-shirt. I grabbed my phone and lay on my bed. There were two missed calls and a text from Matt.

Matt: Are u home yet?
Me: Yes
Matt: Can we talk?
I looked at the message and sighed.
Me: Tomorrow

I killed the volume on my phone and set it on the nightstand. I clicked off the lamp and got under the covers. It was still relatively early for a Friday night, but I was mentally exhausted. All I wanted to do was sleep and leave reality behind. Before I knew it, I'd drifted off into a peaceful slumber.

Tap, tap, tap.

I cracked an eye open and sat up in bed. It was deathly quiet. I looked about in bewilderment, trying to determine the source of the noise that woke me. Thunder rumbled outside somewhere in the distance. A storm was brewing. *It was probably rain drops*, I thought. Just as I was about to lie back down, I heard it again.

TAP, TAP, TAP, TAP.

This time, it was more forceful and persistent.
Someone was knocking on the window. Barring a burglar or something, there was only one person who it could be. I threw back the covers and got out of bed. I cautiously walked over to the window and slowly pulled the blinds to one side. I saw the top of a black hoodie. Matt looked up at me with his signature crooked grin. I let out a long breath. I was annoyed by him just popping up like this late at night, but I was also kind of relieved. I opened the window for him. He jumped up and clasped the window seal. With minimal effort, he pulled himself up and crawled in.

"You know you could have a great career as a cat burglar?" I joked. I turned on the light.

"Very funny," he said in a low tone. He was staring at the floor as if the light hurt his eyes. He still had the hoodie draped over his head. "I just had to talk to you."

"Okay. I'm listening." I folded my arms across my chest. I was still mad at him, but I was willing to hear him out.

He casually walked up to me with his eyes still facing down. "I just wanted to say," he began, "FUCK YOU!" I couldn't believe my ears. Before I had a chance to respond, he roughly snagged me by my t-shirt and yanked me forward. When he finally looked up, his face was twisted with an unnatural rage.

"Matt, what the hell are you--" He suddenly backhanded me. I was so shocked, I couldn't react. I was frozen in place. My heart was racing. I tasted blood. I peered into his eyes. A chill rippled down my spine. Terror gripped me. It was the same fear I'd felt as a child. Those green eyes that were usually bright and full of warmth were now eerily dark and cold.

"You do what I tell you to do! You hear me?! You belong to **ME**!" He viciously shook me by my shoulders and then punched me in the mouth, splitting my lip. He flung me to the bed with superhuman strength. "You are so weak, naïve, and **STUPID**!" He stalked towards me with his hoodie-covered head low.

I frantically scooched backward on the bed to put some distance between us. I couldn't believe he was hurting me like this. I balled my fist. I was scared and in shock, but I knew I had to defend myself.

"Why are you doing this?" I asked as blood trickled from my lip and dripped down my chin.

No reply.

He just stood silently at the edge of the bed with his head bowed like the grim reaper.

Slowly, he raised one of his hands and gripped his cheek. *What the hell is he doing?* My eyes widened in horror as I watched him tug at his face, stretching it until...it came off like silly putty??? He lowered his arm, resting it at his side. A life-like mask dangled from his hand. His true face was obscured by the hoodie.

"Who are you?" I screamed at him.

The mysterious figure let out a sinister chortle. He slowly lifted his head to reveal glowing red eyes and a mocking grin.

Jarell's face sneered at me from beneath the hoodie.

"I got Matt...now it's your turn!" He lunged at me like a panther pouncing on its prey. With blinding speed, he leapt onto the bed and pinned me down. His mouth opened wide like a viper, displaying a row of jagged teeth framed by two long fangs. I tried to push him off, but it was no use. He was a lot stronger than he appeared.

In a split second, he savagely chomped down on my neck! I shrieked in anguish.

"Ray, you all right in there?" It was my mom's voice.

My eyes snapped open. I shot up in my bed. My heart was pounding out of my chest. I desperately felt both sides of my neck checking for bloody bite marks. There were none. I looked about my dark room in a panic. *Relax, dufus, there's no one here,* I reassured myself. I breathed a sigh of relief. "Uh, yeah, ma! Just had a bad dream."

"Oh, OK. I thought maybe you had Matt in there, and ya'll were playing too rough," she yelled from her room. "If you know what I mean."

I rolled my eyes. "Noooo, ma!" I wiped the thin film of sweat from my forehead and plopped back into the pillow. Hamburger Helper, red velvet cake, and fighting with your boyfriend before bed definitely weren't a good combination. I tossed and turned for a few hours before finally getting back to sleep.

The following day, Keon and I had to work the morning shift. On our lunch break, I told him all about my argument with Matt and the crazy nightmare I had after it.

"Bitch, this is a mess and half." He shook his head ruefully. "After I told the boy your secret weakness, he goes and pulls a stunt like this." *My secret weakness?* I gave him a puzzled look.

I instantly caught on. "Ooooh, so that's how he knew about the cake!" Red velvet cake was my kryptonite. It could always make me weak in the knees.

"Of course." He took the lid off of his finished soda. He held the cup up and titled his head back, letting the ice slide into his waiting mouth. "He saw me in the hall yesterday and asked me for advice on how to get back on your good side," he said between loud crunches of ice.

I smiled a little. It was cute that Matt would actually go to all that trouble just to make up with me. But that didn't negate what had happened with Jarell. "I still can't believe he nonchalantly tells me his best friend kissed him, and then turns around and claims it wasn't a big deal!"

"Nope." Ke was slurping on the ice now. I tried to hide my irritation. "You had every right to be pissed to the upper levels of pissivity. "Let the shoe have been on the other foot and see what would've happened." He smacked his lips. "Chile, he would've gone green bananas and then apeshit on your ass!"

"Exactly. But if you believe him and *Jarell*," his name tasted bitter on my tongue, "I'm just overreacting and being *hypersensitive*." I tossed my half-eaten chicken sandwich on the tray.

"I told you that block-headed bitch was going to be trouble, didn't I? You didn't wanna listen though," Keon gloated.

"Well, thanks for not rubbing it in," I said sarcastically.

He flashed a bashful smile. "My bad."

"And to make matters worse, he has to keep throwing Jarell in my face every time we get into an argument."

"So, do you think they actually did more than just kiss?" He rattled the remnant of the ice in the cup.

"Nah." My lips twisted in contemplation. "At least I hope not."

"Do you think you can trust him around Jarell now, knowing that Jarell has feelings for him?"

"I mean, I trust Matt, but..." I sighed. "His friend is a different story." I was never particularly fond of that dude. This kiss had added another wrinkle to things.

"Well, here's what I think--and you can take it or leave it." He threw his head back and put the cup to his lips, banging on the bottom to get the last of the ice. I huffed softly and rolled my eyes. "If he's really serious about patching things up with you, he'll drop Jarell as a friend." He said it without even batting an eyelash.

"The guy is Matt's teammate; it's unrealistic to expect them not to interact," I reasoned.

"That doesn't mean shit. Savion is his teammate, too. You don't see them hanging out anymore though, do you? Just because they're teammates doesn't mean they have to be friends." He shrugged. "I'm just saying, if it was me, I wouldn't want to be with someone who put his friends—who he just recently met—before our relationship. If I were you, I'd tell him to ditch Jarell ASAP. It's either him or you. He can't have his red velvet and eat it, too." He leaned back in his chair and grinned. "Unless you're down with sharing?"

I looked at him in silence. I didn't know how to respond. On the one hand, I agreed with Ke. Jarell was a thorn in my side. He was creating a wedge between Matt and me. But on the other hand, did I actually have the right to force Matt to end their friendship?

*****

Once our shift was over, Keon's mom gave us a ride home. With all of the tossing and turning and crazy nightmares I had last night, I didn't get much sleep. So after a quick shower, I took a nap and recharged my batteries. When I woke up a few hours later, I went to the kitchen to get something to eat. I warmed up some beef stew and cornbread my mom had made the day before.

As I sat at the kitchen table and ate, my thoughts returned to my pending conversation with Matt. I still had no idea how I was going to broach the whole Jarell subject, but it was something we had to address and deal with if we wanted to get our relationship back on track.

"Alright, Mookie. Another early start for me. I'm off to make that paper." Mom came into the kitchen wearing her uniform. "Make sure you lockup and set the alarm."

"Okay, ma," I said in an exasperated tone. She gave me the same admonition every time she left me home alone.

"And don't forget about the secret weapons," she added.

"Yeah. I know, I know." The "secret weapons" as she referred to them, was a break-in-case-of-emergency kit that we kept just in case of a home invasion that was never going to happen. It contained a stun gun and some pepper spray my mom "borrowed" from her job.

She stopped at the table and put her hands on her hips. "That's all you eating?" I just gave her an annoyed looked. She shook her head. "Just like a little baby bird."

"Have a good night, ma," I said, hoping she'd get the hint.

"Boy, stop rushing me out the house. You got Matt coming over here after I leave?" She gave me the side-eye.

"No," I replied in a solemn tone.

She pursed her lips to the side. "Why not?"

"Meh, it's a long story." I shoved a piece of cornbread in my mouth. She stared at me expectantly. "Um, aren't you going to be late for work?"

She glanced at her watch and frowned. "I'll call you on my break to get ALL the details. And if you know what's good for you, you better answer that phone, too."

"Oookayyy, ma," I groaned.

After she finally left, I finished eating and went to my room. I turned on my computer and logged on to my Skype account. I took a deep breath. *Time to get this over with,* I said to myself as I called Matt. His face appeared on the screen with a somber expression.

"Hey," he said in a low-key voice.

"Hey," I replied. An awkward silence filled the air. My throat suddenly felt dry. I wasn't sure how to begin. "Um, I'm sorry about storming off the way I did last night."

"It's okay, man." He gave me a faint smile. "I can understand why you spazzed out about the whole kiss thing." I didn't really think I had "spazzed out," but whatever. I wasn't going to get hung up on semantics. At least he was finally "getting" it.

"So, you don't think I'm being oversensitive or paranoid about you and Jarell's friendship?"

"No," he said with a shrug. "I think you're being jealous for no reason though."

Or maybe he wasn't getting it after all.

"I'm not being jealous, Matt," I said defensively. "I just think you're letting Jarell drive a wedge between us and push us apart."

Hopefully, he would be reasonable and understand my concerns.

"If I remember correctly, it's not Jarell who started all of this drama between us. It was you going behind my back and agreeing to study with Aaron."

And once again, he was back on this.

"We're not talking about Aaron right now. We're talking about your best friend who likes you and KISSED you," I shot back.

"Jesus Christ!" He exclaimed. "You're not going to let that go, are you? I knew I shouldn't have mentioned that to you."

"Oh, so you were just going to act like it never happened?" I glared at him incredulously.

"I probably should have, since you apparently can't handle honesty."

"Trust me, I have no problem with you being honest," I retorted. "What I do have a problem with is you being friends with someone who has his sights set on you!"

"I already told you I set him straight and let him know what the deal was. If you can't trust me to do the right thing, then that's your problem. You're just being insecure!" He folded his arms across his chest and scowled.

"I'm not being insecure. I trust you. It's just Jarell that I don't trust," I tried to explain. "After what he did, I just don't think it's appropriate for you to hang around him."

He raised an eyebrow. "Oh, so you're picking my friends now?"

"Of course not," I replied with a dismissive wave of my hand. "I'm just saying that I don't believe it's good for our relationship for you to continue to be friends."

"Damn, now you're giving me an ultimatum?" His eyes narrowed.

"I'm not giving you an '*ultimatum*,' Matt! It's just a suggestion," I replied, trying to remain calm even though he was thoroughly working my nerves.

"And if I don't follow your 'suggestion,' what's going to happen? Am I going to catch an attitude all the time?"

I exhaled in frustration. I knew Jarell and I weren't in competition, but the way Matt was so stridently clinging to him was beginning to make me wonder who he'd choose if we were.

"You went ahead and tutored Aaron after I asked you not to." And here we go again! "So why should I stop hanging with Jarell just because you're asking me to?"

"You didn't ask me to not tutor Aaron—you FORBADE me," I snapped. "There's a big difference between asking someone to do something, versus commanding him to do it."

"Stop splitting hairs, Ray. It's the same damn thing."

Matt was determined to win this fight at all costs. Like always, he was being pigheaded and combative. It was like we were just talking in circles. I was tired of trying to get through to him, and I was fed up with his stubbornness.

"Since we can't seem to see eye-to-eye on anything, maybe we should just take a break from each other?" I didn't really mean it, but I didn't know what else to say to get him to realize how serious I felt about this.

"So now you're breaking up with me?" His face screwed up.

"I'm not breaking up with you, Matt!" I yelled in aggravation. Why did he have to misinterpret everything? "All we've been doing lately is fight. Maybe it'd do us both some good if we had some time to cool off and clear our heads?"

"Fine. If that's the way you want it." He stood up, knocking over his chair in the process. "Take all the time you want!"

"Matt--" He abruptly signed off before I could finish. I exhaled and massaged my temples. "He's so damn stubborn," I growled to myself. You didn't need x-ray vision to see that we'd reached an impasse. We'd crashed smack dab into a brick wall, and the way things were going, I wondered if that wall would be insurmountable.

Matt and I didn't speak or text for the rest of the weekend. When the week started, we didn't even walk to school together. Monday's always sucked. And with us at odds, this one sucked harder than usual.

At lunch, Keon and I were sitting together at our regular spot. I saw Matt, Jarell, and Quin coming down the aisle with their trays. They sat at a table across the room. Matt glanced over at me with a grimace on his face. I rolled my eyes and shook my head as I turned to Ke.

"So how long are ya'll two going to keep this up?" Ke asked, taking a bite of his hot dog.

I shrugged. "Your guess is as good as mine. As you can see, Jarell is still prominently displayed in the picture. As long as Mr. Immature insists on keeping him around, then I've got nothing to say to him." I casually chugged my chocolate milk. I was trying to put on a cool facade, but in reality, this silent "feud" with Matt was tearing me up inside. Even though I could see him, it was like an invisible force field was preventing me from communicating with him.

"Well, just stick to your guns," Keon replied. "After he suffers through a few days of drought, he'll kick that block-headed bitch to the curb and come crawling back to you."

"Yeah, I guess," I said dejectedly. I just hoped he was right.

Just then, Aaron and his two All-Star cohorts strutted by. He gave me a subtle smile as he passed. I looked down sheepishly. I still couldn't believe Aaron was treating me like a civilized human being. True to his word, he hadn't harassed or taunted me since I studied with him last week. He even gave me a friendly greeting this morning in homeroom. His current reformed behavior was all the vindication I needed. Even if Matt still disagreed, I was more convinced than ever that I'd done the right thing by helping him. Still, it was a bitter-sweet victory. I'd ended Aaron's reign of terror...but at what cost?

After lunch I went to my fourth period Spanish class. As usual, I was the first person there. I pulled out my phone and just stared at it. I was so tempted to text Matt, but I couldn't bend on this. I had to be strong and stand my ground. It was either Jarell or me.

Savion suddenly walked in.

"What's up, Ray?" He said, sitting in the desk next to mine. *Wow, this was early for him*, I thought. He would typically stroll into class just a split second before Ms. Rios slammed the door.

"Sup," I replied, not looking at him. I pretended to scroll through my phone.

"So, when are you gonna give a brotha another chance?" I glanced up to see him with a big smile on his face. I looked at him like he was stupid and went back to playing with my phone. He mumbled something under his breath.

Geez, can he sense Matt and I are going through a rough patch? I wondered. It was like he was a vulture lying in wait. Well, if that was the case, he was going to starve to death. Even if I was having problems with Matt, I still wouldn't go back to Savion.

I was glad when the final bell rang, signaling the end of the day. I just wanted to get my stuff and go home. Once I finished getting the books I would need to do my homework, I closed my locker and turned around. I startled when I looked up into Aaron's face.

"What's up, Reynolds?" He extended his hand to me. Once again, I just stared at it. His eyebrows furrowed. "So, you're just going to keep leaving me hanging every time I try to show you some love?" I hesitantly gripped his hand. He sprouted a toothy smile and forcefully pulled me into a tight bro-hug. "I got an 'A' on my Spanish test!" He was so excited that I thought he was going to squeeze the life out of me. "Thanks for tutoring me, dawg."

"Uh, that's great, man," I replied, feeling a little awkward because he still hadn't let me go. "You're welcome."

"Aye, my birthday is this weekend." He slowly loosened his grip on my hand, but kept his hypnotic gaze fixated on me. "I'm having a big party at my crib. You should come through." Everyone knew that Aaron threw an extravagant birthday celebration every year. I'd heard tales about what went on at his parties, but of course, I'd never been to one. Now, King Aaron himself was giving me an open invite? I was actually being asked to rub shoulders with the "elite"???

"Um, thanks," I sputtered. "I'm not really the partying type though."

"Man, stop being lame and bring your lil' ass to my party. Bring a friend or two, if you want."

I smiled coyly. "I'll think about it."

"You better," he said with a cocky grin. He gave me a wink and sauntered off, dapping up people as he passed. I scratched my forehead in bewilderment. I wasn't sure when I'd been sucked into Bizzaro World, but there was no denying that my life was now topsy-turvy. Just as I was about to pinch myself to make sure I wasn't dreaming, I noticed Matt standing across the hall staring at me. He had an agitated look on his face.

Our eyes locked for a second, and then he disappeared into the crowd.

With a deep sigh, I pulled on my bag. *Well, I guess that was another brick stacked atop the high wall that's separating us*, I lamented. As I made my way out the building, I felt my heart sink. It was beginning to look more and more like this temporary "break" may become permanent.

CHAPTER 26
MATTHEW

I swear, I just didn't understand Ray lately.

After leaving from his locker, I pushed and bumped my way through the crowded hallway. I was feeling some kind of way. *And to think, for a second, I was actually going to try to apologize for everything,* I ruminated. However, when I saw him talking to Aaron, it brought back the reason why we were in our current predicament. He didn't care what I thought. It wasn't fair for him to blatantly disregard my feelings when it came to Aaron and then turn around and give me grief over Rell.

When I walked into the locker room to change for practice, I saw Savion smiling and talking to Aaron. Considering how much he hated Aaron, I found it a little odd. When they noticed me, they both gave me simultaneous smirks. Maybe I was being paranoid, but I just couldn't shake the feeling that Aaron was up to something. I pushed it out of my mind and went to another area to get dressed.

Following another grueling practice, everybody was sweaty and barely able to stand. Once we all managed to catch our breath, Coach blew his whistle. Everyone rallied around him in the center of the gym.

"Alright, fellas, this was the last practice session for the week. I want all of you to enjoy your days off and Thanksgiving. Eat as much as you can and relax, because when you return next week, it's back to business as usual! So, watch those pounds; I don't want to hear any belly aching when I make you run laps. And if you drop dead on the floor, I'm not calling an ambulance. I'm just going to have the janitor sweep your behind up!"

Everybody laughed.

"Aye, can I say something, Coach?" Aaron chimed in, throwing his arm around Coach like they were old chums. He obliged and gave Aaron the floor. "I just want to thank everybody for the great teamwork so far this season. Also, as everybody already knows," he flashed a big grin, "ya' boy's birthday is this weekend!" Everyone erupted into applause. Aaron sucked up the adulation and pretended to bow. "Anyway, I'm having a party. So when you're finished pigging out with your fam on Thursday, you can swing by my crib on Saturday and get your party on! I want to see all of you guys there. And, uh, don't forget to bring presents. I accept cash, clothes, and all major credit cards." Everyone laughed. I rolled my eyes. He was so damn corny.

When Aaron finally stopped grandstanding, Coach dismissed us. Everyone made a beeline for the locker room. After we showered and got dressed, Quin and I accompanied Rell to his car.

"So, we're going to Aaron's party Saturday, right?" Rell's question sounded more like a declaration.

"Are you crazy?" I looked at him like he had octopus tentacles growing out of his box fade. "Why in the hell would I want to go there? I can't stand that dude. And I'm sure the feeling is mutual."

Quinton burst out laughing. "Man, you can just go and eat his food, drink up all his liquor, and bounce. That's what we do." He leaned forward in the backseat and nudged Jarell with his elbow.

"It's a team unity thing," Rell interjected. "All the fellas are gonna be there."

I smirked and puffed air from my mouth. "Not I, said the white guy."

Rell snickered. "Come on, man. You gotta go!"

"Dude, I'm not stepping foot in a place where I'm not wanted." I was adamant.

"That's exactly why you should go," Quin chimed in. "So you can crash the party."

A sly grin slowly crawled across my face. I liked the sound of that. "We'll see."

We dropped Quin off at his house first. As we pulled off, Rell turned the volume down on the radio.

"So, you and your boy still beefing?"

I huffed. "Yeah, I was going to talk to him after school. I just wanted to stop all of this childishness." I had been in a surly mood all day. I hated that things seemed to be in a downward spiral between me and Ray. "Until I saw him smiling in Aaron's face."

"Oh, yeah?" He clicked the turn signal and craned his neck to look out the rear window.

"Yep. And yet, he has the balls to try to tell me who I can and can't talk to."

He chuckled. "Who doesn't he want you talking to?"

I didn't even want to involve him in this silliness. "Nobody."

"It ain't me, is it?" He gave me a sidelong glance.

"Nah," I muttered unconvincingly.

"Stop frontin', dawg--I know it's me. I can tell ole dude doesn't like me."

"Why do you say that?" I asked, trying to sound surprised by his statement.

"I can just tell," he said with a grin. "Did you tell him about me kissing you?"

I slouched in my seat and averted my eyes. "Yeah."

"I thought you said that was between us?" He remarked. I could hear the disappointment in his voice.

"Sorry, man. I kind of let it slip." I felt like shit for violating his trust and breaking my promise.

"It's cool. As long as he doesn't go blabbing it to the whole school."

I shook my head. "Ray's not like that."

"Yeah, but what about that fat dude he hangs with?"

"Keon? Well, uh..." I knew Ray wasn't the gossiping type, but I couldn't truthfully vouch for Ke. However, I doubted he would go around putting anyone on blast either. An uneasy silence hung in the air.

"So, you're in the dog house now because you couldn't keep your big mouth shut." He laughed.

"Man, this shit isn't funny." I was happy to see he wasn't mad about me outing him to Ray, but he had no idea how serious this was. "He's basically threatening to break up with me if I don't stop hanging with you."

"Wow! So he's got you by the balls like that, dawg?" He looked at me with a cocked eyebrow. "That's not cool for him to put you on the spot like that. If you let him strong arm you and shit this time, he'll keep doing it to get his way. Females like to do the same thing, just to see if you're a pushover or not. I don't know about gay guys, but I know girls don't want no dude they can just run over. They all claim to want a nice guy, but deep down, they want somebody who's gonna put their ass in check."

"Um, yeah." I agreed with some of what he said, but I didn't want to turn this into a Ray-bashing fest. "I tried to explain to him that you just kissed me in the spur of the moment and that it didn't mean anything."

Jarell nodded his head as he turned a corner. "And what did he say?"

"He wasn't trying to hear it. He's convinced that you're after me now." I laughed a little. "Crazy right?"

"Definitely," he said resolutely. "Aye, if you want, I can talk to him and let him know it's not even like that."

"Man, you don't have to do all that. He just needs to get over his little jealous streak."

He chuckled. "For real though, I don't want to be the cause of friction in ya'll's relationship." He looked at me with big puppy dog eyes.

I thought about it for a minute. I could tell Ray that Rell wasn't after me until I was blue in the face. It still wouldn't change his mind. But maybe if he actually heard it from the horse's mouth, he'd realize how unreasonable he was being? Hell, it wasn't like it could hurt.

"On second thought," I said, "you wouldn't mind doing that?"

"It ain't no big deal, cuz. Anything to get my boy out the dog house," he replied with a grin.

A few minutes later, we pulled up to Ray's place. We both got out the car and walked up to his door. I rang the bell. I mentally crossed my fingers and toes. I knew this was a crazy gambit, but desperate times called for desperate measures. I nervously tapped my foot on the straw welcome mat. The little drape covering the door window moved slightly, I could see someone peeking out. The door slowly opened.

"Hey, Ms. Reynolds," I said with a smile. "Is Ray home?"

"Yeah, he's here." She cut her eyes at Rell. Judging by her icy reception, I guess Ray had filled her in on our relationship problems. No doubt, he'd painted me as the bad guy. She stood with her back straight and her arms folded across her chest like a bouncer. Man, was she intimidating.

"Uh, can I talk to him?" My voice nearly cracked.

"Hold on," she said curtly. She disappeared back inside.

A few seconds later, Ray emerged. He looked from Rell to me.

"What's up?" He asked, standing in the doorway. I could see the suspicion in his eyes.

"Ray, look, we just came to clear the air. Rell wanted to talk to you real quick." I fidgeted with the zipper on my coat.

"Aye, dawg, I just wanted to say that you don't have nothin' to worry about," Jarell said. "I ain't trying to take your dude. We're just boys. You don't have to be all jealous and shit."

Ray clenched his jaw. "I'm not jealous of anyone, especially you."

I exhaled. Once again, he was taking things the wrong way. "He didn't mean it like that, Ray."

"Yeah, so watch your mouth," Rell interjected.

"No, you watch *your* damn mouth," Ray fired back, his face contorting in anger.

"Why don't you make me?" Rell retaliated. "You better handle your boy, Matt." They were staring each other down. Things were rapidly spiraling out of control.

"Alright, everybody calm down!" I yelled, getting in between them. "We didn't come here to argue. We just came to talk."

Ray's head whipped in my direction. "There's nothing to talk about! It's obvious now that you care more about being with him than with me."

"You know that's not true!" I had lost my cool now. "I just don't think it's right for you to give me fucking ultimatums."

"Oh, like the one you gave me?" He retorted. I opened my mouth to reply, but he interrupted. "You know what? I'm tired of fighting with you, Matt. Since we're obviously never going to see eye-to-eye, why even waste our time?" He began to go back inside. "You and Jarell have a nice life."

Before I could get out another word, the door slammed in my face.

*****

I sat silently, smoldering in the passenger seat as Jarell drove me home. Once again my attempts to reconcile with Ray had blown up in my face.

"Why you over there with your lip poked out, bruh?"

"Take a wild guess," I replied.

"What did I do?" He was clearly playing dumb.

"You know what you did, man. Why did you have to antagonize him?" After the door slammed in my face, I wanted to ring the bell until Ray came back, but I knew that would only piss him off more (and incur the unholy wrath of Ms. Reynolds).

I also wanted to ring Rell's neck.

He sighed dramatically. "Dawg, all I did was tell ole boy the truth. Don't get mad at me because he's all super-sensitive."

"Don't talk about him like that." I was getting tired of him taking cheap shots at Ray. "You didn't have to say anything. All I asked you to do was put his mind at ease about me and you. But instead, you try to fight the dude in front of his own house?"

"Well...he started it."

I just stared at him in disbelief. Why had I allowed our friendship to come between Ray and me again? "Wow. That sounded real juvenile."

He shrugged. "Okay, man. What do you want me to say? I'm sorry, all right?" His apology was faker than a two dollar bill.

"Yeah, sure." I may not have been the sharpest crayon in the box, but even I could see that Rell had pushed Ray's buttons on purpose. Whether he was intentionally trying to break us up or he was just being a dickhead, the result was the same--Ray had dropped me like a ton of hot bricks. I had no idea how, or even if, I could get him back after this fiasco.

A long silence hung in the air before Jarell spoke again. "Aye, you wanna come by my crib and chill for a minute?"

"Nah, I'm just going home today." *Hanging out with you has already caused enough trouble*, I wanted to say.

"Aight," he said, sounding disappointed. When he pulled up to my house, my mom was unloading groceries from the back of her car.

"Later, man." I gave Jarell a halfhearted pound as I got out the car. I watched him drive off and then walked up to my mom. "Hey, mom. Let me help you with that." I grabbed two plastic bags full of groceries.

"Thanks, Matty," she replied with a smile.

I made two trips to the car before I finally finished bringing everything inside. "Wow, this is a lot of stuff, mom." I held a bag containing a huge turkey.

She laughed. "Well, you know how much you and your brother eat."

"Hey, don't lump me in with Ty-Rex." My brother Tyler was a brawny dude who could eat his own weight in grub. "This is a lot of food even for him. What's he doing—bringing his whole platoon with him?"

She stopped putting the canned goods in the pantry and took a deep breath. Whenever she did that, I usually hated what would come out of her mouth next. "Honey, I was waiting for the right time to tell you this...but Joshua is coming to dinner, too."

I glared at her and dropped the turkey on the counter with a thud. I didn't even want to hear her twisted logic for inviting this man to share our table again. I wasn't in the mood for it. I stormed to my room and slammed the door. This was the perfect way to top off a crappy day. Not only had I lost Ray, but now I find out my asshole stepdad was going to be here for Thanksgiving. I flung my bag to the floor. I already knew this wasn't going to turn out well.

My mom knocked on my door later that night and tried to talk to me. I turned up my radio to let her know I was still alive, but I refused to answer. After a few minutes, she finally gave up. I stayed holed up in my room until she left for work. I got myself something to eat and then laid across my bed. Even though I was tempted to Skype Ray, I decided it would be best to just give him some space and time to cool off. With my luck, we'd just end up having another shouting match anyway. I would just wait to talk to him tomorrow, I concluded.

Since we didn't walk to school together in the morning, I didn't see him until lunch. And even that was from a distance. Jarell and Quin were engaged in their usual sports banter. I tuned them out. As their conversation faded into the background, I looked across the cafeteria at Ray. I wanted to go over and sit with him so badly, but I knew it would be awkward. I sighed softly. My heart was heavy. I missed my Mookie. I missed us. I longed for things to be the way they were before last week. He glanced over and caught me staring. He gave me a blank look.

"Yo, you listening, dawg?" Quin's voice snapped me back to attention.

"Nah. What did you say?" I asked, turning my head to him.

"Pay attention when I'm talkin' to you, punk." He laughed. "I said, are you going to Aaron's party?"

I made a face. "Man, I don't know." I was tired of hearing about this stupid party. Everybody was acting as if that shit was the Presidential Inaugural Ball or something. The last thing I wanted to do was look in Aaron's lame face when I didn't have to. But then again, the thought of popping up and raining on his parade kind of warmed my heart. I'm sure I was the last person he wanted to see at his little shindig. That alone made the thought of showing up appealing. "I have to check my calendar."

"Why? It's not like you got a life or anything?" Jarell laughed. He reached over and mussed my hair. I pushed his hand away and cracked a faint smile. I glanced over and noticed Ray was staring at me. When our eyes met, he simply smirked and then turned his attention back to Keon.

Great, I thought. *On top of everything else, he witnesses Rell playing in my hair.* When lunch was over, he walked past me and emptied his tray. He didn't even look in my direction as he and Ke left the lunchroom.

I was determined to talk to him before the day was over. I had to.

When I walked into my fifth period class, Ray was already at his desk. He was looking over his notes. I sat down next to him. He didn't acknowledge my presence. I let out a yawn and stretched. He still didn't look in my direction. OK, this was ridiculous.

"You ready for the test?" I asked hesitantly.

He nodded his head without taking his eyes off his notes.

I cleared my throat. "Um, about yesterday..." I shifted in my seat. My mouth felt like sand paper. "I want to apologize for what Rell said. I honestly didn't know he was going to come out his face like that."

"Okay," he said. He continued to look at his notes. His voice was flat and unemotional. I didn't know how to read his response. I didn't want to badger him, so I just left it alone. I flipped open my book to review the chapter real quick as other students began to trickle in.

Thankfully, the test wasn't too hard. When class let out, Ray gathered his things and made his way for the door. I caught up to him as he left the room.

"So, do you think we can maybe put everything behind us and start over?" I asked with guarded optimism.

"No." He turned and finally looked at me. His face usually beamed when he saw me. Not anymore. The radiance in his eyes had dimmed.

My heart sank. "Come on, man." I gave him a pleading look.

"After everything that's happened...I honestly don't know how I feel about you anymore, Matt." His facial expression was stoic. I opened my mouth, but nothing came out. I didn't know how to respond. He gave me one last lingering look and then faced forward. We walked side-by-side through the noisy hall in deafening silence. I wanted to say something, but I had no words.

What can you possibly say to rekindle someone's loving light once it's been extinguished?

When we reached a certain point in the hall, we parted and went our separate ways.

CHAPTER 27
RAYMOND

Spending Thanksgiving with my extended family was an annual tradition. Since my aunt had a nice two-story house in Marietta and loved to host company, everyone always flocked to her residence for Turkey Day. It was a three-hour drive (or two hours, the way my speed demon, led foot mom drove). My sister was upfront in the passenger seat. I spent the ride in the backseat trying to pay attention to the movie I was watching on my Ipad. I couldn't focus for anything. We weren't even at my aunt's house yet, and they were already gossiping and talking crap about the relatives they expected to see at dinner. Even though I had my head phones on to shield my ears, they couldn't muffle my mind. As much as I tried to fight it, Matt kept creeping into my head. I could still see the deer-in-the-headlights look on his face when I told him I wasn't sure how I felt about him.

A few days had passed since then.

There hadn't been any communication between us. A part of me still loved Matt, but I was just fed up. Ordering me not to tutor Aaron, all the temper tantrums and silent treatment, bringing Jarell to my house to confront me—it was just too much drama for me. Seeing him sitting at the lunch table with Jarell and joking around with him the next day was the final straw for me.

My thoughts were interrupted by a loud chime. I put the movie I wasn't really watching on pause and pulled out my phone. It was a text message from Ke.

> Keon: I can't wait for the party!!!! I've already picked out my dress :-D

> Me: lmao. Of course.

I couldn't believe I'd let Ke twist my arm into attending Aaron's party on Saturday. When I told him Aaron had invited me, he insisted we go. Initially, I protested vigorously. I had visions of *Carrie* and being drenched in "pig blood" while a cruel crowd of gawking onlookers laughed. Ke told me I was just being paranoid and swore he'd whoop anybody's ass who even so much as sneezed in my direction. When I realized that resistance was indeed futile, I acquiesced. He said we had arrived and this would be the highlight of our senior year. I still wasn't sold. I just wasn't a social butterfly (If anything, I was more like an anti-social caterpillar trapped in a concrete cocoon). Maybe I would be able to come up with a convenient excuse to back out. We weren't currently scheduled to work on Saturday, but hopefully that would change before then.

When we finally arrived at Auntie's house, there were a bunch of cars already parked out front. I took a deep breath and readied myself as we got out the car. My aunt greeted us at the door. Like always, she had to dote over me. My mom and sister used this as an opportunity to sneak away. I silently vowed a merciless an unending vengeance upon them for leaving me alone with Ms. Thompson. My aunt was even nosier than my mom.

"How you doing, baby?" She asked, giving me a backbreaking hug.

"I'm great, ma'am," I whimpered.

"You always sound so cute and proper." She laughed and pinched my cheek. I blushed. "No glasses now?"

"Nope, I've upgraded to contacts," I proudly proclaimed.

"I hear that! So how's school? This is your last year, right?"

"Yeah, it's going well. I'll be happy when it's all over though."

"Mmhmm." She proceeded to fire off a rapid succession of questions. I felt like I was being interrogated. All she needed was a bright spot light to shine in my eyes. "You got yourself a little boyfriend yet?"

"Umm...yeah," I replied shyly. "Kinda."

"What's that mean?" She stared at me expectantly. Didn't she have a turkey to baste or something? Ugh, I did NOT want to get into my relationship problems with my freaking auntie of all people!

"Hi, mama!" I was so thankful to hear my cousin Rashad's voice ring out. He'd arrived just in the nick of time. I wanted to wipe my brow in relief. Rashad had just moved back from New York about a month ago. He was a thick, toned dude with my complexion. He had 360-degree waves and a handsome face which was punctuated by a brilliant smile. He gave me a warm embrace. He was accompanied by a tall, good-looking dude who appeared to be Puerto Rican. "Ray, this is Victor." He introduced us to each other. "Vic, this is my lil' cousin, Raymond."

"Sup?" Vic gripped my hand like a vice. He had a thuggish-aura and manner about him.

"Heeyyyy, Victor. Come on over here and let's talk." Ms. Thompson looped her arm under his and proceeded to pull him across the room. "So, how've you been adjusting to Atlanta?" Vic looked back at us with a *please-help-me* expression on his face. I grinned. Better him than me.

"I just sacrificed my poor baby to save you from mama." Rashad sniffed and pretended to wipe a tear from his eye. "So, anyhoo!" He laughed. "What's been going on with you, kiddo?"

For the next ten minutes, we talked and got caught up on each other's life. In particular, we discussed what colleges I'd applied to. He was hoping I would attend his alma mater, Morehouse. I'd applied to schools in GA, NC, and FL. Even though I wanted to get out of Augusta, I still wanted to be close to home. (My mom would probably kill me if I tried to move cross-country anyway.) I always got along well with my cousin. In fact, he was the first person I came out to. He had some fem ways, but he wasn't flamboyant or anything. I was young when he came out to his parents, but I remember it being a huge scandal when his mom told my mom. I remember overhearing Mom talking to her sister on the phone saying that she would love her son even if she found out he was gay. Thankfully, she was true to her word, and accepted me unconditionally when I came out to her six years later.

As we continued to talk, Rashad's sister Tonia and her fiancé Greg came into the living room. She gave me a hug and a peck on the cheek. Greg gave me a half-hug. Tonia was holding a bottle of wine. Rashad snatched it out of her hands.

"Ooh, bitch. This is Moscato? Good job!" He patted her on the head like a puppy. "I'd rather have Hennessey, but this will work, too."

She yanked the bottle back. "That's for everybody, lushy."

"Fine." Rashad folded his arms and turned up his nose. "Nobody wants that cheap shit anyway."

She laughed. "I bet you'll have your glass out and ready as soon as it's open."

"You damn, right." He cackled. "And you better pour it up, too. Thanks!" I just stood by observing and enjoying the banter between them. I wished my sister and I had the same kind of relationship. His sister and her fiancé moseyed over to greet Ms. Thompson.

Rashad and I got back to our conversation. We eventually wound up on the topic of dating.

"So, are you seeing anyone?" He asked.

"Yeah...sort of..." I replied bashfully. Technically, I didn't know if I was still "seeing" Matt or not.

"Whaaat???" His eyes lit up. When I'd last spoken to Rashad, I was still a virgin. (Of course, this was before Savion). "My Lil' Mookie is married now? I don't believe it. Show-me-the-receipts!" He repeatedly smacked the back of his right hand into his open left palm.

"Okay, you are certifiably in-SANE." I could only imagine him and Keon together. Talk about a major mess. I laughed as I pulled out my phone. I scrolled through my photos till I found one of my favorite pics of Matt--modeling the Spider-man underwear I'd bought him. "This is my nutcase right here."

He snatched the phone from me. "Mmph! He's a cutie."

"Yeah." I beamed proudly. "Unfortunately, he's also a thickheaded, stubborn, oblivious, short-fused hothead."

"Mmm." Rashad stroked his hairless chin. "Sounds like you're playing with fire. He doesn't put his hands on you, does he?"

"Of course not," I replied with my face twisted. He handed my phone back to me.

"Okay, just checking. You know I'll go HAM, bacon, eggs, grits, and hash browns on anybody in a second if they mess with my favorite cousin."

"Oh, Lord." I chuckled. "Trust me, there's no need for you to go to jail on my account."

He laughed. "Good. It sounds like we're attracted to the same type of guys."

"Really?" My antennas shot up. Rashad was twenty-seven years old. As a gay man who had been in "the life" for almost ten years (which he joked was the equivalent of twenty heterosexual years and thirty dog years), he was pretty knowledgeable about the trials and travails of being a black gay man.

"Yep. He's pushy, aggressive, and borderline mental." He chortled. "But he's still a good guy underneath all the crap."

I smiled. He'd just described Matt. "Your boyfriend's like that, too?"

"Oh, yeah. Trust me, if you Google 'hothead,' a picture of Vic will come up. Hell, a whole photo album will probably pop up. He came from a pretty screwed up childhood though, so that's to be expected. That doesn't excuse it or anything, but you got to take that into consideration when dealing with some of these dudes out here. They come with baggage and have difficulty connecting, interacting and communicating beyond a certain level." I nodded my head in agreement. I realized how Matt's dysfunctional relationship with his stepfather had probably contributed to his domineering behavior.

Rashad continued, "He's working on that temper though. He's changed a lot since we met." He stopped and smiled. "You've got to be patient with them. He's not perfect--hell no one is--except me." He laughed. "But seriously, if you love him, you'll stick with him. I'm not saying tolerate a lot of BS, but don't just run away at the drop of a hat either. Anything or anyone worth having will take time and effort."

"Do you guys ever have disagreements and arguments? How do you deal with it?" I was eager to get some advice for handling Matt.

He twisted his lips and gave me a look. "Duh. All relationships have those. That comes with the territory. Just try not to go to bed mad at each other, that's all." He waved at Vic who was still being held hostage by Ms. Thompson. He flashed a quick smile, bit his bottom lip, and winked back. Rashad put his hand over his mouth and giggled.

"Awww," I quipped. "That's so cute."

"Stay out of grown folks' business."

"Get a room." I chuckled. "But I hear you though," I said, getting back on topic. "One of the major causes of friction between us is that Matt is just so frickin' overprotective."

"I'm going to put you on to something, lil' cousin." He leaned close and lowered his voice. "These 'alpha-male' types always want to treat you like a damsel in distress. That's just their way of showing love. It makes them feel all manly to be defending your honor. Of course, they always have to feel like they're the boss, too." He rolled his eyes. "The trick is—only let them *think* they're calling the shots to stroke their ego." He grinned mischievously. "When they get angry, you treat them like big ole babies throwing temper tantrums. Instead of spanking them, you just let them kick and scream until they get it all out of their system. When they're finish, you make 'em apologize. Then, you grudgingly forgive them and make them do what you wanted in the first place."

I burst out laughing. "Oh, boy, I'm loving this wisdom. You should write a book."

"I already have! You ain't know? It's called 'Rashad Reads Yo' Relationship'. Available in hardcover, paperback, e-book and audio book. Log on and pre-order your copy today. Thanks. You better ask somebody." He smacked his lips. "And then go run and tell everybody else what you heard."

"Soooo, yeah." I gave him the same blank stare I reserved for Keon's crazy rejoinders. "What if you don't like the people he hangs with?"

Rashad shrugged. "You can't pick and choose his acquaintances for him. You just have to trust his judgment and hope he has enough common sense to discern on his own if he's associating with a snake or not. If you try to control each other, it's only going to breed resentment and strife. Hell, at least his friends aren't trying to kill you."

I looked at him with a stilted eyebrow.

"Only God can judge me!" He laughed and bumped me with his shoulder. "It's a crazy, convoluted 'rated R' story not suited for youngin's such as yourself."

I rolled my eyes. "Okay, grandpa."

"But seriously, when you're in a relationship with someone, there has to be give and take. You both can't have your way all the time. There isn't always a right or a wrong point-of-view. Every now and then, there're two equally valid, logical sides to an argument. In those instances, you just have to reach a compromise."

"But what if there isn't a reasonable compromise?" I soaked up his words of wisdom like an alien parasite absorbing the life force of its unsuspecting host. "What if you reach an impasse?"

"If you truly love each other, you can always find common ground. It may not be easy and it may not be perfect, but you'll eventually reach a solution and come to a mutual agreement." He threw an arm around my shoulder and pulled me close. "So I said all of that to say: There's no such thing as a perfect relationship."

"Yeah, I guess not," I said with a sigh. Rashad gently squeezed my shoulder.

"If you and your boo want a couple's counseling session, I'll give ya'll a discount."

"Gee, thanks."

"You're so very welcome. But let me stop dispensing all this sage wisdom." He withdrew his arm. "I feel like I'm in a damn Tyler Perry movie."

"Yep, all you're missing is the wig, floral patterned dress and wide-rimmed glasses." I gave him a wry smile.

"Boy, don't get cute and get cut." He gave me a playful push.

"Yep, that sounds like something Madea would say." I snickered.

Just then, an older lady walked up. The first thing I noticed was the ill-fitting wig she had on. She gleefully greeted both of us with hugs.

"Hey, Ms. Phyllis!" Rashad said. They talked for a few minutes, and then she went on her way. Once she was out of sight, he gave me a slanted grin. "Now Ms. Phyllis know she wrong for coming up in here with that nest all haphazardly perched atop her head like that."

I tried not to laugh. "Stop being mean, Rashad."

"What?" He shrugged. "I'm just pointing out the obvious." He looked across the room. Tonia, Greg, Kim and Victor appeared to be having a lively discussion. Kim was daintily twisting a strand of hair around her finger while flirtatiously smiling in Vic's face. "Well, let me go over here and get my man before I have to snatch some tracks out this ho's head." Rashad started to leave and then came back. "Oh, yeah, one more thing; always trust your man." He leaned in and whispered. "But make sure to mark your territory when necessary, and beat a bitch's ass when you have to." A broad smile spread across his face. He walked over to them and promptly joined in the conversation. He subtly wrapped his arm around Vic's waist and gave me a wink when no one was looking. I laughed to myself and shook my head.

Feeling parched after running my mouth for so long, I migrated to the kitchen and grabbed a grape soda from the fridge. Just as I took a gulp, my phone chimed. It was another message from Keon. When I opened it there was a picture of a flowing antebellum dress and a big floppy bonnet.

The caption read: *"This is what I'm going to wear to the party. I'm gonna let them hoes have it! What you think? :-P"*

I almost spit soda out my nose. I wasn't even fucking with Ke's silly behind. I shoved my phone in my pocket, went back into the living room, and tried my best to be sociable.

An hour or so later, everybody who was coming had arrived. The food was ready, the table was set, and it was time to finally get our eat on! Once everyone took a seat at the table we all joined hands and bowed our heads. Auntie Thompson said grace. As she droned on and on, and on...and on, my mind drifted back to Matt. I wondered how his Thanksgiving was going. A smile played at my lips as I imagined him stuffing his cute, greedy face. I let out a deep breath. Rashad had given me a lot of food for thought today, but I still wasn't convinced I could work things out with Matt or if it was even worth the headache to try. I was going to have to chew on this some more later.

CHAPTER 28
MATTHEW

"Where the hell is this big headed troll?" I wondered to myself aloud. I checked my watch again. Since Mom was still busy preparing Thanksgiving dinner, she sent me to pick up my brother from the airport. I was more than happy to oblige. The plane had landed and the passengers were deboarding. I was standing in the arrivals area waiting for Tyler to come through the door.

It was a small airport, so there was no way I could miss him. Just as I was about to look at my watch again, people started trickling through the door. Seconds later, Ty entered. He was wearing his camouflage army gear and hat with the big beige combat boots. His broad shoulders and brawny physique filled out the uniform with ease. At 5'9", he was a few inches shorter than me, but a lot more muscular. This guy was a beast in the gym. It looked like he'd gotten even bigger since I last saw him a year ago. Guess that military regimen was no joke. The strap of a carry-on sized duffel bag was draped over his shoulder. He lifted the brim of his hat from his eyes. When he spotted me, his face lit up. He sprouted an ear-to-ear smile. I made my way to him as quickly as possible without running. We clasped hands and pulled each other into a tight bro-hug.

"Damn, you need a haircut, dude." He roughly rumpled my hair.

"Get your stinkin' paws off me, you damn dirty ape!" I laughed as I pushed him off.

"These damn dirty paws are about to knock you out," he replied. We threw our fists up and pretended to spar. We always carried on like this. People were staring at us like we were crazy, but I didn't care. It felt good to finally see my big bro in person again.

After we finished playing around, we walked to baggage claim. When his suitcase finally rolled around on the conveyor belt, I grabbed it.

"Geez, how much crap did you pack? You sure you're only staying for a few days? Or have you gone AWOL?" I asked, struggling to hoist the bag up with one arm.

"Silence, you puny weakling." He did a lousy Arnold Schwarzenegger impersonation. "Even the girl at the check-in counter this morning lifted that bag without breaking a sweat. Though come to think of it, she did have a five O'clock shadow." He grinned.

"You'd probably still hit it."

He shrugged. "Pussy is pussy."

"Still no class, I see." I shook my head.

"Nope." He bared his teeth again. "None whatsoever."

After stopping to buy sodas from the vending machine, we exited the terminal. We walked to the car in the parking lot and stuffed Ty's bags in the trunk. We hopped inside. Once he fastened his seat belt, he took off his hat to reveal his fresh buzz cut. Both my brother and I strongly favored my mom. However, whereas I had inherited her dark hair color, his was sandy brown like my stepdad's.

"So, did you wear your army fatigues to show off, Captain America?" I quipped as I drove out of the airport.

"Yessir. Not to mention, I get crazy telephone numbers dressed like this. I even bagged a few flight attendant digits on the plane ride here. I'm going to be getting that mile high love soon." He licked his lips and rubbed his hands together in gleeful anticipation.

"Whatever." I leaned over and pretended to squint at the rank insignia on his chest. "You're still a Private."

He finished guzzling his soda and let out a loud burp. "Private First Class, to be exact." He smiled triumphantly.

"Same difference." He swatted me on the head.

"Bro, take my word for it; chicks get wet when they see a dude in uniform. They're going to be throwing themselves at you. It's one of the few perks of selling your soul to Uncle Sam." He let out a hearty laugh.

"Yeah, I guess." I gave him a faint smile. Tyler had no idea I wasn't into girls, so the prospect of them throwing themselves at me didn't excite me in the least. "I'm not even sure if I want to join the Army anymore," I confessed.

"What?" He looked shocked. "Why not?"

"Well, lately, I've been thinking about going to college after I graduate."

"Why the change of heart? I thought you wanted to enlist?"

"Actually, I thought that was something that would make dad like me." My voice was somber. "I just wanted him to respect me and be as proud of me as he is of you. I guess it doesn't matter anymore, since he's never going to like me."

He scratched his forearm under his jacket. "You can't live to make other people happy, man. You only have one life to live. So, you've gotta do what's right for you. If you do go to school, you can always join the Army after you finish. With a degree, you'll start off at a higher rank."

"Yeah, I know," I replied.

He got unusually quiet. "I still can't believe what's been going on between Mom and Dad. Well, actually, I can." He exhaled. "Our childhood was seriously screwed up, man. When you're a kid and living in a dysfunctional environment like that, you don't know any better. You think that's how things are supposed to be, ya know? I didn't realize how truly bad it was until I moved away and got a chance to look at it from the outside." It felt weird to hear Ty be so deep. Even though we were extremely close, we'd never had a genuine forthcoming conversation about our home life.

When we were younger, Ty would try to intervene on my behalf. He sacrificed himself to deflect our dad's rage as much as possible. Even though he was subjected to our dad's abuse too, the majority of his wrath was always directed at me. I didn't know why until recently. He hated me because I was a constant reminder of my mom's infidelity. I had to ask Ty a burning question that had been on my mind ever since I learned the truth.

"So...did you know I wasn't really Dad's biological son?" I continued to focus on the road ahead.

"No," he said with a sullen tone. "I can't believe Mom was able to hold something like that in all these years."

"Yeah, tell me about it. And what's even more fucked up is how Dad used the secret to basically blackmail her into putting up with him and taking all his crap. The dude left to be with the woman he was cheating with for a month, and Mom still wants to take him back. I'm telling you, Ty, I don't know if I can keep my sanity if that happens. Sometimes, I just wish I could shake some sense into her."

"Mom is a grown woman, Matt. We both can talk to her until we're blue-green in the face. But in the end, it's going to be up to her to make the decision to leave him alone. In the meantime, all you can do is grin and bear it, or move out."

"Yeah, right." I sucked my teeth. "Move out to where?"

"I have my own apartment off post now. You can stay with me if Mom lets you."

"Really?" I asked excitedly. He was stationed in Fort Hood. As much as I bitched and moaned about hot weather, I couldn't see myself living in Texas. Even though the offer was tempting, I knew I couldn't. There was no way I could leave my mom here alone with that asshole. Not to mention, I couldn't leave Ray (even though I didn't know if we would get back together or not). "Eh, thanks for the offer. I'll just stick it out here till I graduate though." I gave him a sly smirk. "Besides, I can only imagine how crappy you keep your pad."

His shoulders shrugged. "I'm a handsome bachelor, bro. Of course they're panties everywhere." We both cracked up. Our laughter died down again as we approached the house and saw Joshua's car parked in the driveway. Ty let out a long breath. "Whelp, looks like daddy dearest is home."

"Great," I replied with dry enthusiasm.

"Come on, Matty. We'll get through this." He rumpled my hair again. We got out the car and retrieved his bags from the trunk. When we walked in the house, Mom was still in the kitchen.

"Look what I found while dumpster diving!" I announced as we entered. She turned around and her face beamed with excitement. She dropped the spoon she was holding and dried her hands on her apron. She rushed to Ty and they embraced. Seconds later, my stepdad emerged from the living room. He eagerly greeted Ty also. Joshua fawned over him like a groupie. That was nothing new. Why shouldn't he? He was his real son, after all. He had always treated him better than me, but not too much better. I guess you could say it was varying degrees of shitty. I went back to my room and let them enjoy their son's triumphant return.

Once we all sat down to eat, everything just felt wrong to me. I ate quietly with my head down. There was this unshakeable sense of foreboding in the air. Ty joked around, trying to lighten the atmosphere and diffuse the unspoken tension between my stepdad and I. It wasn't working. Sitting next to my father at the small table had put me in an irritable mood. I tried to suppress it, but my anger was simmering below the surface. Having to hear him rant and rave about everything under the sun was only making it boil.

"At least you army boys get to shoot M-16's and shit," Joshua complained. "Meanwhile, over here in the 'good ole US of A,' the government is trying to abolish the 2nd Amendment and take away our guns! I wish some damn Liberal would try to take my baby from me." He patted the gun which he kept holstered on his hip like he was Barney Fife.

"Dad, no one's going to abolish the 2nd Amendment," Ty replied, trying to be the voice of reason. "They just want to restrict access to assault weapons that can slaughter dozens of people in a matter of minutes."

My stepdad let out a bellowing laugh. "That's what they want you to believe!" He took a swig of his beer. "Don't be stupid, Tyler. You can't trust this screwed up government."

Ty had a look of subdued aggravation on his face. "So, how do you like Augusta so far?" He was obviously attempting to get his dad down from his soap box.

"It's not bad," Joshua replied, taking another drink of beer. "It's definitely better than living in that cesspool California with all those damn illegals running around."

I rolled my eyes.

My brother didn't even bother to respond. Instead, he shoveled a forkful of stuffing in his mouth and turned his attention to Mom. "This tastes great, ma! I miss the hell out of your cook--" Before he could get the rest of his sentence out, Joshua interrupted him.

"And if that isn't bad enough—now we've got queers running around trying to get married--pushing their perverted agenda in our faces." He shook his head in dismay. "This country is going straight to hell in a hand basket. I'm telling you, the people of this nation need to rise up and do something about this. If the government wants to outlaw something, then that's where they should start. They should round up all those sickos and put 'em out of their misery."

Bigotry, beer and bullets; those were the only things he cared about. I was so sick of his ignorance. I couldn't keep my mouth shut any longer. I lifted my head and scowled.

"Why don't you just shut up for a change?" I said what everybody was probably thinking.

His fork dropped to his plate with a loud clank. "What did you say, boy?"

"You heard me." I dropped my fork and stared at him defiantly. "Why don't you shut your ignorant, hateful, homophobic mouth?"

He smirked. "Oh, let me guess: you support 'gay rights' now?"

"Yeah, why wouldn't I?" I said it with unapologetic confidence. I took a deep breath and pressed on. "Considering I'm gay, too." I heard my mom and brother's forks drop. Everyone stared at me in utter silence. It was like I'd just announced that I had been diagnosed with a terminal illness. Even I couldn't believe I'd just come out to my whole family at Thanksgiving. Mom was the first to speak.

"I don't agree with that lifestyle, Matthew."

I laughed derisively. "Get off your high horse, Mom. I didn't agree with your 'lifestyle' of being married to an abusive drunk, but you didn't hear me complaining."

"Don't you dare talk to me that way!" She shot back, tossing her napkin to the table.

"See, Sharon?" My stepdad chimed in. "If you'd let me discipline this punk the way I wanted to, he wouldn't have turned out to be a queer." He glared at me. "You make me sick to my fucking stomach."

The look in his eyes and the contempt in his voice made me snap. All the years of verbal and physical abuse at this man's hands had finally pushed me to the breaking point. Without thinking, I dove at him like a rockstar leaping into a mosh pit. His chair toppled backwards and we both fell to the floor. He looked at me in bewilderment as I punched him in the face. We rolled around on the floor taking swings at each other until Ty snatched my stepdad off me. Both of us were breathing hard. He staggered to his feet and wiped his fingers across his lip. When he saw I had drawn blood, his face twisted in anger. He reached under his flannel shirt and drew his gun. He pushed past Ty who was standing between us, and aimed the gun at me. I kept my face blank and resolute. I refused to give him the satisfaction of thinking his words or actions had any power over me. I swallowed and stared at him unflinchingly. If I was going to die, then I would take my bullet like a man.

"Dad, are you crazy?" Tyler asked. My stepdad didn't reply. He just stood there like a statue. "Don't do this," he said in a softer tone. He placed a hand on his dad's shoulder. Joshua didn't budge.

The gun remained pointed at my head.

He kept his gaze locked on me.

I kept mine fixated on him. I could see the murderous hatred in his eyes. I knew if I even flinched, he wouldn't hesitate to blow me away.

Still, I refused to show even a glimmer of fear.

After a tension-filled minute, he lowered the gun and put it back in his holster.

"You're lucky my son is here, boy." He looked at my mom. "Sharon, you better put this punk out of here before I move back in."

My mom's eyes narrowed and shot daggers at him. "You actually pulled a weapon on my son?" She shook her head in disbelief. "You haven't changed at all, Joshua. You're nothing more than a cold-hearted monster. I see now that I was a fool for even considering allowing you to come back here. Not anymore. I'm through with you--for good this time."

My stepdad pointed his finger in her face. "Now, see here, you dumb bitch--" Before he could spew another insult, she slapped the spit out of his mouth.

"Joshua...get out." For the first time I could ever recall, Mom stood her ground. Her face was firm, not betraying even a hint of doubt. My stepdad just stood there like he couldn't believe she was finally standing up to him. Her loud decree snapped him out of his trance. "NOW!"

He huffed and straightened his collar. He sneered and then stormed out the door. Seconds later, we heard the sound of screeching tires. The Monster was gone. Maybe it was for good this time.

My mom buried her face in her hand. Ty embraced her. This was all my fault. Sure, Thanksgiving wasn't going well, but I'd officially ruined it. As my brother consoled Mom, I shuffled back to my room and closed the door. I lay across the bed with my arms behind my head, staring up at the ceiling. I was actually staring off into space. I wanted to be anywhere but here. In spite of everything that had just happened, I was oddly enough thinking about Ray. Hopefully, his day was going better than mine.

A few minutes later, there was a knock at the door.

"Hey, can I come in?"

Before I could even reply, Tyler burst into the room. He closed the door behind him and plopped down on my bed, causing the mattress to strain under his weight.

"Thank God I wasn't in here jerking off when you kicked down the door," I joked.

"Oh, my bad." He covered his eyes with hands. He kept them there for three seconds and then removed them. "Done yet?"

"Asshole." I snickered a little.

"Man, I think this is the craziest Thanksgiving we've ever had. Are you, OK?"

"Yeah, I'm fine." I sat upright. I was anxious to see how our relationship was going to be impacted by my coming out. "So...how do you feel about your little brother being a 'butt muncher'?" I teasingly used the homophobic term that he'd often thrown around when we were younger.

"Well, to be honest, with all these beautiful women out here, I don't know why you'd rather look at another dude's hairy ass." He shuddered and grinned. "I'm not judging though; to each his own. It may take me a little time—and a few shots of Tequila—to wrap my head around this, but I'm cool with it. You're my lil' bro and I'm still gonna love you regardless. " He hugged me. I began to tear up when I heard him say that. However, I didn't want to cry in front of him (because he'd never let me live it down). I serve with a few gay dudes. They're all cool people, so it's no big deal." I was surprised to hear him say that. Apparently, being away in the military and being exposed to different people had made him more open-minded.

"Thanks, man," I said as he let me go. "I just wish Mom felt the same way."

He looked me in the eyes. "Look, I'll try to talk some sense into her before I go. This is a major shock to her, but I know she loves you just as much as I do. She'll come around eventually."

"I hope so," I replied solemnly.

"She will." He cleared his throat. "So, you got yourself a brofriend, a dudette, or whatever you call it?"

"Lame." I laughed. "Actually, I am dating a cool guy named Ray." I lowered my eyes. "Or, at least I was until last week."

"That doesn't sound good. What happened?" He leaned back on the bed, resting on his elbows.

"Well, we kind of had a falling out. I was just looking out for him, but he took that as me being controlling. It's like whenever he asks me to do something, it's automatically a reasonable request which can't be denied. But when the shoe is on the other foot—I'm the bad guy who's trying to boss him around."

"So, um, are you the man or the woman in the relationship?" I gave him an awkward look. "Uh, never mind. I guess what I'm going to say works either way. I can only go on my experience with women, but you can still apply it to your situation. No respectable girl with a good head on her shoulders likes to have some dude telling her what to do. You gotta give him the freedom and space to do his own thing. Of course, that doesn't mean let him run all over you. But if you're too overbearing and abrasive, you're just going to push him away. Either that, or destroy his self-esteem and have him scared of you like Mom was of Dad."

I mulled over his words. It was unsettling to realize that I'd been behaving like my dad towards Ray. But still, the breakup wasn't all my fault, I reminded myself. I had a legitimate grievance too.

"Another thing is he doesn't want me to be friends with someone because I recently found out the guy likes me. So a few days ago, we both went to Ray's house to hash things out."

Ty swiveled his head around like the girl from *The Exorcist* and looked at me like I was crazy. "Wow. That was dumb."

"Thanks for seeing things my way," I replied sarcastically. "Well, it seemed like a good idea at the time."

"You must've been high?" He laughed.

"No, I wasn't," I grumbled.

"Okay...so that was your problem." He grinned. "You weren't in your right mind." I just rolled my eyes. "Seriously, bro, your batting average sucks. It sounds like you've been striking out left and right with this dude."

"Yeah, I know." I sighed dejectedly. Hearing myself explain all my actions aloud really brought home how much of a douche I'd been lately. I didn't blame Ray for dropping me. I wanted him back, but I didn't want to force it. As much as it pained me to do so, I would just have to be patient and wait on him. Hopefully, he would find it in his heart to give me another chance.

My thoughts were interrupted by a loud fart.

My nose crinkled as I looked at Ty in disgust. "Ugh, you're so gross, man."

He grinned and shrugged. "The asparagus gets me every time. I bet you don't complain when Ray lets one fly."

"Nah, he actually has manners." I pinched my nose. "Unlike you, he's not a pig."

"Hey, watch that mouth, Matty. You may have a few inches on me now, but you're still my LITTLE brother." He wrapped his arm around my neck. He pulled my head down towards his lap and gave me a noogie. I pushed him away. "So now that we've had our Hallmark moment," Ty said, "let's finish eating. I got dibs on the drumsticks!" He sprung from the bed and bum rushed the door."

"Oh, no you don't, chump!" I jumped up and grabbed the back of his t-shirt. We wrestled, elbowed, clawed and shoved each other in the doorway before ripping and running down the hall.

Man, I loved my big brother!

CHAPTER 29
RAYMOND

I had just finished brushing my hair when I heard Keon outside blowing the horn like a lunatic. I tossed the brush on the dresser and grabbed my keys. I gave myself a once-over in the floor length mirror. Instead of my usual comic book-themed attire, I put on a button down shirt, some gray jeans and a pair of black leather Converses. This was as high fashion as it got for me. I raced through the hall and out the door, locking it behind me.

It was a calm, crisp and clear night.

A full moon hung low in the sky.

It was a good night for a party (or a zombie apocalypse).

"My, my—don't we look dapper tonight?" Keon said as I got in the car.

"Thanks," I replied bashfully. "You look pretty spiffy yourself."

"Oh, you know I try." He playfully batted his eyelashes.

"Changed your mind about the antebellum dress, I see?" I grinned.

"Chile, please. I have my *Gone with the Wind* ensemble in the trunk. I figure I'll run out to the car and change into it for my second act!" He laughed. Once I buckled up, we were off to our destination. I still couldn't believe I was going to Aaron's birthday party. I was a bundle of nerves the whole ride there. I reminded myself to stay calm and take deep breaths.

Keon followed the directions from the GPS turn for turn. We eventually arrived at a large house in a cul-de-sac. It was located in a nice, well-maintained subdivision. From all of the expensive cars and trucks parked in the garages and driveways, this was clearly a well-to-do neighborhood.

"Bitch, we have arrived--literally and figuratively." He pulled the car along the curb and put it in park. There were already a bunch of other cars parked out front, and people filing into the residence. He pulled down the sun visor and looked at himself in the mirror as he applied some lip balm. "I want to make sure I'm on point just in case the paparazzi try to snap pics." He puckered his lips like a fish and turned his head from side-to-side while keeping his eyes on his reflection.

"By the time you finish primming and posing, the party will be over."

He blew out air. "Don't rush me. Everything needs to be perfect for my grand entrance!"

I snickered. "Take your time, Ms. Gaga." While he continued to poke out and twist his lips in the mirror, I looked at Aaron's house. I let out a low whistle. "Geez, this place is a freaking McMansion."

"Bitch, Aaron is living like the modern day Huxtables'," Keon joked, referring to the upper middle class family from the old *Cosby Show*.

"Tell me about it. I feel like I'm about to step foot on Mt. Olympus."

"Good looking, tall, and rich; now I see why that ho Brianna's pussy stay in a tizzy when somebody else tries to push up on him. Hell, I may have to throw some of my tasty cakes at ole boy."

A few more minutes passed, and we finally got out of the car. Keon adjusted his belt and pulled down his tight shirt as we made our way up the long driveway.

A beautiful woman greeted us at the door. It took me a moment to realize it was Aaron's sister. She was a senior when I was a freshman. *Well, at least the party is sort of being chaperoned.* Hopefully, that lessened the odds of me being stripped down to my underwear, hung upside down from the second floor landing, videotaped and posted on Youtube as a prank, I reasoned. We followed the crowd into a cavernous living room.

The energy in the atmosphere was palatable. Music was thumping from the stereo system. Judging from how the bass seemed to be pumping from every direction, it had to be surround sound. An opulent crystal chandelier hung from the ceiling. The room was decorated with cream colored, leather furniture. There was a 70-inch plasma TV mounted on one wall, while the others were adorned with breath-taking oil paintings. Keon and I stood there looking as if we'd just walked into Wonderland. This place was like something I'd seen on *MTV cribs!*

Keon leaned close and whispered. "Ooohwee! We're honorary members of the Illuminati now. I'm about to log on to *Getmylife.com* up in here!"

I smirked. "Don't get too carried away, Cinderalla. All of this could still be a setup," I cautioned.

"Chile, stop being paranoid." He smacked his lips. "I wish a bitch would try some shit tonight."

We found our way to where everybody else was getting refreshments. After getting our drinks, we meandered back into the open space. We sipped from our cups and looked about like starstruck groupies who'd snuck into a ritzy gala. Members of the basketball team, football team, and all the other popular kids were in attendance.

"So this is how the upper crust lives," Ke said, grabbing a handful of h'orderves off of a tray which sat on the coffee table. He popped one into his mouth. "My dear man, could you please pass the Grey Poupon?" He said with a faux, snobby aristocratic accent.

I shook my head at him and chuckled. Just then, I noticed Aaron's girlfriend sashaying over to us like a super model in Milan. She was flanked by two other girls who looked like cheerleaders.

"What's up, bitch?" She flashed a gleaming smile as she hugged Ke.

"Hey, Bri!" He exclaimed, giving her his fakest smile. "Girl, your hair is sitting lovely!"

"Aww, thank you," she gushed. "Come on, let's take a walk. I'll show you around my man's place."

"Ray, we're about to go for some girl talk. Mix and mingle a little. I'll be right back," Keon said, squeezing my arm.

"Alright. I'll be around." I smiled.

They all walked off arm-in-arm. Ke glanced back at me. He made a funny face and rolled his eyes. I snickered to myself. I looked about uncomfortably, suddenly realizing I was all alone. I tapped my foot and bobbed my head to the music, trying not to appear nervous or out of place. I couldn't really relax because I had been on high alert from the moment I stepped foot through the front door. I pulled out my phone and pretended to be preoccupied. I contemplated texting Matt. I'd spent all day Friday thinking about him and mulling over my cousin's advice. I still wasn't sure if things could work between us, but I wanted to at least give it another try. I knew he was probably spending time with his brother yesterday, so I didn't disturb him. I debated calling him earlier today, but decided against it. If I'd told him I already promised to hang out with Keon tonight and we were going to Aaron's party, my phone would've spontaneously combusted.

I put the phone back in my pocket. I would wait to hit him up tomorrow.

A familiar voice suddenly startled me.

"Fancy seeing you here, bruh." I turned to see Savion leaning against the wall. He was holding a plastic cup in one hand. "What's good?"

"Hey, what's up?" I replied with a flat tone.

"Wow, this is a pleasant surprise." He licked his lips. "It must be fate that keeps bringing us together."

I rolled my eyes and took a gulp of my fruit punch.

"You need me to refill your drink for you, cuz?" He smiled broadly.

"No thanks, I can manage." I gave him an annoyed look. "Um, you do realize we're in public, right?" I said sarcastically, hoping he'd get the hint and leave me alone.

"Man, I told you I don't care about that." He grinned a little and lowered his voice. "So...have you thought about what I said? I mean, about us?"

I cut my eyes. "Nope. I haven't thought about you at all."

"Aight, be that way then." The grin vanished from his face. "Enjoy the rest of your night. And if I don't see you later, get home safe." He shook my hand and walked off. He put his arm around some random girl and started talking to her.

I let out a long breath. *Where the hell is Keon's ass?* I wondered. *So much for him keeping me company.* I went back into the kitchen to get another cup of juice. (At this rate, I was going to OD on the stuff.) When I walked back into the living room, Keon was dancing in the middle of a group of girls. He was shaking it fast and dropping it low. I laughed to myself and shook my head. Well, at least someone was enjoying himself. I wandered over to another section of the room and just watched everyone talking and dancing. I spotted Aaron in the midst of some people, regaling them like a true showman. When he saw me, he flashed a smile. I showed a sliver of teeth in return. He broke away from his adoring fans and approached me. I instantly threw up my force field and readied myself for any eventuality. To say I still didn't trust Aaron was an understatement.

"Glad you could make it, homie." He gave me a warm smile and a bro-hug. He had on a form-fitting, black v-neck sweater. As always, he was impeccably dressed.

"Yeah, I wouldn't miss it for the world," I lied. "Happy birthday."

"Thanks, man." He showed his pearlies again. "Why're you just standing over here holding up the wall?"

"Eh, I'm just getting warmed up. Once I've finished my fifth cup of punch, the party animal in me will be unleashed."

He laughed. "You know there's no liquor in that, right?"

"Yeah, I know."

"You should let me spike it for you." He sipped from his cup and gave me a sly grin. Whatever he was drinking on must've had a kick, because he seemed a little tipsy. "My sister hooked me up with some top shelf shit." He swished the liquid around in his cup.

"Nah, I'm good. I don't drink. I'm the designated backseat driver after all," I joked.

"Aight, I'm not going to pressure you." He smiled. We just stared at each other awkwardly. I looked away sheepishly.

"Um, where's your bathroom?" I suddenly had to pee like crazy.

"Oh, right up there--a few doors down on the right." He pointed to a flight of stairs which led to the second floor.

"Thanks." I hurried off to drain my bladder, quickly ascending the steps. The second floor was dark and devoid of activity. I guess the party was strictly confined to downstairs and the outside patio. Once I found the bathroom, I urinated for what seemed an eternity. When I was finally done, I washed and dried my hands. I straightened my clothes and checked my reflection in the mirror before turning out the light. I opened the door and stepped back into the hall.

"Did you find the bathroom?" Aaron asked, scaring me half to death. He was standing at the top of the stairs.

"Yeah, barely. This place is huge, man."

He laughed a little. "Aye, come here. I want to show you something real quick before we go back down."

"Uh..." I gave him an unsure look. Was this the trap I'd been expecting?

"Dawg, come on." He picked up on my trepidation. "I told you I wasn't going to fuck with you anymore, didn't I?"

My spider-sense wasn't tingling, so it was probably okay. I cautiously followed him. He led me to a room at the far end of the hall.

"Welcome to my humble abode." He pushed open the door and flipped on the light.

"Woah," I gasped. My mouth hung open in awe as I imbibed my surroundings. He had a mammoth king-size poster bed. There was a 40-gallon aquarium, atop a cherry oak wood cabinet positioned against the wall. I walked over to it to get a closer look. It was illuminated with a soft blue light and filled with beautiful, exotic-looking fish. He also had a display case that contained trophies of varying shapes and sizes. Aaron had obviously played and excelled at competitive sports since he was a kid. His wall was covered with posters of basketball players and Manga art. There was also a flat screen on the wall that was just a little smaller than the one downstairs.

He closed the door. I glanced at the closet.

Was someone about to jump out of there?

Aaron walked over to the desk in the corner. He set his drink down and picked something up. He came back to me.

"I wanted to show you this." He slowly unrolled it and held it open for me to see. "This is a work in progress. What do you think?"

It was a detailed drawing of a winged, fire-breathing serpent. It wasn't finished, but it already looked awesome. This artistic side to Aaron was so fascinating. "Geez, that's incredible, man!"

"Thanks," he said with a proud smile. "I'm thinking about using this design for my next tattoo." He folded the poster back up and set it down. "So, are you having a good time tonight?"

I gave him a casual shrug. "Yeah, it's alright." I still wasn't used to Aaron being so nice to me.

"Damn, keep it down, man. You're too excited." He laughed as he looked down at me. "Are you at least feeling the music?"

"Yeah, it's cool." I tried to put a little more enthusiasm in my voice.

"That's what's up. You've got good taste." He flashed a sly grin. "That's my playlist."

"Oh, I take that back then," I said.

He pretended to recoil in offense. "That's cold, dawg."

"Nah, I'm just playing. At least you don't have any *One Direction* on there."

He let out a raucous laugh and shook his head. "Never that."

Once again, an awkward silence settled in. We just stared at each other for a second.

"Aye, I just wanted to say thanks again for helping me ace that test."

"It's cool, man. Glad I could help," I nervously glanced down at my feet.

"And you know when you asked me before why I always picked on you, and I said I didn't know?"

I lifted my head and looked into his eyes. "Um, yeah?"

"Well, I think I figured out why." He paused and rubbed his wavy hair. He took a deep breath. "It's because deep down...I'm feeling you."

All I could do was blink like Bambi in front of an oncoming tractor trailer.

"I just could never bring myself to accept it, until now."

I swallowed hard. What the hell was about to happen?

My heart started racing.

He bent down, bringing his lips toward mine.

It's amazing how many thoughts can flash through your mind in an instant. Depending on which scientist, sci-fi writer, or comic book geek you asked, the speed of thought may actually be faster than even the speed of light. As I stood transfixed, watching Aaron's lips approach mine, all I could do was wonder how I'd gotten myself into this position. When exactly had my life veered from reality into the realm of fantasy and become a gay teen romance novel? Aaron and I were once sworn enemies. Now we were alone in his room-- on the verge of an intense kiss??? This was the stuff of homoerotic fantasy. Was I going to suddenly wake up to find out that this was a dream, or more likely, a nightmare?

This was just too surreal.

Aaron Thomas--the tall, good-looking basketball captain whom everyone swooned over-- had just confessed his true feelings for me.

The same Aaron Thomas who made my life a living hell for the past four years, to be exact, a small voice in my subconscious interjected. With that thought, I snapped to.

At the last second, I turned my head to avoid his kiss. "Aaron, what are you doing?"

For a moment, he looked bewildered. However, he quickly reverted back to his usual smooth game face. "You're smart enough to figure it out." He gripped me by my waist and pulled me into him. His warm body pushed against mine. I could feel his hard dick through his jeans, resting against my stomach. "You feel that shit?" He bent down and grazed his tongue against the side of my neck. The scent of his cologne gently massaged my nostrils. I could feel myself getting hard as well. He nipped my earlobe with his soft, wet lips. My body quivered.

Get ahold of yourself, Raymond. I knew I couldn't let this go any further. I had to stay strong. I had to use the Force! I placed a hand against his firm chest to keep him at bay. "Um, are you feeling all right?" Maybe the full moon was affecting his mind or something?

"I can show you better than I can tell you." He licked his lips seductively as he took hold of my hand. His gaze burned with lust. He pulled up the front his sweater. His erection was standing straight up in his briefs, creating a long bulge which protruded from his pants. "Touch it," he breathed, slowly guiding my hand toward his rigid dick.

"Aaron, that's enough." I pulled away and pushed him back. "I'm not doing anything with you."

His thick, silky eyebrows furrowed. "Homie, I'm giving you a once in a lifetime opportunity, and you're tripping like this?" He stared at me with wide-eyed disbelief. "Are you retarded or something?"

I shot him a dirty look. "Wow, silly me," I said sarcastically. "Let's see; you taunted and tormented me every year for the past four years because you had a secret crush on me?" He remained silent. "Day in and day out, you harassed me about my sexuality, my skin tone, the way I talk, the way I dressed—hell, it was always something new." I was getting angrier and angrier as I relived the memories.

He barely managed to suppress a grin. I guess he still got a residual kick out of his own antics. "I already said I was sorry about all that, didn't I?" He was completely oblivious to the hurtful impact of his actions. His face began to grow impatient. He blew out an agitated breath and squeezed his dick through his underwear. "So, are we going to fuck or not? We don't have a lot of time before people start noticing that we're missing."

I stared at him incredulously. "Let me break it down for you: You won't be fucking me tonight, tomorrow, or ever, for that matter."

Aaron's face softened. "Come on, Ray. I really like you though. Keeping it real, the reason why I asked you to study with me was so I could get at you on the low." He bit his bottom lip and looked at me with puppy dog eyes. He was switching tactics with the precision of a Starfleet pilot shifting into warp drive. He was clearly used to getting whatever and whomever he wanted.

Well, I was going to break that streak tonight.

"You'll have to excuse me if I don't jump at the chance to be taken advantage of by the person who treated me like crap for the past three years." I took a step back to put more space between us. "It'll take more than several weeks of smiles and friendly overtures to make me forget. I have a lot more respect for myself than that," I stated confidently.

He sucked his teeth. "Don't play yourself, dawg. I was just going to fuck you as a charity case because I felt sorry for you. It's not like I wanted to be with you or anything." He snickered derisively. "I mean, why would *I* want to be with a weak homo like *you*?" He smirked as if he'd just delivered a verbal finishing move.

"Whatever, man." I gave him an easy smile. His words didn't faze me in the manner he'd probably expected them to. I knew what he was doing. Since I rejected him, he was trying to save face by putting me down. I'd dealt a blow to his planet-sized ego, and this was his way of retaliating. It wasn't working though. I felt emboldened and empowered. It was my turn to taunt him for a change. "You can call me whatever you want. I don't care anymore. You may think I'm weak, but at least I have the courage to be who I really am...unlike *some* scary homos I know." I folded my arms and flashed a smirk of my own.

"I'm not gay," he replied with his face contorted. He angrily stuffed his dick back in his pants and fixed his sweater. "That was just the liquor talking."

"Okay, if you say so," I scoffed. "Anyway, I'm heading back downstairs." As I turned to leave the room, he grabbed me by the arm. His face warped into an angry sneer. I glanced down at his balled fist. "So what are you going to do?" I asked calmly. Oddly enough, since I knew the truth now, I wasn't afraid of him anymore. "Are you going to beat me up because I turned you down?"

"Nah, I'm not going to lay a finger on you, homie. Like I said, I always keep my word." His scowl faded. "This stays between us, aight?"

"Yeah, sure." I nodded my head. He gave me a lingering glare and then let me go. I casually walked out the room and down the hall. Aaron closed the door and followed a few steps behind. I descended the steps with him not far behind.

As soon as I got to the foot of the stairs, I instantly spotted Matt.

CHAPTER 30
MATTHEW

After spending all day Friday chilling with my brother, I needed a little break. All we did was watch football, play video games, and gorge ourselves on leftovers. When Saturday night came, it was Mom's turn to babysit Ty. I would be attending stupid Aaron's stupid party. By the time Rell, Quin and I showed up, it was in full swing. It was wall-to-wall packed with kids from school.

The inside of his crib was just as expansive and impressive as the outside. Coming from money like this, I could see why Aaron had such a big head.

"This shit is live!" Quinton exclaimed as he turned to us. "Come on, ya'll. Let's find the liquor."

We followed behind him as he pushed his way through the crowd. He stopped abruptly when he ran into Savion, who was all hugged up on some girl. When he saw us, he broke away from her and eagerly dapped up Quin and Rell. He totally ignored me (which was perfectly fine with me).

"What's good, bruh?" He smiled broadly.

"Chillin'. How long have you been here?" Quin asked.

"Not that long. Just been getting my drink and mack on." Savion laughed and held up a plastic cup. "So ya'll gonna pay me back tonight, right?" He looked from Jarell to Quin. Guess it was weed money collection time.

"Yeah, man. I got you," Quin replied enthusiastically. Jarell looked uncertain.

As this exchange was going on, my eyes drifted to the stairs across the room. Someone was descending the steps. I instantly recognized that sexy, slim little body. It was Ray! He had an uneasy expression on his face for some reason. Aside from me, he was the last person I expected to be here. When he got to the bottom of the stairs, he looked out into the crowd. It didn't take long for my eyes to catch his. My heart fluttered. It was like we were the only ones in the room. My lips slowly curled upward, forming a smile. I knew I said I'd be patient and wait until he was ready to come back to me, but I just wanted to run over to him. I wanted to apologize and put all of the petty bullshit aside. I yearned to hug him and kiss him, and feel his love again.

Just as I was about to throw caution to the wind and step to him, another figure came down the stairs. My smile vanished when I realized it was Aaron. Apparently, they were best buds now. Before my talk with Ty, I would've instantly "Hulked up" and started smashing shit. But this time, I was just going to keep my cool. *No more jumping to conclusions and spazzing out*, I reminded myself. I felt a hand rest on my shoulder. It was Jarell's.

"Aye, are you coming to get drinks?" He asked.

"Yeah...let's go." I followed him though the crowd, leaving Quin with Savion. We made our way into the kitchen. There was a marble top island in the center of the room. It was covered with every brand of liquor you could imagine. People were getting soda and ice from the fridge, and mixing their own drinks. Me and Rell followed suit. I made myself an extra potent drink. With beverages in hand, we went back to the living room to join in the festivities.

I'm not going to lie, the music was banging. We stood off in the cut, sipping on our drinks. I was beginning to feel nice. Things had been awkward between Rell and me since the incident at Ray's house. I was kind of uncomfortable being around him by myself now. I was convinced that he'd pushed the confrontation with Ray on purpose. And like a chump, I went along with it to my detriment.

"So uh," Rell's voice got my attention, "do you want to chill back at my crib tonight after we leave here?"

I shrugged. "I don't know, man." I already knew what he had in mind. I peered through the crowd and noticed Ray talking to Keon. He was looking right at me. Our eyes connected once more. It was like neither of us could turn away from the others' gaze. Some of the other basketball players came over and chopped it up with us for a minute. In the midst of clowning with them--out the corner of my eye--I noticed Aaron talking to Savion over in the corner. *Is everyone best buds with Aaron now, except me?* I wondered. As I pondered that question, Quinton came over to us. He had two cups in his hand.

"Damn, dawg. You still sipping on that?" He peaked into my cup. "Here, take this. It'll really get you nice." He flashed a toothy grin.

"Thanks, man." I laughed as I accepted the drink. He raised his cup to toast me. I took it to the head and felt it immediately. We chatted for a bit, and then he moved on.

In spite of the frenetic atmosphere around me, I just wasn't in a festive mood. My mind was still on Ray. We were only a few feet away from each other, but we were still miles apart. I glanced at him again. He was still talking to Ke. He looked away shyly.

Why can't he just come over and talk to me?

Quin came back and started conversing with Rell. I used that as my opportunity to slip away and clear my head. I wandered into what looked like the dining room. There were people in here too, but it was less packed than the living room. I stood with my back against the wall, staring into the liquid in my cup as if it was a magic caldron that could tell the future.

Would Ray and I ever get back together?

I took a deep breath and slowly released it.

"Having fun?" I jumped when I heard his voice. I turned my head to see Ray standing next to me with a smile on his face.

"Well, to borrow your expression; it's kinda 'meh'." I smiled back.

He laughed. "My sentiments exactly." We just stared at each other.

I got serious. It was time to make things right. "Ray, I'm sorry for the way I've been behaving lately. I was just trying to look out for you, but I guess I went overboard. I didn't realize I was acting like such an asshole."

"Yeah, you were sort of a jerk," he said with a snicker. "But it wasn't all your fault. I was acting like an intergalactic warlord myself by trying to dictate who you can be friends with."

"So to summarize: we were both acting like dickheads?" I said. "And not the good kind."

"Yeah, that sounds about right," Ray agreed.

"Does this mean we can kiss and make up?" I extended my hand to him. He gripped it.

"Well, my mom is working a double shift tonight. I guess we can take turns making it up to each other at my house?" His eyes glimmered with flirtatious energy.

"You don't have to ask me twice." I grinned mischievously. I was happy we'd finally begun the reconciliation process, but I was still curious about something. "So, where were you and Aaron coming from when I saw you earlier?"

"Um, you wouldn't believe me if I told you." He diverted his eyes momentarily. "We had an interesting discussion. Let's just say you were right not to trust him."

"Oh, yeah? What do you mean by that?" My heart started pumping faster.

He looked up at me again. "I'll tell you later."

I was tempted to press for more info, but I wasn't going to let my curiosity get the best of me. I would let him tell me in his own time. I mentally took a deep breath and exhaled. If this was going to work, I knew I had trust Ray. And I did.

A girl stuck her head in the doorway. "Hey, everybody, they're about to bring out the cake!"

I looked over at Ray. He rolled his eyes. I gave him an empathetic grin. It felt good for us to finally be back on the same wavelength. We grudgingly went back in the living room.

A hush had fallen over the crowd. I turned my attention to the entrance. Seconds later, Aaron's girlfriend and sister entered. His sister was pushing a metal serving cart with a humongous, rectangular cake on it. *"Happy 18th Birthday Aaron"* was inscribed on the top in red icing. It was covered with flickering candles. Everyone began to sing happy birthday (except me and Ray).

Aaron stood in the center of the room soaking up the attention like a giant sponge before blowing out the candles.

My vision became blurry. "Woah," I muttered. My head suddenly felt like it was spinning for a second.

"Are you alright?" Ray whispered.

"Yeah, I'm cool. Just ready to get you home." I gave him a flirtatious look.

He smiled. "Sounds like a good idea to me." He leaned over and said something to Ke.

"Ya'll trying to go without getting any cake first?" Keon looked at us with a shocked expression. "Chile."

"Get it to go, so we can get the heck out of here," Ray replied.

"If I must." Keon turned his head and pretended to be mad. Ray laughed.

"Where's the bathroom in this castle?" I asked. My bladder was screaming at me.

"Oh, I'll show you," Ray replied. He told Keon we'd meet him outside at his car. I followed him as he led me upstairs.

After I finished draining the one-eyed snake, I shook it twice and put it back in my pants. I washed my hands and dried them off. I opened the door and poked my head out. "Wanna join me in the bathroom for a quickie?" I flashed a crooked grin.

Ray twisted his lips. "Uh, no thanks."

"Wuss."

"You're a perv, you know that?"

"Yep. You know you love it." I reached out and wrapped my arms around his waist, pulling him to me. We stood face-to-face in the hallway with our noses touching. My breathing quickened. "I missed you so much, Ray-man."

He snickered as his hands caressed my back. "I've missed you, too." We stared longingly into each other's eyes. Our lips slowly crushed together in an exhilarating kiss. Our tongues spent a good five minutes getting reacquainted before Ray pulled back for air. "We better get going. I'm sure Ke's crazy behind is already out there waking up the neighborhood with his horn."

I followed him down the stairs. We bumped and shoved our way through the crowd. Just before we got to the door to leave, I felt someone grab my arm. My head spun around.

"You're leaving already?" Rell asked. "You don't want to hang later?" He stared into my eyes almost imploringly.

"Nah, I'm good." I made my choice. "I'm going home with my baby." I took Ray's hand in mine and squeezed it. A disappointed look appeared on Rell's face.

"If the man wanna leave, then let him go," Savion said with a grin. He took a sip from his cup. "Get home safe, fellas." He said to us as he went in the other direction. Rell gave me a lingering look and then dapped me up before disappearing into the crowd.

I looked at Ray. We both smiled at the same time. When we walked outside the cool air hit me. Unfortunately, it didn't do anything to sober me up. I staggered to the car.

"Geez, you look messed up," Ray said, putting his arm around my shoulder to steady me as we walked up the driveway. "How much did you have to drink?"

I had to think about it for a second. "Only two," I replied. And I was this fucked up? *Damn, that last shot Quin brought me must've been strong as hell.*

"And you call me a lightweight?" He looked at me and laughed. Thankfully, he was there to keep me balanced. Man, I was feeling wasted.

When we got to Keon's car, we got in the backseat. I laid down with my head on Ray's lap, staring at the ceiling. I groaned. He gently stroked my hair as Ke drove us home. His tender touch was so soothing.

"Are ya'll good back there?" Keon asked.

"Yeah, we're straight," I replied.

"The hell you are!" He burst into laughter. "FYI, this is my mom's caddie. Don't throw up in it, please. I'm not trying to pay to have this bitch cleaned."

"Aye aye, Captain," I replied with a chuckle. My phone's ringtone started blaring. I pulled it from my pocket. Rell's name was on the caller ID. (Thankfully Ray didn't see the screen). I guess he was calling to see if I'd changed my mind about chilling. I sighed and sent the call to voicemail. I stuffed my phone back in my pocket and rubbed my eyes. I didn't feel nauseous, just a little spaced out and extremely sleepy.

I don't know how long we were moving, but when we eventually came to a stop, I was half sleep.

"Alright, ladies and gents — you're home," Keon said. "I'll invoice you for the ride tomorrow. Gratuity will be included."

"Gee, thanks, cabbie." Ray shook me to wake me up. "Let's go, Sleeping Beauty."

My eyes popped open. I wiped my mouth with the back of my hand. I still felt out of it. We both hugged Ke from the backseat and climbed out the car. We watched as he drove off.

"Let's get you inside and get you some water," Ray said. He placed his arm around my waist to support me.

"Thanks, bae," I mumbled. As I stumbled to the house, I suddenly felt the rumble of bass-filled speakers. A bright pair of headlights came out of nowhere. I squinted and shielded my face from the blinding glare with one hand. I heard a car come to a stop, and then the door open. I opened my eyes to see Savion approaching us. Quinton had also gotten out the car.

"What are you doing here, Savion?" Ray asked with an annoyed tone.

"Why did ya'll cut out so early?" He stopped inches in front of us. His eyes landed on me. "Sup, cuz? You all right? You look paler than usual. Guess that stuff I got from my brother to put in your drink worked." A devious grin graced his face.

That's why I'm so fucked up – that shot Quin gave me was spiked with something! Before I had time to formulate another thought, Savion punched me in the mouth. In the state I was in, I could barely stand. I fell to the ground like a ton of bricks.

"Leave him alone!" Ray rushed Savion, but Quin intercepted him with a punch to the gut and a blow to the face.

"That's what you get, bitch." Savion laughed. He then turned his attention back to me. I tried to get to one knee, but my motor skills were all out of whack. My head was in a fog. He slugged me again, and I went back down. "You thought I forgot about what you did to me? Nah, bruh, I ain't forget how you sucker punched me, how you stole my spot on the team, and all the other shit you did!" He kicked me in the side. "Who's laughing now, huh?"

I looked up at him with a defiant, bloody smile. "You knew you couldn't beat me in a fair fight...so you had to drug me?" I shook my head. "Wow...you are lame."

The smirk on his face turned to a scowl. "Oh, so you think this is a joke, huh?" He reached in his coat and pulled out a gun. He cocked it. He knelt down and grabbed me by my hair. My blood ran cold. "Why aren't laughing now?"

This was the second time in several days that someone had pulled a gun on me. When had I become The Most Hated Man in America? That thought mixed with whatever was in my system must've made me delirious. I couldn't help but chuckle.

"Oh, so you think this is funny?" Savion sneered.

"Yeah, man." I let out a taunting snicker. "You're still a joke--with or without a gun." I didn't know if the liquor was giving me liquid courage or if I just didn't give a fuck. I'd stared down the barrel of a gun a few days ago and defied death. If I did it once, I could do it again, I assured myself.

"Woah, dawg. What the fuck are you doing? Where you get that from?" Quinton asked, his voice full of surprise. He was restraining Ray with a full nelson wrestling hold.

"My brother hooked me up with this too."

"Aye, man, you said you just wanted to get a little payback. You ain't say nothing about no gun."

"Man, shut the fuck up." Savion snapped. "I got this."

"Alright, so what are you waiting for?" I was intentionally goading him so I could get under his skin.

"Shut the fuck up, man." He was rattled. I could see the apprehension in his eyes. Just as I had suspected, he had no intention of pulling the trigger.

Ray struggled to break free of Quin. "Leave him alone!"

Savion turned to face him.

He was distracted.

This was my chance.

I don't know if it was a surge of adrenaline or just my determination to protect Ray at all costs, but I suddenly felt like Super Matt. I gathered all my strength of will and managed to get to my feet. In a last ditch effort, I thrust myself at Savion, hitting him in the jaw. He fell backward on his ass. I wobbled over to him as fast as I could and dove on top of him. I gripped the gun, trying to pry it from his hands. We struggled for the gun as Ray screamed for us to stop.

That was the last thing I heard before...

POP!!!

Savion and I stopped tussling. A heavy silence hung in the air like the smell of gun powder.

I suddenly felt searing pain in my abdomen. Wetness began seeping through my shirt. Savion pushed me off of him. I rolled over on the sidewalk, clutching my stomach. I'd never felt such pain in all my life.

"Oh shit, man! What did you do?!" Quin said in a panic.

"Fuck! It was an accident. I just wanted to scare him," Savion replied.

"Man, you shot the dude!" Quin screamed. "What're we gonna do?"

"He grabbed the gun and it went off," Savion said. "Fuck. Come on, leave him here. Let's go!"

He and Quin rushed off. Car doors slammed, and tires squealed away. I heard Ray's panicked voice as he called 911. After telling the operator what happened, he knelt down next to me. I was lying on my back on the concrete, staring up at the full moon. In spite of everything that had just happened, the night seemed oddly tranquil.

"Stay with me, Matt. The ambulance will be here any second now." Ray gripped my hand tightly. I was grateful for the warmth of his loving touch. "Come on, baby — stay with me!"

As I thought back on my life, this just seemed to be par for the course. Once I cleared one hurdle, a brick wall would pop up in its place. As soon as I resolved one problem, another one, far more complicated than the last, would present itself. So it was only fitting that as soon as I got a seat on the happy train, the whole damn thing derailed.

My mind was bombarded with memories and images of the people in my life I loved.

Mom.

Grandma.

Tyler.

Ray-Rey

In the grand scheme of things, I'd only known Ray for a short time. However, the impact he'd had on my life and my perspective was profound. Where would life have taken us together? *I'll never know*, I lamented.

A solitary tear escaped my eye and ran down the side of my cheek.

Am I really...dying?

I could hear sirens wailing. But instead of coming closer, they seemed to be getting farther and farther away... until there was a calm, eerie silence. I felt a hand softly brush against my cheek. I looked at Ray's tear-stained face, focusing on his beautiful eyes. They were filled with fear. I hated seeing him this way.

"Don't worry, Mookie." I whispered through labored breaths. I forced myself to crack a smile, trying to put him at ease. "It's going to be okay...."

My eyes closed one last time, and my world faded to black.

CHAPTER 31
RAYMOND

I sat in the emergency room with my head buried in my hands. There were people all around me, but I didn't notice them. I was lost in a daze. I uncovered my eyes long enough to take another glance at my shirt and jeans, which were stained with Matt's blood. A burly white police officer was standing in front of me, scribbling notes on a pad. I just kept hoping that this was all a nightmare and I would wake up soon. My mom had her arm around my shoulder, trying to console me. Aside from answering the police officer's laundry list of questions, I had barely spoken at all. I was still in a state of shock.

A few minutes later, Matt's mom arrived. She was accompanied by a muscular man. She looked frantic. In the midst of all the chaos, I'd almost forgotten that I'd left a voicemail on Matt's home phone informing her Matt was in the ER. I stood up, Mom followed suit. The three of us watched as they approached the waiting area.

"You must be Raymond?" The muscular guy asked me. He resembled Matt, but his hair was a different color. All I could do was nod my head in response. "I'm Matt's brother, Tyler." He shook my hand in a remarkably calm fashion. "We got your message and came here as fast as we could."

Mrs. Richards pushed past him. She was nearly hysterical. "What happened to my son???"

"They were attacked by two boys from school after they came from a party." The deputy looked her square in the eyes. "Unfortunately...your son was shot during the scuffle."

Matt's mom covered her mouth and squeezed her eyes shut. "Where did this happen?"

"They jumped them in front of my house," my mom chimed in.

"And you didn't do anything to stop it?" A horrified expression appeared on Mrs. Richards' face.

"I was at work when it happened," my mother answered defensively. "I came here as soon as I got the call from Ray."

Matt's mother shook her head ruefully as tears began to roll down her cheeks. "This only happened because Matt was going against God's will."

"Mom, don't say something like that." Tyler tried to intervene.

"No, if Matt wasn't with HIM," she pointed at me, "then none of this would've happened!" Her outburst caused me to recoil.

"Now hold up," my mom said. "I know you're hurting right now, but don't you dare take it out Raymond."

"Don't tell me what to do!" Mrs. Richards snapped. "You have no idea how I feel!" Her face contorted with anger.

"Now, see here." Mom put a hand on her hip and shifted into a combative stance. Everyone was on edge. Emotions were running high. "First of all--"

"Okay, everybody calm down," the police officer ordered with a forceful tone.

"I've got her, officer," Tyler said. He put his arm around his mom's shoulder. "Mom, this isn't the time or place for this. Come on, let's see if we can get some information on his condition." He led her away to the nurses station. He glanced back at me with an apologetic look on his face.

Once they returned to the waiting area, Matt's mom collapsed into a chair. She ran a hand through her dark hair and wiped tears from her face with a crumpled tissue. The policeman went over to her and they began talking. As they conversed, Tyler approached us. His face was grave.

"I'm sorry for the way my mom acted," he said, massaging the back of his neck with his hand. His voice was laden with concern.

"It's okay. We understand," my mother replied. "I would probably be the same way if the situation was reversed."

Ty let out a heavy sigh. "The doctor is operating on him now. It's going to be a while before we know anything. You guys should probably go on home."

"No, we can't leave." I looked from him to my mom with wide eyes. "I need to stay here. I have to be here for him!" I was emphatic.

"Baby, there's nothing you can do except pray. It's in the Lord's hands now."

"But..." I had to say something to convince her to let me stay.

"Your mom's right, Ray," Tyler interjected. He turned to Mom. "Ma'am, if you give me your number, I'll be sure to call you and update you on Matt's condition as soon as we find out more."

"Yes, please do that," she said. "Thank you." After Ty saved my mom's number, he faced me.

"Don't worry, dude. My brother's a trooper. He'll pull through this." He gave me a reassuring smile and a bro-hug. He then left to rejoin his mom.

I took a deep breath and lowered my head. I felt Mom's hand gently squeeze my shoulder. "Come on, baby. Let's go home," she said softly. "You've had a crazy night. You need some rest."

*****

"Raymond, are you hungry?" My mom's voice awakened me from a deep slumber. Unfortunately, the events of last night were still all too real. I'd been in bed all day. I was mentally and physically drained. I didn't even have the strength to call Keon and let him know what had occurred. I didn't feel like talking or eating. All I wanted to do was sleep. When I didn't reply, she cracked open the door and poked her head in. "You hear me?"

I didn't say anything. I was too distraught. I rolled over in my bed so my back was facing her. I heard her open the door all the way and come into my room. She sat on the edge of the bed. I hadn't spoken or eaten since we left the hospital. All I could do was think about Matt. I just kept replaying the events of last night in the theater of my mind.

When I unexpectedly saw Matt at the party, I feared that he would go into a berserker rage at the sight of me and Aaron coming down the stairs together. Amazingly enough, he didn't flip out. That gave me a small glimmer of hope that we might be able to work things out after all. The question was though, who would make the first move? We kept watching each other throughout the night. Keon urged me to just go talk to him. I desperately wanted to, but I was unsure of how he would react.

Eventually, Matt broke away from his friends. I summoned all of my courage and followed him into the other room. I was pleasantly surprised when he appeared happy to see me standing there. Before I could say much, he apologized. I was flabbergasted. As deep as the rift between us was, all it took was a few words to bridge the gap. That's just how strong our love for each other was. Although I was happy and relieved, I noticed he seemed kind of out of it. It concerned me a little, but I just took it that he'd had too much to drink. I figured once we got back to my place, he would be able to sleep it off. By the time Keon dropped us off, Matt could barely stand up without my help. I still didn't think it was serious though. When Savion and Quin suddenly showed up, I knew something bad was about to happen. I just had no idea how bad.

I hadn't cried since last night when I was there holding Matt's hand. Just recalling the haunting look in his eyes sent a shiver down my spine. If I cried, I told myself, I would be throwing in the towel and conceding that Matt wasn't going to make it. I just couldn't allow that. Besides, what right did I have to cry? I blamed myself for what happened to him. *Maybe if I'd been stronger, I could've done something?* I wondered again for the gazillionth time. *Maybe if I wasn't so damn weak, he would've never fought my battle for me with Savion, and none of this would've happened?*

Then I became angry.

Angry at Savion.

Angry at life.

But most of all, angry at myself.

"Boy, you need to eat something. You know you can't afford to be losing any weight." My mom playfully swatted me on the butt, trying to get me to snap out of my depression. She sighed. "I just got a call from Matt's brother."

God, please let it be good news, I silently prayed. My breath caught in my throat. I slowly turned to face her.

"Thankfully, no major organs were punctured by the bullet. But he did sustain some internal damage," Mom said somberly. "He's still in serious condition." I zoned out. Her voice sounded like it was traveling through a long a tunnel. "The police got the two boys that did it." So Savion and Quin were apprehended? That was one silver lining in this dark cloud, but it didn't make me feel any better. "He said one of them confessed to spiking his drink with Oxycodone." I gasped in disbelief.

A powerful sedative, mixed with alcohol--so that's why Matt was so drowsy and disoriented.

"When you feel up to it, get you something to eat, alright?" She implored me, bringing me back to reality. I mechanically nodded my head to get her to leave me alone. She got up and walked to the doorway. "And you can stay home from school tomorrow, too, if you want, OK?" I just nodded my head again. She finally closed the door and left me to my thoughts.

I took another deep breath and exhaled slowly. After being holed up in my room all day, I wanted to get out. I needed to go to school tomorrow to distract me from the mental flogging that I was giving myself. I also needed to go for another reason:

To confront Jarell.

Something told me he had a role in all of this. And I intended to find out just what that role was.

CHAPTER 32
RAYMOND

It was a cold, gray morning. The gloomy weather matched my mood perfectly. I trudged up the path to school with an impending sense of dread. When I reached the main entrance of the building, I found Keon standing out front waiting for me like he said he would be. When he saw me approaching, he cracked a little smile. I gave him an uninspired greeting.

"Hey, boy," he said as he embraced me. "How're you feeling?"

"Like crap," I muttered. My shoulders slumped as if they bared the weight of twin moons.

"You aren't still blaming yourself for what happened, are you?"

I averted my eyes. "Who else should I blame?" I still felt as if I could've and should've done more to protect Matt.

"You can blame the bastards who did it—Savion, his supposed friend, Quin—and probably Jarell's ass, too."

"I know." I exhaled. "But none of this would've happened if Matt hadn't gotten mixed up with me in the first place. Because of me he's laid up in a hospital bed clinging to life. If he doesn't survive, I'll never be able to..." I choked up before I could complete my sentence.

"Ray, don't even think like that." Keon placed a hand on my shoulder and stared into my eyes compassionately. "He's going to be all right. Both of you are going to make it through this dark tunnel and come out on the other side stronger than ever. Trust me on this." He gave me a confidant smile. "Have I ever lied to you?"

"Well, um..." A sheepish grin made its way onto my face.

"Don't play," he quickly interjected. I laughed a little. "Let's get inside. It's so cold out this bitch my nipples are getting hard." He rubbed my back as we walked into the building.

Once we pushed our way through the heavy steel doors, I felt like all eyes and conversations instantly shifted to me. As we made our way through the hallway I could hear people talking about what had happened Saturday night. Everybody was abuzz about Matt.

"I heard he was there, too," one girl murmured to another while looking at me. Their gazes followed me.

"He shot homeboy pointblank," another voice said as we passed.

"Somebody told me it was because the white dude owed Savion money," some guy I'd never even seen before told his equally obscure friend. "And that's why he bust a cap in his ass." I stopped and glared at the big mouth liar. I felt compelled to set him straight for spreading rumors about my boyfriend.

"Come on, don't pay that buck-toothed bitch no mind." Ke pulled me by my arm to get me to keep walking. "What he needs to be worried about is what random guy's dick his momma was sucking last night!" He said it loud enough for others standing around to hear. Snickers and giggles came from all directions.

Mr. Big Mouth grimaced. Even his friend was laughing at him.

"Thanks," I said dejectedly. "Maybe it wasn't such a good idea for me to come to school today?"

"Don't mind these people, chile. Just remember the real reason why you came here."

He was right. I couldn't allow myself to be distracted from my objective of confronting Jarell. After putting away my book bag in my locker, I made my way to homeroom. Once I got there, I spent the entire time trying to block out the whispering and murmuring around me; all of it was about Matt, Savion, Quin...and me. It seemed like it would never end.

When homeroom finally let out, I felt a tap on my shoulder as I stood up. It was Aaron.

"Aye man, are you all right?" He gave me a sympathetic look.

"I'm okay," I replied unconvincingly.

"Look, I feel bad about what happened to your boy. We had our disagreements, but what they did to Matt was fucked up."

"Yeah." My voice was barely audible.

"Look, if you need somebody to talk to, I'm here for you." He pulled out his iPhone and tapped the screen a few times. "I just forwarded you my number." I'd given him my number when we studied, but he'd never called me. "Feel free to hit me up anytime, aight?" He gently squeezed my bicep and gave me a warm smile.

"Thanks, man." I appreciated Aaron's kindness in my time of distress. We walked out the room together and dapped off before going our separate ways.

*****

I went through the first half of my day on auto-pilot. My body was present, but my mind might as well have been in another galaxy. All I could think about was Matt and my impending talk with Jarell. I was itching to find out what part he played in all of this. He was boys with Matt and Quin, so there was no way he didn't at least have an inkling that something was going to go down. When lunchtime finally came, I strode to the cafeteria with purpose. Keon and I stood at the entrance of the lunchroom, patiently waiting for Jarell to arrive.

A few minutes later, I spotted his high-top fade making its way through the sea of hungry faces. His eyes widened when he saw me.

"I need to talk to you," I said gruffly. The look on my face let him know I meant business. He nodded his head in compliance. We walked over to a quiet area of the hall. Ke followed behind me with his arms folded like an enforcer.

"Look, I'm sorry about Matt," he uttered. He was admitting guilt without me even pressing him.

"So, you did know it was going to happen?" My blood started percolating.

"Yeah--no--kind of," he replied, turning his head to avoid my death gaze.

"What the fuck does that mean?" I growled.

He let out a long breath. "Savion told us about his beef with Matt a few months ago. He talked me and Quin into becoming cool with him so we could set him up at the right time. We were just supposed to rough him up a little. At first, I was down with it." He nervously scratched the back of his head. "But after getting to know Matt, I realized he was actually a cool dude—nothing like the way Savion made him out to be. That's when I started having second thoughts about going through with the plan. I attempted to get them to squash their beef, but Savion wasn't trying to hear it at first. When he didn't mention it for a few weeks, I thought I'd managed to talk some sense into him. But when I saw him at the party, he told me that he was still planning to go through with it that night." He lowered his eyes and shook his head. "I was scared. I didn't know what to do. I tried to stop Matt from leaving, but I couldn't. I begged Savion not to do anything. He told me he wouldn't. When I went to use the bathroom and came back, I couldn't find him or Quin anywhere. I went outside and saw Savion's car was gone. I called him and it went straight to voicemail. I knew what he was up to. I dialed Matt as fast as I could, but he didn't answer. " His voice wavered. "I'm so sorry, man. I can't believe my cousin did some dumb shit like this."

I stared at him incredulously. "You and Savion...are related?"

"He's my first cousin." His head dropped. "He told me not to tell Matt though."

My mind could barely process what I'd just heard. Savion was so blinded by hatred for Matt that he even used his own cousin as a pawn to get revenge. He obviously didn't count on Jarell developing feelings for Matt in the process.

"Since you knew what they were planning, did you also know they put something in his drink?" I grabbed him by his collar and jacked him up against the wall. There was a glint of fear and shock in his eyes. I guess he was just as surprised by my aggressive reaction as I was.

"I-I didn't know anything about that," he stuttered. "I'm being totally straight up with you, man. I didn't know it would go this far."

"Yeah, well it did," I said through gritted teeth. "And if you were really Matt's friend, you could've done a hell of a lot more to warn him!"

"Ray, that's enough." Keon placed a hand on my shoulder. I looked back and saw a lunchroom monitor staring in our direction. I returned my glare to Jarell. I held onto him for a few seconds before reluctantly releasing him. He wasn't worth getting suspended over. Keon and I began to walk back toward the lunchroom.

"Seriously, dawg," Jarell's voice stopped us dead in our tracks. I spun around to face him with a snarl. "None of this shit would've happened if Aaron hadn't put them up to it." He straightened his shirt and grimaced. "All of this was his idea to begin with."

*****

Once school was over for the day, Ke and I went to our lockers. After retrieving our bags, I walked with him to catch his bus.

"You sure you don't want me to come with you to talk to him?" He asked again for the millionth time.

"For the millionth and one time, NO," I replied. "Don't worry, I can handle this on my own." I'd texted Aaron during fourth period and asked him to meet up with me after school. I was determined to find out if Jarell was telling the truth or not. If what he said was true, then Aaron was just as guilty as Savion and Quin in all of this. I tried to persuade Jarell to go to the police and tell them what he'd told me, but he refused. Even though he didn't actually participate in the attack, he was scared that he would be implicating himself if he told them he was initially part of the plot. I might not have been able to compel him to go to the police, but that didn't mean I couldn't go myself. However, I wasn't going to go empty-handed. I had a plan to get a confession straight from the horse's mouth.

"Alright, well call me later and let me know what happens." He began to climb the steps of the bus and then looked back. "And I want every d-e-t-a-i-l, too!"

I rolled my eyes. "OK."

"And be careful, alright?" He added.

"Okaaaay, Mom #2!" I watched as he got on the bus and sat in the middle row.

He peered out the window at me. *"Call me,"* he mouthed, using his hand to simulate a telephone. I gave him a smile and a salute. The second I turned and began to walk to the student parking lot, the smile disappeared from my face. The gravity of what I was about to do had suddenly set in. The mission I was undertaking was risky and a little harebrained, but if it worked, it would be worth it.

My heart was racing a mile a millisecond as I approached Aaron's car. It was easy to find since he always parked in the same place. Apparently, being the most popular guy in school came with fringe benefits, such as an "unofficial" reserved spot. I stood by the front of his car and looked at my watch. I took a deep breath and pulled out my phone. *He should be here any minute now.* I hit the button to activate the voice recorder. Hopefully by putting the phone in my front coat pocket, I would be able to capture the impending conversation without his knowledge.

"What's good, homie?" The unexpected sound of Aaron's voice almost made me fumble my phone. *Fuck!* It was like he had materialized out of thin air. He flashed his typical killer smile and dapped me up.

"Uh, hey, Aaron," I nervously replied. I lowered the phone to my leg and prayed he didn't suspect anything.

"You tell me." He glanced down at the phone in my hand. I awkwardly folded my arms to try to conceal it. I did my best to hide my anxiety. He gave me a peculiar look for a second before continuing. "You wanted to holla at me?"

"Um, yeah. I have to ask you something." I subtly positioned the phone under my armpit. I was careful not to block the receiver or look too suspicious.

"Aight." He stared at me expectantly. "Sup?"

I swallowed hard. "Did you set me and Matt up?"

He snickered. "Of course not. Why would I do something like that?"

"That's what I'd like to know," I replied. I stared into his eyes with confidence. I was about to play detective. "Honestly, why did you invite me to your party?"

"I invited you because I'm genuinely feeling you." He bit his bottom lip. "Like I said, I've had my eye on you for years, dawg."

"And instead of just approaching me like a real man—the way Matt did—all you did was pick on me like an elementary school boy with a crush?" I was trying to turn up the heat.

"I was going to step to you...sooner or later," he mumbled. "But that white boy jumped his ass in the way first."

"And when you saw I was with someone, you went through all of this elaborate crap—pretending to need tutoring, being nice to me, inviting me to your party—just so you could get at me? And when that didn't work, you sicced Savion on both of us?"

He didn't answer, but his facial expression told me he knew he'd been busted. He turned his head and waved at some kids passing by. While he was distracted, I quickly slid the phone in my front coat pocket. When he returned his attention to me, he gave me a strange look.

"Like I said, dawg--I don't know what you're talking about."

He was playing dumb, and it was starting to piss me off. "Stop lying, Aaron!" I snapped. "Savion's cousin already told me everything!"

"Who, Jarell?" He laughed. "Of course that punk had to run his mouth. He's just mad cause I don't want nothing to do with his ass anymore."

I gave him a puzzled look as my mind processed his words. *Does this mean that he and Jarell--?*

Aaron seemingly read my mind. "Yeah, we fucked around a few years ago, but I cut dude off."

So basically, Jarell was Aaron's jilted jumpoff? I was almost having a hard time keeping up. (Where was a holographic flowchart when I needed one?)

"Aight, since you know now, I'll keep it real with you." He stared into my eyes. "Yeah, I had something to do with it."

"But I thought you promised not to mess with me or him anymore?" I threw his own words in his face.

"And I kept my promise. I said *I* wouldn't fuck him anymore. But, I never said I wouldn't get someone else to do it for me." He smirked. "This is my senior year. Everything was supposed to be perfect. This was my school, until your boy came along and started fucking shit up. When he embarrassed me on the first week of school, I started losing credibility. Then he shows me up on the basketball court and steals my shine." I silently listened to Aaron's delusions of grandeur. He paused and swiped his tongue across his lips to moisten them before continuing with his soliloquy.

"There was no way I could let that shit slide. Dude needed to be taught a lesson. The All-Stars were going to beat his ass the same day he hit me, but I didn't want to risk getting in trouble and being kicked off the basketball team before the season even began. So, I knew I would just have to bide my time. It was all good. A month went by and tryouts started. From the first day, I noticed Savion appeared to have a beef with Matt, too. Right then and there, a light bulb lit up in my head. I asked myself, *why should you get your hands dirty, when you could have some no-name losers to do the dirty work for you?* It made perfect sense. So I *suggested* to Savion that he set dude up and handle him off school grounds. It didn't take much to persuade him, he was all gung ho about it from the jump. For whatever reason, he seemed to have more of a beef with ole boy than I did."

"So you had Matt's supposed friends lure him into a trap?" I interjected.

"Nah, I didn't even know he was going to show up. I guess Savion had his boys bring him. But coming down the stairs and seeing him there after you'd turned me down was the best birthday present I could've asked for." A thin smile played at his lips. "All I had to do was give Savion a little 'pep talk.' By the time I was finished, homeboy was hype as fuck. He told me about some shit he'd brought with him to put in Matt's drink. I didn't ask and I didn't tell. I wasn't getting caught up in the details. As long as they didn't fuck up my crib fighting, I didn't give a shit. All I knew was that he was going to follow dude home and jump him. I had no idea that his stupid ass was going to go as far as he did, though." He casually leaned against his car. "Oh, well. Tough titty."

I shook my head disdainfully. "You're even more of a slimy asshole than I thought." I now had all the evidence I needed.

His eyebrows furrowed. "You don't have anybody to protect you now, so you better watch your mouth," he warned as he stood up straight. "I gave you a chance of a lifetime, but you chose to stay with that white boy instead. It's not my fault you put yourself in the line of fire." He shrugged nonchalantly.

Aaron had manipulated all of us ingeniously. Although it was apparent that he was unaware of the real reason for the animosity between Matt and Savion, that didn't stop him from using it to his advantage. And knowing how much Savion detested Aaron, the only reason why he probably conspired with him was because their plans coincided. I highly doubted that he knew Aaron was also interested in me and was just using him to get Matt out the way. All of these machinations were mind-blowing; Hell, it actually seemed like a grand super-villain master plan. And like a true mastermind, Aaron stood before me gloating. I had to say something to wipe the smirk off his face.

"I'm going to the police and tell them you orchestrated all of this," I threatened.

"All I did was plant the seed in homeboy's head and watered it a little. I can't help it if I happen to be highly persuasive."

"We'll see if you can talk your way out of a prison sentence," I said.

He laughed. "Even if I did concoct the whole thing, you don't have any proof."

That's what you think. I had heard and recorded enough. I turned and began to walk away. Suddenly, I felt his forearm wrap around my neck. He placed me in a tight chokehold. I struggled to break free, but it was no use. Aaron easily outmuscled and overpowered me.

It was becoming difficult to breathe.

I felt myself losing consciousness.

He reached into my coat pocket with his free hand and pulled out my phone.

"You think I didn't know you were recording me?" He held the screen up to my drooping eyelids. He used his thumb to hit the stop button on the recorder. "You're lucky I'm still feeling you a little," he breathed in my ear. "But if you ever try some shit like this again, you're going to be laid up in the hospital with your boy." He released the hold and shoved me to the ground. I looked up at him as I gasped for breath. Aaron tapped the phone with his thumb again and then tossed it at me. I managed to catch it before it hit the ground. He gave me a lingering sneer, and proceeded to walk around to the driver's side of his car. He got in and slammed the door.

I watched him pull out of the parking lot as I stood up. Looking down at the phone in my hand, my heart dropped.

All of this was for nothing.

Aaron had deleted the recording.

CHAPTER 33
RAYMOND

The smell of collard greens and black-eyed peas greeted my nose as soon I walked into my house. Mom was in the kitchen cooking up a storm. I tried to sneak by without her noticing me.

"Hey, baby. How're you feeling today?" She asked.

"Fine," I muttered, trying my best to hide my surly disposition. I wanted to say I felt like a dumbass for losing the recording the way I had. Once again, I'd let Aaron punk me. I kept walking to avoid eye contact with her. I didn't feel like answering a litany of questions.

"I've got some news," she called out. I turned to face her. She had a somber visage. "Tyler called me this morning." The beating of my heart came to a screeching stop.

"Yeah?" I squeaked. "W-what did he say?" My breathing quickened. I felt lightheaded.

She came closer and placed a hand on my shoulder. "Matt's expected to make a full recovery."

"Really?" An ear-to-ear smile spread across my face.

"Yep. He's been moved out of the ICU to another unit. I can take you to visit him before I go to work."

"Oh, man. That's awesome!" I was so happy that I could barely contain my glee. I reached out and gave my mom a big hug.

After eating dinner, we drove to the hospital. Tyler greeted us in the lobby. Since only two visitors were allowed in at a time, I went up to see Matt alone. His mom was in his room visiting, too. Ty assured me she'd be cool with me being there, but I was still wary of seeing her again. After our last encounter, I just didn't know what to expect.

Once I stepped off the elevator onto Matt's floor, I began walking through the corridor to his room. My stomach was tied in knots. The closer I got, the more my palms sweated and my heart raced. As soon as I turned the corner and entered his room, I saw his mom sitting by his bedside.

I took a deep breath. "Hi, Mrs. Richards."

She startled. "Oh, Raymond." Her face relaxed when she saw it was me. "How are you?"

"Um, I'm fine, ma'am," I replied hesitantly. She stood up and walked to the doorway where I was standing.

"I'm sorry for lashing out at you the other day," she said as she looked up into my eyes. "When I found out what had happened to Matt, I was just beside myself."

"I understand," I said in a low voice.

"It wasn't right the way I attacked you." She shook her head ruefully. "Matt always spoke highly of you. Even before I knew the...true nature...of your relationship, I could tell that he was very fond of you. When he awakened after the surgery your name was the first thing that came out of his mouth. Well actually, it was 'Where's Mookie?'" She smiled. "It took us a while to realize that he was referring to you." I chuckled a little. "He couldn't relax until we assured him that you were OK. I can tell you mean a lot to him."

I couldn't stop blushing. "How's he doing?"

"Better." She exhaled. "He was awake earlier, but with all the medication they have him on, he was a little groggy. He's been sleeping like a log for the past hour. Thankfully, he finally stopped snoring." She smiled again. "Is your mom here?"

"Yeah, she's downstairs in the lobby with Tyler."

"Okay. I want to apologize to her, too. I'll leave you two alone." She stepped out of the room, leaving me with Matt.

My heart felt heavy as I approached his bed. My body shuddered when I saw him. He had a tube up his nose and an IV in his arm. Seeing him lay there hooked up to machines like a cyborg was both heart-wrenching and unsettling. I stood at his bedside and looked down at him. His chest slowly rose and fell as he slept.

"Hey, Matt," I said. He didn't respond. He looked so serene. I ran my fingers through his hair. He smacked his lips and continued to snooze. I wanted to nudge him and wake him so badly. I yearned to hear his voice again. "Get your rest, Sleeping Beauty," I whispered. I wasn't going to disturb his slumber. I bent down and kissed him on the forehead. A tear rolled down my cheek. I wiped it away with the back of my hand. I felt horrible. It was my fault that Matt was here. He was an innocent casualty of my longstanding conflict with Aaron. I silently prayed for him, and just watched him sleep. Before exiting the room, I tenderly caressed his face. I got back on the elevator.

As the door closed, my jaw clenched and my fists balled up at my side. I let out a long breath.

I was tired.

Tired of being bullied.

Tired of feeling helpless.

I couldn't go on living like this.

Things had to change.

I had reached my breaking point.

If I couldn't get the law to punish Aaron, I was just going to have to do it myself.

I was always the underdog who would endure constant humiliation and turn the other cheek. Well, that was all about to change. Because tomorrow, this lowly underdog was going to bare his teeth and start biting!

*****

Sleep eluded me that night. I tossed and turned for hours on end. I couldn't stop thinking about what I was planning to do the following day. I was going to stand up for myself for a change. And if I lost, at least I would go down fighting.

Keon tried to talk me out of my plan when I got to school. I wasn't trying to hear it. My mind was made up and there was nothing that could deter me. After placing my book bag in my locker, I walked through the hall like The Terminator. My mind was singularly focused on one objective: Taking Aaron down, once and for all.

In homeroom, I sat in my usual seat. Aaron and his boys sat behind me. Throughout the course of the period I heard them cracking jokes.

"Aye, what do you call a homo with three holes?" Aaron queried.

"What?" One of his boys replied with a snicker.

"Matt Richards!" Aaron answered, bursting into laughter. It didn't take long for him to start showing his true colors again.

I was tempted to say something, but I restrained myself. It wasn't the right time. I was going to strike back when I had maximum exposure.

Go ahead and yuck it up, Aaron, I thought. He may've been laughing now, but he was going to cry later...*in more ways than one.*

Once the period ended, everyone got up and made their way to the door. Aaron bumped me from behind with his shoulder as he passed. He was obviously trying to intimidate me, but the only thing he'd done was stoke the flames growing inside of me. In a few hours, I was going to unleash that fire like a dragon. And when it was all said and done, Aaron would to be burnt to a crisp.

I went through the first half of my day with tunnel vision. It was like the clock was counting down to doomsday. Finally, it was lunchtime, aka Zero Hero.

"So, you haven't changed your mind?" Keon stared at me from across the table with a worried expression.

"Nope." I casually sipped my chocolate milk. Considering what I was about to do, I felt oddly calm. I guess it was the calm before the storm.

"Are you sure you want to do this?" He asked.

"Yep." I was eerily confidant. I'd never been more certain about anything in my life. What I was about to do was a long time coming. "I already told you--you don't have to get involved. This is between me and him."

"Chile." Keon shook his head. "And you call me certifiable."

Almost as if on cue, I saw the All-Stars approaching. Once upon a time, the sight of Aaron, Tim, and Michael made my heart sink. Now, it made my heart sing. Operation: Raymond's Revenge was about to commence. I took one more gulp of milk and set the carton down. I calmly pushed away from the table. I got up from my seat and stood in the middle of the aisle, blocking their path. The cocky, ever-present smile on Aaron's face vanished. He looked at me like I was crazy.

"Hey, Aaron." I smiled gingerly. His brow furrowed and his eyes squinted. He had no idea where I was going with this. "Do you still want that kiss?" I puckered my lips. Everyone started zeroing in on the scene that was developing.

"What the fuck did you just say?" His faced scrunched up. The cafeteria became quiet enough to hear a butterfly breathe. Now that I had an audience, it was time for the main event.

"What, you don't want to kiss me now?" I feigned shock. "Like you tried to do Saturday at your party?!"

Everyone's mouths dropped open, including those of his boys. Aaron's nostrils flared.

"Stop lying on me, faggot!" I could see the panic written all over his face. "I'm gonna fuck you up, dawg!" He hastily set his tray down on a table and shoved me.

"The only 'lying faggot' I see around here is you!" I taunted him with a mocking a smile. He snapped and swung at me. I sidestepped his punch. Like a ticking time bomb, I detonated--exploding into action! I charged at Aaron with fists flying.

All the pent-up rage in me was pouring out with each punch. All of the humiliation he'd subjected me to, all of the anguish—everything he'd ever done to me and Matt—I was going to make him pay for it. I carefully targeted my punches while shielding my face, just like Matt had taught me. I'd caught Aaron off guard. I guess he never expected me to do something like this. (Up until yesterday, this was something I never would've imagined myself doing either.) I was a pacifist by nature.

However, peaceful diplomacy had gotten me nowhere. It was now time for war, and I wasn't taking any prisoners. Violence was the only thing that bullies like Aaron understood.

We grappled and pawed at each other, bumping into tables and knocking over trays of food. Students scattered and gave us space to brawl. Aaron and I were going toe-to-toe, exchanging blow-for-blow. I tasted blood, but I couldn't let it distract me. I just kept throwing rapid fire punches at him.

Although I could have been hallucinating, it seemed as if I was actually winning (or at least holding my own)...until I slipped on some spaghetti that had spilled on the floor. I lost my footing and Aaron seized the moment. He punched me in the stomach, knocking the wind out of me. He then slugged me in the face. I tumbled to the floor. I laid there for a second, disoriented and dazed.

Get up, Ray, I said to myself. I sat up and shook out the cobwebs. I grabbed hold of a table edge and managed to pull myself up. I staggered to my feet.

"Yeah, get your punk ass up." Aaron cracked his knuckles as he stalked towards me. "We're not finished yet."

I smirked. "Wanna bet?" With one fluid motion, I reached into my pocket and pulled out my secret weapon--the "Ultimate Nullifer." It was the closest thing to a bully repellant that I could find. Aaron's initial expression was one of bemusement. That quickly changed. With a squeeze of the trigger, I spewed a stream of venom in his face. He didn't realize it was pepper spray until it was already in his eyes. And by then, it was too late to do anything about it. He dropped to the floor, squealing in agony like his head was on fire. Brianna ran over to try to help him. "Careful, you don't want to get too close," I cautioned her in a calm tone.

"What did you do to him?" She screamed, kneeling down next to her fallen boyfriend.

"I'm just letting him see what it feels like to be the one to shed tears for a change." I looked on with smug satisfaction. Who knew the "break-in-case-of-emergency kit" my mom kept at home would come in handy after all? My face donned a sadistic smile. After all these years, Aaron had finally gotten his comeuppance. His eyes were shut as tears streamed down his face. Mucous poured from his nose. He was coughing and gasping for air. Sure, it looked painful, but it could've been worse. *He's lucky I decided not to bring the stun gun instead.*

As I stood there thoroughly enjoying my revenge, Tim charged at me. He barreled towards me like I was an end zone. There was no time to think—I could only react. I aimed the canister at him and squeezed the trigger, firing a stream of OC spray at his face. He dropped to the floor hacking and wheezing just like Aaron. Tim may've been a big dude, but this pepper spray was the great equalizer.

"Who's next?!" I yelled like a man possessed. My eyes scanned the lunchroom to see if someone else would dare come to Aaron's aid.

Suddenly, I felt a pair of hands grab my shirt from behind. Before I could turn my head, I was slung to the floor. The canister of pepper spray slid from my hand and rolled under a table. Michael, the last standing MVP, stalked toward me with a scowl on his face.

Damn, why didn't I bring that stun gun again? I thought. I glanced over at the pepper spray. It was a few feet away. There was no way I could reach it before Michael got to me. I was going to have to rely on my hands. I just prayed I had enough strength left to finish the job. I staggered to my feet and swiped my tongue across my bottom lip. I threw my fists up and glared at him defiantly.

"Come on," I growled. "Bring it."

As he was about to make his move, something slammed into him from behind with the force of a raging bull! I moved out the way just in the nick of time. Michael careened forward and collided with the floor, landing face first in some spaghetti. Keon stood there with his arms folded and his lips pursed.

"Now you know I couldn't let you have all the fun." He grinned mischievously. I returned the gesture and gave him the thumbs up sign.

Just then, four security guards rushed into the cafeteria. Two attended to Aaron and Tim, who were still crying and writhing on the floor. The other two nabbed me. A victorious smile spread across my face as they led me away. I felt like I'd just slayed Goliath with a slingshot. With an assist from Ke, I'd actually taken on the All-Stars...and won! The entire lunchroom erupted into cheers and applause, some even patting me on the back as I passed. The way some were carrying on you would have thought I'd just toppled a brutal tyrant or something. I guess there was an undercurrent of discontent flowing amongst the denizens of King Aaron's fiefdom after all, I mused. I wasn't surprised.

After all these years, it felt good to finally get respect. I didn't know what was going to happen after today (or how many times my mom was going to kill me when she found out), but at least for this brief moment in space and time, Raymond Reynolds was **THE TOP DOG!**

EPILOGUE
MATTHEW

Ray snuggled up to me and rested his head on my chest. A week had passed since I'd been discharged from the hospital. It felt good to be back in my own bed with my baby. We were just chillin', watching the *Justice League* on the Cartoon Network. It was an episode that featured an all-out slugfest between The League and an army of bad guys.

"That's how we trashed the All-Stars." Ray laughed as he pointed at the TV.

"Man, I still hate that I missed it!" I couldn't stop grinning. When Ray had told me what happened, I couldn't believe my ears. My mild-mannered lil' Mookie had morphed into a mace-wielding maniac--I loved it! On the one hand, I was proud of him for finally standing up for himself against Aaron. But on the other, I was worried about how this could potentially affect him academically. Thankfully, Principal Perry was lenient on him. He could've sent him to alternative school or expelled him altogether. However, upon taking Ray's documented history of bullying problems with Aaron into consideration (and after Ms. Reynolds raised all kinds of holy hell on Ray's behalf), he only suspended him for a week.

"Yeah, it was EPIC!" He beamed. "I was like Batman and Ke was like Robin...or Batgirl."

I let out a hearty laugh. "Dude, cut it out! You're going to make me rupture something," I joked as I rubbed the bandage on my stomach covering the surgical scar. I was looking forward to returning to school and finishing out the rest of the year. It was going to be another week before I could go back. And it was going to take several months for me to fully recover from the injury, but it was all good. I was just grateful to be alive. All things considered, I was much better off than Savion.

He was charged with assault with a deadly weapon and illegal possession of a firearm. He accepted a plea deal put forth by the prosecutor and was sentenced to one year in prison. Quin was charged with Simple battery, and was hit with a $2000 fine for his part in the attack. Believe it or not, in spite of what they'd done, I was actually glad that they weren't given outrageous sentences. Sure, what they did was fucked up, but I didn't want to see them suffer for it for the rest of their lives or anything. I guess my forgiving attitude was a by-product of my newfound perspective on life. Lying in that hospital recovering, I had a lot of time to reflect. Almost dying certainly put the world in a different light for me. I came to the realization that I had to let all of the pain from the past go. Life was too short to dwell on shit and get all bent out of shape over things I couldn't change or control. Harboring resentment was fruitless. I refused to allow anger to rule me any longer. For once, I was totally content with my life. For once, I was happy to me.

When the cartoon went to commercial, Ray lifted his head from my chest. He looked up at me. Our eyes met...followed by our lips. Once we broke the kiss, we just stared at each other wistfully. I felt all warm and fuzzy inside.

"Love ya, Mookie." I flashed a crooked grin.

"Right back at'cha, Machine Gun. So, uh, could you shut up with all that mushy stuff now? The commercial break's over."

"Smartass." I gripped him in a playful headlock and tickled him. He laughed and pushed me away.

"Pass me the remote," he said. I reached over and retrieved it from the nightstand. I held it out to him. He just stared at me with a look of amusement. "Um, not that remote, Magic Matt." He smiled seductively as he grabbed a handful of my dick. "I'm talking about this one."

"Alllrighty, then." I grinned and bit my bottom lip. I clicked off the TV. "We'll catch the replay later." I leaned in to kiss Ray again. "Right now, we've got a lot of catching up to do."

###

Thanks for reading! If you have any questions, comments, or suggestions, feel free to reach out and drop me a line. I appreciate and respond to all feedback. You can find me in the cyberverse on Facebook [ReginaldWrite], Twitter @ReginaldWrite, or on my website, Reginaldwrite.com. Also, (pretty) please be sure to sign up to my email list to receive updates on future releases! LOVE YOU ALL, AND THANKS FOR THE SUPPORT!

OTHER WORKS AVAILABLE BY THIS AUTHOR

Beyond the Breaking Point
Teacher's Pet
My Boyfriend's Brother
Playing with Fire
Playing with Fire Pt 2: Friendly Fire
Tempted

AUTHOR ACKNOWLEDGEMENTS

I wanted to give a quick shout out to some important people in my life: My mom, my dad (RIP), my family, my friends, and especially P.K. Stokes☐. I also want to thank the Almighty for blessing me with the gifts of creativity and a vivid imagination. And I especially want to thank all of those who have supported my dream and given me words of encouragement. Without you, none of this would be possible. I LOVE you all!